# Broken Parts

## Gayle Towell

Blue Skirt Productions

Published 2015 by Blue Skirt Productions
blueskirtproductions.com/blue-skirt-press

The Blue Skirt logo is a trademark of Blue Skirt Productions

Book design by Gayle Towell

ISBN 978-0-9907654-6-2

2015908758
First Edition

Printed in the United States of America

For humans (and those who aren't sure if they are).

WARNING: This novel contains material and deals with subject matter that may be triggering to some. For more details and links to resources visit gayletowell.com/trigger-warnings.

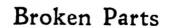

Broken Parts

# CHAPTER ONE

I wake flat on my back in a hospital bed, my shirt lifted, my work boots and socks gone, covered in electrodes connected to an EKG machine, an IV in one arm and a blood pressure cuff around the other. Some woman in pink scrubs and a black braid pushes buttons on the IV pump, while a man who's tall and bald and thick like a weightlifter has his hands all over my chest, disconnecting the electrodes. Fight or flight kicks in, and I shove the man in the gut and try to get away. He grabs my shoulders and pins me down.

"Whoa, whoa, whoa," he says. "Relax."

"What happened?" I say.

"I'm Doctor Olson. You're in the hospital. You passed out in the waiting room."

"Right," I say. I can remember limping through the emergency room doors, but everything's gone after that. And now a throbbing headache and the ache and chill of fever are taking over.

Doctor Olson looks to the nurse. "Can we get a temp?"

The nurse slips a plastic cover on the end of a thermometer, points it at my mouth, and says, "Under your tongue."

She takes my temperature as the blood pressure cuff auto-inflates.

The thermometer beeps.

"Hundred and three point two," she says.

"Get some ibuprofen in that IV," says the doctor. He retrieves a penlight from his pocket and pries my eyes wide open, blinding me with it. He grabs my head, turning it and pressing on a sore spot.

1

"You hit your head when you fell. That's a good-sized knot you got there. Are you feeling disoriented at all?"

I shake my head.

"What's the date today?" he says.

"Um...Tuesday...January thirteenth."

"President?"

"Obama."

"Your name?"

"Jake Smith."

He grabs my wrist and checks my hospital bracelet then looks at me again. "Date of birth?"

"One, six, eighty-five."

"All right."

He opens a cabinet and retrieves a cold pack, bends it in half, shakes it, then hands it to me. I press it against my head and try not to shiver.

"So what's going on? What brought you in?"

"Hurt my leg."

"Hurt how?"

"It's infected. I think."

"You think? If that's what's causing the fever I can guarantee it," he says.

Doctor Olson finishes disconnecting the electrodes and rolls the EKG machine off to the side. Opening a drawer, he retrieves a hospital gown and plops it on the end of the bed.

"Get undressed. I'll come back in a minute and take a look."

Both nurse and doctor leave. I fumble with the button and zipper on my jeans and push them off my hips. A sharp pain rips through my thigh as the fabric tears free from the pus crust. I lie back, close my eyes, and wait for adrenaline to erase it before continuing. I manage to shake free from my jeans, leaving my thigh wound exposed.

The wound itself is the diameter of a quarter. Part crust, part juice—yellow and brown mixed together with red around the edges, peppered with fragments of blue jeans, and all around it is swollen like someone's got their fist buried under my skin.

Tethered to the IV, I can't remove my shirt, so I grab the hospital gown and drape it over my lap.

Two quick knocks, and the doctor reappears. He puts a bed rail down and pulls up a stool. "Let's see this wound."

He grabs the gown and pushes it all the way to my crotch, exposing my underwear and nearly racking me. Poking his finger around the swollen flesh supporting the inch-wide pus crater, he says, "How the heck did this happen?"

"Uh...at work," I say. "A spark burned through my jeans last week when I was welding. It didn't heal right."

"A spark did this?"

"A big spark. Like, a hot piece of metal. From welding."

Doctor Olson nods and prods around the wound some more, his eyebrows coming together.

"You've got quite the infection. We'll need to do a full debridement and get this cleaned out."

The nurse returns, draping me with blankets except for my thigh, and soon Doctor Olson has a wheeled tray full of sharp instruments and syringes at the ready.

As he places a visor with a magnifying glass on top of his head, the nurse dabs alcohol around the festered wound. It burns, and I flinch, sucking in air.

She says, "Sorry about that," but keeps right on dabbing.

Doctor Olson scoots his stool over to my bedside, dragging the tray beside him. I can't stop shivering even with the blankets. He picks up a syringe.

"This is Lidocaine, to get you numb."

He stabs the needle into the flesh above the wound, and I'm hit with a burst of nausea. The nurse shoves a bag in my hand and puts my hand up to my mouth just in time to catch the spew as I vomit and gag. She hands me tissues, throws the bag away, and fills a paper cup with water. I take a drink, swish it, and swallow. She gives me a new bag just in case.

Doctor Olson stares at me. "Better?" he says.

I nod, and he flips the magnifying visor down.

He scores the top crust of the wound with his scalpel, and a pocket of bloody pus breaks free. He blots it with gauze, presses to expel more, and the pressure burns beyond the Lidocaine.

After setting the orange-red gauze on the tray, he slices around the crust, pulling off wet, fleshy chunks with tweezers. The nurse irrigates with saline. He blots with more gauze.

Sharp stabs radiate down to my knee and up to my groin as he digs deeper, hitting live nerves. I look away from the lava flow of blood running down the side of my leg, and push the icepack hard against my head, pressing the welt into my skull so that the headache takes the edge off what he's doing, but if he doesn't finish soon, I just might throw up again.

Dr. Olson pauses. "Are you feeling any of this?"

I shake my head. I'm not sure why. Maybe I just want this to be over, and I'm trying to minimize the complexity.

He instructs the nurse to squirt more saline, and when he blots it with gauze, I wince and arch my back.

"You can stop with the tough guy routine." He grabs a second syringe of Lidocaine and shoves the needle deeper into the muscle. The pain dulls, and I catch my breath.

He scrapes out the last bits, and there's only tugging now—no stabs. The nurse irrigates, and he packs wet gauze inside it. After removing the magnifying visor, he leans back on his stool and says, "Everything okay lately, Jake?"

"Yeah," I say.

"No depression or suicidal thoughts?" He raises an eyebrow.

The nurse has the same expression of questioning concern. My chest tightens, and I grip parts of the bed sheet in my fists, under the blankets where they can't see.

"You know why I'm asking?" Dr. Olson says.

I look past them to the door and think about Ancient Greece. How Hippocrates would have blamed the infection, the fever on an imbalance of humors. He might have even bled me like this guy just did.

"This was no burn wound." Dr. Olson points to the gutted crater. "It's too localized and deep, and I have to wonder why you would lie about that, and why you would let it get so bad before coming in. And this," he points to a round divot scar on my hip. "Don't know what the hell that's from either." Then he points to some stripes on the side of my knee. "But these here, I'd bet money they're from a razor blade. And there're a lot of them, so this habit of yours isn't new, is it?"

He keeps staring at me with the same single raised eyebrow and his mouth drawn flat as if trying to read some meaningful answer from the level of pain on my face. He turns back to the wound, pulls out the gauze, and mops the blood off my leg. "Not much of a talker, are you?"

I look down at the volcanic remains of my thigh—a crater that goes halfway to the bone, bright red swaths of muscle tissue exposed to air.

It was a screw.

I gutted my thigh with a screw.

The screw is now stuck in the bathroom wall in my apartment where I slammed it when I was done. It didn't occur to me at the time that the screw was a cesspool of bacteria. I didn't disinfect the wound, just covered it up and went for a drive to clear my head.

I stopped on a hill outside of the city, turned my car off, turned the headlights off, and laid on the car roof in the freezing cold, staring up at the clear night sky. I was shivering then, too, but the cold made my leg hurt less.

The Quadrantid meteor shower had peaked a few nights before, and I'd missed it. I hoped to maybe catch a few straggler meteors—specks of space debris burning through the atmosphere as the Earth flew through them at 60,000 miles per hour. I finally saw one, streaking toward Arcturus, and decided I could be content in my miniscule existence, here on this tiny planet, because what's a woman's rejection when there's a whole universe? I was perfectly fine living alone. Oh, I was so goddamned profound.

Days later, fed by heat and sweat from work, the wound began to fester, and my delayed cleaning efforts couldn't keep up.

Today when I got home, the fever had me shaking. I sat in my bathroom for a good hour before coming to the hospital, not wanting to move, wondering how deep the rotting pus caldera went. Surely it was spreading, contaminating previously healthy flesh.

"You're lucky," Dr. Olson says. "No major tendon or muscle damage." He crosses his arms. "So what's going on? Should I get a psych consult?"

He waits a moment, then turns back to the wound, packs fresh saline-soaked gauze into it, lays dry gauze on top, and tapes it down.

I slide the icepack over my eyes. "Am I done?" I say. "Are we done?

"I'd like to keep you here until morning. Make sure we've got a handle on the fever and dehydration. You messed yourself up bad enough I suspect you were going into shock—which is why you lost consciousness."

He removes the stained absorbent pad under my leg and throws it into the biohazard bin.

"I need to go home," I say.

"If everything looks good in the morning, we'll get you out as soon as we can."

"I have work in the morning."

"You think you're going to work like this? If you leave now, you're going to end up right back here in worse condition."

My hands shake as I pull the pulse monitor off my thumb. I pick at the tape holding the IV in place, and peel it off.

Doctor Olson folds his arms and nods toward the nurse. "Call upstairs and get a psych consult. This man is a danger to himself and we need to get the ball rolling on a seventy-two hour hold."

The nurse nods and leaves the room.

"You can't do that," I say.

6

"Want to bet?"

And just as I'm trying to figure out if I can fight him off and escape, his pager goes off. He checks it and says, "Damn it." He points at me. "You sit tight. You're not going anywhere like this." Then he rushes out of the room.

As soon as the door closes, I sit up, pull the IV out, and press the blanket against it to control the bleeding. I stand, leaning against the bed, all my weight on my good leg, waiting for the dizziness to subside before bending down and getting my pants. I'm scared enough of being stuck here that I'm able to dress efficiently despite my current condition, but as I reach for my jacket, I see blood running down from the IV site and have to dig through the drawers to find more gauze and tape.

I slowly open the door, peering out into the hall. It's busy enough that I'm able to limp through the ER undetected.

On the drive home, I manage not to crash despite feeling half dead and not having full use of my right leg. It's past midnight and the fever is creeping back up as I pull into the parking lot of my apartment complex.

I step out of my car in the January cold, and like a harbinger of impending doom, my dad is there sitting on the front stairs, breathing white clouds of breath into the frozen night, dressed in slacks and a tie like he just came from work, but his shift would have ended hours ago. My eyes go to the ground as he stands and approaches, his shoes crunching the gravel with each step. He stops beside me, elbows my arm, and says, "You sure get home late. We need to talk."

"About?"

He takes in a deep breath. Lets it out. "Your brother's been telling some stories, and I'm apparently under investigation. Child Protective Services even says I can't stay in my own house right now, if you can believe that."

My heart beats in my ears, fast and loud. My chest hurts, and I can't seem to get enough air, but I just stand there like the bomb Dad dropped is inconsequential.

Dad has that wide-eyed grimace he uses as a sort of mind control. But there's some crack in his composure this time, like he's genuinely worried. I run my fingers through my hair, and rest my palm on the lump on my forehead, pressing the knotted bruise into my skull until the pain nearly blinds me. I don't care to get involved in any of this.

Dad says, "What's wrong? You look sick."

"Nothing. Hurt my leg at work."

He sighs and his shoulders drop, "If you finished college, you'd be able to land a real job. It kills me—your mother, too—watching you squander your intelligence."

"Welding is a real job," I say.

"You scored in the 95th percentile on your SATs for Christ's sake." He stares like he's waiting for me to say something else. When I don't, he says, "How bad is it? You need anything from the pharmacy?"

"It's fine," I say, as much as I'd love to take medication he steals from his work.

"Well...all I can think is your brother's little stunt is retaliation for getting grounded. He kept coming home late and worrying your mother. You remember just last week when you were over, it took him four hours to come home from school? Last night he didn't get home until ten. Your mother was hysterical—you know how she gets—so I told him no friends, no electronics for a week. Then this morning the first thing he does when he gets to school is talk to the counselor. He doesn't know what he's saying. This should all get sorted out soon, but if anyone comes to talk to you about it..."

"Got it," I say.

"This is important, Jacob. I need to make sure we're on the same page. Don't want to give anyone room to twist this into something it isn't."

"Right," I say.

"I can't imagine anyone taking him seriously. Half the people in this city are regular customers at the pharmacy. Everyone knows

I love my kids."

I nod, staring at the ground.

He grabs my shoulder. "You and I both have work in the morning. I'll let you get some rest. I'm going home whether they say I can or not. If they have nothing better to do at this hour than arrest an innocent man for sleeping in his own bed, then so be it."

He pats me on the back, says goodnight, and walks off.

Reality crawls back—the fever, the cold, the throbbing in my head, the burning knot of my leg crater. Dad pulls out of the parking lot behind me, and the world starts spinning again. I take one limping step after another until I'm all the way up the stairs and inside my apartment. Stumbling into the bathroom, I drop to my knees as a sharp pain in the pit of my chest sends me hanging over the toilet, heaving and heaving, but nothing comes up.

# CHAPTER TWO

Sitting in the parking lot at work, I try to visualize the path from my car to my work station. Once there, I can hide under my welding hood and not have to look at anybody. My leg is killing me, I'm still running a fever, and all my brain power is sucked into some panicked void, spinning in circles about Dad's visit. If my brother Ben told someone what I think he's told, then there's about to be some serious shit-and-fan action.

I check the bruising on my forehead in the rearview mirror. Most of it is hidden by my hairline, so at least there's that. But if I limp, someone will notice and there will be questions. If I look too despondent, someone will notice and there will be questions. I'm weak and haven't eaten anything. It wouldn't stay down. And maybe it's stupid to even try to come into work, but sitting at home with my thoughts never ends well.

Out of my car, I let weight on my bad leg, taking a few careful steps and slowly picking up pace as I head toward the front office. When I push through the door, *she's* there, like always, smelling of hairspray and vanilla perfume. Elbows perched on the front counter, chin in her hand. Long, blonde hair teased up and flowing down her shoulders. Her artificially-enhanced melons squished together and popping out of her shirt with a big crack down the middle like someone's giant ass mooning the world. Her eyes filled with judgment.

This is Savannah.

"You're brooding again," she says.

"I'm not. This is my happy face."

I slam myself through the double doors into the shop.

As I head to my work station, Rick, my fat and balding coworker, says, "That night job at the brothel getting to be too much for you?"

I ignore him, don a leather jacket, gloves, and welding hood, set up to weld a trailer, and am about to flip my welding hood down when Savannah enters my peripheral vision.

In those moments when everything in the shop is on pause— no welding, no drilling, no hammering, no yelling—Savannah can be heard running. *Click, click, click, click.* The rest of us wear steel-toed boots, and she trots around in heels. She's only supposed to work in the front office, but the big boss, Dan, puts her in charge of almost everything, so she's out in the shop half the time. Running around. Telling people what to do. And when she runs, those big melons of hers sway back and forth, the faintest fwoop sound with every step. *Fwoop, fwoop, fwoop, fwoop.* Maybe I imagine that part. Maybe it's the sound of her shirt stretching with each shift of those things. Could be the wind resistance, too. She's undergone more than one surgery to get them like that. They're nice enough, I suppose, but perhaps she's gone overboard.

Presently she's *click, click, fwooping* my way, and she's not alone. Some kid barely out of high school is at her side, also with leather jacket, gloves, and holding a welding hood in his hands.

"Hey Romeo, this is Carson," she says. "He's my nephew, and he works here now. Teach him how to weld."

I just stare at her, then she crosses her arms and her weight goes all in one hip.

"Not a problem," I say.

"Play nice, boys," she says and trots off.

This is probably the last thing I need today. I lean against the work bench, most of my weight on my good leg, as Carson stands ready for instruction.

"You ever weld anything before?" I say.

"Savannah said it's so easy any idiot can do it."

"Excellent. Then you don't need my help." I wave at the trailer. "Go ahead. Weld the hitch."

He stares at me like he can't tell if I'm serious, then reaches for the welder. But I grab it first. "Welding is a science," I say. "It is physics, and chemistry, and metallurgy. And if you get your fingers in the way, biology. You ever take a science class?"

"I took physical science at PCC last year."

As I move over to the trailer hitch with the welder, my leg gives out, and I almost fall over. "Tell me," I say. "What's the melting point of steel?"

"I don't know. Like, a hundred degrees?"

"Have you seen steel melt in the sun on a hot day?"

He nods. This just keeps getting better.

"I hope you didn't pay too much for that education."

I carefully kneel on the floor beside the trailer hitch and take a few deep breaths.

"Twenty-five hundred degrees. That's the melting point of steel. Welding bonds two pieces of metal together using intense heat and pressure. Riveting, brazing and soldering can join materials, but none of those hold as strong as a good weld."

Carson says, "Are you sick or something?"

I wipe the sweat from my forehead. It's possible I'm visibly shaking. "When you weld two pieces of metal, joining the original pieces directly to each other, the result is a strong, cohesive bond."

I tap at my hood and nod toward Carson. He puts his hood on, ready to flip it down.

"There are a million ways to fuck this up. Be prepared to discover every single one of them before you get it right."

I flip my hood down, as does Carson, and start the weld. Sparks snap in the air.

I finish, lift my hood, and Carson just stares at me, his hood still on. There's no way he can see me. The lens is made so dark that you can only see the brightest of lights through it so you don't burn your eyeballs while working.

"Cars, buildings, aircraft," I say. "Without welding, none of those would exist. It's crucial to half the gross national product. The art of welding dates back to the Bronze Age. It wasn't until modern times, however, that it got to be as good as it is."

The kid finally lifts his hood. "Is this important?" he says.

"Yes, it's important. You know what's also important? Safety. In the eighteen hundreds, oxidation was a major problem, and brittle welds resulted in failure of bonds causing injuries and deaths. These rods are coated in flux to prevent oxidation. But if you let the flux get ahead of the weld, the weld will be brittle, resulting in failure of the bonds, causing injuries and deaths."

I put my hood down and start another weld. When finished, it's as if my brain isn't prepared for silence and it fills in the gap with Dad's voice. *Your brother's been telling some stories.* My head tics to the side, and I flip my hood up, clear my throat.

"What happened?" says Carson

"Nothing happened." I offer him the welder. "Your turn. Time to give it a try."

As Carson awkwardly determines what to do, I catch sight of Savannah walking across the shop, tossing her hair back over her shoulders. Her heels clicking across the floor.

Red, red lipstick. Blue, blue eye shadow. She might be Helen of Troy under all that, but you'd never know. You might want to know, but she won't let you. It seems contradictory that she spends so much effort covering her face in makeup while simultaneously revealing as much of her body as possible. Maybe I only find her appealing because she's the only female besides my mother I see on a regular basis.

She's the reason for my leg crater, but she'll never know it.

The day I decided to gut my thigh with a screw, I'd had a little conversation with Savannah. It was a moment of weakness—a combination of having just turned thirty and never having been with a woman, let alone asked one out. I'm not one of the assholes who stand around gawking at her fwoopers all day. Or at least, I try not to—they take up enough space, it's difficult to avoid them. I do my job. I'm generally obedient. And I thought maybe all of her odd harassing of me was her way of flirting. Perhaps I fantasized too much about that—read the signals all wrong. But, that day, right after clocking out, I finally found the courage and went up to her and said, "Savannah, can I talk to you a minute?"

Her arms crossed atop her melons, her weight shifted to the right, and her mascara-coated eyelashes opened in wide circles like black daisies, blooming expectantly at me. The full package of Savannah-brand attitude.

Without thinking, I said, "Why do you have to do that?"

She said, "Excuse me?"

Then I panicked and launched into my preplanned dialogue. "Friday night, what are you doing?" It didn't even sound like my voice. I might as well have been twelve, asking my mother what's for dinner.

Her arms uncrossed, her hands went to her hips, and she let out a high-pitched giggle of disbelief, walking away like a cackling hen. That was gutting enough in and of itself, but then on my way to the parking lot, Rick ran up and handed me something silver-gray and galvanized.

"Savannah said you needed a screw," he said, fist up to his mouth, choking back a laugh. The whole rest of the shop was out there, Savannah included, waiting for my reaction.

I stood there like a confused idiot for the longest time before the joke dawned on me. Then I nodded and muttered, "Thank you," calmly tucked the screw into my pocket, and left.

Savannah disappears through the double doors into the front office, and I'm shocked back into the present when Rick shouts, "I still can't believe you had the balls to ask her out last week. Funniest fucking thing I've seen in years. Give it up, buddy. You ain't never getting that."

A loud clanging makes me jump, and I turn to see Carson

dancing around welding rods spilled all over the floor.

\* \* \*

Another harbinger of impending doom awaits me on the front steps of my apartment building when I get home. This time it's my brother Ben. He sits there with a backpack, duffel, and sleeping bag, a string from his hooded sweatshirt hanging from the corner of his mouth, staring at his phone.

"Fuck," I whisper to myself, then look around a moment before limping towards him.

The kid is fifteen, half my age, and looking at him is like looking at my younger self—except, add freckles. Scrawny, more like a twelve-year-old. Short, dirt-brown hair, brown eyes. Plain. Inconspicuous.

He puts the phone in his pocket, then stands in a wobbly, terrified way, dropping the sweatshirt string. "Mom told me to come stay with you."

"Don't you have a friend you can stay with?"

"Dylan's parents don't let him have friends over on a school night. Do you even know what happened?"

I look away.

He says, "Dad...uh..."

"You can stay," I say. "But you're sleeping on the floor."

I hobble past him to the front door, open it, and wait until he grabs his things and walks in.

But he keeps stopping up the stairs in front of me.

First it's, "If you had a cell phone I would have called you."

"I don't need a cell phone," I say.

Then it's, "Don't you want to know what happened?"

"This is between you and Dad. I'm not getting involved."

We almost make it to the second floor when none other than Ronald Duncan, the twenty-something douche-wad building manager who lives in the apartment directly above mine runs into us on his way down. Ron's the sort of person who acts perpetually stoned, except I don't think he actually is. He keeps his hair gelled to a crest down the midline of his head. For some reason it always reminds me of the plumed Corinthian helmets worn by the Spartans—just shorter, and blonde instead of red.

Ron can't just pass by. He stops and says, "Duuude. Hey, yo— is this your kid brother?"

"Yeah," I say. "Ben, this is Ron."

"He looks just like you," says Ron.

Ron holds up a fist for a fist bump. Ben looks to me and then to Ron and then awkwardly fist bumps him.

Ron smiles. "There ya go, little dude."

Ron continues down the stairs, and Ben stops walking yet again and says, "Who was that?"

"Building manager. Lives in the apartment above mine."

"I thought building managers were supposed to be old, and like, mature."

"Can we please keep moving?"

We finally make it to my door, and I let him in.

My studio apartment is tiny and filled with a basic set of yard-sale variety furniture—table, chairs, bed, dresser, nightstand. The only real objects of substance are the overstuffed bookcases along the wall near the window, and Prometheus, my albino leopard gecko, happily sitting on his half-log in his tank on my dresser.

Ben drops his bags on the floor.

"You need another bookshelf," he says.

"Right, and where would I put it?"

"You keep getting more books. You could always just use the Internet or get a kindle."

"I'll keep that in mind."

I grab his sleeping bag and unroll it across the floor in the small space between the table and my bed.

"Look at that," I say. "Luxury accommodations."

He lifts his backpack onto the table with a thud and births his algebra book. "I have a lot of homework."

"I'll let you get on that, then," I say and limp into the bathroom.

I strip naked, sit on the toilet, and gingerly tear off the blood-soaked gauze taped to my thigh. When I pull all the packing out of the hole, my heart starts pounding and my vision goes patchy at the sight of it. I close my eyes until it passes.

In the shower, the metallic smoke grime from work that coats my hair and face runs down my body, black at first, then slowly diluted. The hot water burns residual juice from my thigh wound like somebody's holding an acetylene torch to it, but I have to clean it. I'm not going back to the emergency room. Doctor Olson can kiss my ass.

After drying off, I rebandage the wound and throw on a mostly cleanish t-shirt and shorts from the pile on the bathroom floor.

I leave the bathroom, and Ben watches my every move from the kitchen table, sweatshirt string hanging out the corner of his mouth again.

I hobble to the dresser, dig a spare key out of the bottom drawer, and slap it on the table in front of him. "You're on your own to get to school in the morning. I leave for work at six."

He nods.

I get my plastic bin of crickets, pick some up inside a paper towel tube, open the top of Prometheus's tank, and shake them in there for him.

"That thing's still alive?" Ben says.

"Don't speak of him like that," I say. "It makes him angry."

I watch as Prometheus chomps the life out of a cricket, his tongue slipping around it, his eyes squinting with satisfaction.

The next thing I know, Ben is breathing over my shoulder. "What's wrong with that thing?" he says.

"Nothing," I say. "He's shedding."

"He's ugly," Ben says.

"He can hear you."

"He doesn't have ears."

"He does, too. And he's not ugly." I tap at the glass, and Prometheus looks my way, licking his lips. He gives me his lizardly squint of agreement.

Ben lets out a short laugh.

I wave toward the kitchen. "There's food if you're hungry. Eat whatever."

But that's probably bad advice. Yes, there is food, but I doubt it's safe to eat. I can't remember the last time I went grocery shopping. I've been subsisting on the remaining nonperishable items for the last few weeks, consuming them at a rate that just barely meets the minimum requirements for survival.

Ben wanders back to the table, pulls his laptop computer out of his backpack and turns it on.

I make my way to the bed, collapse, and he says, "Why are you limping?"

I mumble, "I'm not."

And before I can properly fall into a coma, he says, "What's your Wi-Fi password?"

# CHAPTER THREE

A paper towel tears slowly off the roll in the kitchen. Lying in bed, I open my eyes in the dark, squint and make out a time of four-something on the kitchen stove clock. Ben is huddled somewhere near the fridge, sniffling and muttering to himself. It's all high in pitch and weepy and every so often punctuated by a failed attempt at subduing a sob—a sort of sharp, snot-infused explosion, quickly followed by pure silence, as if he's terrified of being found out.

My heart pounds in my ears as a sick hollow fills my stomach. If he finds out I'm awake, there will be some sort of expectation that I should help him in some way—a prime opportunity for me to let him down or screw him up worse, because I don't have a clue what to do. So I close my eyes, pretend to still be asleep, and wait him out, the whole time feeling like a swarm of flies is buzzing in my head.

Over an hour later he's quiet again, and it's almost time to leave for work. I get up and find him back in his forest green sleeping bag, cocooned and curled up all fetal, the same way he slept as a toddler, except instead of a thumb in his mouth, he's holding a wadded paper towel to his face, and he's got a wire coming from one ear going into his phone on the floor beside him.

I limp into the bathroom and redress the wound. The fever's finally gone. That's something. I put on my jeans and work boots, grab my jacket, and leave before Ben so much as stirs.

* * *

At work I watch, cringing, as Carson attempts a weld. The kid has wasted more material in one morning than I do in a month. If my life ever depended on the structural integrity of anything he'd touched, I wouldn't be long for this world.

In the silence just after he ends his latest effort, I hear Savannah talking to someone. I turn around and see her near the double doors with Larry Daly—a buzz cut, angry-looking ex-marine who happens to be our biggest client.

She has her hands on her hips and her large chest aimed right at him. His eyes go down to her boob crack, then he looks up and over at me.

He says to Savannah, "Doesn't look like Mr. Jacob is too busy at the moment."

Savannah walks my way, heels clicking across the floor.

She nods at Carson, "Kid, you're on clean up duty." Then says to me, "You'll have to continue lessons some other time."

"Mr. Larry needs something yesterday?" I say.

"T-braces," she says. "Rick's cutting the pieces for you now."

I look past her, locking eyes with Larry who sports a smug grin of superiority, and say, "I'll get right on it."

Savannah clicks away to the double doors, Larry following, and I nearly jump out of my skin as Rick slams a stack of steel on the table right beside me. Rick shakes his head, laughing.

"You know Larry's fucking her now, right?" he says.

"Shut up, Rick," I say. "You're married to a dog."

"At least I get laid on a regular basis. You know, if you need a screw, there's boxes of them in the supply cabinets. Just saying."

I spend lunch break sitting in the corner of the break room at a small table, hovering over a piece of paper with a pencil, writing and erasing, trying to form words that properly express my interest in Savannah despite the humiliation of last week. All I have so far is: *Savannah, I'm not always good with words.*

Rick plops down in the chair across from me.

"What's that?" he says. "A love letter?"

"Fuck off."

"Oh-ho! It is, isn't it?"

He rips the paper from my grip and holds it up to read while I lunge across the table to get it back. The table breaks, and I fall to the floor as Rick stands up and steps aside, still holding the paper. I get to my feet and grab it from him, but it rips, leaving me with only half of it. Rick balls the remaining half in his fist, and I claw at his hand and shove him into the wall trying to get it.

Just then Savannah shows up and says, "What the hell is going on in here?"

We both stop and look at her. "He has something of mine and won't give it back," I say.

"What is this?" she says. "Grade school?"

Then Rick says, "Romeo here is still in love with you."

She waves a hand around in the air like she's swinging a lasso. "Break's over. Rick, back to work. Jake, my office. You're bleeding."

Rick throws the balled up paper at me as I look at my arm and find a bleeding gash.

In the office, I lean against the desk as Savannah opens a first-aid kit on the desktop and wipes the blood off my arm with alcohol.

"Do we have a problem, Jake?" she says.

"What do you mean?" I say.

"I mean, are you able to pull your head out of your ass and do your job without starting fights?"

"Won't happen again."

"You asked me out last week. I told you no. You need to get over it."

"You didn't say no."

"Bullshit, I didn't say no."

"You didn't. You just laughed."

She rips open a gauze pad. "You should have seen yourself. You know how when a little kid does something they think is serious, but adults find it amusing? That's what you looked like. I couldn't help it. It was endearing."

"Endearing?"

"Forget it, all right? Move on."

She tapes the gauze pad over the wound, then stands upright, locking eyes with me. We're almost close enough we could kiss, and perhaps it's my imagination, but she looks like she might even consider it. But then she just starts packing away the first-aid kit, saying, "Larry needs those T-braces by tonight. And when you're done with that, fix the break room table. No more fights or I'll fire your ass. Got it?"

* * *

I turn off the engine and sit in my car a few minutes when I get home. The car grows cold, and I get out, stopping in the building entryway to fumble a little brass key into my mailbox lock. I'm bumped by Ron coming in the door behind me. He is about to head through the main door and up the stairs, but pauses, nods at me, and grins.

"Dude," he says. "I should, like, warn you—Angie's coming over tonight. You might want to put on some music or something. Especially with the kid hanging around. Won't exactly be G-rated sounds raining down, if you know what I mean."

"Thanks," I say, and he disappears up the stairs.

Right then a FedEx guy comes to the door, and I let him in. He has a package for 2B, my apartment number. But I'm not expecting anything. He hands me the box and says to have a good evening. I look at the label and see the error. It's my apartment number but it's addressed to Ron.

I carry it with me, intending to drop it off at his door, but by the time I make it up to my floor, my leg's on fire, and I can't stomach another flight of stairs. So instead I take it with me as I limp into my apartment.

Ben sits at the table with his algebra homework laid out in front of him. Pencil in mid-factor, he looks up at me and drops the sweatshirt string from his mouth. "Is it okay I'm still here?"

I look away. "That's why I gave you a key."

The apartment smells like pine cleaner. Me and my dirty work boots are standing on a freshly mopped floor. The sink is empty of dishes. The garbage has been taken out. The kid even made my bed. I set the FedEx box and the mail on the counter and remove my boots. The closet door is ajar. My pile of dirty clothes is missing.

"Where are my clothes?"

"I washed them. They're in your dresser."

"You know it's also fine just to leave things alone."

Then before I can even say hi to Prometheus, the buzzer goes off for the door downstairs.

Ben says, "It's Dad."

His eyes meet mine again before his eyebrows start fidgeting, and a series of nervous facial expressions eventually have him staring at the floor.

"He's been trying to get me to talk to him," Ben says. "I told him I'd call the police if he didn't go away."

I'd like to ignore it, but each time the buzzer goes off, it brings me that much closer to an aneurism. I limp over and press the intercom. "Yeah?"

"This is the police. We're looking for Benjamin Smith. We received a call about harassment?"

I turn to Ben. "You called the police?"

"I didn't know what else to do." He looks like he might cry.

I push the speak button again. "Sorry you had to come out here for nothing, but Dad left already."

"Just the same," the officer says. "We'd like to get a statement."

I sigh and buzz them up, open the door, and wait with my arms folded.

Two clean-shaven men in blue uniforms appear in the hall. The one who looks like he's old enough to be the other one's father clears his throat. "I'm Officer Ryan and this is Officer Mitchell. We're looking for Benjamin?"

"He's in here." I step aside.

Ben drops his pencil and closes his algebra book. His eyes run from face to face to face, meeting my eyes every third shift. He looks guilty, but really he's scared. When he was younger, he'd follow up a look like that by wetting himself. He may be fighting the same urge now with the way he's squirming in his seat.

I focus my attention on picking dirt out from under my fingernails.

"What is your name, sir?" Officer Ryan asks me.

"Jake." I point to Ben. "His brother."

Officer Mitchell turns his attention to Ben. "We received a call that your father has been attempting to contact you here, is that correct?"

Ben looks at me like I'm supposed to answer, and the chewed-up sweatshirt string is back in his mouth. When I don't, he looks back at them and nods.

Officer Ryan says, "And there's an order from Child Protective Services that prohibits such contact pending their investigation, is that correct?"

Ben nods again.

"Can you tell us exactly what happened?"

Ben just stares and chews on the string in his mouth. He looks at me again. My guess is he misinterpreted the question, thinking maybe they expect him to divulge all details related to the CPS investigation. The cops follow his gaze. "Can you tell us what happened?"

"Apparently Dad has been ringing the buzzer," I say. "Don't know. I wasn't here."

Officer Ryan looks back at Ben. "Did you let him in?"

Ben shakes his head.

"Did you talk to him at all?"

Ben says, "He said he wanted to talk, but I told him to go away."

"Did he make any threats?"

Ben shakes his head.

Officer Ryan looks to me again. "Can I speak with you in the hall?"

"Why?" I say.

"Because I'd like to speak with you in private a moment."

I follow the officer out.

After closing the door, Officer Ryan says, "He seemed nervous. I know he's going through a lot right now. Kids react differently to this sort of thing."

Staring at the floor, I whisper, "This sort of thing…" and my head tics to the side. Now I'm biting my lip, arms crossed, practically hopping in place with anxiety.

"I assume your father doesn't have a key to the apartment?"

I shake my head.

"How is your brother getting to and from school right now?"

"He takes the city bus," I say. "I leave for work before he gets up."

Footsteps come up the stairs. It's Angie—Ron's girlfriend. She continues on to the third floor only after pausing to look shocked at the policeman in the hall.

Officer Ryan says, "Has your father tried to contact him at all before today?"

"Not here. Ben just showed up at my door last night."

I'm swaying now—leaning onto my right leg until it hurts too much to think, then back to the left. I'm sure I look like a crack-head in need of a fix, all paranoid and agitated. Maybe they'll tell me Ben can't stay here. I'm unfit.

Officer Ryan says, "They'll probably issue an arrest warrant soon. They usually move fast on these types of situations."

I nod, look back down at the floor and whisper, "These types of situations…" as my head tics again. I'm clearly coming down with some sort of neurological disorder. Tourette's, or something on the autism spectrum.

He says, "It might be a good idea to chaperone when your brother goes out in the meantime."

Just then Officer Mitchell opens the door and joins us in the hall. He hands me a card.

Officer Ryan says, "Call if your father tries to make further contact." Then they both nod and leave.

I go back into the apartment, closing the door behind me.

Ben still sits in the chair looking at the floor, chewing on his sweatshirt string, his face burning red.

"I didn't mean to make a big deal out of it," he says.

"It's fine," I say, but my words don't hide my annoyance. "Don't worry about it."

He's practically shaking, about to erupt in some way. He gets up and locks himself in the bathroom.

I lean back against the counter and exhale as if I've been holding my breath this whole time. Maybe I have been. I grab a cup from the cupboard, fill it with water, and drink it down. I fill it again, but I haven't pissed all day and the bathroom is presently occupied.

I scratch my head, and my fingernails come back black with welding grime.

Little whimpering sounds come from the bathroom, and more of the stifled sob-bursts like he did early this morning. I grab the FedEx package, thinking maybe now would be a good time to deliver it—get out of the apartment and away from Ben crying for a few minutes. But that's when the non-G-rated sounds from upstairs begin. A rhythmic creaking of the floor boards, and, good god, Angie's a moaner.

I sit at the table with the package instead, turning it around and around, looking at the address from every angle. Ronald Duncan. Ron the Douche-wad—I squint and that's what it says.

The return address is some pharmaceutical company in Canada. I run my hand over a loose flap of tape. I flick at it lightly with my middle finger, testing to see just how loose.

The noises upstairs alternate between jackrabbit with high-pitched shrieking, and slow motion with deep moaning.

Down here, it sounds like someone's torturing a puppy in the bathroom as Ben continues to despair.

I blink, and for a second I'm in my old room growing up, lying in bed, staring at the ceiling, perfectly still and barely breathing; the door opens and Dad enters quietly with two beers in hand, sits on the bed beside me, taps my shoulder with a beer, leans over, and whispers, "Hey."

I open my eyes, and I can't breathe right.

*Jesus, Benny. Jesus.* I rub my hands over my face. I don't need this.

I fidget with the box until I've got the tape halfway off, then decide, fuck it—Ron can think the box got lost in the mail.

The rest of the tape comes off in one slow, smooth pull. I fold back the cardboard flaps, and there, snug in a mess of packing peanuts, is a sixty-count bottle of Prozac.

I laugh. *Dude*, who still lives off his parents and his only function in life is to caretake a building of twelve tenants, spending the rest of his time at the gym or partying or whatever the hell else he does with his college degree. *Dude*, whose girlfriend screws him so thoroughly that it can be heard from every corner of the building at all hours of the night. *Dude* deems himself in need of antidepressants.

The sounds upstairs culminate in a screaming orgasm as I drop the pill bottle back in the box. Then Ben comes out of the bathroom, his face red at the tips, and shiny, and his eyelashes wet. He inhales slowly through his nose and exhales out of his mouth, working a tenuous composure. Snot drips from a nostril, and he's quick to wipe it with the already slug-trailed sleeve of his sweatshirt. He looks at the box and says, "What is that?"

"Nothing," I say, and shove it in the cupboard above the fridge.

Then he says, "If you want, I can make dinner."

I stare at him a moment. "What, you had time to get groceries, too? Did you even make it to school today?"

He shrugs and looks sideways.

I sigh and make a break for the bathroom before he gets any ideas about going back in there. "I need a leak and a shower."

My bladder is so near bursting that peeing hurts at first, and it takes a minute before I realize there's not a speck of piss or dirt or pubic hair anywhere—in the shower, on the rim of the toilet. No toothpaste blobs in the sink, no water splatters on the mirror, no black layer of grime on the bottom of the tub. The floor's been swept and mopped; the towels are hanging and folded and smelling like fabric softener. Stripping off my work clothes and throwing them in a dirty, stinking pile on the floor feels like desecrating a work of art.

\* \* \*

Dinner is spaghetti and garlic toast and Ben seeking approval. It's the first real food I've had in days.

"This is good," I manage. "Thank you."

Ben settles in his seat. He looks at his plate and back up again like he wants to say something. He takes a deep breath, and opens his mouth. "Jake? Do you take anti-depressants?"

"What?"

"I saw the Prozac in the box you shoved in the cupboard."

"No. That's not mine. I got a neighbor's package by mistake."

"If it was a mistake then why did you keep it?"

"I'm not keeping it. I'll give it to him later. And why are you digging through my cupboards?"

He pokes at his food, then blurts out, "I'm worried about what's going to happen. Dad's really mad, and I'm scared he's—"

"How was school today, Benny?" I interrupt him.

"School?" he says.

"You didn't go, did you?"

"It was just one day."

"If you're not careful your grades are going to start slipping."

"My grades are fine. I made honor roll last term. Besides, you're one to talk. You dropped out of college to weld for a living."

"Now you're sounding like Dad," I say.

"Why are you doing this?" His eyes are watering again.

"Doing what?"

"You've been mad at me ever since I came here. I had nowhere else to go."

I drop my fork on my plate. "I'm tired," I say. "I had a long day at work."

I get up, scrape my food into the garbage, and set my plate in the sink.

# CHAPTER FOUR

My work week is four ten-hour shifts, which always leaves me with Fridays off. But despite it being Friday, I'm awake again at four-something, pretending not to hear a repeat of Ben's sad puppy routine. I lie awake in bed past 5:30, 6:30, until the sun comes up. Slivers of light break through the blinds and illuminate the fetal-positioned, perfectly peaceful Ben on the floor.

"Time to get up," I say.

He stirs but doesn't wake.

"Ben. Get up. You've got school."

His eyes open, and he appears disoriented for a second, then bolts upright. He glances at the clock, and speed-dresses into his clothes.

I grab a pair of jeans from my dresser and put them on. "Don't worry about the bus," I say. "I'm giving you a ride today."

\* \* \*

When I get back from dropping off Ben, I pass Ron in the entryway. He's looking over the mailboxes.

"Dude," he says. "Have you seen, like, a package down here? FedEx said it was delivered, but I never got it."

We lock eyes a moment as I swallow my guilt. "No idea," I say. "I'll let you know if I see anything."

In my apartment, I drop my keys on the table, kick off my shoes, and lie down in bed, trying to fall back asleep, but the phone rings. I try to wait it out, but it keeps ringing and ringing, so I get up and check the caller ID. It's Mom.

I pick the phone up. "Hi, Mom."

What comes through the phone next is hard to make out because it's communicated through a blubbering wetness. I do catch "Police," "Warrant," "They took your father away." And then, "Please come. I don't know what to do."

A half hour later, I'm standing in my parents' driveway in front of their snot green house. The same color it's always been. The color that was pre-mixed on clearance some thirty years ago when Dad bought out the stock and has been repainting with it ever since. The siding, the eaves, the pillars, the steps, all sick with green.

Inside, Mom sits folded up on the peach floral sofa, still in her bathrobe, a tissue box in one hand, a fistful of tissues in the other.

"Hi, Mom," I say.

"They came into our house and questioned us like we're criminals," she sobs. "This is not right. You need to set him straight, Jacob. I can't do this. I can't even look at him anymore."

"Look at who?" I ask.

"Ben!" she outright wails.

It's like the freaking twilight zone, and Mom's in her own alternate universe.

She digs through a box full of prescription pill bottles sitting on the coffee table in front of her, looking at each bottle in turn, setting a few of them aside. Opening a bottle, she pours a pill out, puts it in her mouth, and takes a drink of her tea. I sit beside her and put the bottles back in the box.

"What are you doing?" she says.

"You can't do this, Mom. You shouldn't be taking any of these."

"Your father got those for me."

"Dad's not a doctor. You're going to make yourself sick."

She swats at my hand and starts crying again.

"I don't understand your brother. Is he trying to rebel? Did he get this idea off the Internet? Do we not give him enough attention?"

Clear snot runs from both her nostrils, seeping into her mouth a little and down her chin. Suddenly I'm hit by this all-consuming, chest-tightening hurt—the kind that makes my ears burn, my eyes burn, my gut cramp. That she can whine like this when she's been living in this house the whole time. Benny didn't deserve this. Benny did nothing wrong. I want to be mad at her. I want to say, *You fucking delusional bitch. You're his goddamn mother*, or something like that, but I only nod.

"The pharmacy called this morning and wanted to know why your father didn't come in to work," she says. "I told them he was sick, but what about tomorrow? What about next week? How long do you think before they let him go?"

"Maybe just tell them he's very sick," I say. "Cancer or something. I don't know."

"You think it will be that long?"

"I have no idea."

"Can you talk to the police and ask?"

"Uh...sure," I say.

"We can't afford to have your father out of work that long. Can you tell them that?"

I nod to keep her happy. I don't know how Mom thinks this works.

"Can you imagine if anyone finds out about what your brother's been saying? He doesn't realize words like that can ruin someone's reputation. Everybody loves your father. Customers ask for him specifically at the pharmacy all the time."

That might be because he's willing to fudge prescriptions for anyone who bitches about their idiot doctors. How he hasn't been caught for that yet, I don't know.

What I do know is I can't be here anymore. "I have to go," I say. "I...have errands."

She blots the streaming snot and begs one last time, "Please talk to him." Then she gets up off the sofa and death-hugs me, leaving face-juice all over my shoulder. I don't hug her back. I think I forgot how. I mostly suppress the urge to throw her across the room.

I tell her I'll take care of everything, not that I have any actual intention of doing so.

She seems satisfied that the burden rests squarely on my shoulders. I manage to pry her off me and limp back to the car.

It's three turns of the key before the engine starts. The car's going to die on me any day now because now is the most convenient time for something like that to happen. I pull out onto the street, but the world's a blur. Trees rush by, closing in; my foot is heavy on the gas. This isn't fair. Ben's my brother, not my kid. Dealing with him right now is Mom's responsibility.

A car horn honks, startling me back into reality. The light I'm driving through is red. *Shit.* Breaks squeal, and I narrowly miss being side-swiped. I'm shaking, and the steering wheel is wet with sweat.

I hit every goddamn red light the rest of the way home, and by the time I pull into the parking lot, I can no longer hold a coherent thought in my head. I can't breathe, and my heart's beating way too fast. I can't calm down.

Seconds later, I'm in my apartment grabbing a fillet knife out of the kitchen drawer. Prometheus sits on his half log, staring at me. "Don't look at me like that," I say to him. "Don't you fucking look at me like that!"

Retreating to the bathroom, I slam the door and try to catch a few deep breaths. Stripping off my pants, I sit on the lid of the toilet and use the blade to pry off the bandage on my leg, the wet, tender divot all vulnerable underneath. I know this is a bad idea, but it's the only exit in this whole mess. I can't run, I can't fight, and I can't yell and shout. I can't make anything go away.

I plunge the blade into the center of the wound. Pain resonates like a gunshot. I shiver, and for a few precious moments everything else is washed away. I pull out the blade, and my whole thigh is on fire. The raw flesh bleeds easy. My body doesn't feel like my body anymore. I'm a forest burning down. I'm bones and meat and blood that fail to form a human being.

I sit back and let the rush swallow me. My lungs open wide, getting plenty of air now. Blood seeps down the sides of my leg in a big red web, warm and slow and more of it than I anticipated. I watch it drip onto the floor, blurring. I lean increasingly to one side, unable to stop, arms dropping, the knife lands on the tile, and everything goes dark.

Sucked into some black void, parts of me on fire, parts of me freezing. Sweat soaks the creases of my palms, between each finger. My eyes blink open. I'm on the floor, wedged between the toilet and the tub. Red splotches everywhere. Blood. *Shit, shit.* I'm breathing too fast. Bleeding too much. I pull off my shirt and tie it tight around my thigh as a tourniquet. I watch for a minute to see if it's going to soak through. I pull myself up to the sink, wash my hands and get out the gauze and tape.

When I pick Ben up at school later, I wait for him to buckle, then say, "Dad's been arrested pending charges. You can go back home now."

Ben stares a moment, then drops his head. "Mom hates me."

"Mom doesn't hate you. She's just stressed out."

"She doesn't believe me."

"You have a nice bed at home—a whole bedroom to yourself in a nice big house. I want my apartment back."

"Do you believe me? Do you even know what happened?"

"We're picking your stuff up, and I'm taking you home. You need to make peace with Mom. End of conversation."

He shrinks in his seat, pulls the hood of his sweatshirt over his head, and sucks on the string. I feel like the worst asshole of a brother ever, but all I can think about is getting myself out from all of this before it collapses.

Back at my apartment I lean against the kitchen counter, arms crossed, while Ben rolls up his sleeping bag. The buzzer buzzes. I tense and stare at it. It buzzes again, so I sigh, walk over, and press the speak button. "Yeah?"

"It's the police. Can we speak with you a minute?"

I buzz them in having no idea what this could possibly be now, open the door and wait leaning against the doorframe, arms still crossed. Officer Ryan and Officer Mitchell appear.

Officer Ryan says, "Jacob Smith, correct?

"That's me."

He hands me an envelope and says, "Grand Jury subpoena."

"What?"

Officer Mitchell says, "A grand jury indictment is needed to charge your father with the crimes."

"But I wasn't involved in any of this," I say. My heart pounds, and my chest tightens. "I wouldn't have anything to say."

Officer Ryan says, "It's standard procedure to question family members. Details are in the envelope."

They each offer a nod and a small wave as they head back down the stairs. I close the door, open the envelope, and look over the subpoena, the whole while Ben keeps staring.

Then he blurts, "You know they're trying to charge him with sex abuse, right?"

"I told you I didn't want to get involved with this," I say. "Did you tell them I had something to say? Why am I subpoenaed?"

"I didn't tell them anything. Just that you were my brother."

I walk into the kitchen area and set the subpoena on the counter, my back turned to Ben, but I can still feel him staring, waiting.

"Finish packing," I say. "I want to drive you home before it gets late."

"Dad did it to you, too, didn't he?"

I grip the edge of the counter so hard my knuckles go white and my fingers go numb. "Shut up about it and finish packing."

"But he did."

I turn around and look right at him, my face hot, my eyes burning, and my voice cracks. "Don't fucking do this to me right now. I didn't ask for this." I'm shaking. I can't tell if I'm scared or angry or both. "Just finish packing already."

But Ben fires right back, stone-faced. "Just say it. He did, didn't he?"

"Shut up about it!" I yell, jabbing my finger in the air at him as he shrinks back. "I told you I didn't want to get involved! You went and reported him, Ben. Not me. You made this happen! You deal with it!"

Ben looks like he's been slapped. He grabs his things, including his sleeping bag that's coming unrolled. Then he mutters, "I'll take the bus," and walks out the door.

It feels like I've been punched in the chest. I know I should go after him, but I don't. I just stand there like an idiot. He's gone. I got what I wanted. But I fucking hate myself.

# CHAPTER FIVE

A rhythmic throbbing grows louder and louder until it consumes my head, and I can't tell if it's coming from inside of me or out. It may be my heartbeat, but it feels bigger than that. It grows into a panic, and I'm only vaguely aware that this is a dream.

Someone's being hurt. Someone's screaming. Is it me? No. Ben?

I run through the woods at night like I'm being chased. The sound of heavy breathing is all around. Suddenly I look down and my clothes are gone. I look behind me and keep running. I transform, becoming younger and younger until I'm Ben's age again. I change direction and hide behind a large tree, squatting and out of breath.

More screaming and throbbing. I look all around. "Ben!"

Mom appears in front of me, holding a baby wrapped in a blanket, rocking it and looking down at it lovingly. I cover my crotch with my hands.

"He's only a baby," she says. "You should know better."

It's been a few days since I kicked him out.

The screaming grows louder and seems to be coming from somewhere else. It's a woman. I'm in my bed in my apartment. It's too dark to see. The throbbing is in the walls and ceiling. The screaming feels more real, and my brain is shocked fully awake. But the panic feeling won't leave my chest even after I realize it's just Ron screwing Angie directly over my head again.

They need to stop. I can't breathe right. I feel sick. The clock on the stove reads midnight. Ron and Angie are going at it like jackrabbits, and I fear the ceiling might give out.

I head for the bathroom, turn the light on, sit on the lid of the toilet, stare at the tub. It feels like someone's got my stomach in their fist. I throw up a little in my mouth, get up and spit it into the sink, and wash my mouth out. Finally, a screaming orgasm brings the thumping to an end.

"Jesus, fuck," I whisper, rubbing my face. I still can't breathe. I open the cupboard, retrieve a razor, and stare at myself in the mirror.

I take off my shirt. My chest is covered in old scars.

"You're a sick fuck, Jakey," I say to my reflection. Somehow those words give me power, give me a new resolve. "You're a sick fuck. You fucking goddamn moron."

Without hesitation, I press the blade vertically on the right side of my chest. I pull it out as soon as it sinks into my skin, and I don't even feel it. I see the red, but there's too much in the way for my nerve endings to get a signal to my brain. I'm not real. I'm not anything. Little beads of blood form along the inch-tall line. Some get fat enough to roll down my stomach, leaving crimson trails to my waist.

The sick feeling slowly fades behind the red. My body feels like it's glowing, becoming new, as I press the blade into my skin on a diagonal from the top of the first cut. Another slice and then another and I've made an M. I follow it with a square-shaped O, an R, another O, an N.

It's only after spelling the whole thing out that it starts to hurt. The hurt builds until it feels like I've been stamped with a branding iron. I touch the blood. My insides. My face is red in the mirror, hot and light. My chest is the bleeding title on a horror movie poster.

I wash the sink, rinse off the blade, and put it away. I wet the end of a towel with cold water and hold it to the cuts. I leave the bathroom and sit on my bed, detached from reality, but calmer.

Then my apartment doorknob twitches back and forth like someone is trying to get in. A moment later the lock clicks, and the door opens. Ben steps inside, face chapped from the cold, eyes red.

"I don't mean to break in like this," he says. "But Mom wouldn't let me come home. I stayed with Dylan over the weekend, but because there's school tomorrow his parents won't let me stay anymore, and I thought maybe I'd just try to sleep outside somewhere, but it's really cold. Can I just sleep here tonight? I'll try to find somewhere else tomorrow. I promise."

His eyes move to my chest and the blood-soaked rag I'm holding there.

"You're bleeding," he says. "What happened?"

I look down at myself and then around the room. "Come in. It's fine. Close the door."

He closes the door, drops his things on the floor, and sits in a chair. "I didn't mean to make you mad," he says.

"You didn't do anything wrong, Benny. It was me. I fucked up."

His eyes go to my chest again. "What did you do? Why are you bleeding?"

I watch his face, wait a few breaths, and pull the towel back, revealing the word carved into my chest.

"You did that?" he says.

I nod.

"Why?"

I shrug. "You were right."

"About what?"

"About Dad. He...uh..."

"Did it to you, too?"

I bite my lip and nod.

"Does it hurt?" he says.

I look down at my chest again. "A little."

"Mom says I can't come home until Dad gets out," he says, his voice rising in pitch and cracking. "But if Dad gets out, I don't know what I'll do because I can't let things go back to how they were. Not after all this."

His head is going to explode. He looks so damn hopeless. And I have no idea what else to do about it, so I say, "You want to try it?"

"Cut myself?"

"If you're careful. It'll help you sleep like a baby. I don't know about you, but I'm fucking spent."

He takes off his coat and shirt. I stand, and he follows me into the bathroom. I hand him the blade, and say, "Quick and shallow. You don't want to go too deep. It's pretty sharp. Just start small."

This is all wrong. I grab the blade from him before he can begin, get a bottle of rubbing alcohol out of the cabinet, and pour some of it over the blade before giving it back.

Ben closes the cabinet, looks in the mirror, eyes all big, and drags the blade diagonally across his stomach. He sucks in air and stares at his reflection as blood seeps from the line he just drew. He's buzzing now, too—getting dizzy like I am. He drags the blade the other way, carving a giant X, and I wonder if he's able to feel it yet.

He looks in the mirror once more and lightly traces his fingers through the drips on his abdomen, then holds his red fingers out to show me, his mouth hanging open in excited disbelief. "I'm really scared, Jake," he says.

Looking at the two of us in the mirror with our bleeding labels—Moron and X—I say, "Me, too."

# CHAPTER SIX

Monday morning I wake at 6:00 a.m. Ben is still asleep on his back on top of his sleeping bag, his bare stomach with the big X on display. I let him sleep and spend some quality time in the bathroom cleaning my wounds, bringing the phone with me. I don't know what to tell Savannah about why I'm not showing up for work today. When I finally suck it up and call, I spit out as fast as I can, "Hey, this is Jake. Very sick. Can't come in today," and hang up before she can respond. The phone rings seconds later, but I don't answer.

I clean Prometheus's tank and get him some fresh water. When it gets late enough, I toss Ben's shirt on his face to wake him. He sits up slowly. "Is it time to go?"

"Almost," I say.

He looks down at his red lines. They've started scabbing, but look inflamed in places. I tell him, "There's peroxide in the bathroom. Don't let it get infected. Trust me."

* * *

On the drive to the courthouse, Ben stares at his phone, scrolling through it with his thumb.

"You're leaving that in the car when we get there," I say.

He sighs, then lifts his shirt halfway up with his phone-free hand and pokes at the bottom end of his X, pulling the skin apart so that it bleeds a little, then wiping off the blood with his finger and rubbing it on the car seat.

"Put your shirt down and stop picking at it," I say.

He lays his shirt gently over his stomach and sits upright. "It doesn't hurt."

"That's not the point. Stop wiping your blood on my car."

"Sorry." His hand snakes back under his shirt and rests on the cut. "So," he starts. "You do this a lot?"

"Look, Benny, we don't talk about it, okay? And we don't tell anyone."

He turns away and leans his forehead despondently against the passenger side window.

I really suck at this brother thing.

When we get in the vicinity of the Justice Services building, I realize I don't actually know where I'm going. There are multiple court-type buildings spread over a few blocks. I loop around once, but I still have no idea.

"Let's just park," Ben says.

I pull over into a random parking spot on the side of the street. We get out of the car, and Ben says, "This is two hour parking only."

"And?" I say.

He shrugs and shoves his sweatshirt string into his mouth.

I pull the subpoena out of my pocket, read the address, and make an educated guess about which building it is. I try to stave off the limp for fear of drawing attention to myself. I try to make my head blank and switch to minimal functioning mode because I just want this thing to be over.

"Jake," Ben says from behind me.

"What?"

"It's here, I think."

I was walking right past the entrance. We go up the stairs and through the doors to the security check point.

Ben walks through the metal detector and past security without issue. I set my wallet and keys in a tray and send it through the x-ray machine, then set off the metal detector, loudly, as I try to pass.

Boots. I'm wearing my steel-toed work boots.

"Sir, you'll have to remove your shoes and try again."

I bend over and nearly pass out from the pain in my thigh as I undo the laces and slip them off. Then I gimp my way through the metal detector once more. Clean pass this time.

Ben saves me from face-planting on the floor by catching my arm as I fumble my boots back on. I end up with my jeans half tucked into the tops, the laces knotted poorly and already coming undone. It feels like I've managed to reopen some of the cuts on my chest, and I regret not having bandaged them because now I'm sticking to my undershirt in places.

We find a window with a secretary. I show her the subpoena and she says, "Wait just a moment," and makes a quick phone call. A few seconds later, an older man with blond-gray hair comes around the corner. He's wearing a dark gray suit and a tie with blue stripes. But what strikes me most about him, for some reason, are his shoes. They are black and shiny and laceless, and I find myself wondering where you buy shoes like that. I have never worn shoes like that. He extends his hand and we shake.

"Jacob, is it?" he says.

I nod.

"I'm Steve Warner, the district attorney prosecuting your father's case." He extends his hand to Ben. "And you must be Ben?"

Ben drops the sweatshirt string from his mouth and gives him a limp handshake.

"If you two will follow me back this way, we can talk about what's going on here today."

He leads us past some offices into a room with navy blue couches lit by lamps instead of overhead lighting. "Make yourselves comfortable," He says. "I'll be back in a minute."

Ben and I sit, and I take this opportunity to fix my boots. The kid snakes his hand under his shirt again to fidget with his cuts, and I elbow him to stop. In the few minutes of silence, the volume and rate at which my heart beats has me feeling like my body might bolt from the building on its own. I close my eyes and try to breathe just as footsteps enter the room again. The DA has returned with a woman.

"This is Jane Sanchez. She's what we call a 'victim's advocate,'" says DA Steve. "She's here to help you through this process." He then sits on the couch at a right angle to us and rests an ankle on one knee and folds his hands in his lap.

Jane is dressed to impress in a navy colored skirt-suit that only goes to her knees, and a lime green scarf around her neck. Her hair is short and dark, and her face is clean of makeup. She is tiny, thin, young, and seems to smile as often as most people blink.

"So how are you feeling this morning? A little nervous?" Her voice is directed at Ben, soft and flowing.

The sweatshirt string goes back into Ben's mouth, and he just stares at her.

"Everything probably seems like it's moving way too fast," she says.

Ben still doesn't respond, but that doesn't seem to deter her.

"The good news is, after today you'll get a break from this for a while. We can't promise that you won't have to come back if this goes to trial, but if that happens, it won't be for several months."

Ben finally drops the sweatshirt string from his mouth and says, "Is Dad here, too?"

DA Steve shakes his head. "No. When someone commits a serious crime, a policeman can't just write him a ticket as if it were a traffic violation. First, we have to present evidence to a grand jury. You, your brother, and other witnesses will be called on, one by one, to answer a few simple questions. If the Grand Jury issues an indictment, then your father will be officially charged with the crimes and likely remain in jail pending a trial."

"Other witnesses?" I say.

"The officers and investigators who questioned Ben, his counselor from school who reported the abuse, the doctor who performed the exam—"

"Exam?" I feel like I've been punched in the chest again.

"It's standard procedure to perform an exam and collect evidence following a reported rape," Jane says.

I feel a surge of sick coming on, combined with a desire to attack anyone associated with this exam process. Like an exam is somehow worse than what Dad did.

Ben slouches lower in his seat.

DA Steve says, "Do you have any other questions?"

Ben doesn't budge.

We are then led out of the room, down an elevator, and into a waiting room filled with plastic chairs, old magazines, and a bin of toys. The cops who came by the apartment are there, along with a few other people I don't recognize, some of whom nod knowingly at Ben. We sit, and Jane sits beside Ben.

All the color drains from his face when Mom enters the room, looking lost and dressed for a funeral in her nicest, darkest clothes.

Jane's automatic smile disintegrates into a grimace, and she says to Ben, "Are you okay?"

Ben's face gains color again, slowly boiling to a beet red. He nods.

Everyone in the room watches Mom as she takes a seat opposite us and stares at Ben like he's an alien. Then she opens her mouth. "You are incorrigible. Everyone is going to see this for what it is."

Jane asks Mom gently, "Would you find it easier to wait in another room?"

"I'm fine here, thank you," she says, her lips trembling as though she can barely contain her bitterness. "That's my son. I have every right to talk to my son."

Jane looks thoughtful for a second. "Well, it might be easier on everyone if we talked about something else."

Mom narrows her eyes at Jane.

I really don't need this to blow up right now.

"Mom," I say, and when she turns to me, her shoulders drop. She just stares vacantly at the floor, while DA Steve starts calling people back, one by one, to get questioned behind closed doors.

The waiting room slowly empties over the next hour or so, and soon DA Steve calls on Ben. Ben has that look as if he's going to wet himself, then he stands up and walks out of the room with an awkward gait, leaving just me and Mom and Jane.

He's not gone more than a minute when Mom moves to sit next to me.

"Please tell me you've tried to talk to him," she says.

I don't know what to say to her. I don't want to hurt her, but I can't stand being near her right now. I know she's wrong. I just don't know how much she's aware of it.

"Jacob? Are you listening to me?"

"It's okay, Mom," I say.

"We never even had to ground you once," she says. "But Ben has a mean streak in him. I've never understood why."

Jane looks at me like she wants to say something, but doesn't. The cuts on my chest itch and burn, and I want to scratch them, but instead, I tuck my hands into my jacket pockets and make tight fists, digging my fingernails into the calluses on my palms.

Soon Ben returns with red-rimmed eyes, and sits on the opposite side of the room. He pulls his hoodie over his head and tightens the strings until the top half of his face is hidden, then tucks the end of a string in his mouth.

Mom is called next. I grab an old National Geographic and pretend to read about the oceans of the world. Jane attempts to engage Ben in small talk, but he's checked out.

Then I hear Mom's raised voice coming through the closed doors down the hall. There's a crashing sound, like someone tipped over a chair or dropped a book, and then a chorus of people shouting. A security guard rushes towards the grand jury room, and a moment later, the guard leads Mom past the waiting room, her face soaked with tears and snot and fear. She slows her gait as she makes eye contact with me, and the guard tells her to keep walking.

Then it's my turn.

The grand jury room is a small room with a large white table and a bunch of ordinary people sitting around it. A jury of peers. At the head of the table is a woman with a laptop labeled as being property of the courthouse. I am asked to sit at the opposite end, and

DA Steve begins, "Can you tell us your name and relationship to Benjamin Smith?"

I swallow and rub my sweaty palms on my jeans. "Jacob Smith. I'm his brother."

"Is your brother currently staying with you or at home with your mother?"

"With me."

At that, the jury looks relieved.

"How long has he been staying with you?"

"Since just before our dad was arrested."

"Has he stayed with you in the past?"

"Yeah, for a night or two here and there."

"Is it safe to say you've had ample opportunity in the past several years to get to know your brother and observe his and your father's behavior?"

I nod.

Then he says, "Now, realizing that at the time it may not have been obvious what was going on with your brother, looking back—in hindsight—can you recall any behaviors that might have been indications of sexual abuse?"

I'm taken aback at how effortlessly he drops those words. Everyone stares, waiting, and I mumble, "Maybe."

"Can you describe those behaviors?"

"He'd seem awkward. Insecure. Withdrawn. Too much like how I remember being at that age."

DA Steve, who had been leaning back in his chair, now sits bolt upright, arms folded on the table. "What do you mean how you remember being?"

I wince. *Crap.* "When I was his age," I blurt out, as if that would explain it.

DA Steve is trying not to let on to the jury that this is news to him. But all eyes are on me. I've given it up. They know. I can't look at any of them for fear they'll somehow glean too many details from my eyes.

"You felt the same way?" says DA Steve.

"W-we had the same father," I say, and my voice is barely audible.

DA Steve manages to lock eyes with me now, but I can't stay there. I look down at the white space of the table in front of me.

"So are you saying that your father also abused you?"

My chest is so tight that I can't seem to find enough air to speak. Everyone just keeps staring, waiting. They might as well be asking, *Are you a sick fuck, Jakey? Would you strip please and let us see your scars?*

I finally nod to get it over with, which is followed by a symphony of tiny gasps.

"Was the last incident more or less than six years ago?"

"More."

"And what is your age right now?"

"Thirty."

He then tells the jury that due to the statute of limitations they can't charge Dad with what he did to me, but can consider my statement as evidence he was capable of doing what he did to Ben.

\* \* \*

Jane leads Ben and me back up to the room with the couches to wait while the jury decides whether or not to indict.

"It doesn't usually take more than an hour," she says, and I start to think about my car parked in the two hour parking zone. I don't have a watch, there is no clock in the room, but it must be at least seventy hours since we got here. I probably have a dozen tickets by now.

Jane brings in a stack of magazines and lays them out on the small table in front of our couch. I grab a Sudoku book from the pile. Ben stays hidden under his hood.

"Do you have a pen?" I ask Jane.

She pulls one from her pocket and offers it to me. "I'll be in Room 217 down the hall," she points. "If you need anything, don't hesitate to come find me."

Four five-star Sudokus later DA Steve enters and sits on the other couch. I toss the book on the table and elbow Ben, who has either fallen asleep or died.

"The jury charged your father with sexual abuse. A trial date will be set that will probably get moved a few times before it actually happens—if there isn't a plea bargain instead. If there is a trial, I will be calling you to go over how all of that will work, but otherwise, you can put all of this behind you for the time being. You should know that your father's defense attorney may try to question you as they build their case, but you are well within your rights to refuse."

"Dad stays in jail, then?" Ben says, his voice weak and wavering. The hood of his sweatshirt is falling off his head, revealing his red and glossy eyes.

"Most likely, yes," says DA Steve. He sighs and leans forward. "You did the right thing, Ben. I know it isn't easy to speak about things like this. What your father did was unforgivable and not your fault. And he's now facing the consequences. You did nothing wrong here, okay?"

I'm staring at DA Steve's shiny shoes wondering how many times he says those lines in a given year and if he means them or not, or if they're just automatic to him. Ben sniffs and does his slow, trying-not-to-cry breathing.

Steve extends a hand for me to shake again and says, "Thanks for coming down here today."

Ben and I exit the courthouse and go back out into the wide world, which looks to be about the same as we left it. Except that now, flapping in the breeze under my windshield, is a bright yellow parking ticket.

On the drive home Ben has this thousand-yard stare like he's in shock. I try to distract him by telling stories about all the stupid shit he used to do when he was two. How he would color himself with markers and eat his food without hands like a cat. But none of it registers, and I feel like a dumbass for trying.

# CHAPTER SEVEN

Savannah comes *click, click, fwooping* over to me with a sticky note. Sticky note reads, "Mom says Ben's school called. Pick Mom up and go there ASAP. Cuts on his body."

She says, "Who's Ben?"

"My brother."

"Sounds serious. Remember to clock out."

I do not want to clock out. I do not want to go. I do not understand why Mom is unable to drive herself. "You really want me to leave work?"

One arm horizontal under her melons, one hand palm up, weight in one hip, she says, "He's your brother."

\* \* \*

I spot a police cruiser when I pull into the parking lot and start wondering what sort of punishment razor-sharing incurs.

The eerie familiarity of my old high school hits like an ache. Those were the years it really sank in how everything Dad was doing with me—that I was doing with him—wasn't normal. There's something worse about loneliness when you feel it even in a crowd, and I see corners and walls and benches that I remember standing near, sitting on, as people walked by. Part of me had wanted them to continue ignoring me. I didn't want anyone to know how stupid I was. At the same time some part of me was waiting for someone, anyone, to help somehow. I just didn't know what that help should look like and how it could happen without everything blowing up. Much as it is doing now for Ben. Some of my teachers knew Dad—

were regular customers at the pharmacy. They liked him. They bought his smiles and well wishes. That picture was too convincing. No one would believe me.

Mom follows feebly behind, letting me lead the way to the front office. We are directed to a small conference room. Principal Stenberg introduces herself and shakes our hands. Mom in turn says her name is Helen, and I tell them I'm Ben's brother.

Principal Stenberg is a stout looking woman, approximately twice my age. Not fat, but thick like a tree with deep roots. Her face is gruff, and she has a fair amount of facial hair for a woman, but wears it like it's unimportant. She introduces Mr. Oates, the school counselor. I recognize him as someone who was at the grand jury hearing, though he left before Mom's hysteria.

Mr. Oates is a twenty-something guy with round glasses and straight, blonde hair tied back in a ponytail at the base of his neck. He wears khakis and a button-down, long-sleeve blue shirt, and I get the impression he's the sort that's into dungeons and dragons.

Before he can be formally introduced, the officer nods his head and says, "Officer James." He does not offer a hand to shake. A muscled cop with a military buzz cut, his workout regimen is likely meant to make himself appear as threatening as possible. His face has the early wrinkling of a man in his late thirties, and I don't get the sense that his mouth ever wanders too far from a sneer.

"Have a seat," Principal Stenberg says, gesturing at a round table with evenly spaced chairs.

Ben sits to the right of the counselor. The principal sits on the other side of the counselor, and the cop sits on the other side of the principal. Mom sits by Ben, leaving me the seat between her and the cop.

Ben won't look at me, but everyone else gives me furtive glances.

Principal Stenberg sits upright, her forearms on the table, hands clasped. But she's not the one who leads the conversation.

Mr. Oates begins, "So, what's going on today is that one of

Ben's classmates noticed some large cuts on his stomach when he was in the locker room before PE. Were either of you aware of the cuts?"

Everyone looks at Mom first, but she just stares, wide-eyed, clutching her purse in her lap as though it is a floatation device, and she's treading water in an ocean. She slowly shakes her head. All eyes move to me.

"Were you aware of the cuts on his stomach?" Officer James asks.

His eyes say he knows the answer. He wants to see if I lie. I look over at Ben who has turned so far away that I can't even see his profile. I nod.

"Your brother tells us you gave him a razor and showed him how to use it to hurt himself," Officer James continues.

Ben turns my way the slightest bit. His eyes roll sideways to meet mine, then he turns back. Mom's in a trance, staring beyond everyone at a framed picture of a ship on rough seas hanging on the wall behind the principal.

"Did you?" Officer James says.

"It sounds bad, when you put it like that," I say. "It wasn't really like it sounds."

"Then what was it like?" Principal Stenberg asks.

"It was stupid. A serious misjudgment on my part. But it's not happening again, I promise."

Mr. Oates says, "This sort of thing is very serious. I'd highly recommend trying to get Ben some counseling."

Officer James says, "I'm going to write you up for negligence, so you can go tell a judge about how this was just a misjudgment." His face looks even more dangerous, and I get the sense that he isn't just performing his cop duties, he outright hates me.

"My record's clean," I try. "It won't happen again."

Officer James tilts his head in sarcastic imitation of a parent scolding a child. "And how do we know that? You haven't explained how it happened the first time."

Principal Stenberg seems uncomfortable with the officer's lack of professionalism and turns her attention towards Mom. Everyone else in the room except for Ben follows suit—the whole lot of them staring at Mom and waiting for Principal Stenberg's words. "Ben has told us that he's been staying with his brother and not at home, is that right?"

Mom purses her lips and nods solemnly while staring down at the floor beneath my chair.

"Is there any reason why Ben shouldn't go back home?"

Mom looks at Ben. "This whole thing with his father has been very stressful on all of us. Jake has been helping out," she says.

Officer James says, "His father isn't still in the home, is he?"

She shakes her head.

Ben says. "He's been arrested."

"So presumably there's no reason for him not to go back home, is there?"

"He can stay with Jake," Mom says. "I'm okay with that. They get along well."

Officer James says, "Mrs. Smith, with all due respect regarding the difficulty of your current circumstances, Jake gave your son a razor and showed him how to hurt himself with it."

"Jake is my son, too."

"Is there a reason why Ben shouldn't come home with you? Because if there is, we're going to need to make arrangements for finding a safe place for him to stay."

"Why can't he stay with Jake?"

Officer James says, "Ma'am, is the answer to that question really not clear to you?"

"Jake has been helping," Mom says.

"Helping?"

"People make mistakes," she says.

The cop, the principal, and the counselor all look at each other, trying to figure out who's going to make the judgment call.

If nothing else, while Mom won't be easy to live with, she's also not going to hurt him, and I'll at least know where he is. It pains me to have to do this, but I need to cover for Mom's outright insanity.

"She's just upset," I say. "Ben's fine going home." I immediately get the sense that my words aren't worth much to anyone except for Ben, who turns toward me and slips his sweatshirt string into the corner of his mouth.

Mom has reached the threshold of what she's capable of suppressing, and she bursts, her voice making this warbling wail, like a hand-cranked siren, growing louder until she breaks into a sob, spewing snot and tears onto the table. I am in a dream. A nightmare. I'd like to be anywhere else. Drop me in hellfire.

Principal Stenberg says, "Mrs. Smith, you need to calm down or I'm going to ask you to leave."

Ben is still looking at me, ignoring Mom. "I didn't mean to tell," he says. "They asked, and I didn't know what to say. I didn't mean to." He stares a moment longer, blushing, then he pulls his hood up over his head.

Mom is still sobbing.

Principal Stenberg retrieves a box of tissues and places it in front of Mom. "I'm very serious," she says, but her demeanor is not without compassion. Mom doesn't seem to have the wherewithal to use the tissues, so I start pulling them out of the box and forcing them into her hand.

Mr. Oates keeps saying, "All right, let's all calm down." Then he bobs his head around, trying to make eye contact with Ben. "This is okay. This is all going to get sorted out. We're just trying to figure out what will be best for you."

Officer James shifts angrily in his seat.

Ben's face is all but gone under his now tightened hood. He bobs a knee up and down, and wipes his face with his sleeve.

"Ben," Mr. Oates says. "Let's go into my office for a minute, all right?"

Mr. Oates stands. Ben does, too, and walks behind Mom and me, towards the door. Before leaving, he turns back and shoots me this look like I broke him, betrayed him, abandoned him. And I did fuck up, I really did.

With them gone, Officer James leans forward in his seat, as if trying to intimidate Mom as much as possible. Little does he know, that doesn't take much. Principal Stenberg shifts sideways in her seat, as though attempting to project some invisible barrier between the officer and Mom. "We all need to relax and take some deep breaths here," she says.

Officer James keeps his eyes on Mom and says, "If you don't straighten up and pull yourself together, I will be taking your son somewhere else until things settle down. Is that what you want?"

Mom is no longer crying. She has that repentant dazed look she always gets anytime Dad is upset. And Dad never even yells much when he's upset. He just has this way of spinning things to make you feel wrong.

"The last thing your son needs right now is to have all the adults in his life acting like irresponsible children," the officer continues.

Mom nods as though she's a puppet and Officer James has her strings.

"Should I feel confident sending him home with you? Because right now you're not giving me much of a reason to."

Mom nods again.

I almost want to defend her. I want to tell the officer to shut up. I lock eyes with the principal. Maybe I can appeal to her. Her face almost looks receptive, like she's waiting for me to go ahead. That, or she's studying me. She's assessing what sort of person I am.

"It's okay," Mom says weakly. "I can take him home. It's okay."

Officer James sits back and nods towards the principal. The principal says, "Mrs. Smith, how about you come with me and retrieve your son?"

"I was her ride here," I say.

Officer James says, "Then I'll give them a ride back." He stands. "You made my job easy coming here. Now I don't have to hunt you down to write you up." He tells me to walk with him.

I follow him to the parking lot. We stop in front of his police car, and he asks for my license. I hand it to him and he says to wait. He sits in his car for a minute, talking on the radio, writing stuff down. Then he comes back out, returns my license, explains how I'll have to appear in court, and asks me to sign under the boxed-in bold words, **Without admitting guilt, I promise to appear at the time and place indicated below.** He separates the carbon copies, hands me mine, and says, "All the details are on the back."

I'm about to leave when he adds, "You know, I have a kid your brother's age. If anyone hurt him, do you know what I'd do?"

He looks around the parking lot, and the next thing I know, his fist comes around and hooks me right in the jaw. I almost go down but manage to stay on my feet. Immobilizing pain swallows the whole left side of my face, and my mouth fills with blood. I double forward and spit a big gob of red onto the pavement.

He says, "The kid's already been through hell and you go and teach him that emo bullshit? What the fuck is wrong with you, you piece of shit?"

# CHAPTER EIGHT

I stop by Mom's in the morning and leave all of Ben's things on the porch.

When I get to work Savannah greets me at the front office. "You never came back yesterday."

"You're very observant." I clock in.

"What happened?"

"It's complicated."

"I mean, your face," she says, referring to the swollen, split lip and purple jaw line.

"It's still there as far as I can tell."

Hands on hips shifted asymmetrically, her lips purse flat like a duck's bill. "Are you getting into bar brawls now in your off hours?"

"No, I just sometimes run into walls."

Her arms fold slowly over her cleavage. "Is your brother okay?"

"He's fine."

"Was he hurt or something? What was the whole thing about having cuts on his body?"

"It was nothing."

"Nothing?"

I walk away, and for once she doesn't follow me.

My head is still mush. I grab a handful of welding rods from the cabinet in the back and hold them in my armpit as I drag the welder over, but all the rods fall to the floor.

Fuck it. I'll make Carson pick them up when he comes in.

I move the welder again, and I'm looking up under the trailer to see where I left off yesterday when I hear Savannah *click-fwooping* around the corner. She doesn't see the rods and steps right on them, slick as ball bearings, and goes down with a *click-fwoop-crash*.

Rick drops everything and rushes to her assistance, offering her a hand as she lies sprawled on the floor, her skirt riding up, the brown edge of one nipple peeking over the top of a partially exposed bra. She quickly pops back on her feet like a weeble, and the rods clang loudly against each other as she kicks them in frustration with the toe of her high-heeled shoe before brushing herself off and tucking her bits away. Then she huffs and puffs and clicks back to the office. Rick picks up the rods and looks around the shop with a grin as if maybe this was a gift from the welding rod fairy.

\* \* \*

I spend the evening poking under the hood of my car trying to determine why it fails to start half the time. You might think it would be a problem with the starter, but I replaced that, I replaced the battery, and it's still having issues. Also, it's dark out and starting to rain. Big fat drops smacking me on the head as I stare at the dying innards of the vehicle I've had since I was a teenager.

I hear footsteps crunching on the gravel and look up to see Santa Claus coming to town. A round man with a bushy white beard lurches toward me. But this Santa never bathes and has lost a few teeth; he's wearing a trench coat instead of a red suit and has a drug-shriveled face in place of rosy cheeks. To my surprise, he gets into my personal space, and spits out, "You wanna buy some Vitamin K?"

He towers over me, smelling like ass. I hold up the wrench in my hand like I'm going to hit him, but he just laughs.

"Come on," he says. "I've got surplus to offload, and I'll give you a good price."

"Not interested," I say, still holding up the wrench.

"What?" he shouts. "I didn't hear you."

"You know what?" I say. "Fuck it. How much?"

He blinks his eyes and pushes out his face with the word, "Forty."

I slip him two twenties. He breaks into a dirty grin, presses a small packet into the palm of my hand, and walks off.

Now I'm out forty bucks, have an illegal substance in my possession, and it just won't stop raining. I'm completely soaked and shivering, so I give up on my car for the time being and go inside.

After warming up with a shower, I sit at the table and look at the white packet from all angles. I open it, lick my finger, touch it to the powder, and touch it to my tongue. It tastes sort of like sweet soap.

I rinse my mouth with water and spit it out.

Footsteps come up the stairs, continuing to the floor above me. Ron's door opens and closes. There is giggling. And in less than a minute, the screwing begins.

I start thinking about Ron's magic Prozac in the cupboard above the fridge. I pull out the box and set it on the table beside the Vitamin K packet. I take out the bottle of Prozac and turn it around and around in my hands, passively wondering if it's the sort of thing someone can OD on.

All the while above me Angie lets out deep, lustful moans. Ron starts grunting along with her.

I twist off the cap and shake a pill into my palm. The green and white capsule of magic. Ron's cure-all for the times when he almost feels a little sad. I tug at the ends of the capsule, and it slides apart. White powder drains onto the table. It doesn't look all that different from the Vitamin K.

The pounding continues upstairs. I watch the ceiling, trying to see if it's visibly moving—if it might crack and give way. I pinch some Vitamin K into the white end of the capsule. Capping it with the green, I set it down carefully so it doesn't roll. I feel like I've seen my dad do this sort of thing before—change out what's in a capsule—but I don't recall the context. I splay my hands in front of me. They're shaking.

I get a bowl from the cupboard, pour the bottle of Prozac into it, and put the tampered pill inside the bottle. I continue to slide each capsule open, pour out the Prozac powder, and refill it with a few pinches of Vitamin K.

Ron and Angie pick up pace. It feels like they're having sex inside my head. I contemplate swallowing the whole pile of Prozac powder and letting someone find me dead on the floor only after I've decayed enough to stink up the place. I suppose I could take a few Vitamin Ks and see what they do, but I can't stand the thought of turning into Mom when she's hopelessly addicted to happy pills—all ignorant of reality to the detriment of everyone around her. No, I'm done playing with my toys and should throw it all in the trash—get rid of the evidence, right?

Except I don't.

Instead I wedge the bottle full of altered pills back into the box, refluff the packing peanuts, and seal it up with fresh tape. With a black sharpie, I write the correct apartment number on it.

As Ron and Angie near orgasm, I make a quick limp down the stairs, deposit the package by the mailboxes, and return to sit at my kitchen table. The sex sounds finally stop and blissful silence returns. I sweep the remaining pile of Prozac powder into the bowl and dump it into the garbage.

The base of my skull starts throbbing.

I sit on my bed and stare at Prometheus in his tank. He's walking around like he can't decide what to do with himself, so I remove the lid and pick him up. I lay on my bed and let him crawl around on my chest as I pick the remains of shedding skin off of his toes. He settles somewhere over my heart and closes his eyes. He's so pale, I can see his pink insides through his skin in places.

# CHAPTER NINE

I have a Latin phrase book. It has useful phrases in it like: omnia dicta fortiori si dieta Latina, which means: everything that can be spoken is stronger in Latin. There was a time when I tried to memorize everything I read to see if my brain would reach full capacity and nothing else could get in.

Of course, that's not how it works. Your brain prioritizes. If something more important comes along, your hippocampus says, *Hey, join the party.* At least that's what it says in *Cognitive Neuroscience: An Introduction*, by Henry Falstaff, which sits next to the Latin phrase book on my bookshelf, which sits next to *Probability and Statistics*, by Armond Chev, which sits next to *Ancient Greece*, by Joan Walberg, and I could go on. Half of these books I've read so many times I could recite them by heart. Some I've had since I was a kid—usually presents from Dad. Some are remnants of my attempt at going to college a decade ago, because once upon a time I was smart. The rest, I've picked up at odd bookstores over the years. All of them non-fiction. It's easier that way. No emotional investment required.

I haven't heard from Mom or Ben in weeks. Pretty much that day at the high school was it. No more weeping phone calls. Mom is past weeping. Ben's a ghost—a figment of my imagination. And I'm back to my standard aloneness. Just me and Prometheus. But it feels less okay than it ever did before.

Sometimes at night I hear crashes and thuds from 3B above me, usually followed by a loud, "Shit!" or "Dude!" But mostly when I see Ron, he looks kind of happy, just with abnormally large pupils.

Ron's fuck sessions have decreased in number and intensity—there's something to be thankful for. The Vitamin K is doing something, but it isn't killing him. What I find most interesting is that he doesn't seem to suspect anything is up.

Today I go to court to face my negligence charge. I haven't yet asked for the day off work, and I don't know how to say it right. I'd ask Prometheus for advice, but he's a fucking gecko.

Savannah should be in the office by now, and pretty soon she's going to wonder why I'm not there. I default to the genius last minute plan of calling in sick again. But when I do, I don't hang up fast enough, and Savannah meets my excuse with an indignant, "That's funny, because you don't sound sick, and you were fine yesterday. How about you tell me the real reason?"

"I have to go to court."

"Traffic ticket?"

"Not exactly."

"DUI? Busted for pot?"

"No, it's my brother."

"What's going on with your brother now?"

"I'll be in tomorrow," I say and hang up before she can get another word in.

* * *

I stand like a shamed felon in front of the judge, an angry looking older man with a round face and dark caterpillars for eyebrows. He stares through glasses at the papers sitting in front of him and says, "Jacob Smith. Is that you?"

"Yes."

"It looks like you've been charged with negligence, is that correct?"

"Yes."

"And how do you plead?"

"Guilty?"

"Can you tell me what happened before I make a judgment on

this?"

"I don't know."

The judge takes off his glasses and looks right at me. "You don't know? Then why did you plead guilty?"

I take a deep breath and swallow. "I gave a razor blade to my brother and showed him how to hurt himself with it."

"How old is your brother?"

"Fifteen."

"How old are you?"

"Thirty."

"And why did you show your brother how to hurt himself with a razor blade?"

"I don't know."

"Try again."

I look at the floor. "He was upset. I wasn't thinking clearly. I was trying to help him, I think."

"And why did you think showing him how to cut himself would help him?"

"I don't know."

"Try again."

A lump swells in my throat. "It's something I do to myself sometimes."

"Does it help you?"

I shrug. "Not really."

"Then why did you think it would help him?"

I shrug again. "I didn't."

"Didn't what?"

"I didn't think."

He says, "Do you realize what you did was wrong?"

I nod.

"I can't hear your head bobbing."

"Yes. It won't happen again."

"Have you ever tried counseling, Mr. Smith?"

I shake my head.

"I can't hear you."

"No, I haven't," I say.

"Well, you're going to get the chance."

I don't have to pay any fines, though I'd rather. No jail time, nothing like that. Just a full year of weekly therapy sessions, because telling some stranger my personal shit will solve all my problems.

* * *

I come home to see another little brown box in the entryway addressed to Ron, but with the correct apartment number on the FedEx label this time. My first thought is that this is probably for the best. Now everything will go back to normal for him, and I can stop feeling guilty. But then my selfish side says, *Do you really want the fuck storms to start raging over your head again as you sleep? You've got a good thing going here. Ron's only banging her, like, once a week now.* And my curious side says, *I wonder how long he can keep taking the tampered pills before he figures it out. Surely this is an experiment worth pursuing.* And what do I even care anymore? I already have a record, and my life's a shithole anyway. This will at least keep things interesting. I stack my mail on top of the box and carry it up the stairs with me.

I spend the rest of the day in search of Santa Claus, eventually finding him passed out on a bench a dozen blocks away. The guy stinks like he's rotting so I tap his foot with the toe of my boot.

The first words out of his mouth before he's even conscious are, "Ya wanna buy some Vitamin K?"

I look around to see if anyone might have heard him. But there's no one in sight, so I hand him two twenties.

He blinks and says, "Sixty."

I pull out one more twenty, and he slips me the packet. I go home, repeat the same switch routine with Ron's pills, and leave the tampered package by the mailboxes.

I feel like I'm fucking flying.

* * *

The end of the following week, I manage to find the counseling place without getting lost, but the parking lot is nearly full. I'm early so I wait in my car for a few minutes. A few people exit the building, and for the most part, they look perfectly normal, which makes me wonder why they're even here. I don't want to be here.

I get out of my car and go inside, and it's a repeat of the parking lot: nearly every seat in the waiting room is full. I stand awkwardly at the check-in window for a good few minutes before someone finally sees me and hands me a clipboard full of paperwork. I sit down next to a tired old man leafing through a fishing magazine.

Dear god this is fucked.

Even on a good day, I don't like crowds. My heart is beating loud enough it's possible my whole body is visibly pulsing. This is why college didn't work out. Classrooms always felt like this.

I fill out all of the medical and mental history information, mostly answering no to everything without even reading it. I have this sense of being found out—like everyone in the room is wondering what's wrong with me. I start feeling like everything I do is evidence of some sort of mental disturbance, from where my eyes look to how I hold the pen to my pattern of nervous heel tapping.

Then a door opens, and a woman's voice says, "Jacob?"

I get up and follow her into her office. She greets me with a sympathetic smile.

"Call me Lauren," she says.

The upper half of her stringy blond hair is clipped behind her head. She is covered neck to wrist to toe in a lavender outfit and projects a look of perpetual concern. Her office doesn't have a couch like I imagined, but rather, two comfy chairs. One for me and one for her. In the air is the smell of recently burned incense.

She is quiet at first, leafing through my paperwork.

Being in here is only marginally easier than sitting in the waiting room. I try to breathe normally, but I only make myself light-headed.

Finally she says, "Why do you think the judge decided it would be a good idea for you to be here?" She must have read the "Reason for seeking counseling" section on the paperwork.

"Don't know."

"Can you to tell me what it was you were charged with?"

I sigh and close my eyes. "Negligence."

"Negligence for what?"

"My kid brother."

"What happened?"

"I showed him how to use a razor to cut himself."

I hear her scratch away, making notes. I open my eyes again, and she looks up. "Do you have any thoughts on that?"

"I won't do it again?" I stare sideways at her bookshelf.

She folds her hands on top of the paperwork in her lap. "I'm getting the sense that you're apprehensive. And that's fine; after all, it doesn't sound like this was your idea. But if we're going to be seeing each other once a week for a year, you can choose for that to be an annoyance, or you can choose to make use of it."

"Sorry," I say. Apprehensive isn't the word I would use. Would-rather-be-in-front-of-a-firing-squad fits better. I lock eyes with her a second. Her face narrows in concentration, watching mine too closely. I look away again.

"Let me ask you this," she says. "If you had it to do all over again, would you have made the same choice?"

That question depends on poorly defined variables. If the situation were truly identical, then obviously it would play out the same way it did. It's not like I can change the past. If I could somehow go back to the moment of decision with the knowledge I have now, then the situation really isn't identical, is it? So the question is moot. But there's no sense in pointing this out to her because what she's really asking is will I do it again, and I've already said I wouldn't. Perhaps it's worth repeating.

"No," I say.

"You know, the self-harm behavior you shared with your brother is not that terribly unusual."

"That's not what it was," I say.

She says, "You said you showed your brother how to cut

himself. Could you tell me what was going on with that, then?"

"Stress relief."

"Well," she nods. "That is one reason people do that sort of thing. Other reasons include distraction from overwhelming emotions, self-punishment, attempts to rid oneself of emotional numbness or other uncomfortable feelings. It can be a way of expressing inner pain. Some studies show that as many as one in ten people self-harm at some point in their lives."

This is supposed to make me feel like I'm not a freak. But wrong should also mean rare. Ten percent is not rare.

She runs through a long list of questions about my family and personal history, but I give her little more than pat answers. Everything's fine. Hunky-dory. I can't tell by the end if she's frustrated with me or if her general demeanor is always so tense. Or maybe I'm projecting and reading her body language all wrong—it's been known to happen.

After our little getting-to-know-you session, I leave her office, happy to be free again, and thinking ten percent of the population suffers from anxiety. Ten percent have high blood pressure. Ten percent have fucked up families. What does it matter?

Later, I overhear Ron explaining to Angie that, he's not sure, but he thinks the ghost of Freud may be speaking to him, and I'm thinking ten percent of the population has a drug problem of some sort.

Ten percent of people are morons.

Ten percent of leopard geckos are albino.

\* \* \*

At work on Monday, the sign near the front office says we have gone twenty days without an accident. I am clumsy, and I let some welding rods fall out of my arms again, accidentally on purpose, in the same place where Savannah tripped the other week. Ten percent of people are accident prone.

Not more than fifteen minutes pass before payoff. Again, it's Savannah.

*Click. Fwoop. Crash.*

But she's crying, clutching her side, and not getting up as fast this time. The lens on my welding hood was flipped up so I could watch, but when Rick goes wide-eyed at the sight of a screw impaled in her right boob, I flip it back down, and everything turns black.

I've made an error. A bad, bad error. For some reason I thought she'd just bounce right back up again.

The next day we have a safety meeting. All of us gather around a folding buffet table in the main office as Dan, the big boss, scribbles "Keep walkways free of debris" on one of those giant notepads on a tripod. Savannah sits near the front, leaning a bit to one side, a large Band-Aid clearly visible through her sheer top. She had to go to the hospital and get a tetanus shot.

I stare at her, at the spot of her gore wound. But she never looks my way, even for a second. Dan talks about the importance of keeping a clean workspace, but not the importance of walking instead of running and wearing appropriate clothing for a work setting.

# CHAPTER TEN

The thick scent of vanilla fills the air.

This is a fucking dream. A dream about fucking.

I am sound asleep, but in my mind my dick is wedged between Savannah's oiled melons. We're on a bed of some sort, the sheets of which appear pale green in the dim light of the room. At least I assume at first that it's a room.

Beneath me, her hands with their red painted fingernails press her melons together around my hard-on. Her head tilts back, and her mouth hangs open. Her eyes with their black spider eyelashes are closed. I'm straddled over her abdomen, my hands planted shoulder width apart above her head; her teased, hairspray-sticky blonde hair is all over the place. I grind back and forth between those soft masses, her nipples all hard and pointing at the ceiling.

But I feel like I'm doing something bad. I like it, but I shouldn't. Maybe she doesn't want this and is only pretending to.

My sack tightens. Her hand grabs my ass, and her nails dig sharp into my skin. My half-closed eyes open wide, and I look up, away from the sun of Savannah's hair splayed out in a halo around her head. There are no walls. Everything just fades into a dark oblivion.

There's movement in the shadows.

Her hand on my ass keeps guiding me back and forth between her tits. The wash of her skin sliding over me sends my eyes back to her face, and she's making those little moans like women do in pornos—like Angie does with Ron.

It's slippery, all of this is slippery. Vanilla is becoming not vanilla. It's sweat. Savannah's sweat. She doesn't smell right. There's a hot feeling in my blood, like it's going to burn through my skin. But I don't stop. The shadows in the void. The audience. Someone's there. Watching. My body keeps pumping, keeps going, like it has to, like it can't not.

Savannah's pinky finger inches toward my rear. I pull her hand back. She whispers, "Just relax," which echoes, and the shadows whisper it back in a voice that sounds like Dad's, and my heart slams against my chest. I look all around, Savannah's hand still guiding me back and forth. Her finger snakes around to my backside. I feel it go in, but it's way too big to be her finger, and it's not oil, it's Vaseline, the pasty, plain scent of Vaseline. I can smell it and feel it, and my ass hurts. Somehow, there's pumping at my ass. I squirt, and the pumping at my ass doesn't stop.

Hands come around me from behind, pull my arms out from under me, and I'm slammed down onto Savannah. She dissolves. She's gone. Dad's on top of me, his sweaty, wet chest on my back, shredding my ass. I can't breathe. Dad's voice steams hot into my ear, "Shhh—just relax. You're fine." My face presses into the bed, and the sheets are wet with my own drool. I can smell his salty garlic sweat, hear his skin slapping against mine, and I need to get away.

I try to kick, to fight it, but every time I move, he moans as if he likes it. I keep fighting, and I try to scream, but no sound comes out. Finally I'm able to move, and I'm kicking, and I'm in my bed in my apartment on all fours. I ram my head into the wall above my bed before scrambling sideways onto the nightstand, knocking over the lamp, and crashing onto the floor.

\* \* \*

As I enter the front office at work in the morning, every muscle in my body is prepared to run, prepared to fight at a moment's notice. Savannah says, "Good morning, Sunshine," from behind the front desk, and I flinch.

"What's with you?" she says. "You look like you're about to piss yourself."

Her eyes stay trained on me as I clock in and head through the double doors to my work station.

I get the welder set up and then forget what I'm even working on. Whatever it is, it's not near where I am. I look around the shop, waiting for something to click when Rick walks past, smirking. "You been losing IQ points?"

Then I see Carson over by the trailer hitch, about to burn his fingers off fucking with the welder without gloves. I march over and yank it out of his hands.

"What?" he says.

Everything I do the whole rest of the day feels off. My heart beats at twice the necessary rate, and it's downright exhausting.

When my shift ends, I nearly trip over my own feet on the way to clock out, running into the front desk, knocking over papers, and my hands shake too bad to even properly pick them all up. Savannah kneels down and helps, and her boob crack is way too close. I blink and see the nightmare again.

As I stand back up, Rick appears. "Damn, man, are you even safe to drive?"

His face is filled with pompous pride, and the tension that's been plaguing me all day finally erupts. Loud and clear, I yell, "Fuck off!" lunging at him before promptly leaving the building.

* * *

I sit anxiously in Lauren's office, wondering how many secrets she can guess just by the way I breathe. I still don't understand how being here is supposed to be helpful.

Lauren opens with, "Have you done anything to harm yourself since last you were here?"

"I don't do that anymore," I say. Or, I haven't done it since. Yet. Honestly I have been putting effort into not doing it. Checkmark for progress! Though it's always been cyclical, so it's only a matter of time.

Her eyebrows rise. "May I ask how old you were the first time you injured yourself?"

"No," I say. Though I appreciate her asking if she can ask instead of just asking without permission.

"Since our last visit, what percentage of the time have you felt unhappy or sad?"

I roll my eyes. "Christ."

I imagine being in here, Ben's age, looking like a dopey kid. Suppose she learns what the dopey kid's dad is like behind closed doors—that's no doubt where this is going. If she gets just the bare details, then maybe she feels bad for the dopey kid. Everyone knows grown-ups aren't supposed to engage with children in sexual ways.

"May I ask how you've been sleeping?" she says.

That question makes me tense, and then I smile at the realization that sleep actually scares me.

"How many hours of sleep do you get each night?" she asks.

I shake my head. She jots down notes.

"It's not unusual to experience insomnia or nightmares during times of stress."

"I'm not stressed." My words are so transparent, they aren't even lies. They're just a cowardly way of saying, *Lady, you make me uncomfortable.*

Oh, dopey kid, why the hell didn't you tell anyone? Dopey kid, your daddy didn't even threaten you. You went to school every day. You could have told your teacher. If you wanted it to stop. *If.* So no matter what you say, dopey kid, the fact is you must have been perfectly fine with it.

"How has work been this week?" Her words are intrusions, travelling through the air, right up into my brain without consent.

"Fine," I say.

"Have you seen or talked to your brother at all recently?"

"No."

"What about your parents?" She doesn't even give me a chance to inhale.

I shake my head and start examining the calluses on my hands, picking at the one at the base of my index finger.

"What is your relationship with your parents? Do you get along?"

"It's complicated," I say. It feels like she has her hands on my ribcage, prying it open. Looking at her only gives her more leverage.

*Tell me what your dick did during those encounters with Daddy, dopey kid. Did it stay limp? No? Tell me your real secret, dopey kid. Tell me how you liked being used. Tell me, dopey kid, how you thought your daddy loved you. And you loved him.*

"How would you describe your mother?" she says. I keep picking at my calluses, but my hands are shaking. Does she see my thoughts? Am I generating some sort of jittery Morse code that shrinks can read?

"If you could say just a few words about your mother, what would those words be?"

I shake my head. "Oblivious? Delusional?"

"And your father?"

My face burns. *Goddamn*, dopey kid, you let him make you bleed, and you somehow twisted it around in your head that this was perfectly fine. You like bleeding like that, dopey kid? The rough times—those were true love. Daddy sure smiled proudly afterwards. And oh, how you'd pride yourself on your ability to take it. It was some sick way of proving your manliness, wasn't it, dopey kid? The more you pretended it didn't hurt the more awesome you were.

"How would you describe your father?"

"Incarcerated." My voice fades to a whisper. My ribs crack all the way open and my lungs just dangle, unable to inflate.

"Oh? For how long?"

"About a month."

"What for?"

"He hurt Ben."

"Your brother?"

I nod.

"Has your father ever been in jail before?"

"Nope."

"How was your brother hurt?"

I shake my head. I start working the calluses on my other hand. It feels like the room shrank, and I'm in some cave, Lauren hanging over me. I'm afraid to look up and see just how close she is, her face giving away all of her suspicions.

"The incident that earned you mandatory counseling—that must have happened right around the time of your father's arrest?"

I nod.

"Can we talk about what led you and your brother to self-injure that day?"

"No."

What age did it finally stop, dopey kid? When you moved out? Well, dopey kid, you're either really fucking stupid, or a really sick fuck. I mean, *goddamn*, dopey kid—that was your dad. What were you thinking?

Lauren leaves a pause. Maybe I offended her. I'm being an asshole. But I can't shake the feeling that she wants to drag me into the sewer and drown me in shit. The shit needs to stay where it is. No sense in swimming in it.

"Do you miss your brother? You said you hadn't seen him in a while."

I stop picking at my hands and stare out her window at a tree cast in sunlight. It's sunny outside. I wonder how long it's been like that.

She sighs and folds her hands. Then she gives some spiel about how "this is a safe place," and whenever I feel "ready to talk" she's "ready to listen."

How does it feel to be a moron, dopey kid? The word moron is derived from the ancient Greek *moros*, meaning foolish or dull. You know all about Ancient Greece, don't you? Pederasty. That's the word. Daddy told you all about that once, didn't he? And the Melanesian tribes of New Guinea, and all sorts of traditions around the globe and throughout history. *Goddamn*, dopey kid. You were worldly.

* * *

At home I hear Ron and Angie in heated discussion upstairs. I can't make out the words, but she sounds stern. Not hurt, but annoyed. Ron sounds like he's pleading. A door slams. I go to my window, look outside, and see Angie exit the building a few moments later, walking briskly down the sidewalk.

Over the coming days I become more and more of a hermit. I don't talk to anyone at work. Savannah keeps scowling at me and pursing her lips. My free time I spend at home looking through old books I've all but memorized, like some robot taking meaningless input. I do it enough that I no longer have thoughts.

My sessions with Lauren become dry as cardboard. I refuse to answer any hard questions, ignoring her until she changes the subject. If she presses me to speak with a, "What would you like to talk about today?" I only offer her uninteresting details about things I welded that week. Or if I'm feeling spry, I regale her with tales of the Peloponnesian war, or the etymology of common words, or Gödel's Theorem, or whatever the hell else I read about recently. Sometimes she even gets details about the diet of a leopard gecko and what special care the albino ones need because of their sensitivity to light.

She can't help herself. She yawns a lot.

# CHAPTER ELEVEN

I come home and find someone in my apartment, sitting at the table. My heart makes a quick run up my throat before I recognize Ben. "Fuck," I say, and now I'm all edgy and hyperaware. It's been a few months since I saw him last.

Ben's eyes aren't visible because they're covered in an oversized pair of black-rimmed sunglasses.

"Give me ten minutes. I need a shower," I say and hide from him in the bathroom to get my bearings.

Under the near-scalding water, the black melts off my body and down the drain. My leg crater has healed into a puckered hole. On my chest, where I carved MORON, the scabs are gone and some of the scars didn't stick, so now it reads MO O . And I'm wondering why X is here and what the deal is with the sunglasses. Ten percent of the planet has a sensitivity to light. Or maybe the kid's been sad-puppying again, and he's trying to hide it.

I come out with a towel around my waist, throw on a shirt and some shorts, then sit across from him at the table. Kid looks like a stranger. It's weird having him back here. The apartment's been a dead thing without him, and I've been a zombie.

"Hi," he says, hands folded in his lap. I can't tell where he's looking because his eyes are barely visible behind giant black shields.

"So, what brings you here?"

He pulls off his sweatshirt, rolls his t-shirt sleeves up on top of his shoulders, and lifts his arms over his head, showing me a ladder of meticulous scars near his armpits. His armpits with a total of five hairs between them.

I feel sick.

"I didn't stop," he says. "But no one knows because it's hidden better this way."

The reddish flush of his cheeks and slight upturned corners of his mouth wait for feedback. I'm supposed to commend him. *You're a genius, Ben! That's the best idea ever!*

"Put your arms down," I say.

"What?"

"You shouldn't do that anymore."

"You do it."

"I do a lot of dumb things."

He lowers his arms and stares at the floor.

"Does Mom know you're here?" I ask.

"I don't think she cares," he shrugs. "She doesn't really say much about anything I do."

I fold my arms.

"Are you mad?" he asks.

His cheeks are pale now, and his mouth hangs ever-so-slightly open. Almost like the little "o" he would make with his mouth as a newborn. Dad called it the "where's the boob" face, any time something touched his cheek. Boob into mouth penetration. Bonding. The normal kind of parental intimacy. Ten percent of babies are breastfed through their first birthday. Ben was. Once upon a time Mom actually gave a shit.

I look into his big black voids. "No. I'm not mad." I get up, take the cheese out of the fridge, chop off the moldy bits, and start grating. "Have you eaten yet?"

Ben shakes his head and asks if he can help. I put him in charge of the frying pan and an unopened package of tortillas that aren't too far past their expiration date. He turns the burner on and says, "You remember about next week, right?"

Next week is the trial.

I say, "Yeah," and open a can of jalapeno peppers.

The room fills with the smell of warm melted cheese and the sharpness of jalapenos as everything sizzles on the tortillas in the frying pan.

Ben says, "So, the DA says everything moved pretty fast."

"Pretty fast?"

"Yeah, it's only been three months since they arrested Dad. He says sometimes it can take a year, even. He says he wasn't expecting it to go to trial either—usually there's a plea bargain or something, but Dad's lawyer hasn't offered one. He thinks Dad's probably not listening to his lawyer's advice, which might be a good thing for us."

"For you," I say.

"What?"

"A good thing for you. This is your case."

"Yeah. Well, I was at the DA's office yesterday. That's when he told me all of this. We went over how everything is supposed to go at the trial. Haven't they talked to you about it?"

"Not really," I say. I got a call to come in to go over trial details, too, but I asked if I had to, and they said, "Technically, no," so I went with that.

At the table, not fifteen minutes later, it starts—my body saying, *Don't take another bite, please*, but I've hardly eaten anything. Maybe the cheese was too far gone. Does food poisoning hit this fast? Ben's devouring his with no ill effect. The oil that separated from the cheese drips from the corner of his tortilla in fat, yellow drops on his plate. Every time he takes a bite it feels like it's going into my stomach, and my stomach responds by burning more acid. I take a deep breath and try to dilute the sensation of jalapenos flaming their way up my throat, but all that comes into my lungs is the taste of spicy cheese. I get up, open the window, and inhale.

Ben asks if I'm okay.

I shake my head. It feels as if my soul is trying to leave my body, anchored only by what my stomach is doing.

I go into the bathroom and sit on the floor in front of the toilet, but nothing comes up. The putrescence seeps through my core until it absorbs all the way through me. After a while, there's a faint bird-tap on the door and Ben's voice saying, "Jake?"

I make a moaning grunt that he's supposed to interpret as me saying, "What?"

"You okay?"

I grunt again and open the door.

Ben just stares at me through those giant black shields. He's cleaned the kitchen and done the dishes already.

"Should probably be getting you home," I say.

But he stands there like he's waiting for something else.

Something's not right. There's got to be some bigger reason for him coming here.

I reach out and pluck the shades from his face. Kid looks like a raccoon. Black-purple circles around his bloodshot eyes. "What is this?"

Ben says, "It's no big deal."

"This happen at school?"

Ben shrugs.

"Who did this?"

"Just some friends. They called me an emo fag. I told them to stop calling me that."

They're picking on him for the cutting, and I taught him that. They're picking on him for what Dad did. The pure rage I feel is enough to force the bile back down my throat. "Tell me the fuckers got expelled."

"I didn't tell anyone."

"You didn't tell anyone? You tell everyone about every other goddamn thing that happens to you, but not this? Have your teachers noticed?"

"It sort of just happened right after school today."

"Does Mom know?"

"I haven't gone home yet. And she wouldn't care anyway."

I put one hand on his forehead, tilt his head up, and press around the bridge of his nose, checking all the little pink and blue patches,

"Are you sure nothing's broken in there?" He winces with his mouth hanging open. I stop.

"I mean, it hurts, but I'm pretty sure I'm okay." He grabs his sunglasses and puts them back on.

Do I call the school tomorrow? Would they even care to talk to me after the last time? Mom's supposed to do this. Mom's supposed to take care of this.

"Come with me," I say, grabbing my keys, and he follows me out the door.

*  *  *

When we get to my parents' house, I tell Ben to wait in the car. Inside, Mom sits on the couch watching TV in her bathrobe, knees folded to her chest, a mug of tea in one hand. I shut the TV off. She turns toward me with the unfocused gaze of a blind person and says, "Jake?"

I say, "Benny showed up at my place today with two black eyes. Does this concern you in any way?"

"I'm sure he's all right." She's too relaxed. The fucking Valium again.

"He's staying with me," I say. "You need to stop the pills, Mom. You can't keep doing this."

She looks me in the eye. "Thank you, Jacob. I always appreciate your help." She turns the TV back on with her remote. Ten percent of the population is out of their fucking minds.

I go back to the car and send Ben in to get his things.

*  *  *

I can't hide from Lauren that something's changed. She's just suffered through weeks of me being as dull as a post, and now I'm extra fidgety and weird.

When she says, "How was your week?" it comes out with perky posture and renewed interest.

"Ben's staying with me again," I say.

"What do you mean again?"

"He'd been staying with me before the whole…razor sharing

thing." And now I feel stupid for opening that can of worms.

"Oh, I didn't know that. So what brought him back?"

"Black eyes."

"Someone hurt him?"

"Kids at school."

Lauren is sly. These last few weeks, talking about nothing at all—she got me used to talking to her. It occurs to me that I've probably exchanged more words with her in the past few months than I've exchanged with any other human being in more than a decade. I can't decide if that's a good thing or if I've been tricked.

"What about your mother?"

"What about her?"

"Why is he no longer staying with her?"

I stare out the window trying to decide how far down this road I'm willing to go. "I told you before, right?" I say. "She's oblivious and delusional. She's been actively ignoring his existence ever since Dad's arrest."

"She blames your brother for that?"

"He's the one who made the accusations."

"You've still never told me about that," she says. "What was your father arrested for?"

And there she goes, dropping the bomb. We're back to where we were when these sessions started. *What did your daddy do, Jakey?*

It's getting hard to breathe. My chest hurts. "Why do you need me to say it?" I whisper. "There's no way you haven't already guessed."

"I'm not psychic," she says. "You told me he had hurt your brother. But there are many types of abuse."

"Such as?" I say, folding my arms, my eyes trained out the window.

"Physical, sexual..."

"The second one," I say.

"I'm sorry to hear that."

She lets her words disperse until they're no longer hanging thick in the air around my head. The room fills with a cleansing silence.

Finally I say, "His trial is Monday."

She lets my words settle before asking, "Will you be attending?"

"I'm on the witness list. And someone needs to take Ben there."

"Are you nervous?"

"Um..." I squirm lower in my seat and keep staring out the window. My body starts shivering, but I'm not cold. My stomach is floating. "Yes," I say.

"Do you know what you will be asked about on the stand?"

"I've been trying not to think about it."

She nods and shifts in her seat, uncrossing her legs, then recrossing them the other way. After a few careful breaths, she says, "Was your brother his only victim?"

"He's the one this trial is about."

"Is this because of a statute of limitations?"

"What are you getting at?" I say, looking at her this time, angry, wanting her to stop.

Her posture remains firm, and she doesn't back down. "I think you know," she says, her words somehow coming out softly despite her eyes piercing right through mine into the back of my skull.

I don't know what to say to that. I want to feel relief that the cat is finally out of the bag, but at the same time the fine details paint a picture I don't think she sees yet. She'd change her opinion of me pretty quick. And for some reason her opinion has become important.

So I revert to the tactic I've been using for weeks: deflection. "You know the word 'psychic' comes from the Greek 'psychikos' which means 'of the mind,'" I say. "But it also means 'soul.' In Greek mythology, Psyche was a mortal princess who later became the goddess of the soul."

\* \* \*

In the afternoon when Ben comes home from school, face still hidden behind sunglasses, I say, "You want to come with me to get a new car? Mine's busted, and I'm tired of trying to hold it together with paperclips."

"Sure," he says, and drops his backpack with a thud on the floor.

A few hours later, I've got the keys to a Royal Blue Honda Civic. Last year's model. We pull out of the dealership parking lot and head the opposite direction from home.

"Where are we going?" Ben says.

"You'll see," I tell him. On the edge of town an old strip mall lies empty in wait of a Walmart. I park in the middle of the lot and tell Ben to get out.

I get out, too, hand him the keys, and jump in on the passenger's side.

He just stands there, holding the key out in front of him like it's a dirty napkin. "Get in the driver's seat," I say. "And take the damn sunglasses off."

He takes them off, and that nervous, I'm-going-to-wet-myself look comes over him. "But I don't have a permit."

"So you'll stop by the DMV on Monday and pick up one of those booklets and start studying. Get in."

The kid's got to move the seat forward. He's so short for his age that he can barely see over the steering wheel—like one of those grannies that drive twenty miles an hour down the freeway. And he's got no clue what to do with the damn key.

I laugh at him, and he starts blushing in frustration as he says, "I've never done this before."

I tell him it's okay, and we cover the basics. The pedals, the e-brake, the turn signals, the headlights, the wipers, and then we spend a considerable amount of time lurching across the parking lot—gas, break, gas, break—all the while our heads go back, forth, back, forth.

After I'm sufficiently satisfied with our level of whiplash, we switch back to our original seats.

Ben asks how he did.

I elbow him and say, "Not bad for a first try."

Then he smiles a real smile for once.

# CHAPTER TWELVE

The courthouse is a random slice of the populace. Men in suits so pristine they look like mannequins. People of every color. Santa Claus people. Traffic tickets, parole violations, divorces, sodomy.

I told Savannah I had the measles and needed to be under quarantine for a week. She was unconvinced.

After checking in, Ben and I go upstairs to the room with the couches again to wait for DA Steve. He comes in, looking roughly how I remember him from three months ago, only extra spiffy and mannequin-like in his own right.

"How are you guys feeling this morning?" he asks.

Seriously? We're awesome.

"Okay," Ben says.

"Do you have any questions before we go downstairs?"

Ben says, "You said I can be in the courtroom for the whole thing because I'm the victim, but can Jake be there, too?"

"Because he's on the witness list, it isn't typically allowed, but you are allowed to name a support person to sit with you, and if you want that to be your brother, I'll see if we can get the judge to approve."

Ben looks at me and nods.

"I assume you're okay with that Jacob? Being in the courtroom for the trial?"

Ben looks desperate. "Sure," I say.

We stand up, and DA Steve leads us downstairs to courtroom seven and asks us to wait outside. Ben spends a solid fifteen minutes nervously over-hydrating himself at the water fountain before DA Steve comes back out and tells us it's time.

The courtroom is wood on wood. The walls are wood, the tables are wood, the chairs are wood, the judge's bench is wood, the witness stand is wood, the jury box is wood, the bar and the benches behind it are all wood. The only thing not wood is the ceiling, the flags, and the green carpet. Ben and I sit on the right side, behind the DA. Not a single blond-gray hair on the top of his head is out of place.

Dad sits on the left, on the other side of the bar at a table with his lawyer—a woman in a skirt-suit with her hair in a bun. Part of me wants to run out the door and never look back. The other part wants to jump over the bar and kick Dad in his clean-shaven face until there's nothing but a bloody stump on his neck, but I'd for sure lose my ability to follow through as soon as he got his eyes locked on mine. He just sits there, dressed up in a pressed suit. He looks innocent. But he always has. That's always been the trick of it.

Ben, for whatever reason, looks guilty. He can't look anyone in the eye, and neither can I. We're dressed in plain clothes, but we're clean, and we smell like fabric softener. DA Steve suggested it would be best if Ben didn't wear sunglasses in the courtroom, so Ben is all blinky as his purple-ringed eyes adjust to the light. Dad, upon seeing Ben's beaten-up face, whispers something to his lawyer that I can't quite hear, but the mere sound of his voice triggers a rushing thud of blood in my ears.

Ben keeps looking back at the double doors. Finally he whispers, "Mom's not here."

"Was she on the witness list? Maybe she has to wait outside."

"No. The DA said no one wanted to put her on the stand so they never subpoenaed her."

"Did she say she was coming?"

"No, but I thought she would."

Mom's been avoiding reality for so long that I can't imagine why she'd stop now. It's better for her if she can sit at home and pretend the trial involves nothing more than Ben saying, "Dad was bad," and Dad saying, "I'm innocent," followed by a verdict.

At the front of the courtroom, files are handed back and forth. The judge says a few words to the jury and then to the lawyers.

During the opening statements, Ben elbows me in the ribs and whispers, "I need to pee but I don't want to miss anything. Do you think they'll break soon?"

"I don't know," I say. I've been deliberately not paying attention, and it's not like I've been to a trial before.

So he squirms, and I find myself thinking about his algebra homework. How *was* the quadratic formula derived? Once upon a time I knew.

The DA and Dad's lawyer spend the next bit of forever whispering angrily in front of the judge. The judge's face is a weathered stone, indifferent to the seasons. Then the court is in recess until after lunch, and Ben and I are in the restroom.

At the urinal, Ben pees a half-gallon of water. I'm locked in a stall as the granola bar I ate for breakfast makes its way back up my esophagus. It comes with such force that it shoots up my nose, burning my sinuses and making my eyes water. The little granola bits all stick in my throat, the itch of them causing me to cough.

"Jake?" Ben says, knocking on my stall door.

"What?"

"Are you okay?"

"Yeah, fine."

"Can I borrow some money for the vending machine?"

I pause my vomiting to fish a few dollar bills out of my wallet and throw them under the stall door. Ben disappears, and I spend the whole rest of the break gagging and hacking.

When I come out, I find Ben at the water fountain again, refilling.

Court resumes and DA Steve calls his first witness. Mr. Oates, the counselor from Ben's school.

Ben is wearing this jean jacket today. It's been bothering me all morning because somehow it looks familiar, but I'm pretty sure I've never seen him wear it before. He's got his right hand up inside the sleeve while his left twists the sleeve's outside button back and forth. Back and forth, back and forth.

They swear in Mr. Oates. DA Steve asks him how he knows Ben. Nothing terribly interesting until Steve wants to know what happened on January thirteenth of this year.

Mr. Oates says, "Ben came into my office. He looked nervous, and I told him to have a seat. I asked him what was wrong, and he said he had something he needed to tell someone. He told me his father had raped him the night before, and he said it wasn't the first time."

"And you believed him?"

"I had no reason not to. He looked very upset."

"In what way did he look upset?"

"His eyes were red like he might have been crying."

Ben folds his left arm under his right elbow, and the fist hidden inside his sleeve is now up by his mouth. He leans back, slouching more and more with every line of testimony that goes by.

"And what did you do after he told you about his father?"

"I said he did the right thing and discussed it with the principal and then called the police."

"And what happened after that?"

"A representative from DHS showed up and drove him to the hospital."

The button on Ben's sleeve is in his mouth. The juror closest to us isn't listening to the testimony anymore, she's watching Ben. He's biting the button; all he's missing is his blankie.

"Thumb?" I whisper.

His eyes move sideways, and he drops his fist in his lap, wiping his mouth with his other sleeve.

I shift in my seat until I'm as upright as I can get, and Ben copies.

DA Steve finishes his questioning, and Dad's lawyer declines to cross examine.

Next witness is the doctor who examined Ben. I'm sweating, and my eyes still burn from throwing up earlier. I stare at the back of DA Steve's chair again.

The doctor explains the damaged state of Ben's rectum and anus, and I start feeling pains in similar places in my body, and it's so real that I might just throw up again. I bend forward, my elbows on my knees, my head in my hands, staring at my shoes, and trying to think of anything else. Quadratic formula. Coefficients a, b, and c. Completing the square. It's algebra, simple algebra. Once upon a time I was in college and I took math as far as multivariable calculus. Not that I remember any of it anymore.

When I look up, someone new is on the stand. A forensics person. Semen. They're discussing semen, but it's all technical.

DA Steve asks, "What exactly is P30?"

And the guy on the stand says, "It's a prostate specific hormone found in high levels in seminal fluid."

"Where did you find the sample that tested positive for this hormone?"

"From rectal swabs taken from the victim."

Dad's lawyer stands. She asks, "Is it possible that the hormone—this P30—actually came from the alleged victim's own body?"

"It's only found in these concentrations in seminal fluid."

Ben leans forward with his elbows propped on his knees and the button from his sleeve is in his mouth again.

"But the alleged victim is male. Could it have been from his own seminal fluid?"

"Technically, yes, but highly unlikely given the location—"

"Was any DNA evidence found?"

"Unfortunately the sample was too degraded to produce any useable DNA."

"So the only forensic evidence is seminal fluid?"

"Yes."

"It could have been anyone's? It could have been his own?"

"In theory."

"Seminal fluid on a fifteen year old male."

And she's done. Apparently they think Ben must have fucked his own self in the ass. Didn't know the kid was so talented.

They call for a short recess before the next witness. DA Steve turns to Ben as everyone files out. "You're up next. Are you ready for this?"

Ben nods.

"Remember what we talked about—the type of questions that will be asked? It's not too late to give your testimony from another room via closed circuit television."

Ben turns toward me as if I should answer for him. I don't. He turns back to DA Steve. "No, I'm okay."

"If at any time you need a break when you're up there, don't hesitate to say so. Don't let the defense attorney get to you. Just answer anything she asks as best you can."

Ben nods again.

"All right. We're reconvening in twenty minutes."

Ben and I hit the restroom again. I wash my face, and swish water in my mouth. Ben looks as though he's expecting words of advice, but I don't know what to say. He drowns his anxiety at the drinking fountain.

When we walk back into the courtroom, he's doing that deep breathing thing he does when he's trying not to cry.

Up on the stand, sitting in a wooden cage with a glass of water in front of him, Ben looks smaller than usual.

DA Steve asks, "Can you tell the court what happened on the night of January twelfth of this year?"

Ben takes a sip of water and then spits the words right out. "My dad raped me."

"Can you tell us how it happened?"

"It was late. The door to my room opened, and I knew it was him. He, uh, had two beers—one for him, one for me, like always."

This is too familiar. I can practically taste those shitty beers.

Ben takes another sip of water and stares at the glass. "He told me to stand up, then he pulled down my shorts."

DA Steve says, "What happened after that?"

Ben lifts his head and takes another sip from the glass in front of him. "He started touching me."

I turn toward the double doors at the back of the courtroom, and when my eyes go front again, Ben is looking right at me. His mouth drops into a little "o" for a second, and Steve says, "Where did he touch you?"

"My nuts and my penis."

My head jerks to the side, and I blink hard. Colors in the room blur to a spotty fluorescent green, and there's a fist in my chest, right above my stomach, strangling my esophagus. Ben is still staring at me. I wipe the sweat off my forehead and shoot him the only smile I can muster, then get up and walk out.

I'm in the bathroom puking, in the end stall. Literally, my guts. Certainly no food is left in there. I sit on the floor and lean against the wall. I just ditched Ben. The kid's going to hate me. But I can't go back in there right now. I don't have it in me.

All of a sudden I hear his voice. "Jake?"

I get to my feet, open the door, and there he is, all red-eyed and stoic. "We're done until tomorrow," he says.

I say, "I didn't mean to run out like that."

And he says, "I still have to testify more tomorrow."

* * *

Back at my apartment the first thing I do is get in the shower. I'm all gross from spending so much time hanging my face over a men's room toilet, and I really need to be alone.

Hot water sprays on my face, and I hear the door open. I peek through the shower curtain, and Ben puts the lid down on the toilet and sits.

"What are you doing?" I say.

"I just want to talk."

"It can't wait until I get out?"

"Why do you think Mom didn't come?" he says. Apparently the answer is no—no, it can't wait until I get out.

"Did you really want her there?"

"I don't know, I just thought it was weird she didn't come."

"Call her," I say.

"It's not worth it."

Then I remember that jean jacket. I know why it looks familiar now.

"Where'd you find the jacket, by the way?"

"In the closet in your old room. Is that okay?"

"Yeah, fine. I just, didn't realize I still had stuff back there."

"Jake," he says. "After you left the courtroom today, I didn't do so well."

"I'm sure you were fine."

"I cried."

"Okay."

"Why did you leave?"

I shut the water off. "I wasn't feeling well."

"Do you have the flu or something?"

"Or something."

"Are you mad at me?"

I pull the curtain back and wrap a towel around my waist. "No, never, I'm not mad at you." And he stares long and hard at all the scars on my chest.

\* \* \*

Ben is back on the stand in the morning. I'm weak from not eating or just from everything, and this all feels like a dream or maybe a nightmare. But I promised myself I would keep it together today.

DA Steve says to Ben, "Yesterday you described the incident which occurred on January twelfth. Have there been other similar incidents?"

"Yes."

"When?"

"I don't even know. It's happened a lot."

"How often?"

"A couple of times a month he would go all the way like he did that day, but he was usually in my room once or twice a week."

"And when did it start?"

"I'm not sure, exactly. I think maybe I was eight the first time."

The jury collectively winces. All eyes are locked on Ben.

"Had you ever tried to tell anyone about the abuse before this last time?"

"No. Not really."

"What do you mean 'not really'?"

"I mean, I thought about it and almost did a couple of times, but I guess I was too scared."

"Why were you scared? What were you afraid might happen?"

"I don't know."

"Did your father ever threaten you in any way?"

"He said it was a secret. I was embarrassed."

"And why did you choose to speak out now?"

"I just," he sighs. "I needed to. I couldn't do it anymore."

Now Dad's lawyer gets a go at him.

"Do you get in trouble much?" she asks Ben.

"What do you mean?"

"Do you come home late, talk back to your parents, things like that?"

"Sometimes."

"Do you remember the last time you got in trouble?"

"I was grounded back in January."

"What for?"

"I came home late from school."

"How late?"

"Nine or ten."

"And what were you doing during that time?"

"Just walking."

"Walking? Where? Wasn't it cold out?"

"I was just walking around town so I could think."

"How often have you done this—stayed out late and been grounded for it?"

"I don't know. A few times."

"Can you tell the court how you got those black eyes?"

"Objection, irrelevant," says DA Steve.

"Sustained," says the judge.

"Do you get angry at your dad when he grounds you for staying out late?"

"Sometimes."

"Let's go back to the night of January twelfth. Were you grounded then?"

"Yes."

"Now, you say your father came into your room that night. About what time was that?"

"I'm not sure. Maybe a few hours after I went to bed. So maybe, like, midnight."

"But you're not sure?"

"No."

"You said your father brought you a beer."

"Yes."

"And you drank the beer."

"Yes."

"You said shortly after that, you were fondled, and he pushed you down on your bed, is that correct?"

"Yes."

"Did you still have the beer in your hand?"

"I don't remember."

"Did the beer spill?"

"No, I don't think so."

"So you didn't have it in your hand when you were pushed onto the bed?"

"Maybe not."

"Where did the beer go, then?"

"Maybe I set it down or he grabbed it from me. I don't know."

Let's get to the bottom of the case of the misplaced beer. Clearly this is important and a sure sign that Ben is lying because he can't remember where he put the fucking beer.

She keeps on with this endless string of nitpicking questions. The kid is strong, though. He answers everything.

The judge calls for recess until tomorrow. The kid, of course, needs to piss a gallon. I'm too weak to hurl anymore. Or too empty.

As we leave the courthouse, Ben says, "I'm hungry."

I have no intention of refilling my vomit reservoir, but I say, "Pick a place," and soon we're in a cheap restaurant, me sipping on a sprite, and him eating a burrito in silence.

After only a few bites, he starts frowning at it, and poking around the insides of it with his finger.

"What's wrong?" I say.

"It has onions," he says.

* * *

I'm first on the stand the following morning, and I'm not the least bit ready. The room is cold. Or maybe it's me. The jury's eyes are all on me as I take a seat.

DA Steve says, "What is your relationship to Benjamin Smith?"

"He's my brother."

"What is your relationship to the defendant William Smith?"

"He's my father."

"And as a child, you grew up in the same house with your mother and father as your brother Benjamin did, is that correct?"

"Yes."

"How old were you when you moved out?"

"Eighteen."

"How old was Ben at that time?"

"Three."

"Did you still maintain a relationship with your family and regularly visit them after moving out?"

"Yes."

"Looking back, were there ever any signs that might have been indications that your father was abusing your brother from around the time he was eight?"

I nod and my head floods with vivid memories of Thanksgiving that year. It was one of the times Mom had begged me to come over. *We're your family* and all that. Ben kept looking at me like maybe he wanted to tell me something. I played let's pretend. Let's pretend everything is normal and the kid is being weird for no good reason. Look, Mom's all happy and proud of that fat, glossy turkey. Dad looks hungry and innocent. Ben is too young. These suspicions are all in my head.

Ben followed me around like a puppy the whole day—like he couldn't be left alone for a minute.

"Could you speak into the microphone, please?"

And I say a reverberating, "Yes." Ben is looking right at me, fist with button up to his mouth.

"Can you describe what these signs were?"

"It was just...the way he acted. He changed and seemed like... he was thinking more. I don't know. Less secure, maybe."

"Mr. Smith, when you were a child living at home was there ever any inappropriate sexual contact between you and your father?"

I close my eyes and nod.

"Can you speak into the microphone please?"

"Yes," I say, and it comes out weak. I clear my throat.

"Can you tell the court how old you were the first time this inappropriate contact happened?"

"Ten."

"Can you describe what happened between you and your father when you were ten?"

Ben's waiting. I can hear his words, *My dad raped me*, over and over in his kid voice. I try to say it, but each word bites before it can roll off my tongue. The letters are sharp bits of glass I keep cutting my mouth on. They get stuck in my throat.

"Mr. Smith, are you able to answer the question?"

Everyone wants to see me stripped naked. Everyone wants to

be horrified. They want to sneer in disgust. I open my mouth, and nothing comes out. I stare into my lap and shake my head.

"Okay. Can you tell us how long the inappropriate contact by your father went on?"

I look up, and the jury appears sympathetic, but Dad looks so average, so innocent. As if Ben's words were lies. As if this was nothing more than father-son bonding, and we're making it into a catastrophe.

"Long enough," I manage to whisper. "Longer than it should have."

I can feel every muscle in my jaw, my mouth, my tongue, as if cement has been poured into the tissue. My lungs ache.

"Mr. Smith, do you need a break?"

I shake my head. I can hear every blood cell flowing past my ear drums, grating on the walls of my veins.

"Can you describe what happened between you and your father when you were ten?"

DA Steve is right in front of me. His eyes are white surrounding brown, surrounding black, locked onto me as if to pull me back into reality. Pleading. *Say it. You can do this. Say it.*

"He-uh." My hands tremble in my lap. My whole body might be shaking, I can't tell. I close my eyes, then open them again and look at Dad. His eyes say, *Keep your mouth shut. This is between you and me.*

DA Steve steps strategically to the side to block my view of Dad—like I don't have object permanence, and I'll believe he's disappeared. But I can feel when Dad's in a room whether I see him or not. He changes the taste of the air somehow.

"Mr. Smith, can you tell us where the abuse took place?"

I nod. "Usually my bedroom. Usually at night." My voice shakes as if I'm crying.

"Can you tell us anything at all about what happened in your bedroom at night?"

The judge seems resigned to what's happening here. Nothing is a surprise. The jurors shift uncomfortably in their seats.

I open my mouth but nothing comes out. I can't say it. Ben could, but I can't. "I'm sorry."

"That's okay. I realize this is difficult. Take your time."

"No, I'm sorry. I-I can't. I don't remember the details," I lie.

"Can you tell us anything at all? Anything you remember?"

I shake my head. "I'm sorry."

"Take your time."

I close my eyes again. I hear Ben's testimony. I hear him saying the words. I whisper the word "rape" into the microphone, and my head ticks hard to the side. "Touching a-and his mouth..." and that's all I've got. My throat is numb, and I can't open my eyes.

"Mr. Smith?" DA Steve says. "Can you tell us anything else?"

"I-I don't remember details," I lie again.

"Can you tell us how frequently these incidents with your father occurred?"

"Couple of times a week, maybe."

"Is there anything else at all about these incidents that you can recall?"

"I'm sorry," I say.

DA Steve waits for what seems like forever, hoping I'll spill out more details. When I don't, he sighs and tells the judge he's finished with the witness. The judge asks if I'd like a break before cross-examination. I shake my head. If I get a break, they'll have to drag me back into the room kicking and screaming. I take a deep breath, open my eyes, and steel myself for the queen of pointed questions.

"Mr. Smith," she says. "Did you ever tell anyone about the alleged abuse by your father?"

I swallow. "No."

"Your mother lived in the house with you growing up as well, is that correct?"

"Yes."

"Did you ever tell her about the alleged abuse?"

"No."

"Did she ever ask you if anything was going on?"

"No."

"Did anyone else ever ask you if anything was going on?"

"No."

"Have you ever told anyone at all about the alleged abuse before the current accusations against your father?"

"No."

Her questions are bullets, and she just keeps firing. "How old were you when your brother Benjamin was born?"

"Fifteen."

"Still living at home?"

"Yes."

"Did you care about your brother when he was an infant?"

"Yes."

"Do you still care about him now?"

"Very much." My voice keeps growing higher in pitch with each answer, and I'm almost falsetto.

"If you feared harm might come to him, would you take measures to protect him?"

"Yes."

"Would those measures include lying if you feared your brother would get into trouble?"

"That depends on the circumstances."

"Given the right circumstances, would you lie to protect him?"

"Technically, yes, but—"

"Now if, as you claim, your father sexually abused you as a child, did you not worry he would do the same thing to your brother?"

I nod, eyes closed.

"Can you speak into the microphone please, Mr. Smith?"

"Yes." I open my eyes and stare at the table in front of me—whirls and knots and grain like the fingerprint of a tree.

"Did you take any measures to protect your brother from what you claim you feared might happen?"

I can feel Dad's glare. I can feel Ben staring. My heart is pounding so fast, so hard, that it's bound to give out soon. I draw in my breath slowly.

"No."

"Why not?"

There's no sound in the room. Ben looks to Dad, then back to me, pokerfaced. Doesn't even have his sleeve in his mouth anymore. "I don't know." My voice is shaky again. A fire builds between my eyes, in my sinuses.

"Your brother has testified that your father allegedly began abusing him when he was eight years old. How old were you when your brother was eight?"

"Twenty-three."

"What was your relationship with your brother at that time?"

"I didn't live at home anymore, but I would see him every few weeks or so when I'd visit my parents."

"You still visited your parents even though your father had allegedly been abusing you since you were ten?"

"Yes."

"Did you work and support yourself when you were twenty-three?"

"Yes."

"Did you rely on your parents for any support at that time?"

"No."

"Had your father threatened you in any way?"

"No."

"Did you care about your brother's well-being?"

"Yes."

"Did you suspect he was being abused at that time?"

"Yes."

"Did you tell any authorities about it?"

"No."

"Why not?"

"I don't know." *Guilty. Guilty. Guilty.* I feel like I'm on trial.

Guilty of negligence. Guilty of screwing up my kid brother's life forever. Guilty of being too scared to do anything about it. Guilty of being a coward who thought that saying anything would make it real in a way that it wasn't already.

"What *do* you know, Mr. Smith? Do you really know that your brother was being abused?"

"Yes." My face is hot. My heart is pumping so violently that my blood might burst through my skin at any moment.

"So you really suspected he was being abused for the last seven years?"

"Yes." I didn't just suspect, I damn well knew.

"But at the same time you have told us that you would take measures to protect your brother if you feared harm would come to him, is that correct?"

"Yes."

"And these measures include lying under the proper circumstances?"

"I'm not making this up. Ben's not making this up."

"You claim to have believed abuse was taking place, yet you did nothing about it?"

"No."

"I ask you again, why?"

Her "why" is sharp enough to cut the ties holding back the bitter anger. My voice doesn't come out weak this time. I'm practically yelling. "Because it was too late! It was too late. I was going to, but it was too late. I don't know. It was too goddamn late!" My whole body stiffens, then begins to shake, and my head jerks hard to the side. I blink, and my eyes stay closed. I thought I had another year or two before Dad would try anything with him. I was going to do something about it before then. But I didn't. Then it happened. And it was too late.

I bend forward until my head touches the desk.

The defense is done with the witness.

The judge calls for recess.

* * *

I manage to slip comfortably into a state of dissociation, existing in some numb purgatory separate from the here and now.

Dad's testimony is a buzz in my head. They ask him what happened, and he says Ben made it all up. Ben was upset at being grounded. He's a difficult kid, but Dad loves him anyway. Of course he does.

DA Steve gets up and says, "We have seen evidence presented that suggests physical trauma to your son's anus as well as semen in his rectum. Was this a result of you sodomizing your son?"

"Absolutely not."

"Then how did that evidence get there?"

"Objection. Calls for speculation."

"Sustained."

Ben won't sit near me. His arms are crossed, and he's staring stone-faced up at Dad on the stand.

DA Steve asks Dad, "Have you provided your son with beer before?"

"I've let him have a taste a few times. I didn't figure there was any harm in it."

"Did you provide your son with a beer on the night of January twelfth?"

"No."

"Did you enter your son's room after he had gone to bed on the night of January twelfth?"

"No."

"Did you put your son's penis in your mouth on the night of January twelfth?"

"No."

"Did you sodomize your son on the night of January twelfth?"

"No."

And while the faces of the jurors say they aren't buying any of it, this whole production is pointless now. All the dirty laundry has been aired. This isn't going to get us anywhere, regardless of the verdict.

Next they call a character witness for Dad. Someone from Dad's pharmacy. I guess Mom didn't go with the cancer story after all. Dad's dirt is out in the open. But I can't even imagine trying to convince anyone who knew him that Ben's story is true. Everyone always thought Dad was some wonderful human being—whether they found him simply pleasant and caring, or whether they appreciated his willingness to help them obtain medications that the "stupid" doctors wouldn't prescribe, or that "stupid" insurance wouldn't pay for. It was community service, not criminal activity.

The witness gushes over Dad's delightful personality and the kindness he extended toward each and every customer. The witness says he's worked with Dad for over a decade.

But then DA Steve asks, "Have you ever been to the house of the defendant?"

"No."

"Not once?"

"No."

"Have you ever met any of his family? His wife or his sons?"

"They've come by the pharmacy before."

"How often?"

"I don't know. A few times."

"You talk to them much?"

"Well, no, but—"

"Thank you."

And that's it. We're at recess until tomorrow morning for closing arguments.

* * *

Ben can't look at me. The sunglasses go back on as soon as we leave the courtroom. When we enter my apartment, the jean jacket comes off and drops to the floor. He splays his homework across the table but doesn't do more than tap at it with a pencil. Then the laptop computer comes out, and he starts angrily clicking through the vast resources of the Internet.

I shower with a razor blade for the first time in weeks. I thought I'd be disappointed in myself when I finally caved and self-injured again—after all, Lauren has seemed so pleased at how "good" I've been—but all I am is relieved. Hot water and little cuts on the inside of my upper arm and red streams wash down to my fingertips. I want all the blood to drain out of me. I want to be emptied.

* * *

The sobbing puppy makes another appearance in the four o'clock hour, but I don't pretend to sleep through it this time. I turn the lamp on. Ben stops and stares at me with the same blank expression he had in court, except his face is soaked. In the next second, he disappears, burrowed inside his sleeping bag.

Sitting up on the edge of the bed, I say, "I'm sorry, Benny. I'm really sorry."

"Fuck you," he says, and his words burn into every bone in my body like a disease, a marrow-eating bacteria, and suddenly the whole mess is brutally real again. All I can do is sit paralyzed, staring at the lump of Ben under the green sleeping bag, knowing any expectation of forgiveness would be absurd.

My whole body feels as if it's vibrating at high frequency. I'm bound to hit resonance and shatter. My fists grip the edge of my bed until my fingers go numb. My head tics, and my eyes shut tight.

* * *

In court the closing statements go much like the opening ones. They take about half a day. Ben has to pee about five times. I only throw up once.

The kid is mute until we get home. I tell him he doesn't have to stay with me. I'll understand. He can go back home and stay with Mom.

He looks at me and says simply, "She hates me. And we don't even know if Dad's going to be let free or not."

The jury spends the rest of the day in deliberation. We are called back to the courtroom the following morning. Again we sit behind DA Steve, but Ben makes sure to leave a good five feet between him and me. He keeps his sunglasses on.

As the jury files in, Dad turns around and stares hard at Ben and then at me, and his eyes scream betrayal. His face is foreign somehow, but also hyper-familiar. It finds friends in every corner of my hippocampus. Dad doesn't look forward again until the judge begins to speak.

The judge asks the jury foreperson to check the condition of the verdict forms. He then instructs the bailiff to bring him the envelope. The judge, with his same-as-always face of indifference opens the envelope and examines the forms himself. The envelope is then passed along to the court clerk, and the judge asks Dad to stand as the clerk reads the verdict.

It suddenly hits me that if he is found innocent, then he goes home right now. He won't let Ben stay with me. I'll have to fight him. I'll have to do something big to keep Ben safe. I imagine Dad turning around, grinning because he won, walking back toward us, grabbing Ben by the arm and taking him away. Ben isn't within arm's reach of me.

Dad and his lawyer stand simultaneously. Dad's hands hang in tight fists at his side.

Ben stares straight ahead. If I hear the word "innocent" I'm prepared to grab him, drag him out to my car, and drive off before Dad can catch up. I estimate the distance between me and Ben, between Dad and Ben. Between Ben and the door.

But after a long spiel—the county, the state, the defendant, the case number—"we the jury" find Dad guilty on all counts. Rape. Sex abuse. Sodomy. *Guilty. Guilty. Guilty.* But Dad doesn't budge.

Ben, too, shows no sign of reaction that I can see.

The judge sets a sentencing date one month out, and Dad is ushered out of the courtroom. He doesn't even give us one last hard glare. The last I see of him is the back of his head. My whole body floods with relief.

Before we leave, DA Steve has some victim impact statement for Ben to complete before Dad is sentenced.

"Take it with you," he says. "You don't have to do it now."

Ben still shows no sign of reaction.

As we walk to the car, I tell him, "At least it's over now," but those words hang lamely in the air between us, and his silence is more than enough to let me know that's hardly true.

# CHAPTER THIRTEEN

It's Monday, and my shift is almost over. Savannah leads Larry Daly around to inspect the progress on the handrails he ordered. I'm presently fixing the ones Carson attempted to weld in my absence. Larry is irritated at me—the "damn welder" who "needs to get his ass in gear" because Larry "needs this shit done by the end of the week."

"Who takes time off in the middle of a fucking project?" he asks Savannah.

Savannah's hands go palm out on her ass with her elbows bent behind her back, her chest puffed out like a pigeon's. She blinks and smiles while Larry stares down her tit crack, softening briefly before he looks my way. She uses those melons as a weapon. It isn't just about self-esteem or vanity; it's leverage. Her enemies look there and get all distracted, then she quickly disarms them and wins.

Larry gets a good surly stare into my eyes before I flip down my hood and let some sparks fly.

When my shift ends, Larry is still yakking it up with Savannah by the front office, but the conversation is excessively flirtatious on Larry's part, and Savannah plays into it, because by that power, she has him hypnotized. I clock out, sit in my car, and wait. Another ten minutes pass before Larry emerges, striding toward his silver BMW.

He starts his engine.

I start my engine.

He pulls out of his parking spot.

I pull out of mine.

At the first traffic light his right blinker goes on, and I'm behind him in the turning lane. Larry's eyes in the rearview mirror form their piercing ever-squint of superiority.

What Larry doesn't understand is I would have loved to have been at work last week. What he doesn't understand is I can't keep my food down anymore.

Now we're on the freeway. Larry rides bumpers in the fast lane. He checks his rearview mirror a lot, so I let a few cars slip in between us. The constant stream of cars switching to the slow lane to get out of his way serves as the main indicator of his location.

Larry takes exit 62B.

I take exit 62B.

He cruises at 45 in a 30 MPH zone, and I stay an inconspicuous distance behind him. Traffic zips past on the other side of the yellow line. Such a weak boundary. Just a painted line. So easy to cross. Ten percent of all traffic fatalities are the result of head-on collisions.

I follow him down a side street, being sure to leave enough space that he doesn't see me.

Larry pulls into the driveway of a brown, two-story house.

I park around the corner.

Out of my car, I walk on the side of the street opposite his house. I scale a scotch pine in a small park and sit on a branch some twenty feet up. From there, I have a clear view of the house, but I'm pretty sure no one has a clear view of me. I see his wife with a rigid, toothy smile that hangs there even when she talks. She has light brown hair, straight and cropped at the shoulders. Her breasts aren't nearly as large as Savannah's, but then, not many are. His daughter, who looks maybe eight or ten, follows him around the house like a puppy, but he ignores her.

I have no idea what I'm doing here. Maybe it's that I don't want to face Ben. It's getting late, so I climb down and go home.

Ron fumbles his way past me down the stairs. Dude doesn't much resemble a Spartan anymore. Even his plume crest of hair is gone and looks unbrushed, unwashed. I haven't seen Angie or heard the sex pounding in weeks. He doesn't ask about Ben. Doesn't say so much as, "Dude."

Ben is sound asleep when I get home. I nearly trip over him in the dark. I flick the red lamp on by Prometheus's tank. He slowly meanders out from his half-log, tongue lapping out at the air. I think I forgot to feed him yesterday. I toss a few extra crickets in for him.

\* \* \*

Savannah says she needs to know what was going on last week or I will find myself out of a job.

"I had to be in court," I say.

She crosses her arms and shifts her weight into her left hip. "What'd you do?"

"I was not the one on trial."

She says, "Mhmm," her lips pursed flat again. "Then why were you there?"

I stand at my station, my hood flipped up, my rod clamp in my hand like a gun. In some fucked up way I almost want to tell her every detail. If no one else was around, maybe, just maybe I would. It would blow her caustic little mind.

"I have a lot of work to catch up on," I say.

"You need to take some time and properly train Carson. Then we wouldn't have to worry about falling behind when you don't show."

"Aren't you the one who told him welding is so easy any idiot can do it?"

"We'll talk later," she says and leaves.

When Carson strolls in past nine, I make him polish the sheet metal. This isn't actually a thing, but it keeps him out of my way.

I place a rag on the floor near the tripping corner. Just one. It sits there crumpled and inconspicuous. For now it's a target, and I'm practicing. When I get to the end of a rod—the end glowing a red hot 2,500 degrees Fahrenheit, I unclamp and launch it toward the rag. A quick flick of the wrist. No one sees. No one cares.

The first few times the hot rod end only lands as far as the end of the table, skates off the edge and bounces on the floor, missing the mark by at least five feet. By the end of the day, my rod ends are making it past the table by a few feet with each flick, but still nowhere near target.

On my way home, I drive past Larry's house again, park around the corner, and resume my perch in the tree. He's not home yet, but I can see his wife and kid. Mrs. Daly appears unhappy except when the kid looks at her. Ten percent of women are not satisfied with their marriage.

\* \* \*

At home in the apartment, Ben looks older. Or angrier. He's back in his green hooded sweatshirt, string hanging out the corner of his mouth.

"How was your day?" I say.

He spits the end of the string out, and it fires my direction before reaching the end of its rope and falling.

I never see him without sunglasses now. Behind his black shields he could be looking anywhere at any given time, and I would never be able to tell. Kid hardly speaks to me. Kid hates me. But kid still sleeps on my floor.

It takes me a few minutes to notice that his sunglasses are different. No more black rims. Now they're aviator frames.

"Those new?" I ask pointing at my eyes while looking, possibly, towards his.

He nods.

"Where are the old ones?"

"Broken and in a toilet."

"You do that?"

"No."

"I see."

"You see what?"

"Was it the same kids?"

"Was it the same kids what?"

"The same kids who punched you a few weeks back?"

He shrugs. "So what if it was? Maybe I don't care."

"Yeah? Well maybe I do."

"Prove it."

"You want me to call the school in the morning?"

"Don't. You. Fucking. Dare."

* * *

On Friday I'm being swallowed by the rose-colored chair in the floral themed office of the sympathetic Lauren. I missed last week because of the trial, and she wants to know how that went.

I shrug. "It's over."

"Do you feel any sense of resolution?" she asks.

"He was found guilty."

"And how do you feel about that?"

I shrug.

She scratches away on her notepad.

"How have you been coping with the stress?" When I don't answer, she adds, "Have you done anything to hurt yourself since we last talked?"

"I'm sorry," I say.

"There's no need to be sorry," she says.

That answer makes me angry. I needed her to be disappointed in me.

"Do you want to talk about what you were feeling when it happened?" she says.

"No." The last thing I need is her trying to validate any dumbass thoughts I may have had in the past week.

"How is your brother?"

My eyes burn, my sinuses burn, and my mouth drops open as I try to get enough air. I already had to deal with Benny and a whole courtroom full of people finding out that I knew what Dad was doing to him the whole time. Lauren can't know this now, too.

"Jake?"

"No...he's uh...I don't know. It's been...difficult. He's been struggling with math—algebra. Did you know algebra means 'reunion of broken parts?' It's an Arabic word, but it was a Greek mathematician—Diophantus—who laid the foundation. Anyway, I don't want to talk about this anymore."

Lauren spends the next few minutes digging through files in a cabinet by her bookshelf, amassing handouts about healthy coping mechanisms. Then she jots down the web addresses of some forums for abuse survivors.

"Some studies," Lauren says as she hands me the papers, "say that as many as ten percent of men have been the victim of sexual abuse at some point in their lives."

Those have got to be the most irritating words in the English language. I do one of those really long blinks, and Lauren asks if I'm okay.

I fold the papers in half so I don't have to see any of the words on them. When our session ends, I shove the papers into the glove box of my car.

* * *

Ben is on his third pair of sunglasses when I get home. "Again?" I ask.

He doesn't say anything. Maybe he's plotting to blow up the school. Maybe he's hoping I'll die.

He's hunched over his algebra book again. "Don't you have other classes?" I say.

His face turns toward me.

I point to his book. "That's all I ever see you working on."

"You're not here half the time, so how would you know?"

"So how is school, anyway?" Ben tosses his pencil down on the table so hard that it bounces and lands at my feet. He turns red and breathes hard like an angry bull.

He stands, kicking the chair back and nearly tipping it over, slams his textbook shut with all his papers inside, and sends it flying like a Frisbee toward the bookcases. It smacks hard into the shelves then changes course to explode on the floor. He brushes past me and leaves the apartment, slamming the door behind him. I almost run after, but don't really know what I would say.

I walk over to the bookcase and pick his book back up. The binding has separated at the spine and is a few small tears away from falling off completely. I close it, set it aside, and pick up all the papers. Looks like he's copied all the problems out of the text but hasn't worked any of them out. There's also a couple pages of scratch work and some artwork consisting primarily of dismembered bodies bleeding grotesquely in piles. I stack the papers neatly and set them on top of the book.

I get in my car and head out to find him. I spot him walking down the sidewalk not more than a dozen blocks from the apartment, hunched over with his hands in his pockets, sweatshirt string hanging out of the corner of his mouth. I pull up next to him, roll down the window, and say, "Get in."

He says, "I'm not going home. Or to your place. Whatever."

"Fine," I say. "Get in."

He stops walking.

I stop the car.

He gets in and sits in the passenger seat, arms crossed, jaw clenched, every square inch of exposed flesh blushing red with rage.

We drive to an old riverbed and park. He follows me out of the car to the water's edge where we stand on a large deposit of rocks. I pick up a plumb-sized stone, grab his hand, place it in his palm, and say, "Throw."

He sends it flying down stream and embeds it in the muddy bank on the other side.

"Again," I say, and we both pick up rocks and chuck them.

And again. And again.

Stronger. Faster. Farther.

He throws all his weight into it each time, and his rocks soar like launched missiles.

I point to a tree across the stream a dozen feet back from the bank and say, "Target. Think you can hit it?"

It's getting dark. He pauses to push his shades to the top of his head. His eyes are still lined with purple rings, but they've faded. They're yellowing.

It takes a few throws, but soon he's smacking the tree trunk dead center each time, the crack of the bark echoing against the water. The riverbed is going to run out of rocks before he's through.

"I'm failing algebra," he says.

"Failing?"

"I mean I'm getting a C," he chucks a stone. *Zip—crack.*

"Ben. Fuck algebra."

He shakes his head and lets another stone fly. *Zip—crack.*

He says. "Do you hate me?" *Zip—CRACK.*

"No." I hand him another rock.

"Because it's okay if you do. I've decided I don't care." The sunglasses come back down.

*Zip—crack.* Right on target.

# CHAPTER FOURTEEN

The shop seems unusually quiet as I prep for my first job of the day. Rick and Carson are smirking. Some prank is afoot. I look around at my station, but can't figure what it is.

Then I put my hand in my glove, and something inside is wet and greasy. I pull my hand out, and all over my fingers is the clear slime of Vaseline. Fucking Vaseline, of all things. The shit doesn't come off by wiping, but I wipe anyway, and it's all over my jeans, both hands, my shirt. I look at my hands, palms up, fingers open, and some sick magic turns the Vaseline into sweat and cum. I rub it around in my palm trying to convince myself that it was some optical illusion, but I still see thick white streaks in my hands. And blood. My blood. And I smell him. I smell the old man. This can't be right. What's wrong with my head? There's laughter. Everyone in the shop laughs at me, bending over, hands on their knees, trying to catch their breaths.

I lock eyes with Carson. "Was it you, you little fucker?

Rick shouts, "Learn to take a joke, man."

*Click, fwoop, click.* Savannah comes around the corner, looks at me, looks at them. Air trembles in and out of my lungs, and my chest tightens until it burns. I'm hunched over, ready to collapse, with my messy hands held out in front of me like dirty rags.

Savannah scrunches her nose. "Get over it, and go clean yourself up."

I step-fall my way into the bathroom, start running the water. I blink, and Dad's behind me, his hot breath on my neck. His sweat hangs thick in the air. The whole room smells like him.

It's all over my skin. It's all over me, and I can't get it off. I am small, and his weight is on top of me. I'm being crushed, and I can't breathe.

Soap and water go everywhere. I'm making a bigger mess than I'm fixing. I want to get this crap off, but it's not just on my hands now, it's all over my clothes. My eyes are hot, my cheeks are hot. I look in the mirror, and there're tears all over my face. I didn't even know I was crying. Like a fucking baby. Like Ben at 4:00 a.m. And I can't make it stop. My head tics to the side, and I blink. It tics to the side again.

Savannah knocks on the door. "Zip it up, I'm coming in," she says.

I want to say *No, go, please, you don't need to see this*, but I can't get enough air to form words.

Savannah comes in. She smells like vanilla, but vanilla turning into his sweat, and I don't want her any closer.

"What the hell is going on?" Her words echo in Dad's voice, and I know there's no way he can be here right now, but I hear him. It fucking feels like he's fucking here.

My legs tremble. He's inside of me. I can feel it. My legs give out, and I drop to my knees, hanging onto the edge of the sink.

This isn't real.

This can't be real.

Savannah puts a hand on my shoulder, and I jump, push myself back hard against the piss-stained wall near the urinal, slide to the floor, facing her. Her hands come up as if to indicate she won't hurt me. My head keeps ticking to the side. I keep blinking. Tears drip into my lap. I'm not getting enough air.

My arms tremble now, too. Savannah's black-lined spider eyes stare. She tries to step closer, and I scream "No!" except I didn't mean to. It's my voice but it's not me. I try to shove myself farther from her, but I'm already backed against the wall. I lean my head forward, swing it back, crack it hard against the tile.

The smell, the oily slime of Vaseline, cum and sweat. I feel like someone shoved a knife up my asshole, and Savannah can see it in me. The door is open, and a crowd has gathered.

I look down into my lap as more tears drop off the end of my nose. I wipe my face with my arm, but now I've got Vaseline on my face. I crack my head back again, crack it harder. I say, "Don't touch me, don't touch me," but I don't mean to be speaking. The words just spill out, and I keep rocking forward, smacking my head back on the wall, repeating, "Don't touch me, don't touch me." Because it's all I can do. It's all I can say.

I don't remember much after this. Everyone stares at me from the doorway, Savannah screams at them to get back to work, paramedics arrive, the steady blow of oxygen through a mask on my face, walking assisted through the shop as if it's some sort of tunnel, the outside a bright light at the end, and then I'm in the hospital with an icepack on my head and Lauren sitting on a nearby stool with a notepad, looking at me with her head tilted to one side, her stringy hair pulled back into a ponytail.

"I don't want to talk about it," I say.

I don't want to talk about the Vaseline. How my coworkers must be sadistically psychic to have made such a choice. The shit Dad did. The fucking trial. Ben hates me, and I totally screwed the kid up. Mom's lost her fucking mind. The whole world's gone to shit.

The room I'm in is white on white and smells like disinfectant, and somehow that's calming this time around. Muffled hospital sounds come through the door. Shoes squeak up and down the hall, sets of double doors open, then click slowly closed on their own, the distant ding of an elevator, people mumbling, and Lauren, in my room, jabbering at me, but I don't care what she's saying. My eyes close. Rent's due today, and I haven't paid it yet. Need to go grocery shopping soon, too—almost out of food. Prometheus is almost out of crickets. Need a nap. Need to go home and take a nap.

I look at Lauren. "What time is it?"

She looks at her wristwatch. "Almost noon, why?"

"Okay." I sit up, hang my feet over the edge of the bed. "I need to get going."

"Do you think that's a good idea?"

I plop the icepack on the side table. "You going to stop me?"

* * *

I'm coated white with soap lather in the shower trying to wash away the remainder of the Vaseline. The steam coming off the hot water displaces the air enough to make breathing difficult, but I don't stop until I've rubbed every inch of my skin raw and rinsed my mouth, nose, ears, and eyes.

Naked on the toilet, with razor in hand, I lightly trace the scar from my leg crater. It's so tight, the scar tissue thick and stiff and drawing the edges of the surrounding skin in all puckered. Really, I need a new spot, so I turn to my other leg. All the scars are smaller there, little lazy gashes, and I add a few nicks. But my heart's not in it.

Over by my dresser, I take Prometheus out of his cage. I haven't held him in a while. He's squirmier than usual. He rides on my shoulder as I go to the kitchen for some water, and he bites my ear, like he means to tell me something. Perhaps he's mad I've been ignoring him.

I bring him up to my face, looking into his red eyes. He sighs and squints. I'm exhausted, and my head hurts. After petting him a few strokes over the top of his head, I set him back in his tank and go to bed.

* * *

The intentionally loud thud of Ben's backpack hitting the table wakes me where I've been sleeping, my mouth squished open and drool all over my pillow. Ben stands there expressionless, his sunglassed face turned in my direction.

"What's wrong with you?" he says.

I wipe my mouth, roll onto my back, and rub my face. "You really want to know?" I ask.

He nods.

"I hit my head at work and had to go to the hospital."

"What, did you get a concussion or something?"

"No, I don't think so."

He stares for a minute, then sits at the table, unzips his bag and pulls out his books.

Then he says, "That guy who lives upstairs—is something wrong with him?"

"Something's wrong with everyone."

"I think he was sleeping on the stairs," Ben says. "I mean, he was sitting, and, like, leaning against the wall with his eyes closed."

"Is he still there, you think?"

Ben shrugs, "Probably."

I start thinking maybe Ron's not okay out there. So I get up to check.

Halfway down the stairs between the first and second floor, is the emaciated figure of a fallen Spartan propped up by the wall, and I approach slowly, trying to detect breathing. At first I can't make out any signs of life at all, and I get a little dizzy with the thought that I may have done something very, very bad. His skin, his lips still look pink, so he must be getting oxygen. Looking closer, his chest is rising and falling, but it's subtle.

"Ron?" I say, but it comes out so weak and uncertain that there's no way he would have heard it even if he was conscious. I place my hand on his shoulder and give it a little shake. He squeaks with his next exhale. I shake him harder, "Ron?"

His eyes peel open. His pupils follow the lids up for a moment before they settle unfocused in front of him. "Huh?" he says.

"You okay?" I ask.

He sniffs, leans away from the wall and rolls towards the stairs. He manages to push himself to standing, clinging to the wall, and he stumble-steps up the stairs. I follow right behind in case he falls, all the way to his apartment, which smells like rotting take-out. Gray-blue worms of lo mein and furry stir fry fill the sink. Garbage, dishes, and dirty clothes all over. He falls into a chair, on top of a hamburger box that crumples beneath him.

"So," I slip my hands into my pockets, "can I get you anything?"

He perks up, reaches across the table to drag over a little box and pulls a bottle out of it, shaking it. He starts to open it, and I say, "Are you sure that's a good idea?"

His fingers try repeatedly to get the lid off, but they keep slipping. He hands the bottle to me. I set it on the counter and check the dirty cups for the cleanest one, fill it with water, and hand it to him. "Wait, where's my pills?" he asks.

"You just took them."

He looks confused a moment, then says, "Oh," and takes a sip of water.

"Why do you do that?" I say.

"Do what?"

"The pills. Why do you take them?"

"Beause," he takes another sip of water, and it spills a little out his mouth, making a dark circle on his Hollister t-shirt. "They help."

"Have you looked in a mirror lately?"

He squints at me. "Dude, have you? Oh, and I've been covering for you, just so you know. Haven't said anything to the landlord about you not filling out a new tenant form even though your brother is living here again. What's with that anyway?"

I grab at the back of my head, at the big bruised spot the headache's emanating from.

"Something wrong with your head?"

"Accidentally hit it at work today."

"You know, Freud said that there are no accidents."

"Is that so?"

"So how did you hit your head? Maybe I can help you figure out why it really happened."

"Maybe you should give up the pills."

"What do you know about it?"

"Doesn't look like they're helping you much."

My fingerprints are on his cup and in his apartment and on his pill bottle—heck, they're probably on the pills themselves. If he croaks, it all points back to me.

* * *

5:30 in the morning I'm awake, puking, getting ready for work. Today I bring my own gloves. My goal: to get in the building and get my welding hood on before anyone can say anything. Does it work? No, because Savannah's leaning against the counter in the front office, arms folded around her fwoopers, waiting for me.

"I thought for sure you'd call in today," she says, clicking behind me as I clock in. "You don't look so hot."

I head for the double doors, but she moves to block my way. "In the office. Now."

I follow her in. She points to the chair in front of the desk. "Sit."

I sit, and she faces me, leans her ass on the edge of the desk, and shakes her hair behind her shoulders. Her spider eyes blink. "You want to tell me what happened yesterday?"

"Allergic reaction."

"Allergic reaction?" Her arms cross. "Right. Is that why you were crying?"

"I wasn't crying." Her melons are at eye level, and I think about that dream where everything was good until she turned into Dad.

"What did the doctor say? At the hospital? Are you even okay to work right now?"

"I'm fine."

"You don't look fine." Her head dips down to move my eyes away from her chest. "You're not on drugs are you?"

I stare at her red lips. "No."

Her weight shifts into her right hip, and now I'm getting a boner. One might think exhaustion and stress would make that impossible, and yet there it is. I fold my arms down in my lap and stare sideways at the wall. "I'll take a piss test for you, if you want. I'm not now, nor have I ever been, on anything."

"Are you honestly okay to work today?"

"Wouldn't be here otherwise."

"You really had me worried, you know."

And for some reason that makes me crack a dumbass smile.

"Look, Larry Daly's pissed about the delays so we need you right now. Otherwise, I'd send your ass home. Get to work, and don't go psycho on me."

\* \* \*

Lauren starts with, "Can we talk about what happened at work on Monday?"

I shrug.

"You were pretty spare with your words at the hospital. Can we start from the beginning?"

I hold my hands palm up in my lap, close them into fists and open them again. "It was a harmless prank."

"What was the prank?"

"Vaseline in my work gloves."

"Is that what triggered everything?"

I nod.

"What do you remember about what happened after you put your gloves on?"

I shake my head, still staring at my hands in my lap, opening and closing them.

"Do you want to talk about it?"

My hands start to shake. I close them tight into fists.

"How does your head feel?"

I look up at her. "It's fine."

Then she says, "Do you know what a flashback is?"

I look back down in my lap.

She says, "A flashback is a sudden, involuntary recollection of a past experience or elements of a past experience. You can feel like you are reliving it. And it can be so intense that it's hard to distinguish it from present reality. Does that sound like what might have happened?"

"Maybe," I whisper.

"Do you have any idea why the Vaseline might have been a

trigger?"

My head tics to the side, and I blink. "Yes."

"Do you want to tell me about that?"

My heart pounds in my throat. I close my eyes and swallow. "Nope."

# CHAPTER FIFTEEN

Rick walks by with a rag in hand on his way to clocking out, and he drops it on top of my target rag. This happens a few more times, more people add to it, and my singleton rag becomes "the rag pile." No one questions how this came to be. It's just there now as a fixture in the shop.

I've been getting close with the rod ends. I've been holding back because the target got so large I didn't want to actually land one on it yet, but I feel like I could make it now.

When I get home, Ben's, of course, there, and for whatever reason, he's examining the contents of my bookshelves.

"Mom called," he says.

"Mom called?"

"Mom called."

"And?"

He shrugs and stares at the book in his hands.

I sit on the foot of my bed. "What are you reading?"

He slaps the book shut and reshelves it.

"I need a shower," I say. "Then do you want to come to the store with me?"

"Sure." He plucks another book from the shelf. How he reads anything through sunglasses in the dim light of the room, I have no idea.

Later in the store I follow behind him with the cart as he tosses things in. He bags half a dozen apples. I add a few bananas. He grabs carrots. I throw in an onion.

"What do you need an onion for?" he asks.

"You don't like onions?"

He keeps walking.

"Right. I knew that." I put the onion back.

Frosted flakes, ramen, soup, bread, peanut butter. When we walk by the pharmacy, he tosses in a handful of cheap sunglasses. Down the next aisle, he throws in a jumbo pack of paper towels.

"We could always just get tissues," I say, but he ignores me.

In the checkout line, the checkout lady looks at Ben and says, "You're William Smith's son, aren't you?"

Ben just stares.

"I used to always get my prescriptions from him. He doesn't work at the pharmacy anymore?"

"He's tending to other obligations," Ben says.

Ben selects a lighter and tosses it onto the conveyer belt. After the checker rings it up, she sets it on the check writing shelf. He reaches for it, but I grab it first and shove it in my pocket.

Back in the apartment, once the groceries are all put away, we sit at the table. I pull the lighter out of my pocket. Flicking it on and off, I say, "What do you need this for?"

He holds his hand out, and I place it in his palm. Then he flicks it on and holds his palm over the top of the flame as his mouth spreads open in a pain grimace.

I snatch the thing from him and chuck it into the kitchen sink. "What the fuck, Ben?"

He just sits there, breathing fast, smiling, his burnt palm wrapped under his fingers.

My little brother is out of his little mind.

I throw some ice in a towel and grab his hand. He opens it up, revealing the red-black mark, and I set the towel in his palm. I yank the sunglasses off his face and toss them on the table.

Just then, the phone rings.

I answer.

It's Mom.

* * *

"Cheerios were on sale last week," Mom says, sitting in the recliner in her living room, legs crossed, both arms leaning on one arm of the chair. "Two dollars a box—the big boxes. That's even less than the store brand." The foot of her crossed leg shakes back and forth. The house smells like vanilla candles.

I nod. Ben nods.

Ben and I sit on opposite corners of the peach floral sofa—me leaning forward with my elbows on my knees and Ben all slumped, his hands in his lap, fidgeting with the bandage covering his self-inflicted lighter stigmata, his sunglasses back on.

Mom's silvering black hair looks clean and brushed. She smiles, and it goes all the way to her eyes.

"I should send you kids home with some." She gets up. "I've got more than I'm ever going to eat." I follow her into the kitchen. She opens the pantry door, revealing not just a dozen boxes of Cheerios, but every sale item from the past month in a minimum of triplicate. There's pasta, soup, can after can of beans, peas, corn, cases of macaroni and cheese, crackers, cake mixes, oatmeal, granola bars, and the list goes on. Mom will never have to worry should a major disaster befall the region leaving her housebound for a year or more. She plops a rattling pair of boxes on the counter, goes back in for two more, goes back in for another, making it five boxes of Cheerios and asks if there's anything else we need. I tell her no, they can detonate the nukes now.

"Jake," she says, her eyes look out the kitchen window, smile fading. "I'm going to be out of Valium next week, and with your father gone, I don't know how to get a refill."

Well, Mom. Perhaps you could go see an actual doctor and get a legitimate prescription and take it to an honest pharmacist. Or perhaps you could stop taking the fucking stuff all together. "I don't know, Mom," I say. "Maybe go to the doctor?"

She nods. "I'll call them in the morning."

Mom's going to run out of money at some point. I can't picture her holding down a job. Don't know how much savings they have. Dad was still more than a decade away from retirement.

"Well, how's work?" she says. "How are things?"

Scratching at the corner of my eye, I shrug. "Work's work."

"Oh?" she nods. "And Ben," she calls into the next room as she walks back in to take a seat in the recliner once more, "how's school?"

Ben says, "You know. School's school."

"Uh-huh." She nods again, eyebrows coming together, tongue pushing her cheek out on one side. "How are things otherwise?"

And Ben, the great philosopher, says, "Life sucks, but hey, at least I'm not getting fucked in the ass anymore."

"Well," she starts, but leaves us hanging, losing herself in the distraction of her fingernails, folding herself up in the recliner. She becomes particularly concerned by a hangnail on her right index finger and proceeds to bite at it. Trying to flick it up with her thumbnail, trying to come at it from a good angle.

I try to give Ben a glare of disapproval, but it's impossible to tell if he's even looking my way. "So, Mom, how have you been?" I say.

"Oh, good," she pops up. "Well," her head tilts to the side. "I-I've decided to divorce your father. You know, for tax reasons mostly. It just made sense."

"Really? To escape the IRS?" Ben crosses his arms.

"Ben—" I say.

"Shut up, Jake." His face turns red behind his black shades.

"Ben, follow." I motion towards the hall, and start walking. He gets up, and stomps along behind me. Down the hall is my old room, now primarily used for storage. My old bed lies buried under boxes of crap, a few of which I move to the floor. "Sit," I tell Ben, and he does.

I lean against the wall, blow out a long breath.

Ben says, "What—you going to tell me to be nice? You going to tell me not to hate her? You going to tell me she didn't do anything wrong?"

"I get that you're mad."

"You don't have any idea."

I shake my head. There's something about seeing him on my old bed. Leaning back on his elbows like that. And my eyes go to the door to make sure it's closed, like I'm worried Dad might walk in.

"Whatever," he says. "Why are we even here? Why did you make me come with you?"

"Mom wanted to see us," I say.

"Why?"

"Because she's human?" I say. "Because she's lonely? I don't know."

"She doesn't even like me," he says.

"Granted, she's a little fucked in the head. That doesn't mean she hates you."

"I thought you were on my side."

"There aren't sides, Benny. A lot's happened. But everything's over. Dad's in jail. Maybe it's time to start trying to get back to normal."

"Back to normal?"

"You know what I mean."

"If you want to kick me out, just say so. That's what this is, isn't it? You want me to move back in with her."

"That's not it at all," I say.

"Then what is it?"

"She's your mother. She's my mother. We're visiting her. That's what people do. Can you just try to be nice? There's no reason to turn this into some big argument."

"She doesn't believe us, Jake. You don't think that's a big deal? She thinks I lied about everything."

"The court doesn't think you lied. I don't think you lied."

"Whatever," he says.

I sigh and shake my head. "You don't remember what she used to be like."

He cocks his head side to side while mocking, "I don't remember what she used to be like."

"Stop being a smart ass."

"I'm not. What did she used to be like?" He looks right at me, waiting.

I wet my lips and close my eyes. "I was about nine when she got hooked on Valium the first time. It was, of course, Dad's idea. For nerves, right? Except it wasn't nerves, it was him. It was being married to him for ten years."

Ben just sits there, waiting for more.

"Do you know why your bedroom is yellow?"

He shakes his head.

"She painted it yellow for you, before you were born. It used to be white." My room was the same yellow. "She wanted it to be sunny or something. So you'd grow up happy."

"Point?" He stares up at the light bulb through his sunglasses.

"Point is, she gave birth to you, she fed you, she wiped shit off your ass, she got up with you in the middle of the night every time you made so much as a peep."

He takes in a quick breath, "She hold my dick, too?"

I step toward him, ball my hand up into a fist, punch the box closest to him, and he flinches. "Damn it, Ben! I could hear her through this wall, you know, singing to your screaming self. All calm. And you would fall asleep to that."

Ben shakes his head, then he turns to the side, trying to look away from me. From behind his glasses, a tear rolls down his cheek. His hand moves fast to smack it away as he sniffs. He reminds me of myself at that age, right around the time he was born, and there's this weird feeling that I'm forgetting something about then—about how I used to be.

"What do you want from me?" I say.

He shrugs, his head still turned away.

"Who do you have in this world, Ben? Me? You think I'm worth a shit? You also have her. And she may be out of her fucking mind half the time, she may be in denial, but somewhere in there, she cares about you even if she doesn't know how to show it anymore. You have to believe that. You have to."

"You're not helping," he says.

I sit on the floor and lean back against the wall.

He stares at the light bulb through his shades again. "I don't forgive her," he says. "I don't forgive you, either. And I never will, so you can stop trying."

# CHAPTER SIXTEEN

Larry Daly paces back and forth in his yard, backlit in the dark by every light in his house, shotgun in hand. He looks ferocious, like a caged beast.

I'm up in my tree, and I won't be coming down for a while. He doesn't know I'm here, and I'd like to keep it that way.

"Where you at, you fucker!" he screams.

When the police pull up, they unholster their weapons and walk toward him with one hand held palm out, saying, "Put the gun down, sir."

Larry sets his weapon against the wall of his house. "I have a license for it. I have a right to protect my family."

Every night Larry comes home late, his wife leaves the garage door unlocked. Don't know why he doesn't have an automatic opener, but he doesn't. Tonight when Larry got home, sometime around 10:30, he opened the garage door to park his car, but there was no room. Every item that had been carefully shelved was now lying in a giant pile in the middle of the floor.

I did it.

Because Larry is too uptight. Because Larry works too late. Or maybe I'm just bored.

Really, it's that the more I can distract myself from my actual life, the better. Ben and his resentment hang on me like a weight, and I can't even close my eyes half the time without seeing Dad. Besides, it's nice to watch someone else feel not in control for once.

I waited until the lights went off in the house. Larry still wasn't home. I dropped out of my tree, crossed the street, rolled under the garage door, and got to work emptying odd boxes of junk, dumping tools, a bike, some old rolls of wallpaper, skis, golf clubs in the middle of the floor. Then I went back to my tree and waited. He got home half an hour later, pulled the garage door open and stood frozen for a minute. Then he went in the house, all the lights came flickering back on, there was yelling, and he returned out front with his shotgun.

The cops stick around for a while writing a report, looking at the stuff in the garage, telling Larry to calm down. When they leave, he starts putting things back on shelves, all the while, holding the gun in his right hand and every so often pacing menacingly at the garage entrance, scanning the street for the perpetrator. His wife pops out at regular intervals asking him to come in, but he ignores her.

It takes a lot longer to create order than to create a mess, particularly if you're only working with one non-dominant hand, and I start to wonder if he'll ever get it all done.

Once Larry finally has everything put away, he closes the garage door and sits on his front step, gun across his lap. It's been hours, sitting on this tree branch. My tailbone feels spurred on the end. Segments of my back and rear take turns going numb in between each subtle shift of position. I'm hungry enough that my stomach is eating its own acid, and it occurs to me I haven't eaten a thing in over twenty-four hours. It's well after midnight, and I still need to get up at 5:30 and go to work. Larry's got to go inside sometime.

Mrs. Daly saves me. She cracks open the door in her bathrobe and frazzled puff of brown hair, sighs, and says, "Come inside, it's late." Larry stands and takes one last piercing look into the darkness and finally grants her request. A few minutes later all the lights flick off one by one. And I am free.

I get home to find Ben at the table, face down, sleeping in what else but his algebra book, all of the lights still on. His right hand holds a pen and rests on a half-finished drawing of an army of zombie farm animals.

Starving, I throw some deli meat and mustard between two

slices of bread and sit across from him. His eyes blink open, squint, and he lifts his head up, rubbing his neck. His face is all scrunched and bright pink on one side from peeling off the pages of the book.

"What time is it?" he says, looking over at the clock on the stove, answering his own question. He stares at me eating for a minute. "Why are you up?"

I chew and swallow. "Just got home."

"Where were you?"

"Kind of a long story."

He leans back in his chair. "So tell me."

"It's complicated. Anyway, how was school?"

"Fuck you." He shakes his head, slams his book shut, and disappears into the bathroom. Until recently I don't think I'd ever heard a curse word out of him in his entire little life. Now there's at least one in every conversation.

Prometheus is sitting on his half-log despite all of the lights being on. I stand up to go feed him and accidentally knock a new pair of sunglasses onto the floor.

# CHAPTER SEVENTEEN

They say depression is anger without enthusiasm. Well, Ben is far too enthusiastic to be depressed so check that off the list of concerns. He comes home on a Friday afternoon, slams the door behind him, rips the backpack off his shoulders, and slingshots it into the wall by the table. His breath is heavy, and he pauses, facing me as I lie reading on the bed before he disappears into the bathroom, slamming yet another door.

In the bathroom, there is plenty of enthusiasm. Kicking in the cabinet door, some animalistic growls and screams. I get up and make an attempt at the knob, but it's locked, so I let him be.

About thirty minutes later, he opens the door, all sweaty with his hair messed. He leans on the door frame and turns to face me.

"You okay?" I say.

He smiles huge and nods.

He walks across to the other side of the room, then slides down the wall to sitting on the floor, still smiling. His legs out flat in front of him, his arms at his side, and I think he's looking at me, but it's hard to tell.

He's not happy, he's dopey.

"What'd you do?" I say.

"Nothing."

I go into the bathroom, check the trash bin, but it's empty. I come out and dig through all the pockets in his backpack, but don't find anything. Then I drop to my knees beside him and dig through his pants pockets and pull out a baggie full of pills. He doesn't fight it. Just watches.

"What the hell are these?"

"Percocet," he says, his head bobbing around.

"Where'd you get them?"

"At home. You know Dad's got drugs all over the place."

"How many did you take?"

His head stops bobbing and slowly moves to upright. He holds up three fingers.

"Fuck, Ben—why?"

He shrugs. "It's only three."

"It's a fucking narcotic." I pull off his sunglasses and toss them clattering across the room.

He says, "Hey," and just stares at them as his eyes droop. His hands rub across his face, he scratches his arms, and says, "I'm itchy." He rubs his face again.

I stand. "Come on off the floor. Can you even stand up?"

He looks at his feet like he's trying to figure out how standing up works. He brings up his knees, plants his hands, and shifts his weight onto his feet, then reaches back for the wall as he gets to standing. I give him an arm, and he grabs it. I guide him over to the bed.

He says, "I feel really good right now, just itchy."

I leave him and flush the remaining Percocet down the toilet.

Lying in my bed, Ben isn't smiling anymore. His mouth is open, he's pale, and he keeps scratching at his arms. "I think I feel sick."

"How sick?"

"Uh..." He puts his arm over his eyes and tips to one side.

"Lie down all the way before you fall out of bed."

"Uh..." he whimpers again.

"You're not about to hurl, are you?"

He drops his arm off his face, blinks, and smiles. "I don't know." He scratches his arms, still leaning.

"You're falling out of bed."

"No, I'm good." His eyes droop even more.

I pull his legs so he slides down mostly horizontal with his head on the pillow, and I sit next to him. He keeps digging his nails into his arms, so I grab his hands. "You're not going to have any skin left if you keep that up."

"It itches."

"Here, just don't scratch it. I'll be right back." I go to the kitchen area, fill a bowl with ice cubes, and grab a dish towel.

I sit next to him and set the bowl on the floor. When he scratches again, I grab his hand, pull his arm toward me, and rub an ice cube up and down the red marks. It melts and wets his arm, drips onto the bed, and I blot the water with the towel. I do the same with his other arm. "How's that?"

"Better." He turns his arm over, wrapping his fingers tight around my hand. I try to move my hand away, but his grip tightens. He says, "Stay here," and reaches up with his other hand to scratch his face.

I pull my hand free. "I'm not going anywhere." I rub another ice cube across his forehead, down the bridge of his nose and on his cheeks, drop the cube back in the bowl.

His eyes are trained on mine—his brown eyes and skinny wet face. I look toward my dresser at Prometheus in his tank.

Ben whispers, "I don't want to go to school anymore."

"Why's that?"

"I'm failing everything." I hear him scratching again. "Can you do my stomach, too?"

I look at him. He's got his shirt pulled up, scratching at his belly. "I could help you with your homework if you'd just ask."

He digs his fingernails into his stomach, scratching hard. I pull his hand away, grab another ice cube and rub it across the new red marks. As it melts, his skin goes to goose bumps. I drop the cube back in the bowl and look toward Prometheus again. He's hiding just under his half-log, staring out at me with his red eyes.

Ben says, "You know what they did last night?"

"The same kids again?"

"I told Dylan all about everything a while back. He wasn't

supposed to tell anyone, but he did. They started a tumblr all about it and called it 'Ben-Gay,' and they're putting everything I said up there, but changing it to make it sound like I'm some sort of porno king. Dylan is telling everyone I hit on him. He just doesn't want people to know about him. I thought I loved him."

"Loved him?"

"I thought," Ben says.

"Like, as a friend, or...?"

"Doesn't matter anymore," Ben says.

My lungs hurt. I don't know how to protect him from any of this. I listen as his breathing slows and he sighs like people do when they've just fallen asleep. Prometheus retreats all the way into the dark.

I move to the table, turn on his laptop, and find the tumblr site. It's just as he described. There are even poorly rendered MS Paint cartoon sketches depicting everything. The cartoon faces are all smiling.

This is the exact thing I always feared would happen if I told when I was his age—everyone would turn on me, expose me, hold me accountable for every act. And I kept coming to the conclusion that they'd be right in doing so.

Ben looks at peace in his drug-induced coma, but I can't stare at him too long or my eyes start to water. He doesn't deserve this. He's just a kid.

* * *

Ben's been out for almost twelve hours straight when 4:00 a.m. comes around. I've been up all night making sure he didn't stop breathing. He rolls onto his back, lets out a long breath, breathes in deep, then lets out a shaky breath. The beginnings of another sad puppy episode. I turn the light on, and his arm goes over his eyes.

"How are you feeling?" I say.

He pulls the blankets off, sits up, and a small tear drips out his left eye. "Are you mad at me?"

I shake my head. "Just don't do it again."

He nods.

"Get your shoes and jacket."

"Why?"

"Just do it." I pull my shoes on. He does the same. He grabs his hooded sweatshirt from the back of a chair and slips it on. Puts on his sunglasses.

Outside I give him the car keys. He holds them for a minute, staring at them in his open palm, then wraps them in his fist and gets in on the driver's side.

He pushes the sunglasses on top of his head, starts the car, and says, "Where to?"

I shrug. "East." I reach over to show him where the headlights are, and we're off with a sudden reverse, abrupt stop, turn of the wheel, and a lurch forward onto the street.

At first there's a lot of yelling back and forth.

"Turn signal!"

"I can't do that and turn at the same time!"

"Supposed to do it before you turn. Stop sign!"

"I see it!"

"You didn't see the one we just passed. Left lane—check your blind spot!"

"I can't look and drive at the same time!"

Eventually we make it to open freeway, and he has hundreds of miles before we'll encounter anything.

Streetlamps and approaching headlights break up the darkness. The buzzing whir of the tires puts me in a trance, and I fall asleep.

I wake later with my arms folded, head wedged into the window, the hot, stale air from the vent burning my face. The sun is out now. I sit upright, rub the stiffness out of my neck, and blink at the daylight. Ben looks briefly in my direction, then returns his death stare to the road, white knuckling the steering wheel. He's got his sweatshirt string hanging out the corner of his mouth again.

We pass brown hills with dormant grass and sagebrush. A lowly tumbleweed rolls by. Rock and dirt and brown. Hill after hill, dry and blank. We pass the occasional smatter of houses here and there sometimes labeled as towns. The odd clump of cattle. Ridges etched in the hillsides from where the cattle have walked.

A sign up ahead claims the next right leads to a state park, so I tell him to take the exit. He successfully manages the turn signal but doesn't start slowing fast enough until I yell.

The park consists of little more than a sign stating that it's a park, a gravel parking lot, and a trail leading off into the vast nothingness. So we take it.

Everything all exposed for lack of trees. Nothing on this trail but dirt and rock, dry and brown. And we're cold in the morning air.

Ben says, "Haven't filled out the victim's impact statement yet."

"What?"

"For Dad's sentencing—remember? It's next week."

"Right."

We approach a trickle of a stream where the trail ends. Rocks cover the bank beneath our feet. I look over at Ben, and we both reach down and grab one. He throws first, down the stream, splashing into the water. "Oh come on," I say. "You can do better than that." I chuck mine farther.

"I don't think I'm going to—fill out the statement. I don't want to." He picks up another rock and launches it, throwing all his weight into it.

"Have you talked to the DA about that?"

"I don't need to. It was optional anyway."

"Are you sure you don't want to?"

He nods. "They have minimum sentencing rules. He's getting at least twenty-five years."

Ben is fifteen, and twenty-five years is still forever in his world. He chucks another rock, letting it go with a grunt that echoes off the water.

"Do you think that's enough?" I say.

"Do you? Anyway, I don't care." He picks up another rock, and another, and another.

# CHAPTER EIGHTEEN

*Alpha*

The door opens in the night and the old man whispers, "Shhh..."

*Beta*

I prop myself up in bed on my elbows, and my head shakes no in two quick jerks, not a conscious reaction, but a tic.

*Gamma*

He holds a pair of beers in one hand, and when he closes the door behind him, it's so dark in the room that I mostly make out his location by scent and sound. The caps twist off the beer, and I know to sit up and put my hand out for one.

*Delta*

The old man gulps, and there's that hollow plunking sound when his lips leave the bottle. A small sigh after he swallows, then a cold hand traces below my belly button, slips inside my underwear, and cups my nuts. *Tic.*

*Epsilon*

The old man says, "Shhh... You're fine." That's my cue to relax, and the tension moves down to my curling toes. I take another sip and wince at the malt aftertaste.

*Zeta*

He towers over me, breathing his sour breath into my face. I look away, say nothing. I know he's not going anywhere.

*Eta*

Take another sip of beer. *Tic. Tic. Sip. Sip.*

*Theta*

He swallows the rest of his brew in a single go and sets the bottle on the floor. Halfway through mine, I'm back on the bed on my elbows, and my shorts are coming off. *Tic. Sip.*

*Iota*

A cold hand grabs my thigh, and a hot mouth swallows my dick. *Tic.* My whole body feels like a numb limb waking—pins and needles all over, and moving will only make it worse. But there's pleasure mixed in, and I'm getting hard. *Sip.*

*Kappa*

My toes curl so tight that the stabbing pain of a muscle cramp takes over my right foot, and I'm grateful for the release of adrenaline that takes me out of myself just a bit.

*Lambda*

*Sip.* As soon as the bottle leaves my lips, it's grabbed from my hand and set aside.

*Mu*

It's dark in the room, but I close my eyes anyway in case any light at all makes its way in. The pop of a button, the zip of a zipper, the old man's pants come off. A hand on my hip rolls me onto my stomach.

*Nu*

A buzzing sensation grows in my head. My ears burn. I grab my pillow and wrap it up close to my face. My gut is all mixed up— the butterflies of excitement, the want to please, the expectation of pain, the swirling cyclone of confusion—words and pictures and feelings that don't know where to land, how to line up, how to form something I can call me.

*Xi*

A cold hand rubs Vaseline right up my crack. *Tic.* I know to draw my knees up under me. I hear the wet smacking sound of the old man rubbing himself with more lube in preparation.

*Omicron*

He presses into me. I can't help but tighten, cringe, and he says, "Shhhh... Just relax, you're fine." And part of me wants him to hold me, cradle me like a baby, comfort me. I move the tension to my jaw, bite hard on the pillow.

*Pi*

My body goes away. I'm not there. I'm the things I know and those only. Facts pour themselves in organized lists on the inside of my eyelids, and I run through them.

*Rho*

I run through the facts faster and with a rhythm that matches his. As his breathing gets louder, so too does the buzz in my head. The confusion grows, and I can't properly classify everything I feel. I want it to all be bad, but then I want my dad to love me. I start to love him. I'm back in my body, all damp. His sweat coats my back.

*Sigma*

My belly cramps, my ass feels like it's tearing. Now I'm on fire, and I've got to get away. Back over the list—what else do I know? Give myself a number. Two. Run through the Greek alphabet twice and maybe it will be over.

*Tau*

Try three. *Don't cry, Jakey. Don't cry.*

*Upsilon*

Four, and it ends. He's spent. His hands next to my shoulders. His weight on top. His breath on my neck. He pulls out. A towel is rubbed over me.

*Phi*

I keep my head buried in the pillow, my face soaked in my own drool, until he kisses the back of my head, lays down beside me, and pulls me into his arms. He says, "You're fine. You're fine." And I am warm with relief. I lay with my head in the sweat of his armpit, but I'm leaving my body again. He slips away from me, and his jeans come back on with a jingle of the button and zipper. He tucks my blanket up to my chin and leaves. I run one last round of the Greek alphabet through my head.

*Chi*

I get up, pull my shorts back on, and run to the bathroom.

There I sit, in the dark on the toilet, let it all out of me until I feel emptied. I think about what Mom will say if I don't eat breakfast in the morning, and try to breathe right so the nausea will go away.

*Psi*

I grab a washcloth, wash myself down. Repeat quietly. *Don't wake your mother.*

*Omega*

I see Dad's face, close-up, his mouth forming the words so loud it shakes me, "Don't wake your mother!"

I stop breathing.

I'm suffocating.

I'm dying.

I can't move my limbs.

There's a gasping sound. A cry.

It's me, sucking in air.

I regain control of my limbs, flail around in bed, tangled in the blankets. A light comes on. I open my eyes, still panicking for breath, breaking free of the sheets and falling hard onto the floor, hitting my dresser and nearly knocking Prometheus's tank to the floor. I'm in my apartment, and Ben is standing by the light switch, staring at me like I'm some monster.

* * *

"Why do you do that?" I say after Lauren quotes another statistic. Apparently ten percent of the population suffers from depression.

"I'm not depressed." I'm wedged into the cushy chair with my arms crossed. "I'm not anything. Everything, these names and numbers that you give me, they don't make sense."

"How do you mean?" She sits more upright now.

The room feels like it's narrowing, but it might just be me sinking further in this chair every time I shift position. "I don't know."

"Depression often goes hand in hand with PTSD," she says.

Post-Traumatic Stress Disorder.

She dropped that "diagnosis" a while back.

She says, "It's understandable that you're angry."

"I'm not angry."

She jots down some notes, recrosses her legs, rests her elbow on the arm of her chair, and props her head with her hand. "So how have things been with Ben lately?"

"I don't know. He's just a kid, still."

"What do you mean by that?"

"I mean I don't think he knows what to think, and I don't think he knows who he is, and I don't think he knows what he wants, but he has time to figure all that out."

"What about you? Do you still have time to figure all that out?"

"What?"

"What you think, who you are, what you want?"

"I sorted that out years ago."

"So who is Jacob Smith, and what does he want?"

"He's a thirty-year-old loner who welds for a living."

"And is that what he wants?"

"It doesn't matter what he wants. That's what he is."

"And none of those things can be changed?"

"No."

"When you were a child, what did you want to be when you grew up?"

"A welder."

"That's what you are now. Is that what you've always aspired to be?"

"Why do people have a problem with this? What's so wrong with my job?"

"I don't have a problem with it," she says. "But I've gotten the sense on more than one occasion that you might."

I pick at the calluses on my hands and shake my head.

"My only intention here is to help you, Jacob—not judge you. I only want you to get better."

"You make it sound like I have some sort of disease. There's nothing wrong with me, except I'm an asshole."

"Do you think that the self-harm behavior is healthy?"

"It does what it needs to."

"And what is that?"

"Didn't we already have this conversation?"

"Maybe you can refresh my memory."

I shrug. "I don't know. Gets me out of my head."

"Why do you feel the need to get out of your head?"

"Just do. It's like a sinkhole sometimes."

"Can you give me an example? A situation when you felt compelled to hurt yourself—what was going through your mind at the time?"

"I don't know." As I squirm in my seat from the itching burn of fresh cuts on my lower abdomen near my groin, all I can figure is she must be psychic.

"Can you remember the last time you did so?"

"I don't know."

"It's not an uncommon thing in abuse survivors. It's not strange at all given what you've been through. My concern is that it isn't healthy in the long run. There are better ways to deal with what you've been feeling. Getting to the bottom of it can help you move forward."

"I'm fine." This chair has smells—hairspray, like Savannah's hairspray, but also the burn of incense.

Lauren has this look like there's something I'm not getting. She crosses her legs the other way.

"Did you burn incense in here again?" I tap my heel on the floor, my knee bobbing up and down.

Lauren gets up and opens the window. "How are you sleeping?" she says.

I pull the bags down under my eyes with my fingers and let them spring back up.

"Nightmares?" she says.

I look out the window.

"Have you been having nightmares?"

# CHAPTER NINETEEN

Ben's looking very unabomber today with sunglasses on and his green hooded sweatshirt pulled over his head. Hands in pockets, he's slumped as low in the chair across from the counselor's desk as he can go without falling on the floor. The left corner of his mouth is puffy and split and there's a triplet of blood drops on the neck of his sweatshirt.

It's the middle of the day. I got a call from Mom, who got a call from Ben's school, who said he'd been in a fight and a parent needed to go deal with it.

The counselor looks sorely disappointed when he sees it's me who showed up. His mouth in a pursed frown, he shakes my hand.

"Was your mother unable to make it?"

I look over at the busted lip, down at the tiled floor, then back up at him, "She's a little confused, so Ben stays with me right now."

The counselor avoids looking my way altogether and instead stares despondently at Ben.

"So what happened?" I say.

"Well, Ben?" The counselor says.

Ben shrugs.

The counselor waits.

"Was it the same kids?" I ask Ben.

He shrugs.

The counselor says, "We have reason to believe he initiated the fight."

"He initiated the fight?" I say. "Do you have any idea what

those little assholes have been doing? This isn't the first time they've roughed him up. And you should see the shit they've put on the internet."

The counselor stiffens in his seat. "Ben?" he says. "What's been going on?"

Ben shrugs again, then tips sideways until his head meets the wall. No one is going to get anything out of him like this.

"Can we talk in the hall?" I ask the counselor.

He stands, gestures towards the door, and we both exit.

"Well?" he says.

"You know the situation with our Dad?" I say. Except the word Dad comes out with an extended, stuttered "a" unexpectedly *Daa-aa-aad* like I'm a sheep.

The counselor nods and can't bring himself to look at me. "I was at the grand jury hearing. I was at the trial," he says.

I nod. "So, you've got kids in the school posting sick shit about that online. Did you know this?"

"There really isn't anything I can do about what happens on the internet unless they're using school computers for it."

"Glad to hear you don't give a shit."

"That's not true. Maybe you could try contacting the police."

"Maybe you could try making sure those assholes leave him the fuck alone!"

He squirms at my choice of language. "With all due respect, I have not been made aware of any other incidents, and there was more than one witness who saw him throw the first punch today."

"If he did, they deserved it."

His arms cross. "Has he been getting any help? Seeing anyone about the whole situation?"

I shake my head, "That's not what he needs."

"His teachers have been expressing concerns about his academic performance. He can come to my office and talk to me any time. We can make arrangements with his teachers to allow extra time on tests. But there's only so much we can do here."

"None of this was his fault."

"Mr. Smith, it really sounds like you've been thrust into the caregiver role—"

"That's my brother," I say, my eyes burning.

The counselor says, "Can you really handle him on your own? Because there are programs designed to—"

"That's my brother!"

He looks at me as though I slapped him, his mouth still hanging open because he wasn't able to finish his words. "Well, because of the fight, he's being suspended for three days."

I can't tell if that was the plan all along or if he's only now deciding this because he doesn't like me. I shake my head, go back into his office, grab Ben, and leave.

# CHAPTER TWENTY

Ben pushes the lawnmower across Mom's overgrown lawn with such vigor that mostly he's uprooting and not merely trimming the grass. He's flushed, and sweat drips in fat beads down his face. The grass is so tall that he keeps getting stuck, and he has to yank the thing back and forth violently, the mower always on the verge of getting away from him as he struggles along behind it.

I lean against the house, shovel in hand, taking a break from dumping good dirt on top of bad dirt so Mom can plant a garden. The pale green paint on the side of the house is blistering in spots. I peel off a few loose patches, crumble them in my hand and let them fall to the ground.

Mom materializes beside me. With the buzz of the mower, I didn't hear the door or her steps. She watches me dust the remaining paint chips off my palm. Her arms cross, she smiles. Her mouth forms the words, "Time to repaint again soon," but the mower's too noisy to hear them.

I nod.

She waves down Ben, yelling, "Lunch."

Can't tell if he doesn't see her or just doesn't care. Can't see his eyes again. On another pass, he comes right at us like he intends to mow us over, then he veers around us at the last minute and keeps going. I grab Mom's shoulder and yell in her ear to go in, we'll be there in a second. She disappears into the house.

I shout Ben's name half a dozen times, but he doesn't respond, so I grab the back of his shirt with one hand and kill the mower with the other. "Time to go in," I say, his shirt still balled up in my fist.

He shakes free and yells, "Sure thing, Dad!"

"What did you just say?" I rip the shades off his face and stare right into his dilated pupils.

He steps back looking at the ground and marches inside.

At the table, Mom has prepared a feast. There is macaroni and cheese, chicken breasts, peas, corn, garlic toast, and the list goes on. She's trying to put her pantry stock to use. The sunglasses have found their way back onto Ben's face, and he sits slouched as low as he can go, steadily shoveling in food and chewing loudly with his mouth open. I rearrange the food on my plate to give the appearance that it's being worked on. Mom keeps looking back and forth between Ben and me, confused. I fork a singleton noodle into my mouth and chew it around a bit.

"How's school?" she says.

Ben doesn't speak, just keeps chewing loudly.

"Ben's got credit recovery next year if he doesn't ace his finals," I say.

"Oh," she nods. "Well, I guess with all that's happened..." she trails off.

"What happened?" Ben says between bites.

"Ben, don't," I say.

He looks my way, closes his mouth, chews slower for a few seconds, and then reverts to his original mode.

Mom keeps looking from my plate to me. "What's wrong?" she finally asks.

I shake my head, "Just not hungry."

Her face wrinkles, "You're not sick are you? You look so pale."

Then Ben says, "Jake doesn't eat food anymore."

I drop my fork and turn toward him. "Ben."

"Doesn't sleep much either," he continues. "And when he does, he's always falling out of bed."

"Ben! Cool it."

Mom says, "Have you tried Tylenol PM?"

"I'm fine. I'll be fine."

Ben says, "No you won't."

I sigh and look at him.

"You won't. We won't." His fist grips and ungrips his fork as his knee bobs up and down, his heel tapping the floor. He slams the fork down on the table and stands up, knocking over his chair.

I stand, too, grab the back of his shirt in my fist again, and say, "Outside. We need to talk."

He shakes free of my grip and runs out the door. I follow him to the edge of the dirt-filled patch slated to become a garden.

"Take off the shades," I say.

"No."

I reach over, rip them off, and throw them over the fence. He crosses his arms and looks to the side.

"What's your fucking problem today?" I say. "Spill it."

"Maybe I don't get how you can just sit at the table with her and act like everything's all normal."

"You're mad at her. I get that. We've been over this."

He shakes his head.

"You've got more than that, what else?"

He just shakes his head.

"Say it," I tell him.

He works his jaw around, face turning red, breathing hard. "It's just that," he takes in a deep breath, looks right at me. "You knew." He waits a moment, takes a deeper breath, and then yells, "You knew! You fucking knew! More than anyone, you did!" His voice is shrill and so loud, the entire neighborhood can hear. "You knew what he was doing to me the whole fucking time! You even said so in court!" His eyes water, his lip quivers. "I'm just supposed to be okay with that?"

"Have I ever said that?"

His chest rises high and falls hard with each breath. "Why did you let it happen? I don't get it. Why? You're even worse than Mom."

I hold my arms out to the side and say, "Take it. Take a shot."

He looks away.

"I'm wide open. Go for it."

He looks at me, then away, then back, uncrosses his arms, and lunges, shoving me with both hands, causing me to step back.

"Oh, fuck it, Ben. You can do better than that."

He walks away a few steps then comes at me running, knocking me down into the dirt. He beats my chest with his fists, knees me in the side, pops me in the jaw, gritting his teeth, grunting angrily the whole time.

The kid is strong. Enough rage makes anyone strong. Each hit, each impact takes me out of myself a little more, and pretty soon I am detached. The soft dirt on my back, the fresh cut grass in the air, the sun up high in the sky. And all I can think about is the last time it happened to me. The last time Dad happened to me. I was twenty. All grown up and not even living at home anymore. It was a camping trip. Dad wanted to take his boys camping. Ben was only five.

Back on his feet, Ben kicks dirt in my face, kicks me in the gut.

Thing is, I only went on that camping trip because of the kid.

Ben sits back in the dirt, spent, panting, and says, "I hate you. I fucking hate you sometimes."

I sit up, spit dirt and blood into the grass. "Fair enough."

"I just don't get it. If you knew, how could you not do anything?"

"There's a lot you don't know."

"Oh, really? Like what?"

I shake my head. "You looking for me to say sorry? Does that word cut it—sorry? And then we can be all happy and you'll forgive me? Sorry is not what you want. Sorry is not what you need."

"Then what? What do I need?" he asks.

There's a ringing in my ears like a mosquito buzzing. "Fuck if I know," I whisper.

I remember the smell of Dad's beer breath, his sweat, and how icy cold his hands were in the tent that night. I remember thinking

Ben's too young. I remember thinking we needed to be really quiet or we would wake the kid up. I remember thinking I was too old for this. I remember thinking I was supposed to know better.

Everything's a tunnel, a mile off, unreachable, dizzy. I hate myself. I get to my feet, then double over, vomiting up the sparse contents of my stomach mixed with blood onto the grass. My gut keeps contracting long after I'm coming up dry. Back upright, I stand, swaying, wiping my mouth with the back of my hand.

I remember thinking never again. I remember thinking I didn't care what happened to the kid, it wasn't worth it. Ben wasn't worth it.

Ben says, "You okay?"

"Yeah, fine," and I hate that word fine. Dad always told me I was fine. That's why I'm fine. Fine. Fine, I'm leaving the scene now, going into the house, past Mom doing the dishes, down the hall toward my old room.

But I stop.

At the end of the hall, the door to Mom and Dad's room is ajar, and there's an itch at the back of my head like a memory, and I go to the open door to see if it will come to me, the whole time feeling like it's something I should be avoiding. I stand in the doorway, hand on the knob, and stare into the room, the disheveled bed and piles of dirty laundry. Mom's old underwear on the floor, and I can't be here anymore. I double back, into my old room and slam the door, kick the bed posts, kick one until it buckles under. Two fists overhead, I land them on the wall that separates my room from Ben's. I slide down the wall as my eyes close, melting to the floor because my legs won't hold me up anymore. I wedge myself into the back corner of the room and curl up, face in my knees, arms bent, elbows at my ears.

# CHAPTER TWENTY-ONE

She was a spider. Her eyes were spiders. Or something. Don't know what they are now. If she even still has eyes.

Savannah tripped again. At the same corner. The one with the rag pile. Except the pile had caught on fire. And she burned.

While I can't be positive, it seems the odds are pretty great that I was the cause. After all, I'd made a habit of flicking the hot ends of my rods that direction. I didn't mean to land one. Not like that. Then again, it could have been Carson. Or, I could at least blame it on Carson.

She hasn't been back to work since. That much screaming, she may never be back. But I'm trying not to think about that.

Before me are last week's newspapers. I'm on my bed with scissors cutting out words and letters because there's no room at the table with all of Ben's homework. I have on gloves so there won't be fingerprints. Glue and paper. Newspaper confetti all over the sheets, falling to the floor. Papers spread open, unfolded, crumpling, headlines all sliced. I'm making letters for Larry Daly because sleep deprivation has convinced me that this is a perfectly sane thing to do.

"A poem," I tell Ben, "I need a poem."

"Roses are red," Ben starts. A pencil plops on the table. He turns around, rests his chin on the top of the chair. "Violets are blue. What are you doing?"

"Roses—that's a good start," I say. Looking for r's now.

Ben gives up and turns back around, hunching with a sigh over his textbook, holding his head with both hands. A few seconds pass and he picks his pencil back up and twists it between his toes.

To Larry, I cut and paste letters of differing sizes and fonts to form an ominous poem. Larry has been more pissed than usual because Savannah's not around and the "damn welder" got lazier in her absence. If anything, I've been more productive, but productivity without melons to stare at isn't as satisfying.

I rip open a box of envelopes.

Ben says, "How do you find a vertex?"

"Like for a quadratic?" I unbury myself from the clippings and walk over as h's, i's, j's, k's fall from me like snow. I lean over the table and leaf back a few pages in his book. "Formula right there." I point my gloved finger to the middle of the page.

"Yeah, but how do I use it?" he asks, elbow on the table, head in his hand, eyes going from my hand to my eyes. "Why are you wearing gloves?"

"The coefficients—a, b, and c are just the coefficients."

"What?"

"a is the number in front of $x^2$, b is the number in front of x, and c is the constant. Figure out what a, b, and c are and plug them in."

He looks back at the formula. "That's it? What's the point?"

"Don't know that there is one." I stand upright. "Except passing algebra is probably a good idea."

"So I can become all knowledgeable and weld like you?"

"That's exactly right," I return to the bed, set an envelope on top of a book, and write Larry's address on it in block letters.

* * *

The next week at work Larry comes in, fuming beneath his smiling request to speak to Dan, the man in charge. He thinks nothing of outright yelling at Dan, owner of this wonderful establishment and our temporary Savannah until she comes back. If she comes back. Dan has enough on his plate, worrying if she's going to sue, but Larry needs his handrails. He does not feel this point has been made until Dan's face is coated with spit and an accusing finger has stabbed the air in my direction for a good ten minutes.

Larry must have received the letter by now, making him even less reasonable than usual. Paper can't hurt him, but he's scared anyway. Fuck him. Fuck Larry the prick.

I go to Larry's house after work again, sit in the tree and wait. He gets home while it's still light outside, and within minutes, he's sitting on the front steps, pump action shotgun in hand, cleaning kit by his side. He removes the barrel and proceeds to shove a cleaning rod through it, stopping every so often to leer at the neighborhood. All the drapes, the blinds in his house are closed. He rubs the parts of the disassembled weapon down with oil and proceeds to put it back together.

In a window on the second floor the drapes part in the middle and give way to two small hands holding a pair of binoculars. It's his daughter. The little fingers adjust the focus as she looks down the street, then down at the ground, then up and out, stopping at my tree. I freeze. My heart hits loud against my ribs. Larry's on the steps, his gun upside down between his legs, feeding shells into the barrel.

Up at the window the binoculars come down and curious eyes squint in my direction as the girl's hand comes up like a hat brim above her brow. Her hand goes back down, and she disappears behind the drapes.

Do I drop out of the tree now and run, hoping to get a head start before Larry finishes loading? Or do I wait on the off chance she's not tromping downstairs right now to say, "Daddy, there's a man in the tree," so Daddy can blow my head off?

I get my feet under me and squat on the limb. A long minute passes, and nothing happens. Another, then another, until I slowly feel confident that my cover hasn't been compromised. My mind wanders, and I start thinking about Savannah, wondering how bad she was hurt, if she'll be okay, feeling *guilty, guilty, guilty.*

I break a small twig off the tree, sit back down, and hold it between my thumb and forefinger, moving it back and forth, tapping it against my chin. I examine the twig closer, and remove some of the bark on one side to sharpen the tip, then trace lines with it on my forearm. No blood, just little white marks where the very surface layer of skin tears. With each pass I press a little harder, and my whole forearm is sore, covered in fading streaks. I grab the twig in my right fist, sharp end down, roll the sleeve all the way up to the shoulder on my left arm, and stab it into my bicep. My mind's a wash, and all I can do is inhale. I pull the twig out, rest it in the fork of a branch above my head, and touch the warm blood leaking from the wedge of displaced meat. I smear my hand all over it, and make a fist. Opening my fingers, I see the red settled in all the creases of my palm. I taste the tip of a crimson-coated finger.

*  *  *

I fall asleep in the tree and wake up on my way to the ground. That stomach-floating freefall feeling, and my eyes open only to see the mud and pine needles coming up too fast. I land on my side with one arm folded under me, all the air gone out of my lungs.

My first instinct is to arch my back around to see if Larry is still on the front steps. It's dark, and the lights are all off, but maybe he's in the shadows. There's a throbbing at the base of my skull again, louder than ever.

Then it's gone. All of it. Suddenly it's later, and I'm sitting in my car with a splitting headache wondering how I got here. Must've hit my head good on the landing.

It's getting light outside, though the sun's not yet peeked above the horizon.

My neck, my whole body, is stiff. The arm I landed on feels oddly not there. I lift it, and it tingles. I make a fist, and it still seems to be working, but maybe I pinched a nerve. I blink the fog from my eyes, taste earth and grit, and spit and wipe my face with my sleeve.

Spitting wasn't enough. I open the door, lean out, and vomit. Sitting back in the car, I look in the rearview mirror. Dried mud cakes the side of my face. I rub it off, try to rub it off my clothes, too.

Keys. Keys. That's the sharp pain under my thigh—keys. I grab them and start the engine. The clock on the dash reads 5:23.

I dig through the glove box to see if there're are any napkins or the like that I can use to clean myself up before heading to work. All I find is the wad of papers Lauren gave me a while back—various handouts on strategies for coping with stress.

I laugh. Meditation, exercise, and deep breathing activities are clearly for those who lack creativity. I cope with my stress by hiding in trees, sending ominous letters in the mail, and performing medical experiments on my upstairs neighbor.

Sleep deprivation can give a person all sorts of crazy ideas. But the more crazy ideas the better because it means I don't have to think about Ben, about Dad, about Mom, about what happened to Savannah. No, this is all way more interesting than sitting at home while Ben fumes, or curling up in bed to wait for a nightmare. I don't know if I could even begin to recognize what's normal anymore, and it's possible I don't care.

I shove the papers back in the glove box.

I can just watch Ron fall apart. I can watch Larry fill with rage, and it isn't even that I feel accomplished. It's that I don't even care. There's some level on which they deserve it because they're too blind to see around it. Like I was once. There's always a way out. Ron could stop taking the pills. Larry could ignore the mail. I could have ran away. I could have told someone like Ben did.

Releasing the e-brake hurts, gas pedal hurts, steering wheel hurts, daylight hurts, and I'm off to work.

When I enter to clock in, Rick laughs and says, "Dude, you look like shit! Rough night?"

Dan looks me up and down, making a motion inside his mouth like maybe he's trying to eat his own tongue. Hood, jacket, gloves, and today I am a zombie.

\* \* \*

Still sore from my night spent in the tree, I come straight home after work. Ben's there, sitting on his sleeping bag against the wall, laptop in lap, and I feel him glaring even through the sunglasses.

"I'm stupid," he says. "Do you want to know why I'm stupid?"

"Benny, you're not stupid."

"I'm stupid because I was up all night worried. Do you know why I was worried?"

If I fucked up again, I'm too tired to care.

"You didn't come home," he says. "The whole night. Where is it you even go?"

"Nowhere," I say. "It doesn't matter. You're fifteen, Benny. You don't need me here at night. And there's no reason to worry. Why would you worry?"

"I told you," he says. "Because I'm stupid."

"I'm sorry, okay? I didn't think it was a big deal. I won't do it again, all right? I'll call you or something if I'm going to be out that late."

"What's even with you?" he says. "It's like this last week you've been even more of a fuckhead than usual."

"I've got a lot on my mind."

"Like what?"

"Personal stuff."

He scoffs, shuts his laptop and stands up. "I'm going for a walk, if you don't mind," he says, heading for the door. "And I'll come back whenever I feel like it, because what does it matter to you?"

\* \* \*

On Friday, I get a call from Lauren. I forgot about my appointment.

"Is everything okay?" she asks.

"Yeah. I just…overslept."

She expresses her satisfaction that I've been getting good sleep, and I assure her I won't miss next week.

But the reality is I've hardly slept at all. Too many things in my head. Ben stayed out until 2:00 a.m. the other night to prove his point. And the more he fluffs up his cloud of vitriol, the more I feel compelled to distract myself with my Larry and Ron experiments. I'm a goddamn scientist these days.

I take Prometheus out of his tank, lie on my back in bed, and set him on my chest. "What the hell am I doing?" I ask him.

He flicks his tongue at me.

"I should stop, right? I should stop before I get myself in trouble."

His head dips forward as if nodding in agreement. But I'm far too restless. It can't be as simple as stopping. I need one last hurrah. I need to make something happen—some big thing to break free, but with a satisfying ending.

Larry with his khakis and his ties. Larry with his buzzed bulldog head. Larry with his gun. Larry needs to make a mistake with repercussions. I put Prometheus back in his tank and get out my stash of newspapers to generate a new message for him. *Guns don't kill people. People kill people.*

Ronald Duncan won't stop taking the stupid pills. Sure, I could just stop switching them out, but you can't change a person—they need to change themselves. If I cut him off, he'll just find something else. It's what people do. Stand in front of their train, and they might slow down and stop, but it doesn't derail them. As soon as they start up again they're on the same track, heading the same way. You've got to do more than jump up and down and wave your hands.

I use Ben's laptop to type up a letter to Ron from the pharmaceutical company stating that they can no longer ship the medication for legal reasons, but that a representative would be in the area to facilitate direct sales later in the week. I give him Larry's address, a date, and a time of 9:00 p.m., then print the letter out at the local library on my way to the post office.

It all falls into place like an odd dream. A few days later, straddling the tree branch, watching through the pine needles, I see Larry on the front steps of his house, gun resting across his lap, beer in hand. It's been a warm day, but there's a breeze and the air carries a hint of pollen and impending rain.

Down the street the city bus screeches to a stop, pauses, then the engine revs as it moves on. A rush of adrenaline lets loose as Ronald Duncan emerges from around the corner. His t-shirt stained, his hair a greasy mat with tufts pointing every which way. The streetlamps blink on, and he appears jaundiced in their yellow glow. He stops, pulls a piece of paper out of his pocket, examines it, and continues. I pull up to standing on my tree limb, grab the branches on either side of me, and dig my nails into the bark until my fingertips burn.

Larry, scowling at the world, spots this figure shuffle-stepping down the street, and sits bolt upright. Ron approaches, seemingly unfazed by the firearm in Larry's lap. Larry's fist goes tight around the barrel, and he stands tall, his chest puffed out, his eyes in perfectly round circles.

Ron says, "Hey, this the place, dude?"

"What place would that be?" says Larry, deep and sharp.

"Like in the letter," Ron says.

"Letters?" Larry lifts the gun, holds the base of it in his left hand and the barrel with his right diagonally in front of him, like a soldier holding his gun at port arms. "You have something you want to tell me about the letters?"

Ron's hands come up, and he takes a step back. "Whoa, dude, I'm just here for the pills."

Larry pumps the barrel with a loud *shick, shick* sound. "Was it you?"

I'm dizzy, hanging on tight, hoping not to fall out of the tree.

The answer Ron spits out is, "Yeah." And Larry takes aim.

I don't know what I had in mind for this encounter, but I'm sure this wasn't it.

"Don't fucking move, you mother fucker!"

Larry's wife pokes her head out the door, and he tells her to call the cops.

Ron squirms like he might piss himself, turning his head side to side, checking up the street and down before making the decision to flee.

Larry lets out one warning, "Stop!" before his finger pulls the trigger, firing a loud crack. Ron appears to explode at the calf and collapses to the ground, grabbing his leg and screaming as blood pools around him.

# CHAPTER TWENTY-TWO

Hot water trickles into the bathroom sink, gurgling down the drain. I tuck my lips in and rub a white foam beard onto a week's worth of stubble, rinse my hands, and grab the razor. The blade grates across my cheek, severing the course hairs from their base. The skin on my face hangs looser than I remember. My eyes are darkly haloed from lack of sleep. I don't remember my ribs being so visible, but there they are. I have to wear a belt to keep my pants on my ass. Can't seem to keep anything down. The situation with Ron and Larry made it all that much worse, but what I find myself thinking about more and more is Savannah—wondering how she's doing. If she's okay. If I'll ever see her again.

The next pass with the razor lands me a triple blade gash under my chin. It stings with the shaving cream, and I let it come, let it bleed. Let the red mix pink in the cream.

Does she still think she's beautiful, I wonder? If she even thought she was before. Covered herself up too much with colors—her face, her fingernails. Her hair always teased to an aerosol stiffness.

I splash water on my face, then dry off, leaving red smudges on the nicely folded towel that Ben washed, dried, and put away.

One more glance in the mirror. The figure staring back resembles a decaying carcass. Skin so pale, it's nearly blue. Guilt. Maybe that's it. This is what guilt does to you. Funny how Dad never looked this way.

Ben takes his final exams today. He spent plenty of time hanging out with his textbooks, but I'm not sure how much studying went on. I should have been around more—tried to help him with his schoolwork more. I should have encouraged him to spend less time drawing heads impaled on fence posts and poking around on the Internet, and more time writing essays and factoring polynomials. But I'm his brother, not his father. I was never supposed to take care of him.

I get dressed and head to work.

There is, once again, no Savannah waiting at the front desk, just an empty seat.

With her gone, I start to realize what I saw in her. There's a way in which she can make anything normal. And not normal like it's acceptable, but normal like there's no point in hiding it and once it's out in the open you just fucking deal with it and move on. Something I can never seem to do.

Probably no makeup to hide her face, now after she caught fire—not even skin. Savannah's insides exposed. And maybe Helen of Troy was in there after all.

I clock in and push through the double doors. Another day of the same old same old. Time slips by, one minute to the next to the next.

I think about the night Ron's calf exploded, after the ambulance came and went, after Larry left with the police. I was shaking so bad I couldn't drive for a while.

I half expected Larry to be stuck in jail after it all happened, but only a week later he was poking around the shop again, spitting at Dan and pointing at me.

Late morning, Dan walks over to check my progress, grabs a handrail, bangs it loudly against the work table, and it separates at the weld. I've been letting the flux get ahead of the metal, creating a bubbling, brittle mess out of everything, but I stopped caring about this hours ago.

He says, "Fix it, Jake. I don't want to fire you, but any more crap like this and I will." No scoff. No arms crossed tight around boob crack. No weight all resting in one hip. No Savannah here, just

Dan.

"Wasn't me," I say. I nod towards Carson, who's busy picking at his fingernails over by the milling machine. "Kid shouldn't even be working here. He can't weld for shit, and I thought nepotism was against company policy. You do know he's Savannah's nephew, right?"

"I also know you're in charge of training him," Dan says. "So I say again—fix it, Jake." He tosses the pieces clanging against the concrete floor.

After work, I send Savannah roses with no card.

Ben doesn't come home until after seven. I don't ask him how finals went, just leave him to pluck away on his laptop with shades on again. I shower, let the water come out hot as I can stand it and imagine what it feels like to get burned all over, to have my flesh seared and turned inside out on itself. Steam fills the room until it's difficult to see, and I sit down in the tub, let the scalding water flow over me, let it turn my skin a lobster red. The heat, the steam, the exhaustion, all of it has me lightheaded. I close my eyes in the hiss of the spraying water and fall asleep.

I wake a bit later, shut the water off, wrap a towel around my waist, stumble out and collapse face-down on the bed for the night. I fall asleep to the sound of Ben still clicking away on the laptop keys.

* * *

A week later Dan says, "Listen, Jake, here's the deal." We're in his office, sitting across from each other at his desk, having a special pow wow. "Larry Daly is breathing down my neck. Now, the guy's seriously got a bug up his ass, and he's clenched too tight for the thing to ever get loose, but our contracts with him make up a huge part of this business, so we really need to keep him happy. Do you think we can make Mr. Daly happy?"

"I don't think Larry is capable of happy."

Dan smiles a second before his mouth turns flat, and his brow drops, "He's about to take his business elsewhere. And if he does, we're going to tank. Jake—you've missed over two weeks of work in just the past couple of months, and your quality has taken a nosedive. And don't try to blame it on Carson. I haven't seen him touch a machine in days."

"Sorry."

"Savannah told me about your little meltdown-had-to-call-an-ambulance the other week. If you've got personal shit going on, it needs to stay at home."

"Sorry."

He props his elbows on the desktop, hides his head and runs his fingers though his black hair. "I honestly don't know how Savannah keeps this place together like she does."

I nod. "Do you know if she's coming back?"

His eyebrows lift before his eyes do, "She hasn't said either way."

"How bad was it?"

"Haven't seen her. Don't know."

That frying bacon smell of her burning skin and the billowing smoke filling the shop—in the month that's passed since, the scent still hasn't left me.

I remember the screaming, remember flipping up my lens and not being able to tell the difference between the flames and her hair. Couldn't tell either if I'd done it or not. Couldn't move at first. The smoke was so thick, everyone was choking. Rick attacked the flames with a fire extinguisher. When I got free of the shock and could move again, I ran into the bathroom and hid in a stall until the sirens came and went, until the screaming stopped, until everyone started going home early for the day. Because that's the sort of moron I am—an utterly gutless fuckwit.

* * *

When I get home, Ben is sitting on the floor, huddled in his hoodie, staring at his phone. He doesn't acknowledge my arrival. I check on Prometheus and go to feed him, but the cricket bin is empty.

"What happened to all the crickets?" I say. "There were still plenty in here last I checked."

"Last you checked," Ben says. "I've been feeding your stupid lizard for you."

"Overfeeding him," I say, staring at Prometheus, whose eyes are squinted, tongue flicking out.

"Not hardly," Ben says. "The cricket box has been empty for three days."

"Three days?" I say. "Why didn't you say anything?"

"Are you fucking kidding me? He's your damn lizard!"

# CHAPTER TWENTY-THREE

Lauren says, "You look very thin."

"Isn't that a good thing?" I say. "Aren't people supposed to be thin?"

"There's a point where it becomes unhealthy. You've been losing a lot of weight in the last few weeks. How has your appetite been?"

"Everything's shitty right now. Is that what you want to hear?"

"Perhaps we should consider the possibility of medication."

"Oh, come on now. Drugs are for losers."

"Certain drugs can be therapeutic."

"Did I ever tell you what my dad did for a living?"

"I don't believe so."

"He was a pharmacist. Heck, maybe you've even talked to him on the phone before. How about that?"

"Well, I suppose that's possible."

"He was always very good at keeping Mom drugged out of her gourd. No depression in our house. No, sir!"

She sighs. "You've been going through a very difficult time. Proper medication might provide you some relief."

"Drop it," I say. "I'm not taking a damn thing."

I shift around until I'm slouching the way Ben always does in his seat, sinking ever further into the chair. I am cocooned, in a womb here, and in some ways that's kind of nice.

Lauren says, "Perhaps you can tell me what's on your mind this week."

I blow out a breath and shrug. What's there to say, really? It's all the same. Can't sleep ever, can't eat, breathing's been getting a bit rough. "This chair," I say. "Can it swallow a person?"

She looks up from her notepad.

"If I slouch lower, do you think it will eat me? And if it does, where will I go?"

She goes back to scribbling. Her stringy blonde hair, only partially held back by a single clip on one side today, falls in her face as she writes.

"Have you been thinking about your father a lot lately?" she asks, recrossing her legs.

Only every time I look in a mirror. Only every time I look at Ben and wonder if I will become Dad. Any time I ever touch the kid, I think, well, this is how it starts, all innocent and then it morphs over time without you realizing it.

"You know, I've never fucked a girl? Made love, I mean. Never had sex with a woman, and I'm thirty. What do you think that says about me?"

"I think it says you're a thirty-year-old virgin. What do you think it says?"

I laugh. "A virgin. Right." I look right at her but can't stand it long, so I look out the window again.

I start thinking about that weird itch of a memory I had at Mom's house, standing in the doorway to her and Dad's room. Déjà vu maybe, but worse. Something happened there. Something bigger than everything else.

"Jake." Lauren sounds stern, and I look up at her anguished face. I get the sense she's been trying to get my attention for a while. "Where did you go? What were you thinking about just now?"

\* \* \*

At home in my apartment all I want to do is break a limb, but that would require a hospital visit so it isn't an option. Instead I frantically pace, almost hitting things, pulling back, all the while Prometheus watches with his lizard eyes, judging, wondering what the hell my problem is.

A pit grows in my core. I'm being hollowed. I finally pull a knife out of the kitchen drawer, march into the bathroom and stare at my pale, withering self in the mirror, trying to decide what needs to be stabbed. My heart, I think. I take off my shirt. Placing my hand over my chest, I try to feel it beating, try to find exactly where it is. I place the knife dead center of the suspected location and press the tip of the blade in. It takes a good deal of pressure before the skin gives. A razor would cut better, but there's something satisfying about gripping a knife handle. I let it sink in only a millimeter or two, but it's enough for the endorphins to kick in. I twist the handle, and in one quick, breath-holding motion, carve out a small chunk. Blood leaks down my emaciated ribcage. I get my breath back, my head feels like it's been rinsed, and fire bursts from the hole, runs up my neck, sideways into my armpit, and down to the bottom of my ribs.

I dip my fingers in the blood and use it to draw a happy face on my stomach. My belly button is the nose. I coat my hand with the rest of the red stuff leaking from the hole and smack a giant handprint on top of the smile. The blood doesn't even seem like mine.

The apartment door opens, shuts, and Ben appears in the bathroom doorway. No sunglasses. He looks me up and down and says, "That's fucking fantastic."

I consider rushing to clean up, to hide everything, to apologize and make excuses, but instead I salute him before washing the blood off my hands.

I point to my eyes, then to his. "Where are your shades?"

He crosses his arms and leans against the door frame, "I give up."

"Huh," I look him up and down as his brown eyes squint back. "Me, too. Good to know we're on the same page."

"Knife?" he asks and holds out his hand. The responsible part of me, however small it may be, seems to think it would be unwise to comply with his request. The responsible part of me should say something lame about how he shouldn't do it, even though I do, and how it is unhealthy and wrong. But so many other things are far more wrong.

I hand it to him and say, "Just don't go overboard."

He removes his jeans and sits in his underwear on the edge of the tub, leaning back against the wall, one foot on the edge with his knee up. He makes superficial stripes with the back edge of the blade down his thigh. I put the toilet lid down and sit, rest my feet on the edge of the tub. His eyes peer sideways at me, his lips part. He looks like a reverse raccoon now. The rest of his face more tan and freckled than the skin around his eyes.

Sighing, he chucks the knife clanging into the tub, leans back, and wraps his hands around his knee as if he decided to do the right thing even though his older brother was too much of a flake to.

Still under the spell of the brain rinse, I gain a smidgeon of perspective. I'm back to where I was months ago on my birthday, before Savannah's rejection, deciding *fuck it*—nothing will change unless I get my shit together and do something. Maybe it will turn out better this time. It couldn't possibly be worse.

* * *

Some days you have to let your curiosity win. You have to know what happened to her. You have to see if maybe, just maybe, she can stand to look at you. Some days you have to act because inaction is eating away at you, and you're losing flesh both inside and out. Some days you have to go for a walk instead of taking the car because you're so jittery that driving's not a good idea, while maybe walking will burn some of the shaking off. Today you walk the thirty blocks to Savannah's house all sweaty and sick.

You try to focus on the rhythm of your steps, because thinking about your destination sends your heart into your throat, and for a quick second the impulse to run the other way takes hold. It's a hot day, and even the small wind gust from each passing car is a relief, but the stench of your armpits seems to grow, and you wonder how noticeable it might be to others.

Lawnmowers run here and there. Fresh cut grass smell mixing

with exhaust fumes. Your fingers smooth back your sweaty hair, and you only now realize how long it's been since you had a haircut. Haven't shaved all week either. Why these things didn't occur to you before you left, you don't know. No turning back, though, because you know you'd never go through with it a second time.

Sometimes you just have to move forward.

Then you're there. You breathe in and knock on the door. The knob turns slowly. The door pulls back, and there she is, and you have no idea what to say.

# CHAPTER TWENTY-FOUR

When she smiles, her bottom lip pulls inside out on itself. The roped webbing of scar tissue across the side of her face draws tight and looks on the verge of tearing near her eye. She holds a wine glass to my lips and tips it up a bit fast, laughing as she drowns me. I grab the glass, pull it out of her hand, wipe the spilled purple off my chin, and smile back. I'm sure her drinking pace has been matching mine, but she's much more steady and sober.

"Why do you do that?" I say, "Laugh. Why do you laugh?"

"I've never seen a man get drunk so fast," she says. "Not surprising. I'll bet you don't weigh more than a buck twenty."

"Oh." I smack at my face to test the numb feeling in my skin. I turn toward her, rest my head on the back of the couch, rub my cheek into the coarse fabric.

She's only wearing mascara. The smooth side of her face looks like real skin for once. But the burns and scars are very wrong. There's pain behind the spider eyelashes, and I fear I put it there. I broke her. Yet she's still in there, somehow not broken, somehow more real than she's ever been. And sitting here—with me of all people. Does she know what she's doing?

"I like you like this," she says. "You're always so uptight and brooding at work."

The lights from the kitchen glow in a halo around her. Instead of hair now, she wears a scarf wrapped around the top of her head. A blue scarf with yellow flowers. Yellow like her hair used to be. My eyes wander past her shoulder to her dining room table, and there are the flowers I sent, unwatered and dying.

Reaching up, I touch her face, her scars, her skin all turned inside out on itself. Her crooked smile goes flat, and she grabs my hand.

I say, "Sorry—does it hurt?"

She shakes her head, throws back a swig of wine, and looks away.

"Nah." I reach my hand back up and let my fingers fall over her face. "Beautiful."

She pulls the wine glass out of my other hand and sets it on the coffee table. Leaning in, her half-scarred lips press against mine for a moment, soft on one side, stiff on the other. I feel like I'm being electrocuted.

Maybe this is relief that I'm here with her, and she looks right into my eyes when she smiles. But there's this pain sitting inside the fact that I've wanted her attention for so long. That this is the only time she's ever touched me, hurts somehow.

"Gotta pee," I say.

She sits back up, blinks her big spider eyelashes, cracks an awkward grin, "Your face red from the wine or the kiss?"

"Oh, wine's going right through." I stand, sway, look around. "Where's it?"

"Down the hall. First door."

I walk down the hallway, but I'm not lined up right. I seem to be heading for the corner, and the signals I'm sending my body to correct itself are delayed. I manage to steer clear of the corner but over-shoot the door and run into the doorframe. Savannah laughs.

I have to brace myself on the countertop as I lift up the toilet seat, and fumble a good minute with my zipper before I'm ready to take aim.

When I return to the hall, Savannah grabs my elbow. She leads me through another door. To a room with a bed made with red sheets.

We sit on the edge of the bed, and she takes off her shirt. Her bra is filled with her giant melons. Overflowing. I reach out and touch the top of one. Through the drunken numbness and calluses on my fingertips, her skin doesn't even feel like it's there. She reaches behind herself. A moment later the bra hangs loose, and the straps fall off her shoulders. Then the bra's on the floor and those massive domes are exposed, nipples pointed and hard. She reaches for the bottom of my shirt and starts to lift it.

"Arms up," she says and pulls my shirt off over my head and throws it to the floor.

I want her to touch me more. I want her to shock the life out of me. I want her to hurt me and never let up.

But her eyes go to my chest, and she says, "You've got some scars yourself." Her finger outlines the faded M, and I realize how bad I must look. Now I'm embarrassed. Little nicks and razor gashes all over, the scabbed hole I carved above my heart—her finger finds that next.

"You do these yourself?" she says.

"Mostly." My eyes close.

"Why am I not surprised?" she says.

I open my eyes, and she's staring me down.

She says, "You look terrified," and pushes me back until I'm lying on the bed.

I say, "I've never really done this before."

"Very funny." She laughs.

She places her hand on my neck, traces it down my chest, down my stomach. She gets to my belt, and I freeze. She says, "You weren't kidding, were you?"

I shake my head.

She sits up. "Jesus, Jake, are you serious? What are you, twelve? This should be interesting." She leans back over me and says, "First thing you need to learn is to relax."

Relax. I can relax. Her fingers trace the lowest part of my belly just below the waistline. My body shivers, and there's the pressure of the growing lump in my pants. She grabs my crotch and says, "Even with all that wine? Impressive."

I'm tensing back up again.

"Relax," she says again. "You're fine."

And like a Pavlovic response, my body goes dead, and my eyes close, and I'm not there anymore. My mind starts running the stupid Greek alphabet. But I force my eyes open, reach out and touch a breast, cup it in my hand, and she leans in for another kiss. Her hand undoes my belt, my button, my zipper.

She tugs at my jeans, pulls them all the way down along with my underwear, and throws them aside. Drunk as I am, I'm still nervous as fuck. I don't know why. I've wanted this for years, but I'm petrified. Savannah kisses me, and I kiss back. She bites my bottom lip.

She's on top of me, and those melons are in my face. She slides herself over my hard-on, warm and wet, and my hips can't help but push up into her. She says, "See? That doesn't feel bad, now, does it?"

I'm scared her voice will change, and I look around the room to make sure this isn't a dream. Her back arches, and she grinds into me. She bounces up and down, and her melons bounce all over. I reach out and grab one again.

She says, "How about we switch."

"Switch?"

"You be on top." She rolls off and lies on her back with her legs spread. I turn onto my side, and her arms are out, coaxing me.

My hands go by her shoulders, and my knees go between her legs, but I'm unsteady holding myself up like that.

Her hand reaches down, grabs my cock, guides it where it's supposed to go, and the warm wetness of her slides over me again. Her arms wrap around, and she pulls me in close. Her hips push up against mine. Instinct takes over. I rock back and forth, hypnotized by my own rhythm. But she starts making sounds, and I can't tell if they're good sounds or bad sounds, and I say, "Am I hurting you?"

"Don't stop." She grabs my ass with both her hands and pulls me into her. I don't like her hands there, but I do as instructed. I keep going, and then all of a sudden her back arches up, and she presses hard into me. Squeezes me like a python, then relaxes with a sigh.

I stop.

She says, "You didn't finish, too, did you? You can keep going, you know."

I try a few more thrusts, but I'm going limp.

She says, "What's wrong?"

"Maybe I had too much to drink." My voice catches on a lump in my throat that I didn't know was there, and worse than that, my eyes are burning.

"Jesus, Jake. It's nothing to cry about." She pulls me close. I lie on top of her with my dick sliding out and my head on her shoulder. She strokes my hair and rubs my back like she's my mother and I'm her upset child.

* * *

In the morning my mouth tastes bitter, and my teeth are coated from the sweetness of the wine. There's the smell of wine in the air, but also a perfume, a sweat other than my own, a woman's sweat— Savannah. My head lies between her breasts. My eyes blink open, everything blurry at first, clouded with sleep, and I breathe her in. I run my tongue over my teeth, work my mouth around to get rid of the staleness. Her skin is warm against mine, a smooth, gentle warm. My bare nuts and dick squished up against her leg.

This is not so bad.

She stirs, and her arm—the one resting against my back, comes up, and her fingers comb through my hair. I move to prop myself up over her, lean down and kiss her broken lips.

She whispers, "What were you dreaming about last night?"

I shake my head. "Nothing."

"You talk in your sleep, did you know that?"

I roll onto my back. "I'm sorry."

"For what?"

"If I woke you up."

"Oh, seriously, Jake. Lots of people talk in their sleep."

I'm afraid to ask her what I said.

Her hand reaches down and grabs my dick. My eyes close, and I shiver. She strokes me up and down. My fingers wrap around the bed sheets to my side, gripping a wad of blanket in my fist. Her other hand reaches over and pulls the blanket out of my grasp. "Relax, already."

"Sorry."

"Hush." She starts kissing my stomach.

"Oh fuck," I say and sit up.

"What?"

"Can I use your phone?"

"My phone?"

"I need to call my brother."

"Your brother? You need to call your brother all of a sudden right now?"

"I didn't tell him I wouldn't be back last night, and I don't want him to be worried."

"Does he live with you or something?"

"Yeah."

"Is this the same brother whose school you had to go to in the middle of the day a while back?"

"Only got the one. I really should give him a call."

She sighs. "Phone's in the kitchen." She throws on a robe, and I put on my jeans and follow her out. She points a finger toward the phone on the counter, and I grab it and dial.

She peers at me out of the corner of her eye as she fills a coffee pot.

Ben answers, "Hello?"

"Hey, Benny, uh, look, I'll be home in a just a little bit—you okay? Everything okay?"

"What, did you get lost or something?"

"I'll explain later. I just didn't want you to worry."

"Yeah, whatever," he says.

"Okay, so see you after a bit then," and I hang up.

Savannah's got her hip cocked, arms crossed. "I'm sure that's a lot—taking on a teenager."

"He's a good kid."

"So why is he staying with you?"

"Kind of a long story."

"You're just full of mysteries aren't you?"

"Mysteries?"

"Mysterious family situation, unusually low sobriety threshold, extreme awkwardness around others." She steps toward me, puts her hand on my chest. "And then there's all of these." Her fingers trace all the little scars. "And I still don't understand why you came over last night." She pats me on the chest. "Go get dressed. I'll make you some breakfast before you leave."

* * *

Daylight leaks through the blinds in my darkened apartment when I come home. Ben's sitting cross-legged on my bed in just a pair of shorts, face bathed in yellow light from his laptop computer screen. He hunches himself around the screen as though protecting his nest of eggs, but his eyes are trained on me.

"So where were you this time?" he says. "Or is it complicated?"

"You really want to know?" I pour myself some water.

He scoffs and looks sideways. "Uh, yeah?"

My head and mouth still feel stuffed with cotton from so much wine. I swish cold water around and swallow. "A girl," I say.

"A girl what? Is that where you always are?"

"No, just last night."

"Did you fuck her?"

I pour the rest of my water in the sink and set the glass down hard on the counter.

"You did, didn't you?" he says.

He stares at me like I hurt him. "I'm sorry I didn't at least call you or something. Everything kind of happened fast. I wasn't expecting to get back so late."

Ben is a knot in my chest behind my sternum. That look in his eyes makes me want to get him a new pair of shades.

"So, what've you been up to?" I ask.

He blinks and looks down at his computer screen. "I don't know."

I check the clock on the stove. It's a quarter to twelve, and I promised Mom a weekend visit. "You coming with me to Mom's?"

"Are you asking me or telling me?" He leans forward, elbow on knee, head in hand, "Because I don't want to go."

"We're helping her with her garden thing."

He taps a few keys on the keyboard. When I walk over and sit on the edge of the bed, he casually turns the screen away from me. I grab it and turn it so I can read it, and he glows nervous-red beneath his freckles.

This seems to be his attempt at retaliation for the Ben-Gay tumblr. He's titled it "Dylan Likes Cock But He Doesn't Want Anyone To Know," and it details all the ways Dylan engages in cock-related activities.

"This might not be the best idea," I say.

He pulls the computer back and hits "post". "Doesn't matter anyway," he says. "You have to have friends first before anyone will read your blog."

His legs uncross, and one foot drops to the floor.

I stand and start toward the bathroom. "Get dressed. We're leaving when I finish my shower."

* * *

Mom comes out of the house, seed packets rattling in her hands. "I know it's a bit late in the season," she says. "But I think we can still get some things to grow."

She hands a packet to Ben. Ben's eyes are all squinty—still not used to the light. She smiles at him. "It's so nice to see your face."

I hoe the rows.

Ben plants the seeds.

Mom directs.

Ben blurts out, "Jake's got a girlfriend." His eyes dart back and forth to gauge our responses.

Mom's piqued curiosity.

My disdain at his reveal.

"Oh?" Mom's eyes widen as she looks at me.

I stand upright, hoe dangling from my grasp, and stare him down. "Ben doesn't know what he's talking about."

Ben squats, and carefully places seeds in the dirt. "Well, Jake has a fuck buddy, then."

I throw down the hoe and start marching toward him.

Testing—he's testing me.

Lauren said something about testing once, but I wasn't listening.

As much as I want to scream some sense into him, engaging him is only going to reinforce the behavior, make me look like a dumbass, and give him yet another reason to hate me. It takes every ounce of willpower to walk past him and instead head to the tool shed, shutting the door behind myself to pace in a circle under a dangling 60-watt bulb.

# CHAPTER TWENTY-FIVE

Dan sent everyone home early because he fucked up ordering parts, so no one has anything to do until tomorrow. Savannah never once made a mistake like that.

As I enter the apartment building, I hear a *click-fwump* sound coming down the stairs. It's Ron on his crutches. It was nearly a month ago that he was shot, and this is the first time I've seen him since. He looks more put together than usual—dress slacks rolled up on one side over his bandaged, reassembled leg. A button-down shirt. His hair gelled up in its Corinthian crest.

The stairway is narrow, and with the broad stance of his crutches, there isn't room for me to get by, so I wait at the bottom for him to descend.

He sees me. He says, "Dude."

He stops, pats his pants pockets, says, "Ah, shit—forgot my wallet," turns around, and starts back up the stairs. I follow.

I say, "What happened to your leg?" because of course I shouldn't know the answer.

"Dude shot me," he says.

"Oh."

He fumbles his cell phone out of his pocket and checks the time. "Damn. I'm so not making my bus." As I round the top of the stairs, ready to head down my hall, he says, "Could you give me a ride? You so owe me—not saying anything about your brother and all."

"Uh...sure."

He gets his wallet and follows me out to my car. "Where to?"

I ask as I start the engine.

And he says, of all places, "The courthouse. Got a court date with the dude that shot me."

Perfect. That throbbing at the base of my skull is back. That whole scene with Dad and the fucking trial. Prostate specific hormones and Ben's black eyes, vomiting in the restroom, and *Do you love your brother?* I don't need this today.

As we drive, Ron says, "Stopped taking the pills."

"Oh?"

"Yeah, got Vicodin now anyway—for my leg, you know?"

"Oh."

I pull over right in front of the building and stop. Ron undoes his buckle and points his finger down the sidewalk. "Hey, that's the dude."

Sure enough, Larry is walking toward the building as well.

I nod and flip the sun visor down in hopes of blocking my face from view. But Ron is so slow and disorganized getting out of the car with his crutches that he makes a scene, which causes Larry to look. And while one would think Ron is distracting enough that no one would look further, Larry's eyes go my way, and he bends down as if trying to peek under the visor. But then he checks his watch, and goes up the steps to the building. Ron finally departs the car, says "Thanks, dude," and follows behind Larry.

* * *

Midday on a Friday I'm reading about cognitive dissonance in a social psychology textbook while trying to reconnect with Prometheus, who's resting happily on my shoulder. Ben comes home from who-knows-where, slamming the apartment door. His face is all red like he's pissed again. He gets a cup out of the cupboard, pours some water, swallows it all in one go, and tosses the cup into the sink.

His cell phone chimes, he checks it, lets out a frustrated grunt, then walks back out the door.

I set my book down, put Prometheus back in his tank as he bites at my finger in disapproval, and follow Ben—far enough behind that he doesn't notice. I sit at the top of the steps, where I can just see his right arm as he opens the door.

Some other kid is there just out of my sight. He says to Ben, "They saw you, you know."

Ben says, "What's your point?"

"Why were you following us again?"

"I wasn't."

"So you just happened to be all the way over by the dump near Tim's house for no reason?"

"It's a free country. I can be wherever I want."

I hear the *click-fwump* of Ron's crutches coming down the stairs and turn around just before he says, "Dude." I pat my hands palm down at the air to tell him to keep it quiet.

The kid talking to Ben says, "They hate your guts. Don't you get that?"

Ben says, "Why do you even hang out with them?"

The other kid scoffs. "They're my friends."

"And what am I?"

Ron whispers, "What's going on?"

I say, "Shhh."

The kid talking to Ben says, "Look, they said they're going to kick the shit out of you next time they see you. They sent me here to warn you."

Ben says, "You're lying."

"It's what they said. You should know, they'd do it, too."

"No—they didn't send you here to warn me. You came on your own. Why?"

Ron sits next to me with a thud, lays his crutches down hard, peeks his head down the stairwell, and whispers, "That your brother?"

Ben takes a couple steps back and looks up at us. He turns to the other kid and says, "My dumbass brother is spying on us. Let's talk outside."

The other kid says, "No, I'm done. Just, no more stalking, all right? And they won't punch your face in. I'm not going to warn you again."

The kid leaves, and Ben screams, "Yeah, fuck you, Dylan!"

Ben stomps up the stairs, forcing his feet down harder than gravity alone would with each step, but we've got him blocked. He crosses his arms and stares right at me, deliberately ignoring Ron's presence, and I get up and step aside. He blows past, hooking me in the gut with his elbow. I let out a grunt but he doesn't look back as he marches down the hallway, goes back into the apartment, and slams the door.

Ron says, "What's with him?"

"Many things." I lean back against the wall. "You have a brother, Ron?"

"No. I'm an only child. Had a dog once, though. People aren't much different than animals. You know your brother? He's all battling with his id. That's, like, the animal part of him."

Thank you, Freud. "I should have gone down there and told off the little shit that came to the door."

"Don't know about that," Ron says. "Sometimes sticking your nose in makes it worse. Kids like that, they'll use it as more of a reason to keep picking on him."

"I should talk to him." I start back down the hall.

"You can't talk to the id," Ron says. "Got to talk to the super-ego."

"Thanks."

In the apartment, Ben's standing by the sink, arms still crossed. He says, "I told you not to follow me."

"The kid Tim you talked about. That was one of the dickheads who gave you the black eyes, right?"

"Why do you care?"

"What were you doing following them anyway?"

"I don't know, Jake. It's complicated."

He pushes past me elbowing me in the ribs again, and then he walks over by my bookcase and starts pulling books out and pushing them back in.

"Look—if you want to talk about it, I'll listen, right?"

"Sure thing, Dad. I'll tell you everything, Dad. You going to help me with my problems, Dad? You want to share secrets, Dad? You want to get all close and personal with me, Dad?"

"Yeah, that's enough."

Ben grabs a book off the shelf and holds out in front of him. "Sorry, Dad. I won't do it again, Dad." He drops the book and lets it splay open on the floor.

"Pick it back up."

"No."

"I could kick you out, you know. You don't have to stay here. You could go live with Mom."

"You want me to go?"

"I want you to stop being a little shit."

"Whatever. You don't want me here. You never did. Nobody fucking wants me around. You can have your place back—just you and your stupid lizard. You know, he's the perfect pet for you. He's all pasty and likes to hide in the dark, too."

Ben beelines for the door, but I block him. He says, "Move, Dad."

"I'm not moving."

He steps to my right and tries to reach around, but I grab his arms.

"Let me go!" He windmills his arms free and steps back.

"I'm not letting you run off all stupid."

I lean back on the doorknob, and he returns to the bookcase, pulling every single damn one of my books out and dropping them on the floor.

\* \* \*

Lauren asks if there's anything new this week.

"I-uh...sort of had an encounter with a female," I say.

"What sort of encounter?"

"One I hadn't had before."

"Oh?" she says. "How did that go?"

I roll my eyes and look sideways. "Awkward would be a good word for it."

Lauren blushes a little but smiles like she's happy for me. "So who was this woman? How did you meet?"

"Someone from work. Savannah—she was my supervisor."

"Was?"

"She's been...taking a break."

"Will you be seeing her again?"

"I think so," I say. "I want to."

"Well, good for you. That's great that you're coming out of your shell a little."

"My shell? I'm not a turtle."

"No," she says. "I've always thought more of an oyster."

"An oyster?"

"Pearl inside." She smiles.

I laugh. "Right." I look around the room trying to think of a new topic. "You said something before," I say. "About testing?"

She narrows her face in a squint for a moment, then all the wrinkles smooth back out. "About your brother?"

I nod.

"You said that he's been talking back, acting out?"

I nod.

She folds her hands on top of her notepad, leans back in her chair, "Your brother relies on you right now as a primary source of guidance."

I laugh. "Of misguidance."

"Misguidance is still a form of guidance."

I sit up, "I mean, I try. I just don't seem to know what to do, ever."

"And your brother is seeing how far he can push before you push back." Her pen comes to the corner of her mouth.

"Yeah, why?"

"Because he's insecure. He feels out of control."

"And what do I do about that?"

"You set reasonable and consistent boundaries."

"Isn't that the textbook answer."

She leans forward and folds her hands on top of her knee. "You know he'll always pay more attention to what you do than what you tell him to do."

"How do you mean?"

"It's what children do. It's how they learn—by modeling the behavior of others. That's why role models are important."

"You don't think Ben's a little screwed in that department?"

"That's a choice you make."

"What choice? I don't fucking know what to do, ever—how's that a choice?"

# CHAPTER TWENTY-SIX

I knock on Savannah's door again. A minute goes by before she opens it, slowly. About the time it would take to register who I am, her face falls into a frown. "What are you doing here?"

I've miscalculated somehow. I mutter, "Sorry," and turn to leave.

But she grabs my shoulder. "Wait," she sighs. "Come in a minute."

I go in, and she closes the door. She points to the couch. "Have a seat." She walks to the kitchen. "Can I get you something to drink?"

My mouth is dry, but I say no.

She pours two glasses of water anyway, comes back, and sets one in front of me.

She sits beside me. Her arms cross, her legs cross. What remains of her hair is wrapped up in a scarf on top of her head just like last time. "Look—I don't want you to have the wrong impression," she says.

"Wrong impression?" I try to glean some understanding from her half-scarred face.

"Yeah. About last week."

"What impression do you think I have?"

Her blues eyes rimmed with their spider eyelashes look me over from one end to the other. "Don't know. Hard to tell with you. Could be anything." She takes a sip of her water. "I'm not in the habit of shagging any guy that comes to my door. That's not what you're looking for today, is it?"

"No." All the blood in my body rises to the surface, and I can feel my face burning red. "Just wanted to see you again."

She runs her tongue over her broken lips. I bite my bottom lip, remembering her electric kiss. She shakes her head, "Because last week wasn't anything."

"It wasn't anything?"

"Wow, are you for real?"

"I should go." I start to stand.

"Sit," she says, and I do. "Look, I'm sorry I ended up being your first, kid, but those feelings you have, they're not what you think they are."

This couch, I wonder, can it swallow a person? It would be nice to disappear about now.

"Don't feel bad. It's normal. If anything, I'm flattered given my current state."

My face stings like I've been slapped. My head is hollow. I can't even speak.

She puts her hand to her face, squinting so it's all tight on the damaged side. "Look at me, Jake, I'm a freak. Is that what you want? A freak? You don't even know me."

"But I'd like to," falls out of my mouth.

"You're nothing if not persistent." She swishes the remaining water in the bottom of her glass around. "Can I get you a beer?"

"No, I'm good."

She goes to the fridge, brings back two beers, sets one in front of me, and pops it open. She opens her beer, takes a sip. "You want to know me? I want to know you. Tell me something. You're not allergic to Vaseline—no?"

I shake my head.

"Then what was that about?"

My head tics to the side. "What are you doing?" I say.

"Am I being too direct? If you can't handle that, then why are you here?" She takes another sip of her beer. She blinks.

So I tell her, "It was like a stress reaction, like a flashback kind of. I don't know."

"Flashback of what?"

My head tics, and I close my eyes. I grab my beer, swallow half of it in one go, and set it back down. My eyes won't open back up. I'm frozen.

"Well, family then. Tell me about your family. How's your kid brother—what's his name?"

"Ben."

"How's Ben?"

"You know," I open my eyes. "He's a teenager. He's kind of screwed up."

"And what's the deal with your parents?"

I stare at my beer. "Mom's kind of confused, and Dad's kind of in jail."

"What'd he do?"

"He, um," my head tics hard to the side again. "He hurt Ben."

"Why do you keep doing that?"

"What?"

"Shaking your head like that."

"Can't help it." My face feels hot.

She picks up my beer and hands it to me, but I fumble, and it spills all over the carpet. "Shit—sorry," I say, and she's off to get a towel. I hold my hands out in front of me, and they're shaking. I don't feel so good.

She comes back, and I help her mop it up. The both of us on the floor, kneeling, she says, "I don't mean to be such a bitch all the time."

"You're not."

"Seriously, Jake? You're so, just, raw, aren't you?"

"Can I ask you something?" I say.

"Fire away."

"How come you always wore so much makeup?"

"What the fuck kind of question is that? You're not drunk off half a can of beer, are you?"

I reach out and touch the unmarred side of her face, let my fingers fall down to her lips. Her lips part, and I feel her breath on my fingers as she stares at me. She doesn't back away, so I lean in and kiss her. Her hand grabs my jaw, and she kisses back.

# CHAPTER TWENTY-SEVEN

Yesterday was the beginning of a late June heat wave—a weekend's worth of three digit temperatures. Ben and I lie sprawled on our backs in our underwear, sweating like we've been all night. It never really cooled off even with the window open and a fan going. But it's a Saturday, so at least there's no work.

"I'm not about to stay in this apartment all day," I tell Ben. "What do you want to do?"

He doesn't move.

"I know you're not sleeping."

"I was trying to."

"Get up. Get dressed."

I leave Prometheus with a couple of ice cubes on one side of his tank and cover his tank with a towel.

We stop by Mom's first and find her out back on her knees weeding the garden. She sits up, her hair stuck to her face with sweat, her mouth hanging open. "Can you believe this weather?" she says, wiping her brow with her forearm. Then she stands and dusts her hands off. "You boys had breakfast?"

"We're good, Mom," I say. "Just stopping by to say hi before we head to the river for the day."

We follow Mom inside. "We're going to the river?" Ben says.

"It's hot," I say. "We're going to the river."

Inside Mom's house is nice and cool thanks to an overworked air conditioner in the living room window.

"Those weeds out there," Mom says, "growing like crazy and

barely a sprout coming up from anything we planted."

"Have you tried weed killer?" I ask.

"I think we've got some in the shed. I just haven't gotten around to digging it out yet."

"I'll look," I say, edge out the door, and cross the yard.

The shed has a musty chemical smell. It's a mess, everything in piles around the edges or on the few shelves. Fragments of destroyed furniture, lawn tools, an old wadded up tent and stakes, tin pots and plates. I start shifting piles around from one location to another. Under the tent I find a pair of machetes in their sheaths. I sit on a five gallon paint bucket and pull one out of its cover. A big, curved, black blade. The Spartans had a short sword of about the same length they would use in close combat after discarding their spears. It was double-edged, though, and leaf shaped with a diamond cross section. But sometimes the cavalry would use a short sword called a makhaira, almost exactly like a machete with its curved blade on one side.

I put the blade back in its cover and set the machetes on a clear spot on one of the shelves. Down on a bottom shelf in the back I come upon a bottle of Weed-B-Gon. Grabbing it and the machetes, I head back to the house.

The house is filled with the warm, sweet smell of pancakes and syrup. Ben's at the table eating his way through a small stack, and Mom's at the stove, flipping a pancake onto a plate.

Mom turns around, grabs the weed killer, says, "Oh, thank you," and sets it down right next to the pancake batter. I grab it and set it on the floor. She sets a plate in front of the seat next to Ben. "Come eat."

I sit, smear on butter, pour on syrup, and fork a bite into my mouth. My mouth is so not used to food that salivation is initially painful.

After shoveling in his last bite, Ben goes straight for the machetes, pulls one out of its cover, and says, "What are these for?"

"Cutting brush. The river, remember? I don't want to go where there'll be people."

* * *

Out a ways is an old logging road, dusty with the gravel all worn into the ground. We pull off to the side where a painted yellow steel gate blocks the way. There's a "No Trespassing" sign all warped and shot up. I hand Ben a machete, grab the other for myself, and we duck under the gate and start walking further up toward a bridge that crosses the river.

Ben squints. The reverse raccoon mask around his eyes from overuse of sunglasses is nearly gone now, and a constellation of freckles grows darker in big clumps across his nose and his cheeks. Little speckly brown patches. His narrowed eyes keep looking out sideways into the trees as we walk. He fiddles with the handle of his machete, trying to hook it into a belt loop, but it keeps slipping out.

We're soaked with sweat when we get to the bridge, so we take our shoes and socks off and wade across instead.

The ice-cold mountain runoff comes as a refreshing sting. Each step takes us deeper into the river. Out in the middle with it up to his knees, Ben leans forward and dips his head in the water. His hair has grown shaggy, just long enough to get into his eyes, and when he flings his head back up, he sends an arc of water through the air.

On the opposite shore I dig my hands in the dirt to climb up, and I'm muddy. Ben follows, and we put our shoes back on minus the socks stuffed in our pockets.

A leafy patch of wood sorrel covers the ground beneath the shade of the trees. I pick a handful, shove the leaves in my mouth and chew on the sour-sweetness.

Ben makes a face. "You know some animal's probably pissed on that."

I tuck the chewed wad of leaves between my cheek and gums.

I pull out my machete and start hacking through the brush overgrowing an old path that runs along the bank of the river. Ben pulls his machete out, too, tucks the cover in the waist of his shorts, and starts swinging all crazy and uncoordinated at the tangle of spindly branches and weeds. I let him ahead of me for fear of being hit.

"So what's the deal with this girl?" he says. "Why is this all top secret? Why won't you tell me anything? Is she a dog or something?"

"I don't even know what the deal is with her."

"But she's your girlfriend, right?"

"I'm not exactly sure."

"Liar. You never want to tell me anything."

He stops his uncoordinated brush hacking and glares at me. I pretend not to notice. He lifts the blade back over his shoulder and starts waving it around into the brush again as if trying to ward off a swarm of bees.

We come to a fallen limb maybe six inches in diameter lying diagonally in our way, the upper end of it resting against a tree. Ben widens his stance and brings his machete straight down on it. The blade gets stuck, and he seesaws it out.

"Don't bother with it," I say. "Just go around." I duck under the branch and work my way forward. There's another loud crack, and Ben's blade is stuck in the limb again. I blow out a long breath. "You're doing it wrong."

"Shut up." He yanks the blade out and stumbles backward. I step forward lifting my blade over my shoulder. I make sure he's out of the way and come down on the limb a bit from the side. My blade pulls out easy, and I lift it back over my other shoulder and come down at it from the other direction. A few more times and there's a sizeable dent.

"You've got to come at it at an angle," I say. "Works better that way." Sweat drips down into my eyes, and I wipe my forehead with the back of my hand. "Seriously, though, it's not worth it." I cut a path through to the river, figuring we're far enough upstream anyway.

Ben keeps hacking away at the limb, not giving up. I take seat on a large boulder near the shore, pull the blade cover out of the waist of my shorts, slide the machete back in, and toss it aside. My shoes off, I step ankle deep into the cold stream. I rub water on my arms, face, and behind my neck.

A dozen feet behind me, the struggling hacking of Ben's blade against the tree limb goes on and on, echoing off the water's surface. I imagine that might be Dad there that he's hacking at, over and over, with everything he's got. Or maybe it's me. Then it stops with a crack as the limb breaks and falls. I look back, and he's picking the limb up in a bear hug and hauling it off to one side. I turn again to the river, dip my hands in, and rub the water on my arms and neck once more.

Ben kicks his shoes off and drops the machete on the ground beside me. His shirt comes off next, tossed on top of his shoes, and he walks into the slow-moving deep portion of the river halfway to the opposite shore. He inhales and ducks under the water. A minute later he pops back up to the surface and rolls over to float on his back. He's out where the shade of the trees doesn't reach. The water carries him like driftwood downstream, turning him around.

The sun bright, almost blinding, reflects off the water on his skin. A shimmering Ben comes to a stop as the river pushes him near the bank on the opposite side. He crawls to shore, on a patch of rock and sand with no shade. He picks up a rock with his right hand, puts his left hand up to his brow as a visor, then chucks the rock across the stream, sending it smacking into a tree a couple feet to my right as I duck.

"Watch it," I say.

"Shut up," he says, "I know what I'm doing. I've got better aim than that."

He picks up another rock, and sends it flying to my left.

"Damn it, Ben." I stand up, ready to cross the river to where he is, and look up just in time to see a third rock coming right at my head. It cracks into my jaw, sharp, and with it a flood of anger.

Ben says, "It wouldn't have hit you if you wouldn't have stood up."

His visor hand and his throwing hand down at his sides, his eyes narrow from the sun burning on his face. His reddening skin heaves up and down with each deep breath.

A blood-metal taste fills my mouth, and I spit what's left of the wood sorrel leaves into the stream—red mixed with the dark green. My jaw stings with an ache that spreads across the entire side of my face and down my neck. My eyes burn, and I don't know if it's from the sun, the anger, or the hurt. I start wading across the river toward him. Everything I've been suppressing for months bubbles right up to the surface, and I'm transforming into The Hulk.

He just stands there, clenching and unclenching his fists at his sides. If he wants a battle, I'm so ready for one.

When I reach the halfway point, he comes at me. We meet in waist-deep water, Ben's hands lifting up like he's ready to shove me in. But I grab him by the shoulders and pitch him sideways into the stream. Water bubbles up like it's boiling, and Ben gets his feet under him and breaks back through the surface, his mouth open for a big inhale.

I grab him again, this time closer to his neck, and force his head back under the water. His hands pull at my hands, trying to bend my thumbs back, but my muscles are tensed solid. I am stronger than him. Bubbles keep rising to the surface—tiny bubbles from his thrashing, big bubbles from his mouth, all sparkling in the sunlight, obscuring his face under the water. He finally hooks me behind my knee with his foot sending me crashing into the water, and I lose my grip. I go under, and when I come back up, Ben's doubled over, crawling to the shore, coughing and choking.

I damn near drowned him.

My anger drains into the river, leaving an all-consuming knot of guilt and regret in my chest.

When he pulls up on land, he turns to look at me. I don't know which he is more, scared or angry, his jaw clenched tight. He sits in the dirt and slips his shoes back on. I wade through the water towards him, and his eyes go to the side, searching. He finds his machete, white-knuckles the handle, and holds it out at me.

"Don't fucking come near me!" he screams, his mouth in a

sneer, his breath heavy.

I put my hands palm out in front of me. Moving my tongue around the aching side of my mouth, I swallow my bloody spit. "Ben—"

"Shut up!" he screams, still holding the machete out in front of him. He crouches down, grabs his shirt, and throws it over his shoulder. He backs up a few steps, then turns around and starts speed walking back down the trail.

On shore, I put my shoes on and follow, matching his pace but letting him keep several yards in front of me. He looks back every so often, but never slows. His hand holding the machete lashes out periodically at stray branches on the side of the path.

Across the bridge, and down the road, he reaches the old gate. He doesn't stop. He ducks under and keeps walking past the car.

I move faster to catch up. Almost at his heels I say, "Ben, I'm sorry."

He doesn't slow.

"Turn around and get in the car," I say.

"I'm not going home with you."

"Then where're you going?"

"Why do you care?"

"We're fucking miles from anywhere, Ben. Just get in the car."

I grab his shoulder, and he pushes my hand away. He turns around and walks past me, keeping his same pace, but toward the car. I follow, and we both get in.

The drive home is painful silence. As we get near town, he finally speaks. "Drop me off at Mom's."

"Ben, I'm sorry."

"I'm not going home with you."

I sigh. "Fine."

We pull up to the pale green house, he gets out, slams the car door, and walks away without looking back.

Driving to my apartment alone, my heartbeat throbs up in my ears, my eyes burn, and my nose is running. It gets so bad that I have to keep blinking to see the road clearly. I shove my knuckles in my mouth and bite down hard, letting the ache in my jaw spread out along the side of my face and down my neck.

Lauren said to set reasonable and consistent boundaries.

Lauren said to set a good example.

It's all a joke.

# CHAPTER TWENTY-EIGHT

Shimmering mirage pools vaporize in front of me in the parking lot on the way to my car after another hot-as-fuck workday. My jeans stick to my legs, rubbing them raw from the sweat. My shirt clings like plastic wrap. The smoke coating all over my body, greasy and thick, burns my eyes. I shove a sweaty hand in my pocket and dig out keys.

I get to my car, about to push the unlock button, and a shadow materializes behind me. A vice-grip hand clamps my wrist, twists my arm at my back, and I'm body slammed into the car. My keys hit the ground.

My heart bangs around in my chest like it's trying to get out. All the air leaves my lungs, leaves me gasping like a shored fish. Someone's massive body leans on mine, his other arm horizontal across my shoulder blades—right at my neck. He's got my wrist bent past ninety degrees and the second knuckle of my thumb pinched between my hand and a bony knob of my spine.

I try to fight back with my free arm, swinging it behind me as best I can, but I've got no leverage. He yanks my arm up tighter.

I use my free hand to push off the car just enough that my lungs can still inflate. I try to twist my head around and see who it is, but he's pinned my arm so tight that any little movement sends a sharp pain all the way through to my neck.

"I knew that car looked familiar," he breathes in my ear, and I recognize his voice.

It's Larry Daly.

Shit.

"I could have swore I saw you in this very car in front of the courthouse last week. You want to tell me how you know Ronald Duncan? Because it's an awful coincidence that I know you, and I know him, and you know each other."

His sweat and my sweat mix between the skin of his hand and mine, the skin of his arm and my neck.

"I asked you a question, asshole!" Larry slams me hard into the car again and knocks any breath I did have right back out.

I try to say, "He lives in my building," but it comes out something like, "Huh lih mbih."

"Speak up!" He gives me another hard shove.

My eyes close. I try to swallow, but there's nothing in my mouth to swallow except my own tongue. "He lives in my building."

Larry tightens his grip and pushes my twisted arm higher. I'm on my tiptoes trying to keep from breaking. I can't tell if the fuzziness of everything I see is from heat mirage or if I'm about to black out.

"Now, you know and I know that Ronald is too dumb to do shit. So I want to know how your neighbor ended up at my house." His hot breath fills my ear, goes all the way up the canal to my brain. "Better yet, I want to know what you know about these letters I've been getting, because you know what? I don't believe in coincidence."

"I-ah n-no."

"What?"

"I-I don't know anything about it."

"You're lying, you little shit, and you can bet I'll fucking find a way to prove it." He leaves me with one last shove and a grunt, and walks away.

My feet go back to flat on the pavement. Blood flows again into my arm and my chest. I double forward, grab my knees, lungs on fire, and pick the keys up off the ground.

Once in the car, I start the engine and run the AC a minute before closing the door and locking it. I rest my palms on the steering wheel, fingers spread out. My hands shake like I've got some sort of neurological disorder. Sudden onset Parkinson's.

I turn the vents at my face and pull out of the parking lot.

Larry's only seen me at the courthouse. Ron doesn't know shit, right? No fingerprints on the letters. No one's seen me in the tree. But what did Ron tell them about why he was at Larry's that day?

When I get home I head straight for the shower.

Grease and grime and black crap from work all melt off in the spray, run in streaks down my body, circle black around the drain.

My sweat. Larry's sweat. Larry's breath in my ear like a buzzing mosquito. Water gets stuck in my ear canal as I try to wash it out, and I go a bit deaf with it. I like it that way. The whole outside world is gone, and I don't need to think about all the stupid crap.

That salty metal taste at the back of my tongue, I wash it out with a mouthful of gargled shower water. Water goes up my nose, and I let it drown me, let it burn up my sinuses, and I cough and snort out more black.

A palmful of liquid soap on my head, lather. I close my eyes, and the soap falls down my face, down my body.

I scrub everything, and rinse, and rinse, and rinse.

The whole bathroom is a cloud of steam when I shut the water off and step out. I wipe the mirror, and there I am. Naked. Still looking like I walked out of a prison camp. Loose skin that holds only skinny bones inside it and a torso that resembles a horror movie prop. I'm tired of it all. All the stupid crap. All the scars, the knots, the scabs.

I want to be happy. Normal. Human, like the other humans—the ones that can take their shirts off in front of a girl and not feel like they have to explain themselves.

My fingers move across the rough bits of scarred skin. The remains of MORON, faded to MO O . The label that says I didn't know what to do. Ben and the family secret. I couldn't handle it. Any of it. And now it's stuck there forever.

There's the dime-sized gouge above my heart from the day I wanted to carve the beating fucker out. A little dashed line at my waist from pinching bits off with nail clippers after that last camping trip with Dad. And too many others to even list.

I close my eyes and suck in a lungful of humid shower air, hold it there. Rub my fingers down my chest across the bumps and ridges. Try to stretch the skin flat with one hand and test if that makes it smooth with the other. It doesn't.

Eyes open, looking in the mirror again, I'm different now. I'm red, and that throbbing at the base of my skull is back.

I go to the kitchen area, get a bowl from the cupboard, and fill it with ice. Prometheus can't tell me this is stupid because he's hidden under a towel. I take the bowl back into the bathroom and get a new razor blade out of the cabinet. I lay out gauze pads and tape.

I pinch a slippery ice cube tight in my fingers and press it hard against the M on my chest. Drips of water tickle down my skin, and the place where I hold the cube feels like a bruise burrowing itself into my flesh. My fingers get numb, and I switch hands.

Maybe this is fucked, but I'm thinking I can slice the scars off. Smooth everything over and leave it new again.

I drop the melted cube back in the bowl. A red halo surrounds a white circle of numbed skin centered on the M. It won't stay numb for long so I move fast, pressing the blade flat against my chest above the two top humps of the letter. The blade, cold on cold, smooth metal on the numbed skin. I slowly slide it down.

A flat noodle of scar tissue separates and sticks to the outer side of the blade, wrinkling and bunching as the razor moves down further. This skin is alien to me. I can't feel it.

But halfway through the M, sensation starts to return as a sting. Blood bubbles up around my fingers holding the razor, but I can't stop now. Pins and needles on top of a fire. I move fast, hold my breath, and saw through the rest of it, but on the way, the razor changes angle and goes even deeper before I get to the end. I fling the chunk of flesh into the toilet, toss the razor into the sink, grab the countertop tight with my hands. My eyes close. My mouth hangs open, sucking quick, shallow breaths as all the feeling comes back, ripping through me like an explosion before I'm used to it.

Opening my eyes, I look at what used to be the M in the mirror. Makes it easier to see it like that—in the mirror. Like looking at a picture.

A big red bleeding patch.

"You little fucker." My voice is a whisper, all the air in my lungs gone. "What did you just do there?" I grab another ice cube and press it on the wound. It stings, then feels like a punch, and I'm dizzy.

Blood mixes with the water melting off, runs down my chest and down my arm. I toss the ice in the sink. There's blood all over the place, dripping down my stomach, onto the counter, and onto the floor. Things start looking patchy, and I can hear my heartbeat.

Then the buzzer for the door downstairs buzz-buzzes. That bad adrenaline—the someone-sneaking-up-on-me adrenaline. Makes my head throb even more.

A towel tight in my fist, I wipe my arm off first, then mop my chest from the waist up. The towel burns against the cut when I hold it there. Removing it lets more blood leak out. I grab a gauze pad and press it tight against the wound, but it soaks through in seconds. Maybe pressing hard is causing too much tension in my chest muscles, making more blood flow. Maybe my heart's still beating too fast from the buzzer scare, I don't know.

The buzzer again.

Maybe it's Ben. He's come back, but he's lost his key. I grab a couple more gauze pads and stack them on top. Flatten my palm over them, pressing hard.

The buzzer.

I grab the roll of tape and bite the loose end of it, unroll and tear a couple pieces off with my teeth, stick the tape on tight as I can to keep pressure on.

I walk out to the main room, one hand cupping the wound, trying to keep the hurt from spreading. Over at the buzzer box, I press the speak button, "Yeah?"

"Jake? It's Savannah."

Savannah.

Without giving it a thought, I press the button for the door downstairs. But I'm naked, and the bathroom looks like a crime scene, and the wound hurts so bad now I can't think straight.

I flush the flesh chunk down the toilet, then dump the ice and leave hot water running over it while I search my dresser for something to wear. I find a pair of cargo shorts and put them on. Back in the bathroom, I wet the end of the towel, wipe the counter and the floor off one-handed. My hand cupped over the wound feels wet. The blood is soaking through again.

Then there's a knock on the door. I shout, "Just a sec." Blinking my eyes hard, I fumble open a couple more gauze pads, press them on top of the saturated ones, rip some more tape off the roll with my teeth and hope this is enough to keep the thing contained. I wash the blood off my hands quick as I can, but it's under my fingernails.

I grab a dirty t-shirt off the floor by the bed and slip it on. The wad of bandage bulges fat underneath the thin cotton, and I fold my right arm over it thinking maybe she won't notice. The lights are off, and I leave them off. I make a point of facing away from her as I open the door.

And not only is there still missed evidence in the bathroom, but there's dirty dishes in the sink. My dirty laundry is spread across the floor—my work clothes from the past week all sweaty and nasty. And underwear. She doesn't need to see my dirty underwear. I open the closet door and start kicking all the clothes in there.

"Don't spaz," she says. "You're a guy. I expect you to be a slob."

"Yeah, I'm not usually."

"Hey," she looks at me with her crooked frown. She grabs my left hand. "Babe, you're shaking."

I stare at her eyes, and for whatever reason, all I feel is confusion. The good side of her face is squinted with concern. Looking down at my fingers in her hand, they've gone sudden onset Parkinson's again. I close my fingers into a fist and turn away from her, walk toward my bed.

I shake my head. "It's just hot in here." My chest is on fire.

"I'll get you some water," she says.

Her heels *click, click, click* along the floor, and that sound is soothing somehow, something familiar connecting me to the real world. I turn back around, my right arm still folded like a chicken wing over the wound. Her short blue skirt clings to her ass tight enough that her underwear shows through as she turns into the kitchen area. Something about her is different today. Her hair—she's wearing a wig that looks almost like her hair used to.

Part of me likes that she's here right now, likes that she just might find me out. Maybe she can understand the things about me that I can't. It feels like she has that power. The other part of me is terrified she'll see too much and won't like it. She'll see down to my piece-of-shit core.

I'm breathing out of my mouth. I close my mouth, but don't get enough air like that, open it again. I sit on the edge of my bed, and Savannah hands me the glass of water. She sits next to me, staring at my chicken wing. She moves to rest a hand on my shoulder, and my head tics hard to the side.

"What?" she says.

I take a sip of water.

She slides her fingers down to my arm, and I pull back.

"Let me see," she demands—like the old Savannah who always got all bitchy at work.

I set the glass down on the floor, stare into blue spider eyes. I lower my wing.

"Jesus, you're bleeding."

I take that to mean it's soaked through again.

She pulls at the bottom of my shirt and starts to lift it. Raising my arms makes the burning sting even worse, but she's gentle as she pulls the shirt away from the bandage before peeling it over my head. I don't want to look.

"Oh my god—what did you do?"

"It's not what you think," I say.

She reaches a hand toward the wound. I close my eyes and wait for her fingers on my skin. Her tiny fingers with their long, sharp nails touch the tender area around the bandage, and I am scared. A nail digs under the tape. She pulls at the edge of it, and all the skin around feels as if it might come off with the adhesive. But I bear it unflinching. I let her hurt me because somehow I want her to. I hold my breath until she's peeled it back far enough to examine.

"You did this?"

"Yeah, but it's not what you think."

"Jake, you need to see a doctor."

"No."

"Jake, look at this. You're bleeding all over the place."

"It'll stop."

I feel something drip down my chest from where the bandage was. Everything's foggy and far away. I stand and walk to the bathroom, cupping the warm outflow with my hand.

I run cold water on a washcloth, look up, and see the red in the mirror, leaking out from under the soaked, fat flap of the bandage. No more white anywhere on the gauze.

Savannah stands behind me as I pull the bandage the rest of the way off and throw it in the trash. She grabs the cloth and tells me to take a seat, pointing to the toilet. I put the lid down and sit. She kneels in front of me, wiping my spill and pressing the cloth on the wound, and I feel so stupid.

"It's not what you think," I say again.

"Well, whatever it is, we need to get it taken care of."

She holds pressure on it for several minutes without saying anything, then pulls the cloth back, and carefully rebandages it. She then makes me sit in bed, propped upright on pillows, and instructs me not to move anytime soon.

She lies beside me on her back, her head near my feet. Her knees bent, and one leg folded over the other. Painted toes make figure eights in the air near my head. But she's looking at the dresser.

"What is that?" she asks.

I turn and see Prometheus staring right at me through the glass of his tank where the towel doesn't cover. "Prometheus," I say. "He's an albino leopard gecko."

"An albino leopard gecko? Why am I not surprised? You're seriously one of the oddest people I've ever met, and I've met some odd people."

"He's just a lizard," I say. And then I feel bad—like Prometheus heard and understood and might be sitting in there feeling belittled.

"Anyway..." she says. "I'm curious about something."

"What?"

"Your dad." She looks at me now. But her eyes crawl up my skin, climbing around in search of something to bite. She's a black widow. She wants to eat me.

"Why?" I ask.

"Why not?" One of her eyebrows raises, the other one—the burned one—tries. "I'm still trying to figure you out."

I sit upright, put my feet over the edge of the bed onto the floor. Every slight bend or slouch, and the wound on my chest stings. But the pain takes me out of myself for a bit, makes me not here, not quite so much an embarrassing display of my own stupidity.

"Not much to tell. He's in jail." I stand up and step to the dresser. I pull Prometheus's towel back and see that he's still got at least one live cricket hopping around in there, and there's still water in his dish.

Savannah sits up and peeks into the tank from a safe distance. "That's probably the creepiest looking lizard I've ever seen. Those red eyes—he's like Satan."

"He's albino," I say in his defense. "He doesn't have pigment." I try to telepathically communicate an apology to him, but he only flicks his tongue around and ignores me. I cover him back up.

Savannah reclines on my bed again. I move over to my bookcases and trace my fingers along the bindings of the books.

"So why exactly is your dad in jail?" she says. "What did he do?"

"I told you before. He hurt Ben." I turn back her way. She's rolled up onto her side, propped up by her elbow, burning through me with her eyes. I turn away again.

"Was he hitting him? Smacking him around? Is that what the cuts on his body were about when you had to leave work that day?"

I shake my head.

My fingers come across the fat, red spine of *Ancient Greece*, by Joan Walberg. I've read this one cover to cover at least a dozen times. Got it when I was Ben's age. "Do you know about the Spartans?" I say.

"Spartans? Like in Ancient Greece?"

I look back at her, weaving my fingers along the smooth gold lettering embedded in the hardcover spine. "Exactly."

She moves to the head of the bed, sits next to my stack of pillows, and pats the place where I was sitting like she wants me to come back.

"In the fifth century BC Sparta was, well, it's where you'd want to live if you were in Greece at the time, and you know why?"

"Why?" She folds her arms and leans back against the wall like she's preparing to tolerate, but not to care.

"It was safe," I say. "Their army was pretty much undefeatable. They were all about their military. Boys started training when they were just seven. They had this guy, the paidonómos, who'd take the boys away from their families to live together in herds. They'd underfeed them so they had to learn how to steal food without being caught. They had to make their own beds out of reeds from the river. They learned how to hunt and everything else so they were pretty tough by the time they grew up."

She clicks her tongue on the roof of her mouth.

I can't stop myself. "Each member of their army alone was tougher than anything, but they were even stronger because of how they'd fight together. It was like a wall—they'd all pack in side by side in a phalanx formation. They'd have their shields on their left arms." I put my left arm horizontal out in front of me. "And each man's shield would protect his own left side as well as the right side of the man next to him. Then they'd each have a spear—a doru—in their right hand." I lift my imaginary doru above my shoulder. The bandage pulls tight, and I feel the parts of the wound that are stuck to the gauze tearing away from it again. Probably bleeding again.

"Careful, Spartacus," she says. "Don't hurt yourself."

I drop the spear and shield. "Spartacus was a gladiator."

"Do you have any beer?" she says.

"No," I shake my head. "I don't usually drink."

She lets a single syllable laugh out her nose. "I guess that's no surprise."

She's uncomfortable. I make her uncomfortable.

I look back at the bookcase. "The Spartans—their training went on until they were twenty-nine, if you can believe that."

A handful of red fingernails hovers in front of her mouth as she yawns. "Why are you telling me all this?" She moves her eyes side to side like she's checking if someone else in the room is interested in what I'm saying. "You were going to tell me about your dad."

"When the Spartan boys were twelve..." I say. I lick my dry lips, look at her, then at the gold lettering on the spine of *Ancient Greece* again. "They'd get involved with an older male. For educational purposes. Pederasty." I still remember reading it for the first time and adding it to the evidence Dad always presented to rationalize what we were doing.

"So what you're telling me is they were a bunch of pedos? That's messed up, Jake."

"No, it wasn't like that." There's a weight between my sternum and heart. So heavy it hurts, worse even than the wound on my chest. It wants to drop me on the floor. "It's just what they did. It's how things were back then." My jaw clenches tight.

"Why are you telling me about this?"

Like she doesn't know. I pull the book halfway out and then shove it hard back into place.

The room is humming. My ears are on fire.

I hear her sit upright, her feet touch the floor, the floorboards creak as she steps up behind me. I smell her vanilla perfume as her hand grabs my shoulder, her voice a whisper in my ear, "Come sit."

My arms cross, my jaw clamps so tight my teeth hurt. I step like a stiff-legged robot over to the bed, sit, and stare hard at the floor. Savannah beside me. Her fingers run through my hair and comb out the heavy feeling in my head. I close my eyes.

"Your dad," her voice so gentle, soft like her skin, not at all how she always was at work. "Why he's in jail... Jake, what did he do to your brother? What did he do to you? He didn't molest you, did he?"

I tilt my head to the side, eyes still closed.

"Did he rape you? Good god."

The hum of the room gets louder, my breathing faster, shallower. The fist of pain in the center of my chest twists and grows, and there's that hot feeling behind my eyes.

She lays her head softly on the top of my shoulder, one arm trails down my back, and her other hand is careful to give the bandage a wide berth as it moves over the scars on my chest, on my belly, melting me.

"That's horrible," she says. "I didn't know."

"No one did," I whisper.

* * *

The doorknob clicks, and I wake. It's dark in my apartment but for the light of the clock on the stove and the streetlamp coming in through cracks in the blinds. At first I'm not sure I actually heard anything—maybe Savannah made some noise in her sleep, or it was a dream, but the door opens. This sends me instantly upright, stepping fast to the bookcase, grabbing for the machete on the top shelf. I get the bedside lamp on about the time a voice from the doorway says, "Jake?" and it's Ben, and I'm naked, and so is Savannah, tucking the loose blankets around herself. I flick the light back off.

"Sorry," the Ben silhouette in the doorway says. He doesn't

sound right.

"Benny? Come in, and close the door. Just wait a sec." I pat the floor in the dark for a pair of shorts. The adrenaline wears off, and the rip-burn of my chest wound gets me for moving too fast.

"What's going on?" Savannah asks.

"It's my brother."

She says, "Oh, hi, Ben. Jake's told me a lot about you."

The door clicks shut.

"Ben, let's talk in the bathroom, okay?"

We run smack into each other in the doorway making the wound on my chest feel torn again. "Watch it," I say and let him step in ahead. I close the door behind us and flick on the light. We meet each other with narrow slit eyes until we adjust to the brightness.

He's bright red with sunburn, but it's more than that. His eyes are red, too, and watery.

I lean back against the counter, and Ben stands near the tub, hands on his hips, elbows back, his brown hair sweaty and messed and slept on. His right knee bobs back and forth like he needs to pee. He looks all around the room, everywhere but at me.

Then he points to the door, whispers, "Is that—"

"Savannah."

His brown eyes shoot quick into mine then to the blood-soaked gauze taped to my chest.

"So, what's up?" I say. "Why are you here so late?"

He crosses his arms. "Just so you know, I'm still mad at you. I just didn't know where else to go." His voice is so quiet, so barely coming out, it's not even fair to call it a whisper.

He brings his hands up over his eyes, hides his face, and sits on the edge of the tub. His head drops low, and he rocks back and forth slowly as if trying to calm himself. My hands grip the edge of the counter so tight my fingertips go numb.

I look around the room like a magic answer might appear on the blank white of the walls. Maybe the shadow behind Ben moving in time with his rocking will tell me what to do.

He says, "I know it's stupid, but..." takes in a deep breath, blinks up at the ceiling, bounces the heel of his shoe off the tile floor, "I couldn't stay in my room anymore."

My head tics fast to the side, my eyes close, and I'm thinking about my old bedroom. How often I used to wash my sheets, and Mom always thought it was funny. How she'd always tell me I was using too much soap, too much fabric softener.

He shakes his head, "I can't go back in that room ever—I'm never going back in that room." His eyes close, and he takes another deep breath.

He's still just a kid, and I still don't know what to do. I know what he's feeling. You never forget the sound your bedroom door makes opening in the night when you know he's coming. All the parts of you that are going to get messed with, and it doesn't matter how tight a ball you curl yourself into. And how you hear that sound even when he's not there, wide awake in your dark room, trying to spot the moving shadow.

Ben says, "It just makes me sick."

My limbs are numb and tingling. My lungs are on fire. I nod, "Yeah, I get you."

"I hate Dad," he says. "I hate him. I hate him. I hate him! I hate him..."

My eyes burn. "Yeah."

He came to me for this. I thought he'd hate me forever, but he came here like I'm something.

My skin all over doesn't feel like part of my body anymore. The base of my skull buzzes like a headache's on its way. I'm breathing too fast.

There's a knock on the bathroom door and Savannah's voice, "Jake?"

I look at the door, to Ben, then to the door, wipe my sweaty palms on my shorts. My limbs are stiff from being so tense, and it's hard to step at first. I open the door a crack, lean my head out, and say, "Yeah?"

"Everything okay in there?" She looks right at me with her crooked face under her crooked wig.

I blink and a drop rolls out of my eye. *Shit.*

"What's going on?" she whispers.

I have to inhale deep so snot doesn't roll out my nose. All I manage in response is a high-pitched affirmative grunt. I look only at the burnt side of her face. There's not as much expression there. She can't get that sympathetic look to come out through the scars.

Her hand goes to my face. She runs the smooth backs of her fingernails down my cheek. "You want me to stay, I'll stay. You want me to go, I'll go."

I look toward the front door.

She presses her crooked lips against my forehead and says for me to call her later.

I nod and close the door. Ben's leaned sideways against the wall, staring at the counter. Red eyes. Brown freckles against a sunburnt face.

"I know it's stupid," he says again. "But I had a nightmare, and it was so real I thought..." and his voice goes quiet.

I know those nightmares. The ones where you wake up and can swear you smell his sweat on your skin. Swear you just felt his hot, hairy body on yours, his burning breath on your neck, in your ear.

Everywhere—my arms, my fingers, my head, my ears, my legs, my toes. My skin. It's like little bugs are burrowing in it. The wound on my chest feels like it's hatching fire ants. Little baby ones with concentrated venom that keep biting.

I look over at Ben. I would erase it all for him if I could. I may have been a fuck up in the past, but I'm not letting a damn thing in this world ever hurt him again. No one gets to hurt him. No nightmares get to hurt him.

"It's not stupid." I drop to my knees, hard on the blue tiled floor, pull him off the edge of the tub and grab him in close. His face against my bare shoulder. My arms tight around his scrawny body. The gauze on my wound bunches and rips away, but I don't care. It's like fire, but he's my brother. My hand on the back of his head, his hair in my fingers. The top of his head tucked under my face.

He's more than my brother.

He cries in my arms, and I whisper, "It's okay, it's okay." And that's a lie because what has him here like this will never be okay. But I have my brother back. I didn't think I'd ever have my brother back, and there's no way I'm letting him go again.

# CHAPTER TWENTY-NINE

There's ringing, but it's muffled. My eyes open to a wad of blankets piled on my head. I know it's the phone, but I'm confused, and I'm tired, and I have no concept of time. The phone rings again, and I claw my way up for air, get to standing. A sharp pain bursts from the bandage on my chest just below my right shoulder and spreads fast like an electric shock all down my front, up under my armpit and up my neck, and I can't help but gasp. The phone rings again, and I nearly trip over the sprawled mass of Ben on the floor on my way to check the caller ID. It's Mom.

"Hi, Mom."

"Jake," she says, "Benny's not here. He wasn't here this morning when I woke up."

"He's here," I say. "He came over last night."

"What?" There's a pause. "What's he doing over there so late?"

"It's nothing, Mom. He's fine. I've got him again for now, okay?"

Ben sits up, rubbing his sunburned face, blinking.

When I hang up the phone, he says, "Don't you have work?"

I look at the clock and see that it's almost nine and panic for a second before I realize what day it is. "No, it's Friday."

The bandage on my chest has old browned blood and new reddish pink juice soaking through. In the bathroom I try to gingerly tear it off. The problem is it's stuck to the wound in places. A warm wet washcloth pressed to it loosens it enough that I can remove it, but the wound seeps yellow-pink liquid and fresh red blood. It's so raw and tender I worry it's getting infected. I fish through the drawer and find a can of antibacterial spray. I blot the wound with the washcloth, spray the stuff on, and tape a new patch of gauze over it.

Back out of the bathroom I find Ben sitting crisscross on the floor, staring at his phone.

"Breakfast?" I say. "You hungry?"

His shoulders rise and fall in a shrug.

I nod toward the kitchen area, and he gets up and follows. "Get a skillet," I say as I reach in the cupboard, shaking an old box of pancake mix.

I mix the batter. Ben heats the pan and gets out the cooking spray. We are a machine, quickly stacking more pancakes than we will likely eat.

I have no syrup, so we eat them with butter and jam in silence, both of us still trying to wake up.

Soon Ben is staring me down. He takes a drink of milk, clears his throat.

"What is it?" I say.

He bends a knee up, rests his foot on his chair and his chin on his knee. "You can't get mad."

"I won't. Promise."

He starts pinching and unpinching the edge of the table between his thumb and forefinger. "I just still don't get why you never told," he whispers.

This again. I sigh, lean back in my seat and run my fingers through my hair, gripping it tight at the roots, pulling hard enough to make it hurt, but not come out.

"I knew you'd get mad," he says.

"I'm not mad. I just...don't have a good answer."

He keeps pinching the edge of the table, his eyes staying there.

"I wasn't brave enough," I say. "Not like you."

He shakes his head.

"I don't know. I was scared." I plant an elbow on the table, hold my forehead in my hand, "And there's some other things."

"Like what?"

"Um." My hands and my voice are both shaking. There's something I'm not remembering. "It's not important anymore."

I get up, walk over to the bookcases, and start running my fingers down the spines of the books. Ben's chair squeaks as he turns to stare at my back. I want to tell him I won't crap out on him again. No one's hurting him ever again. Never. Not Dad, not those dickheads at school, not Mom, not me, not anyone. But I can't get any more words out. There are too many trying to come at once, and they're not in the right order and aren't saying the right thing. Words aren't enough.

I try to read the titles on the spines of the books one at a time, but they're blurring. And Ben's sitting there, waiting for me to do something. "You staying with me again, yeah?" I say.

"Is that okay?"

I turn around. "How about we go apartment hunting today? Some place bigger and with two bedrooms?"

* * *

Ben's sunburned skin is peeling. He pulls off big patches of it and lets them drop to the floor of the car. I think about how all the dust you see on surfaces in a house, in a car—it's mostly dead skin cells. Dead skin cells flake off all the time, we just don't notice because they're small. Ben's pulling his off in big patches because he burnt himself, and now they're collecting like the shed skin of a lizard all over my car.

A couple hours later I'm filling out an application for a town home rental. The rent is near double what I pay now, and I don't have much in savings anymore after buying the car, but I can swing it. I write a check for the application fee, and we're off, headed back home before I have to go see Lauren.

* * *

Lauren, with her narrow posture, stares with narrow eyes like maybe she doesn't recognize me. "You seem in good spirits today," she says.

I shrug. Her eyes squint, and her face doesn't budge, like she's waiting for me to say something, ready to see words as they come out of my mouth. None do. She looks down at her notepad, then back up again.

"How was your week?"

"Um…might be moving to a new place."

"Oh?"

"A bigger place—so Ben can have his own room."

"That sounds like a big step. You're considering that he'll stay with you on a permanent basis?"

"He…uh…tried going back to Mom's, but it didn't work out. Too many bad memories there, and Mom can't seem to handle him."

"Does he act out a lot there?"

"No—she can't handle him, as in, she doesn't seem to want him around."

"That must be very difficult."

I nod and start picking at the calluses on my hands.

"How does Ben feel about all of this?"

"I don't know. Hard to tell."

"How do you feel about taking care of your brother long term?"

"He can't stay with Mom, so where else is he supposed to go? A bigger place should make it easier. I think it will do us both some good to have our own rooms."

"I can imagine things were getting pretty claustrophobic."

I nod.

"What else has happened this week?"

I immediately think about the giant wound I created on my chest. The thing burns even when I'm sitting still. But I don't feel like getting into that. "Not much," I say.

She shifts in her seat, stares down at her notebook a minute as though collecting her thoughts. Then she says, "I was wondering if we could talk about your father a little today."

My head tics fast to the side, and I switch to staring out the window. My fingers drum on my knee. I don't think I have it in me to start digging up that dirt.

"Your relationship with him has no doubt had a significant impact on your life. Maybe it's time to start working through that. What do you think?"

"I think you don't want to know any more than you already do about that."

"There isn't anything you can say that will be wrong," she says. "We don't have to go into any detail, but we can if you want. This is all confidential, and I'm certainly not here to judge."

"That's great," I say.

She sits upright and waits a moment. "How have you been doing with nightmares?"

I shrug.

I'm trying to think of ways to change the subject, but she continues, "One thing that abuse survivors sometimes find helpful is to remind themselves that they're safe now. The reliving—in flashbacks or in nightmares—can make it feel like you're a child, that you only have the power of a child. But if you can remind yourself that you're an adult and the danger isn't there anymore, you have the ability to stop it now that you did not have then."

"Tell me, would you consider twenty years old to be adult?" I say, examining all the little imperfections in the white painted windowsill, which is difficult to do from across the room.

"Adulthood is generally regarded as eighteen and above."

"And thirty?"

"I'm not sure I'm following," she says.

"I've never had the guts to stop it," I say. "Not then and not now. Ben did. I'm a coward. In fact, I'm so much of a coward that..."

"That what?"

I look right at her. "I'm the whole reason it happened to him in the first place." I thought those words would come out strong and angry, but instead they emerge quiet and wobbly.

"What do you mean by that?"

"I knew. And I said nothing. You want to know why Ben hates me so much? Because that's what came out at the trial. That I knew the whole fucking time what Dad was doing to him."

Lauren is silent a moment, staring through me like she's trying to figure out what to say.

"I told you that you didn't want to know any more about it than you already did," I say. "I've told you I'm a piece of shit. You believe me now?"

"Let me ask you this," she says. "Do you love your brother?"

Now she sounds like Dad's lawyer. "Of course I do. I'd do anything for him."

"So if you could have stopped it, then you would have."

"You just told me that adults can do that. Adults have that power."

"Only if they realize they do," she says. "Something kept you from that. I have no doubt that you love your brother. But that doesn't mean you don't make mistakes, and it doesn't mean you are always capable of doing what needs to be done. Something made it too difficult."

"I was a dumbass. That's what made it too difficult." Leaning back, I embed myself even further in the overstuffed chair. I cross my arms, cross my legs, and close my eyes.

"Calling yourself names is the easy way out," she says. "Here's a question for you: Suppose your father, for whatever reason, wasn't found guilty. What would you do, then? Would you let your brother go home?"

I shake my head, and keep my eyes closed. Adrenaline opens my lungs, and each breath floods my body so full of oxygen I feel dizzy. "I wouldn't let Ben near him. Dad could call the cops on me for all I care. We'd run away if we had to."

"So you're an adult now, and you realize you have the ability to tell him no. You have the ability to stop it."

My face is getting hot. The wound on my chest is at once stinging and itching, but I'm afraid to scratch it. I suck in a deep breath, sit upright, open my eyes, and say, "I'm not talking about this anymore today."

* * *

In my dream I don't know where I am or who the man standing in front of me is, but I'm sitting or leaning back on something. Savannah is next to me, almost behind me, maybe supporting me in some way. I'm wrapped in a sheet or a light blanket.

Under the sheet I am naked. The man pulls it open at the top and stares at my chest. The man is Dad. He reaches a finger out to touch the spot on my chest where I cut off the M, and I say, "Don't."

He sticks his finger in his mouth to wet it and reaches it out, rubs his wet finger across my nipple, back and forth and then in circles, and I say, "Don't" again. But my words mean absolutely nothing to him.

I just sit there. Savannah doesn't do anything but watch, solemn, like maybe she's observing a medical procedure. My nipple hardens. Dad pulls his finger back and says, "That's better." Then he does the same to the other nipple. I get the sense that this is the way it should be.

He pulls at the sheet around my waist until I'm all the way exposed. He puts a hand on my inner thigh and rubs slowly up and down, each time getting closer to the undercarriage of my nut sack. When he gets there I cringe and say, "Don't" again.

I think about Lauren telling me I'm an adult now, and I can tell him no. I can stop it. But she's wrong. Maybe I want this. Maybe I'm a sick fuck.

He cups my nuts in his hand, rubs his hand up over them, and grabs my dick. Then I start to let myself go. I start to let it feel good, and Savannah just sits there watching. He rubs my dick up and down until it's hard and then says, "That's better."

He taps Savannah on the shoulder but it's not Savannah anymore. It's Mom. I reach to wrap myself back in the sheet, but it's gone, and Dad just says, "It's fine, she won't remember." He says this will make her happy.

I blink, and I'm standing in the doorway to Mom and Dad's room watching Mom sleeping on the bed. Dad whispers something behind me but I can't hear it. I feel his breath in my ear, and everything is garbled like it's in a foreign language. I blink, and Mom's naked on that bed. I blink, and the blanket covers her.

I blink, and I'm lying on my back in my bed in my old room, naked, and the old man's hot mouth is on my dick. I feel like I'm falling, and I kick and wake, bolt upright, and suck in air.

"Jake?" Ben's voice says in the dark.

"Hmm?" I say between breaths.

"You were talking in your sleep again."

"Yeah, it's nothing. Just go back to bed."

"I can't."

I sigh and flick on the light.

# CHAPTER THIRTY

On Monday I walk through the front door of the shop and stop in my tracks. For the first time in weeks, Savannah is there. She leans against the front counter, arms crossed, in a wig and makeup to hide the melted side of her face.

This is so unexpected I don't even know how to process it. I haven't called her since she left Thursday night after Ben came home. I feel like some robot in a bad sci-fi movie whose signals get overloaded and just stands there saying, *does not compute, does not compute*, until sparks start flying, and he shuts down.

I say, "Hi, Savannah," and immediately push through the double doors to the shop.

"Excuse me?" She follows, her shoes clicking behind me. I beeline to my station, start setting pieces on the table, and get some rods out. She stands there, arms crossed, waiting.

I look at her, then away. I keep thinking about how she caught me slicing my skin off—how she knows about Dad. "I'm actually a bit behind here," I say. I put on my jacket, my gloves, my hood. I flip my hood down, and she's gone.

I totally fucked that up. I don't know how to fix it, so I just weld.

Three handrails later, I flip my hood up. Over by the double doors Savannah stands with her back to me. She's standing in front of someone, hip cocked to one side, waving her hands around in active conversation. I step to the side and see that it's Larry Daly. This can't be good. I set up another job at my table, flip my hood back down and work another weld.

The next time I flip my hood up, Savannah's right beside me. "In my office, now. We need to talk." She marches off, pauses to look back and make sure I'm going to comply. I take off my hood, gloves, and jacket and follow. When I catch up, she's holding the door open for me. I step in. She closes the door, points to a chair and says, "Sit." Then she leans back on the desk in front of me, crosses her arms tight around her melons, and I can't help but stare at them, yearning to burst out of her tight, black top. She must be wearing her black bra underneath. I've seen that bra.

"Larry Daly was just here," she says.

I nod, prop my elbow up on the arm of the chair, and rest my chin in my hand. Now I'm staring at her tiny ankles. She's wearing Capri jeans today.

"I'm perfectly willing to consider that Larry's just plain crazy, but I thought I'd see what you had to say about it first."

"W-what did he tell you?" I look up.

Her eyes narrow at me, and the caked-on makeup on the burnt side of her face cracks. "He claims that you've been sending him threatening letters in the mail." She waves a handful of red painted fingernails through the air. "There was something about a certain stoned neighbor of yours coming to his place."

I shrug. "You're right. He's crazy."

She sighs and tilts her head to the side. I wonder how she keeps the wig on. "Jake, there's work and then there's personal life. At work, I'm responsible for keeping this place afloat. I can't let one of my workers fuck with one of our biggest clients. At the same time, I know you need this job, and you've got all sorts of other shit going on."

"Larry's not going to go anywhere else," I say.

"Oh, and why is that?"

"Well, because you're back."

The scars beneath her foundation emerge through cracks in the makeup as she contorts her face.

"I've seen how he looks at you," I say.

"Oh, seriously, Jake."

"You know it's true."

"What, are you jealous? Because I don't get the sense otherwise that you're even still interested. You don't call me all weekend. You blow me off when you come into work today."

"Sorry," I say.

"That hurts."

"I was going to call."

"You know I've been worried about you?"

"Why?"

She hangs her mouth open in disbelief. "Oh, I don't know. Maybe Thursday you tried to hack off a chunk of skin, and then your little brother comes over having a meltdown in the middle of the night."

Her arms aren't crossed anymore. She's gripping the edge of the desk on either side of her. I stare at her ankles again.

"How'd you deal with that, by the way?" she says.

"Ben's fine. Everything's fine, he's just staying with me again."

"Look, I don't mean to be a bitch, I just need to know where I stand with you."

I open my mouth to speak, and all that comes out is, "Uh."

"Where do I stand with you, Jake?"

I lick my lips and try again, "Ah." Still not working. I want to say the right thing, but I don't know what it is. I try again, "I—I just..." And that seems to be all I've got. I lean forward, elbows on my knees, head in my hand.

"What? You don't want to date a freak?"

"No—" I sit up, wave my hand around at her, "You—you're fine. More than fine." I bury my head back in my hands. I smack myself on my forehead with my palm and sit back upright. Her spider eyes burn a hole into my brain. "I was going to call you. I didn't know you would be at work today."

"And what is that supposed to mean?"

"I'm sorry. I just..." and that's all I've got again, but I leave my mouth hanging like I might say more. *I'm embarrassed that you know too much? I feel like a dumbass?* Nothing comes, but Savannah keeps staring expectantly.

"Look, just tell me—are we still together or not?"

"Sure," I say.

"Sure?" she says.

She nudges my work boot with the toe of her red high-heeled shoe and makes a come-here gesture with her finger. I stand, but lock my eyes sideways at the wall. Her hands grab my face, turn it towards hers. She pulls me in close and presses her broken lips against mine, rough and warm and wet. I close my eyes, and her tongue slides into my mouth.

# CHAPTER THIRTY-ONE

While I'm on my way up the stairs with an armful of packing boxes, Ron comes part way down toward the second floor and says, "Dude—can you help me a sec?"

"Uh, sure." I leave the boxes in the hall and follow him up to his apartment.

Ron's hair is washed and gelled, the dilation of his pupils appears standard for the ambient light, an aftershave cloud radiates from his stubbleless face, and he limps with the aid of a cane now. He's in shorts, and his leg is no longer bandaged.

He shakes his cane at a new TV lying flat on the floor, and says, "I need to get this up on the wall. I've got the wall mount up, but I can't lift the thing myself."

I do most of the lifting and hold the TV in place while he attaches it to the mount. My arms are shaking and about to give out by the time he's done.

"Thanks, man," he says.

I'm about to leave, but he says. "Dude, you moving out by the end of the weekend?"

"That's the plan," I say.

"Sit a minute before you go," he says, shaking his cane at his table. I comply, and he takes seat as well, propping his leg up on a spare chair.

While still a mess, his apartment has been cleaned since last I saw it. The smell of old take-out is fresher and not laced with overtones of decay and rot.

"It's going to be weird not having you around," he says. He sees me looking at his leg and adds, "Oh, dude, you want to see the scars?"

Before I can answer, his leg is on the table, set before me as a gift in all its glory, pushing aside a pizza box and some empty glasses. A sizeable chunk of his calf muscle is missing. In its place is a five-pointed star of a stitched up scar surrounded by a constellation of puckered divots.

I nod. "Nice."

"Dude that shot me? He had this douche bag lawyer and said it was self-defense—like I was going to hurt him or something. Least they made him pay for pain and suffering and all the medical bills. And like forever, too. And I've got all this physical therapy now, so I know it's costing him." A surge of guilt runs down into my gut as I look toward his grotesquely displayed limb. He takes it off the table and sets it back on the spare chair.

"So, what was your story?" I say. "What did you tell the court?"

"Well, I didn't really tell them much." He tips his head to the side, jerky like the movement or a rooster, and folds his hands across his lap. "I just told them I was supposed to meet a friend, and I had the wrong address. Walked up to this Larry dude, and he's all threatening me, and he has this gun. I got scared, and I ran, and that's when he shot me."

I nod again, vigorously, like my head is on a loose hinge. "And the real story?"

"The real story?" He raises a single eyebrow, his eyes flit around the room like he's trying to make sure we're alone. "See, you know about my depression thing, right? And the pills I was taking?"

I nod.

"See, something wasn't right with those pills. I was getting them in the mail, right? And it was like they changed what they were putting in them. And I didn't complain, right? It was, like, trippy. The stuff was good. Well, I get this letter says they can't mail it anymore, and I've got to meet some dude to get it. I thought Larry was the dude, but I must have had the address wrong. Didn't want to tell the court that because I think something wasn't legal with those pills, you know?"

"Huh." I fold my arms, each hand holding the opposite bicep.

"Yeah. Messed up, right? But it's cool because it was like a near death experience almost—getting shot like that. I'm just happy to be alive, right?"

"So how bad is it exactly? Is it supposed to heal right again?"

He drops it back up on the table with a thud, and my chair legs squeak as I jump. He places a finger on the star and weaves it around in the little valleys and craters, peering up at me, like he wants me to lean in and inspect.

"It's like the muscle's all fucked," he says. "They're going to do, like, another surgery here in a month, and they say that after that it'll get most of the way to working if I do all the exercises, but it's always going to be a bit messed up."

"Wow," I whisper, and my head feels like it's lifting away from me.

"Dude," his mouth peels open in another toothy grin. "Don't get sick on me, man." His hand smacks the back of my shoulder. "Hey, just don't ever let anyone shoot you with a shotgun, is all I can say."

I'm about to get out of my seat to make an exit, but he says, "You know something weird, though, is he asked about you."

"He what?"

"Yeah, he stopped by just a couple days ago. He was all nice and everything saying how sorry he was and that it was all a misunderstanding. Then he asks me about you. Asks if maybe it was you that told me to go to his house that day."

"And what'd you say?"

"I was like, no? And then he goes on about the letters again."

"Letters?" I say.

"Yeah, they asked about that in court. About if I had been sending him threatening letters. Of course I don't know anything about that, but Larry asked me when he was here. He asked if my neighbor maybe was doing it."

"And what did you tell him?"

"I was like, how should I know? I was like, Jake's only ever been nice to me. Don't think he'd ever do anything like that."

I nod.

"You haven't been sending the dude weird letters or anything, have you?"

"Uh." I shake my head, "Larry's a pretty crazy guy. I mean, who sits on their front porch with a shotgun around here? Something's not right with him."

Ron nods, but the skin wrinkles around and between his eyes like he might be thinking. "Why would he think it was you?"

My shoulders bunch up to my ears in a shrug, and I tell myself to tone it down a bit.

"Yeah, how does he even know you anyway?"

"Oh. He's a customer where I work."

"Wait, how did you know I was even talking about the Larry that you know?"

"What?" Sweat creeps out the pores in my forehead. The palms of my hands are moist. I tense my muscles to keep from fidgeting, and strain my eyes by forcing them not to shift around. "You told me his name was Larry."

"Yeah, but lots of dudes are named Larry. How did you know it was the same one?"

"I saw him. When I dropped you off at the courthouse—he went in just ahead of you."

"Oh," Ron shakes his head. "Small world, right? Crazy."

"Well, I've got to get going. My brother's packing and probably wondering where I went." My hands plant on my knees. I scoot my chair back, and stand. I've successfully dodged enough bullets for the day.

"Oh, yeah. The little dude. You know he looks a lot like you, right? It's crazy—it's like you could have been twins."

My head bobs one more rubbernecked nod, and I edge my way to the exit. Ron hobbles behind me.

"See you around," I say.

"Yeah," he says. "Still crazy."

"Huh?"

"That you know that Larry dude and all."

Back downstairs, Ben grabs a box from me, and I take the rest to the bookshelves and start packing my books. Plates clank and newspapers rustle in the kitchen area as Ben packs the dishes. Savannah will be over soon with a borrowed truck. There's not a whole lot to move, but I've sprung for a new bed for Ben and a used sofa.

When Ben finishes boxing the dishes, he sits on my bed and watches me.

"What?" I say.

"Can I ask you something?" he says.

"What?" I say.

"Grandma and grandpa on Mom's side are both dead now, but what about Dad's side? I could never get him to say anything about his family. Are his parents dead, too? "

"Honestly? I have no idea. All I know is Dad has a brother. Why are you asking?"

"We have an uncle?"

I nod.

"Then why have we never met him?"

"I've met him. But the last time I saw him, I couldn't have been more than five. He and Dad had some sort of falling out. Haven't seen him since."

"What do you think it was about?"

"I was five, Benny. I have no idea. Why are you so curious about this all of a sudden?"

"You don't ever wonder how Dad got the way he is?"

"I don't think speculating on such matters is a good use of my time or yours."

"Do you think our uncle is like Dad? Do you think Dad's whole family was like Dad?"

"I think Dad's whole family is either dead or they can't stand him."

"You think he abused other kids?"

"I don't think speculating on such matters is a good use of my time or yours," I say again. "Come on. Let's finish packing."

It doesn't take long before everything is boxed up and ready to go. When Savannah arrives, we manage to get all of it loaded in one trip in a truck and trailer. Ben and Prometheus ride with me in my car, and we get everything unloaded into the new place before sunset.

The new place is so much larger. Two bedrooms and a bathroom upstairs, and a living room, dining room, kitchen, and half bathroom downstairs.

We stand in the living room, just finished with the move and Savannah says, "Clearly, Jake, you were a pack rat. It's good that you've expanded into something bigger so you have room for all your stuff." She struts around the room with hands on hips. Poking her head around and making a little warbling giggle. She's in pigeon mode.

Ben crosses his arms and looks from her to me. I'm supposed to read his mind. Probably something about her being annoying, and can she go already.

"Seriously, though," she says. "If you want, after you get unpacked I can help you decorate—fill this place out a little more and make it look like people live here."

Ben turns toward her, opens his mouth, and inhales like he's preparing to say something.

I beat him to it. "No, we're good. We kind of like it this way, right Ben?"

Ben appears satisfied, if not deflated, that he didn't get to say whatever it was he was about to. Now I'm getting a squinty-eyed look from Savannah's half-crispy face, and her weight shifts to one hip. "Well," she says, "I've got to get going. I need to get the truck back." Her eyes go up and down over me, and she looks to the door. I walk her to the exit, my hand on the small of her back. Ben's eyes trained on us the whole way.

In the doorway, Savannah leans in for a kiss. She says, "Call me. I'm serious this time."

When she's gone, Ben says, "Sorry."

"For what?" I say.

He sighs. "I think she hates me."

"I wouldn't read too much into her body language. It doesn't usually make any sense."

Then he says, "What happened to her face?"

\* \* \*

On Sunday, Mom's in distress about all the weeds in her garden. Ben and I stand in her yard as she waves her hands around at the dandelions and clover choking off the heat-withered crop of vegetables she's attempting to grow. Ben fetches a pair of hoes from the shed, and I tell Mom we'll fix it.

Ben attacks the garden with vengeance, swinging the hoe fast and hard, pulling up weeds and tossing them into a pile. He's missing a lot as he goes through, and I follow behind him, getting the little difficult-to-get bits and returning the dirt to a nice smooth surface.

Mom brings out sunblock and says she doesn't want us to get burned.

I tell her it's a bit late for that. This far into the summer we're both pretty tan anyway.

We return home in the afternoon, and Benny looks like his mind is elsewhere. He finally says, "I'm going for a walk," and leaves.

After two hours go by, I start to wonder when he might come back, and once it gets dark, I can't help but pace and peek out the window blinds every five minutes to see if he's coming home yet. Coming on 11:00 at night, I hear the door open and click shut. Then I catch the green streak of Ben in a hooded sweatshirt disappearing up the stairs.

I follow and knock on his door. "Where the hell were you?" I say.

He doesn't answer so I try the doorknob and peek in.

He's sitting in the dark on the corner of his bed, knees to his chest, back against the wall, his hood pulled up and tightened so that it covers most of his face. "What happened?"

I sit on his bed, and he presses himself farther into the wall. I pull the hood off his face, and he doesn't protest. Something isn't right. I flick the light on. His left eye is bruised and swollen, and his eyes are watering.

My heart drops into my gut. It doesn't matter what I do, the kid still gets hurt.

"Who did this?" I say.

"Doesn't matter. It was stupid."

"What was stupid?"

"You wouldn't understand."

"Try me."

He shakes his head. His face has lost color despite his summer tan. "Let me get you some ice," I say and run downstairs to throw ice in a towel for him. When I return he's exactly as I left him. I hand him the ice, and he holds it to his eye.

"Are you hurt anywhere else?" I say.

He nods.

"Where?"

He sighs, then whispers, "They called me a fucking fag. Said he'd shove his foot up my ass but I'd like it too much. Kneed me in the nuts instead."

"Who?" I say. "Tell me who. I'm calling the police."

"It doesn't matter. I'm leaving them alone. It won't happen again."

"It *does* matter," I say. "Was it the same kids from before? Dylan and Tim or whoever?"

"You don't understand," he says. "I think Dylan just wants to be cool, which is why he keeps going along with whatever Tim says."

"You still like him?" I say.

"I told you it was stupid," he says.

"You were good friends? I'd never heard you talk much about him before all of this."

"You never cared before all of this. Anyway, no one knew about us. They still don't because he denies it."

"Denies what?"

He sighs and glares at me.

"Sorry," I say.

"I told you, you wouldn't understand."

"Give me a little more credit than that. Which one of them hit you? Or was it both?"

"Dylan wouldn't hit me."

"So Tim, then. Does Tim have a last name?"

"No, Jake. He's just Tim. Like Kesha or Bansky."

"Who?"

"Seriously?"

"We're going to the police station," I say.

"It's the middle of the night."

"I'm pretty sure they're open."

"I'm not getting up," he says.

"Why?"

"Because…it hurts too much to walk right now."

# CHAPTER THIRTY-TWO

It's Friday evening and Savannah is coming over to hang out with me and Ben, but all I feel like doing is hiding in my room under my blankets. There's something missing inside. I am hollow. My chest hurts. My teeth hurt. I don't brush them enough, and I never go to the dentist. I get scared to. Some stranger opening my mouth up like that and messing around inside. I don't want anyone to see me. I don't want anyone to touch me. I don't want anyone to need anything from me. I might even cry if it wasn't so exhausting. I don't know where I got the idea that I could make an improvement on anything. Why I bothered moving into a place that's too big. I could easily live in a closet.

I force myself out of my bedroom sanctuary and downstairs. Savannah will be here any minute. Ben is sitting at the table pecking despondently at his laptop.

Ostensibly life is on track. Ben's back with me. He has his own bedroom. Dad is convicted and sentenced. Heck, I'm even dating Savannah. But maybe the problem is that I don't deserve any of it.

I still can't protect Ben. He's not happy, and I can't make him happy. Maybe I'm just a dumbass who was never meant to be around people. Whatever it is, I feel like any little thing might set me off. I'll toss my hands up and say fuck it and jump off the nearest cliff.

Part of me wants to go to Lauren's office. Not actually go there, but teleport there. And I almost laugh at that thought. I'd always considered the court order requiring counseling to be some form of inhumane torture. But it's grown on me. It feels like the tables are turned when I'm there. Instead of the world against me, it's me against the world, even if it's still a losing battle. I was just there this morning, but wasted the entire hour extolling the virtues of my new living quarters as though trying to convince her that the move solved all of my problems. It's a long way until next Friday. I have to go to work between now and then, and I don't think I can do it.

There's a knock on the door, and I let Savannah in, hauling a large case of beer. She sets it on the table, then takes one look at Ben and says, "Oh my god, kid, what'd you do to your eye?"

Ben says, "What makes you think something is wrong with my eye?"

Savannah pops a blue-jeaned hip out and plants a handful of teal fingernails on it.

"He got in a fight," I say.

"Well, shit," she says. "You've got to be careful out there, kid!" She waves a hand around and says, "You guys eat pizza? I'm ordering your scrawny asses some pizza to go with this beer. Put a little meat on you and maybe you can be on the giving end of the next black eye." She points a teal fingernail at me. "Where's your phone?"

Her high heeled shoes click behind me in the kitchen. I hand her the phone by the fridge. She says, "Okay, what do you boys like for toppings?"

Ben folds his laptop closed and sits with chin in hand. He shrugs. I tell Savannah, "We're up for anything." Ben sits upright, scowling at me because I didn't properly read his mind. "But no onions," I add, and his scowl melts away.

Savannah dials and orders something with a lot of meat.

When done, she rips open the case of beer, hands one to me, and says, "Can the squirt have one?"

I turn to Ben, "You want one, Benny?"

His head moves side to side very slowly. Savannah pulls one out for herself. Cracks the tab back.

I pop my can open and stare at it a minute. I bring it close to my lips for a sip, but the smell of it makes me think of Dad.

Savannah's watching me. "What's wrong?" she says.

She leans over the edge of the table, her cleavage spilling out of a low cut brown top right at eye level, and then Ben says, "Dad used to give us beer before he'd fuck us."

"You know what?" I say, "Fuck Dad, all right?" I take a big swig of beer and plop the can back on the table. "And fuck the dickhead who thumped you in the eye. Today is a new fucking day." I reach into the case, pull out another can and slide it down the table toward him. "Besides this is Coors in a can, not fucking Budweiser in a bottle." I chug down most of the rest of my can in the next go.

Ben narrows his eyes at me, cracks open his can, and takes a big swig himself.

Savannah says, "Easy, boys," and pats her hand on my back. "It's not a contest."

I wonder how long Ben's eye is going to look like that this time. At least the swelling's gone down, but the black runs all around his eye and across his cheek.

Savannah pulls another can out of the box and places it next to my nearly empty one. She puts the rest of the case in the fridge. When she sits back at the table, she gives a nod in Ben's direction. "So—school starting up again in a month?"

"Am I supposed to be looking forward to it, do you think?" And I don't know if he's aware he's doing this, but he's directly addressing her cleavage.

"Well, I wouldn't know, would I?" she says.

I tell her, "Ben's got credit recovery, and the kids that got him in the eye are kids from school," and pop open my second can of beer.

Ben just glares at me. He does not approve of me divulging those details, but maybe it will make him think twice before bringing up Dad in the presence of company.

"Ah, that sucks," Savannah says. "Those little punks didn't get arrested for that?"

"We filed charges," I say. "Waiting to see if anything happens."

The pizza arrives, and we eat. It's hot and cheesy, and not having eaten much all day, it's unusually good. I knock a few more beers down and am thoroughly buzzed. Ben never gets past his first. Probably a good thing.

Savannah says, "So, Jake, not to bring up work on the weekend, but what do you think the deal is with Larry Daly? Is this just his standard paranoia?"

I nod and crack open another beer. Maybe I should be concerned she's bringing that up, but I don't feel it. Fuck Larry. Fuck the asshole kids who fucked with Ben. Fuck Dad.

My bladder is an overextended water balloon, and I'm going to need a piss break soon.

"There's more to the story, though, isn't there?" Savannah says. She leans back in her chair, crosses her legs, lets one of her shoes dangle off her toe.

"What do you mean?" The shiny shoe oscillating at the end of her foot makes me think of those little cardboard birds you cut out in grade school, put pennies on their wingtips and balance them by their beaks on the end of your finger. They look like they should fall off but they don't. Something about the center of mass.

"Oh, come on. The letters. Don't tell me that wasn't you."

I take another sip of beer. "Uh. What?"

"I'm not going to tell anyone, I'm just curious."

"I need to piss." I stand, and the room moves. I try to walk one way, and my body seems to go another, yet I manage to stumble into the bathroom successfully.

I lose a gallon of liquid in the toilet and come back.

I feel a bit like I'm slipping between worlds. Half of me is in the surface world with Savannah and Ben and pizza and beer, but part of me is falling into some hollow space where nothing quite feels right and any memory I've ever had could be no further than five minutes ago.

Savannah watches me as I fall back in my chair. "Yeah," I say, "Larry's a prick."

"And?" she says.

I pour what's left of the can before me into my mouth. "And I need another beer."

I close my eyes a second, my head falls back, and I'm blank. A wordless mute. Numb. In my mouth a bitter aftertaste, salt and spunk. And peppermint. I am fourteen, and I had a peppermint candy hidden under my mattress. But it's as if the skin flavor, the dick flavor is deep in the flesh of my mouth, and the mint only serves as a garnish. I want to brush my teeth, to rinse my mouth out with Listerine, but I don't feel like moving.

"Who's Larry?" Ben asks.

My eyes blink open. "A prick."

"Does this have anything to do with those letters you were cutting out of newspaper a while back?"

"Dunno," I say. I grip the edge of the table, stand and step carefully until I can brace myself with the handle of the fridge. I pull the door open and grab another can of beer.

I stumble over and plop myself down on the couch, pop the top off the can, and spill a little taking a sip. Savannah abandons her shoes under the table and moves like a dancer toward me, her toes always touching the floor before her heels do. Sometimes she reminds me of Mom. How Mom used to be.

She sits by my side. "Jake. Babe. Pace yourself. You're going at the drinks a bit fast. You'll make yourself sick."

My eyes roll up, and I see Ben sitting sideways in his chair, one leg folded up in the seat, the other on the floor. He looks right at me like he saw where my mind slipped a minute ago. I take another big gulp and say, "I feel good right now. I'm pretty happy."

Then Ben says, "Did you send this Larry guy those creepy letters you were making?"

"Uh, yeah. Maybe."

"Why?"

"Don't know. Just felt good. Just stupid stuff mostly. It's not like a threat or anything. Just to mess with him a little." I down the rest of the can, lean my head back, and close my eyes again. My skin feels separate from my body. A strange casing holding me captive. I smell things in the room that I know aren't here.

Savannah's cool, thin fingers comb through my hair. "Jeez, you probably shouldn't mess with the guy too much. You don't want to get in trouble, you know?"

"No. No one knows. No evidence."

I open my hands and turn them over in the dark. I don't need to bring my fingers near my nose to smell them. To smell him on them. But there's something else there, too. And every second that passes I can feel it seeping deeper into my skin. I am a sponge. I have soaked it up. So it doesn't matter if I brush my teeth. If I shower with a Brillo pad. It's all gone too deep to be washed off. Worse yet, it's become me. I am every bit the evil he is. And I can't even care.

I open my eyes and shake my empty can. Savannah grabs it from my hand. "I think you've had enough."

I say, "No."

She says, "Yes."

I say, "Sorry."

She says, "For what?"

And I stare into her eyes. She blinks, and her left eye doesn't close all the way—it can't because of the scars. "The fire," I say.

Her fingers in my hair stop moving.

I am fourteen and in my bed, and as long as I don't have to move, to stand, to speak, to see another person, I will be okay. I can handle being alone and quiet and numb. I can't handle anything more. Something happened right before this, but the details fade like chalk drawings in the rain. I can't speak about what I've done, what I've become. I can't speak with all that's on my tongue. I am ruined and covered in dirt. I've done something very wrong.

"What fire?" Ben says.

"At work," I say.

"Jake, that was an accident," she says.

"Maybe. But I'm sorry about the screw then. The one that got stuck in your boob. I feel really bad, and I'm sorry."

"What are you saying? Because that was an accident, too."

"Sorry," I say.

"For what?" she says, but not as a question so much as a demand. Her face looks not soft, even on the not burnt side. She has that scary, mean look like at work. She sets my empty can on the floor. Her arms cross and her legs cross.

I am standing in the doorway to Mom and Dad's room, and I can't look at the bed. I remember watching him put white powder in a pill capsule right before this. There's a feeling that this is the time to tell him no, but I won't. Somehow I can't.

"Sometimes I do stupid things," I say.

Savannah says, "What stupid things? Tell me what stupid things you've done."

"*Goosey, goosey gander,*" I say and start laughing.

"What?" she says. "What the hell, Jake. What do you know about those rods being on the floor? What do you know about the fire?"

"Benny, you remember goosey, goosey gander?" He sits up like he's on alert. He shakes his head and looks to Savannah then back to me. "*Whither shall I wander? Upstairs and downstairs and in my lady's chamber.*"

Ben says, "Stop."

"You don't remember? I used to say this one to you all the time when you were a baby—*There I met an old man who wouldn't say his prayers.*"

Savannah says, "Cut the nursery rhyme bullshit. I know you're not that drunk. Did you have something to do with the fire? My fucking face is fucked up forever. Did you have anything to do with that?"

"*So I took him by the left leg and threw him down the stairs!*"

"Say something that makes sense," she says. "Say something right fucking now or I'm gone!"

It's always hours, and I always fall asleep, and one way or

another morning comes. Mom knocks on my door, says it's time to get ready for school. I shower and brush my teeth. She says I should eat some breakfast. She is cheery. She is normal. No hint in her that anything happened. No hint in her that she thinks anything might be going on. She places her hand on her belly. Ben's in her belly, but we don't know that he's Ben yet. He's just "the baby."

And I wonder about that baby and how it was created. And why Dad needed me.

I'm fucking terrified of the baby.

*Upstairs and downstairs*, and I look at the pain in Savannah's face. My mouth opens and my voice cracks but nothing comes out. Savannah slips her shoes back on, grabs her purse from the table, and stomps out the door.

I said too much. It all hits me at once—I just hurt Savannah, and she walked out. She hates me. The baby—what I let Dad do to the baby. Benny just stares at me like I scare him.

A fire bursts in my chest, and I can't keep it in. I crumple forward, my head falls into my arms, and I start sobbing. I can't stay in my seat and end up on the floor, drunk and dizzy and dying inside, crying my eyes out like a sad puppy.

# CHAPTER THIRTY-THREE

Savannah.

She pops into my head, then fades like a whisper when I open my eyes. I'm waking up on the floor staring under the sofa. My eyes hurt, my face hurts, and there's way too much pizza and beer fermenting in my digestive system.

I push myself to sitting. Ben's in a chair, watching me.

I'm positive I said something to Savannah about the fire, but can't piece together what it was.

"What time is it?" I say.

Ben looks over at the clock in the kitchen, looks back at me. "2:00 a.m. You've been out for four hours."

"You been sitting there this whole time?"

"No. Tried to sleep. Couldn't sleep."

I rub my hands over my face and back through my hair. "Ben, what did I say? Before she left—what exactly did I say?"

He draws his shoulders up in a shrug, and his head leans to one side, "I don't know. Some stupid nursery rhyme."

"Shit. Does she think it was me?"

"The one talking like an idiot? Yeah, I'm pretty sure she thought that was you."

"No. Her face. She got burned at work. Fuck." I stand up. My head is mush. "I put one fucking rag on the floor, and everyone decides to add to it and make it a fire hazard."

I walk to the window by the back door, peek through the blinds and see nothing but the reflection of my eyes peeking through the blinds. I don't know what I'm looking for.

"But this was back when she hated me," I continue. "Every fucking day, hated me. Damn it." I turn back around, cross my arms, and pace to the other side of the room. I lean my head forward into the wall and stare at the carpet. "What do I do now? What do I even do?"

"Did you start the fire?"

I push off the wall and look back at him. "Don't know. It was near my station. It could have been me." I stagger over and slump in a chair across from him at the table. "Thing is, she tripped over there twice before." I shake my head, pinch the edge of the table with my fingers.

"Just tell her it wasn't you."

"You think she'll believe me?" I look up at Ben, at the giant black eye swallowing half his face. "There's nothing I can say. Not a thing I can say to her. This is so fucked. So, so fucked."

I get up and head for the fridge, pull out a can of beer, and crack it open.

Ben watches me take a sip. His mouth parts like he has something to say.

"What?"

"You don't think that's maybe not a good idea?"

I throw the can hard against the bottom cupboards, and it splatters all over the place, foams up, and hisses out onto the floor.

"Sorry," Ben says, flinching.

"No, I'm sorry." I throw a towel on the mess. "You're right. I just—maybe I need to go for a walk. Get some air." I grab my wallet off the counter, shove it in my pocket, pick up my keys. "Try to get some sleep, okay?" I lock the front door behind me as I leave.

Across the dead-silent parking lot, across the street, down the sidewalk in the cool night air.

Maybe I should go to Savannah's house, knock on her door, tell her I'm sorry some more. I could tell her my mind wasn't all there, and so I wasn't making sense, and I was just sorry she got hurt, not that I might have had anything to do with it. Like that would be convincing.

I walk past a park, so dark away from the light of the streetlamps. A black oblivion held in the trees. Black like Ben's eye that I let happen. Roped and twisted like the scarred side of Savannah's face that I let happen.

I can't lie to her. I don't have it in me.

I step out onto another street, into blinding headlights and screeching tires, and a bumper just nudges me at the knee before I jump out of the way. A fist turned up, middle digit pointed skyward comes out the driver's side window before the engine revs, and the car speeds off. I walk faster and shove my hands in my pockets.

Does she know she crushed me that day Rick give me the screw? Does she remember laughing in my face? But even still, I'd give her my own flesh to fix her face if I could. I never meant for her to get hurt like that.

I smack at an itchy sting on my neck. Pulling my hand back, I find a popped mosquito in my palm—a little red squirt of my blood making the line of the exclamation mark. I walk so fast I get a stitch in my side. I'd like to think I'm wandering aimlessly in the night, like I could end up anywhere, but I'm not. Past buzzing streetlamps, across a strip mall parking lot, I follow the sidewalk on Main Street down a mile.

I reach the 7-Eleven, turn the corner, and slow my pace.

The street lights reflect dimly off the pale brown of her house. Weeds protrude from cracks in the pavement in her driveway. Fat dandelions gone to seed. The grass in her yard looks unwatered, dormant and dry.

I don't walk the path to her white front door, shut tight and locked. Instead I stand, stupid and at a loss, on the sidewalk. Every light in her house is off. She's curled up inside somewhere thinking I'm a psychopath, thinking I'm way more fucked up than she could have imagined, thinking I'm evil. Thinking I don't love her.

Do I love her? Is that what this is?

It's something, anyway. It hurts.

I don't know what to do with myself, but I don't want to go. It's all I have of her—her door to stare at.

The sky is dark blue and lighter on the eastern horizon. People will see me soon. Savannah might see me.

I turn and walk back home. Slowly.

When I get there, all the lights in the house are on, and Ben's passed out on the couch, his face towards the back and an arm dangling on the floor. I grab a pen from the counter in the kitchen, turn the lights off, and go up to my room to write Savannah a letter. All these things I never seem to say right. All these things I want to tell her.

But I don't have any paper.

Prometheus stares at me, his head tilted to the side as if to say, I know you think what you're doing is really important, but I haven't had a cricket in two days.

So I feed him, and as he flicks his tail around, happily in pursuit of his hopping prey, I grab a book off the shelf and look through it for any blank pages. There are none. I toss it to the floor and grab the next book and find a single blank page on the inside of the back cover. I tear it out and set it on the bed. I go through my shelves until I've got a fat stack of blank pages and a mountain of books on the floor at my feet so large I nearly trip stepping out of it. I grab the largest hardcover off the pile to use as a writing surface and sit on my bed with it.

I start off pathetic:

*Savannah, your voice is like birds singing, and you are beautiful as a rose...*

What is that? Savannah's not a beautiful rose. She's a freaking sunflower with sharp seeds. And her voice cuts like a hawk. It's all too dumb to even come across as real. But I can't seem to stop.

Soon I'm on the next page, still going strong, fingers growing numb from gripping the pen too tight. Maybe I'll fall into a groove and it will start coming out right.

I look up, and Prometheus is watching me, his chest heaving like he's laughing. Really, he's probably just breathing. Maybe he's mad at me. We were supposed to be best buds. I wasn't supposed to have humans in my life. Can a lizard feel jealousy?

I hear Ben downstairs, awake now, moving around.

I do my best to keep my hands from shaking, to keep the writing legible.

*Savannah, I swear to god I'm not crazy...*

Yeah, that's convincing.

There's a knock on my bedroom door.

I don't answer. I shake the stiffness out of my wrist.

*Savannah, I've done stupid things, but I regret every single one of them.*

Ben says, "I know you're in there. I saw your keys and wallet on the table."

"It's open."

He enters, leans his shoulder into the door frame, and crosses his arms. His half-shadowed black eye face stares at me.

I write: *Please read on, all the way to the end. Maybe there'll be something somewhere in here that will explain it all the right way. Everything I've done and everything I've thought. I know I can be a fuck up, but I don't want to be anymore.*

Ben stares at the pile of books on the floor and asks, "What are you doing?"

I say, "I don't know."

He moves over to the disordered book mountain and stacks the books back up in neat piles.

I write about the day Rick handed me the screw and how that felt. And how alone I felt. I tell her how I was angry, and the rods fell on the floor. How she tripped, and I let them fall there again, and she tripped again. How I set the rag down for target practice, but stopped when the rag became a pile. That would have been too far, so I stopped. How really, tripping her in the first place was too far. How on that day she caught fire, I threw up afterwards and sent her flowers. How I came over to see her because what I was feeling was much more than guilt. That I loved her then. That I loved her even before she ever tripped, and that I was too stupid to go about anything the right way.

Then I tell her I've hurt other people, too. I tell her about Ron and Larry and the letters and the drug switch. And I tell her I hadn't been sleeping, hadn't been eating, but that's not an excuse. I tell her I'll never do anything like that again. Ever. Fucking ever.

Ben loads the books back onto the shelves, all the spines lined up like before. When he finishes, his hands go to his hips, and he looks my way again. "I think I'm going to get some more sleep," he says and leaves.

I tell Savannah about Ben. How I knew. How I let Dad get him. How living with that burns like acid in my gut. How I was numb for so many years until the kid started sleeping on my floor, and I didn't know what to do.

Then I beg her to understand that I'm sorry. I won't ever keep any secrets from her again. I won't do anything that might hurt her or anyone else ever again.

I tell her sometimes I'm scared. Really, I'm scared every day. Of who I am. What I've done. Where my life is going. I'm scared to sleep at night. I tell her I'm terrified. Fucking terrified. I tell her I don't feel like a man, always. I tell her most days I feel like a ten-year-old boy, stupid and ashamed. And fucking terrified. But I want to be done with all that.

I write until my hand cramps so bad it doesn't work anymore. Until there are impressions left in the pads of my fingers from my death grip on the pen. Until the ink runs dry. Until I've used up all the paper, and I've written everything I could think to write.

* * *

On Monday I pull into work, all my notes stacked together. It's early morning, but I'm sweating already, down my back and in the palms of my hands. I'm shaking as I walk toward the building, my heart pounding somewhere up in my throat. I push through the front door, expecting to see Savannah, ready to hand her the letters and see what she does with them.

But she's not there. Dan is.

Dan's black hair is slicked back with either hair gel or his own head grease, I can never quite tell. The skin above his eyebrows wrinkles when he sees me. He stares sideways at the wall and says, "Jake. In my office, please."

In his office Dan says sit, and I sit. He walks around behind his desk, stands behind his chair and grips the back of it with both hands. He says, "There's reason to believe that the safety of everyone here might be at risk with you around. You want to tell me about that? I assume you know what I'm talking about."

I nod, but I can't look at him.

"You going to tell me your side?"

I open my mouth to speak but there are no words. My letters are still gripped tight in my sweaty hand. "Am I fired?" I whisper.

"What? Well, not yet. I couldn't do that. You've done good work here for ten years." He licks his lips. "But I am suspending you for now."

"Who's going to take my place? Carson? You know he can't do shit."

"Go home," he says. "I'll call you once this gets sorted out."

I get up and march back out to my car. I really can't afford to lose my job. Not now with the new apartment and Ben.

I sit in my car and the minutes keep ticking by. I hadn't given any thought to my life beyond getting those letters to Savannah.

Everyone's coming into work, heading inside to clock in like any other day, like everything's normal. I put my key in the engine, turn it, and drive slowly to her house.

I park by the curb and turn the engine off. Her house looks so quiet. The driveway cracks are still full of weeds, and there are weeds in the dead lawn, too. Weeds seem to do that—grow where nothing else will and take over.

I get out of the car and walk up the path to the white front door.

The throbbing at the base of my skull is back. I knock, so nervous and knotted inside.

Nothing happens. No noise at all from the other side of the door. Just outside noises—cars passing, the hum of insects in the trees. Some obnoxious squawking bird. I knock again. From inside there's a creak this time, like someone's walking, but it's so faint I might be imagining it.

Then the doorknob turns, slowly, until it clicks. The door cracks open, and I see Savannah's face, her head wrapped in the blue scarf with yellow flowers, her body wrapped in a soft pink robe. The door opens all the way, and she leans against the frame. The scarred side of her face shows no expression, but the normal side hangs loose in a frown. She crosses her arms. Her bare feet cross at the ankle, toenails painted red. She says nothing, stares right through me.

"Um, hi," I say. "I'm so sorry." But she doesn't budge, doesn't flinch. She is a sphinx, guarding the entrance to Thebes with her riddle. She'll strangle and eat me if I get it wrong.

I extend my hand with the wad of letters. "I suck at saying what I need to. I wrote it all down. Everything." The papers shake in my hand. Her blue eyes are the only part of her face that shift, they move to focus on the scribbled stack in my fist.

She reaches her red-tipped lion's paw out and grabs them from me, sending my insides in freefall.

She holds the wad between her hands, stares me right in the eye, and proceeds to rip it in half. The long, slow tearing sound is so loud, like it's ripping inside my own skull. My mouth drops open, and all the air leaves my lungs, all the blood leaves my head. She takes the two ripped halves and stacks them, rips them into quarters, tosses them at me, and they flutter to the ground like fat snowflakes.

She slams the door shut, and I fall to my knees hard on the concrete, and pick the scraps of letters back up. I hold onto them, wadded in my fists, still shaking.

# CHAPTER THIRTY-FOUR

"What are you doing?" It's Ben, and I'm jerked back into reality. Standing at the kitchen sink, water pouring into a glass in my hand, overflowing, and I freak for a second at the cold liquid running over my fingers, or maybe it was the suddenness of Ben's voice. I drop the glass, and it shatters in the sink.

I turn to Ben's freckled, black-eyed face giving me the what-the-fuck look. He reaches across and turns the water off. I lost time again like I've been doing all week.

Jagged glass fills the sink, and Ben just stares at me, that stupid stick in his hand again.

The stick first showed up on Tuesday.

On Tuesday I was hiding in my room like I had been since Savannah ripped my soul to shreds and threw it in my face the day before.

Ben came in to bug me and stood in my doorway with a five-foot stick in his hand. He had it grabbed at the middle, holding it down in the way you might hold a sword pointed at the floor. He asked if I had work that day.

Of course I didn't.

He asked how come, and I said not to worry about it.

"Did they fire you?"

"No, I'm just...not coming in for a while."

"Is this about Savannah?"

"Can we not talk about her? Please?"

He leaned his back against the doorframe and snaked his arm

in a spiral around the stick. He lifted and lowered it as if it was an extension of his own limb.

I was hoping he'd leave, but he didn't. So I asked him how his eye was doing.

And he said, "It's good I guess."

"And everything else?"

He nodded and panned the room as if searching for clues. He stopped when his eyes got to the dresser and the bits of my soul Savannah tore to shreds. I couldn't just throw them away, so I set them near Prometheus's tank for safe keeping. Ben stepped that way, touched the scraps, and spread them out.

"Stop," I told him. "Leave things alone."

He turned back my way and unspiraled the stick from his arm. "So, what are you doing today then if you're not working?"

I wanted to say let's go for a drive. Something. The kid looked bored and worried. But I didn't have it in me.

"I guess I'll leave you alone to mope." He gripped the stick again as if it were a sword at his side, tapped the dresser with it and left the room, closing the door.

Back to right now, and I'm pulling the trash can over, picking the glass shards out of the sink, and tossing them in.

Ben says, "That's going to cut the trash bag. You should put the glass in a paper sack first."

I continue to put the glass in the trash can.

I'm not terribly happy with him. Not after Wednesday.

Wednesday I'd come out of the shower, and when I got back to my room, the letter scraps were missing. But I was stupid at first and thought maybe they'd fallen behind the dresser—like some freak gust of wind came through the room and blew them back there. Of course they weren't there. Which meant Ben did something with them. And how could he? How dare he fuck with my shit?

I didn't feel up for a fight. Instead I sat on the floor in front of the bookcase, grabbed a paperback off the shelf. Stupid Latin phrase dictionary. I tore the cover off and quartered it. Tore the next page out and quartered it. Repeat. Repeat. And the sound of paper ripping felt good. Felt right. Just over and over. Each one slow and loud, the sound sinking into my skin. I could feel it in my chest in that place where my heart was supposed to go.

I get a new glass out of the cupboard and return to my original task of getting water. Ben says, "Have you even eaten anything all week?"

I shrug. He's twirling the stick around again. I go to the cupboard and pour some Cheerios into my hand. Put a few in my mouth and crunch. He follows me around like a puppy, always two steps behind.

That stick of his makes me nervous, and I'm waiting for him to lose control of it and have it hit me in the head. And if that happens, at this point, I just might snap.

Yesterday he was in my room again. He felt the need to tell me Mom called. He saw the pile of torn papers on the floor but didn't ask about them. The destroyed books—six in total. Hours of meditation. Then he looked up at me, and I looked to the dresser and gave a bit of a nod. His eyes rolled sideways to face the opposite wall, avoiding me and the dresser entirely. His face turned red. Then he left the room.

He knows what he did.

I sit at the table, put my feet up on a spare chair. Ben sits across from me, the stick propped up beside him in his hand like a staff. "You're going to your therapist today, right?"

"What's with the stick?" I say. "Are you a samurai?"

"What's with the beard?" he says. "Are you a mountain man?"

I run my hand across the stubble on my cheek and chin. "What's with the stick?" I say again.

"I found it." He tilts the stick toward me as if to emphasize its awesomeness. "There's a path that goes off into the woods at the back corner of the apartments. Found it in the woods." He tilts the stick back. "You didn't answer my question."

I shrug. It hadn't even occurred to me it was Friday already.

"Oh, come on. You can't just keep being this way," his voice tries for a higher pitch but fails and cracks, as happens at his age. More so lately it seems. The kid is finally catching up with puberty.

I take another bite of Cheerios. His bottom lip quivers, and he bites it.

"You think going to the stupid therapist fixes anything?" I say.

"I don't know. I figure she can do more for you than I can." He leans the stick in toward himself, hooks his elbow around it, and lets the top rest on his shoulder.

"I don't need anyone to do anything for me."

"Well... What are you going to do then when you don't have a job and bills are due—rent is due?" His chest heaves up and down, and as much as he pisses me off, I still hate seeing him this way. "Should I go get a job?" he says. "Should I move back in with Mom?" His eyes grow red around the rims.

He stands up and jabs the end of the stick into the floor.

"You know!" he says. "You of all people know I can't sleep in that house."

I brush the rest of the Cheerios off my hand onto the table, sit upright, and rub my hands over my face. "Benny, don't freak on me here. You're not going anywhere. Everything's good. I've got it, all right?"

"No, you don't!" His face is bright red, and he lifts the stick up over his head in both hands. He walks slowly around the room taking big steps like he's looking for something to hit with it. Giving up with a guttural roar, he throws the stick down on the couch. It bounces off onto the carpet. "You're flaking out again like always!"

"Fine. Tell me what you want me to do, and I'll do it."

"Go to your therapist today. Do that for starters."

I sigh, get up, and go back to the kitchen for some more water.

"Fuck you!" Ben picks the stick back up, stabs it into the floor. "Fuck you!"

"I'm going, all right? I'm going."

* * *

I'm embedded in the rose-colored chair while Lauren stares at me again, asking how my week went.

I tell her it's not even worth mentioning.

After we run through the routine questions about sleep and nightmares and appetite and self-injury and etc., she leads with, "What do you want from life?"

"To feel human," I say.

"Why don't you feel human?"

"People don't talk to me. I don't talk to them. I can't keep anything together. At best I'm invisible, at worst I piss people off and fuck up their lives."

"And how is it you feel you've ruined people's lives?"

"Well, for example," and I try to sit more upright—no easy task in the overstuffed chair. "This guy I know shot this other guy I know in the leg because of me. And the shooter guy really wants to kick my ass. The guy he shot—his leg is fucked for life, and he's only in his twenties. Not only that, but Savannah got burned at work a few months back—badly—and now half her face looks like Freddy Krueger, and it happened near my work station and maybe even because of something I did. Got drunk last Friday and told her it might have been me. And now she hates me. She told my boss that maybe the fire was my fault, and he suspended me. Ben's going out of his mind again because I can't seem to get my shit together. I'm supposed to be taking care of him, but I'm his burden half the time."

"And what do you plan on doing about all of this?"

I like how she doesn't ask why I did any of it. She doesn't so much as bat an eye. Like this is normal, and she hears this stuff all the time. "What can I do? Find a new job? Forget about it all and try not to fuck up again?"

"So, run away and leave it all behind you?"

"Wash the slate clean, and start over. Try not to lose Ben on the ride."

She gives me a look like that's the wrong answer.

"What?" I say. "What else am I going to do? None of it's really fixable."

"Has this method worked for you in the past?"

"What do you mean?"

"When you left home, didn't you essentially do the same thing then? Try to forget and move on? It's a natural human response, Jake. Fight or flight. You flew."

"So I'm a coward," I say. "I think that's already been established. Ben's the strong one, right?"

"You did what you felt you could do at the time. Consider the fact that when you were Ben's age, you didn't have an older brother."

"There's more to it than that. You don't know. You have no idea."

She uncrosses her legs, leans the other way, recrosses them, and folds her hands in her lap on top of her notebook. "Tell me this, does Ben have any close friends?"

I shake my head. "I think maybe he did, but he doesn't anymore."

"And where did he stay after he accused your father?"

"He had nowhere else to go. It's not like he came to me for help. He spoke out and then stayed with me after because Mom didn't want him."

"Have you considered that knowing you were out there might have played a role in his bravery?"

"I'm the whole reason the kid got fucked in the first place. It's not like I'm some great asset that's made his life wonderful."

"You ran away from it when you became an adult, but you did not rape your brother. That was your father. You are not responsible for what your father did."

I shake my head. "But I am responsible for what I did."

"You feel you let it happen to your brother? That you condoned it in some way?"

"Yes."

"And how is that?"

"Because maybe," and I look away, "I let the old man think I

was okay with it. I never once told him no. Not even the first time."
I lean forward and rub my hands over my face. "So maybe I made him that way."

"And what happened that first time?"

I tell her, "I don't remember." Which is a lie. And I said it too fast, so she knows it's a lie.

She scribbles in her pad. Maybe writing down something like: *Subject expresses signs of avoidance.* Like this is a new behavior.

"I was ten," I say.

And I have her attention.

I grab a tissue out of the box on the small table to my left and rip it down the middle. "Kids at school, you know, tell jokes about sex. How do you teach a girl math? Subtract her clothes, divide her legs, and square root her. And I didn't get it—I didn't get the joke. So..." I take one half of the tissue and tear it in strips. "Mom was out of the house one evening visiting her parents—my grandparents. I didn't want to go because I wanted to ask Dad about that joke."

I spend a minute tearing the strips of tissue into impossibly small fragments, letting them pile on my lap. Lauren waits, then finally says, "And did you ask him?"

"So... Dad had a few beers in him, watching the news. And, yeah, I asked him." I pick up the pile of snow in my lap, set it on the side table, and grab another tissue.

"And what did he say?"

I rip the new tissue down the middle. "You know I loved him? My Dad? I mean he'd never hurt me. It would never have occurred to me not to trust him—not even a hint. Everyone always seemed to like him. We'd go grocery shopping, and his customers from the pharmacy would recognize him and say hi and smile. Anyway... I asked him about the joke, and he gave me a beer. Said I was getting older. Probably old enough to know about these things. So of course I feel amazing. I feel like that's some special good thing. Then he starts telling me all about how sex works. Lots of detail. Everything. And uh..." My hands shake as I tear the tissue into snow. My head feels hot. But all of this, the nervous reactions of my body feel separate from my mind somehow. They feel separate from my ability to speak for once.

"And what?" she says.

"I got stiff," I whisper. "And he could see it through my shorts."

I look up at Lauren. Her head rests in her hand, her elbow propped on the arm of her chair. Hanging on my every word.

"You don't want to hear this," I say. "You don't want to know where this goes."

"You're fine, Jake. You can keep going."

I start picking all the snow off my lap again. "He could tell I was embarrassed, and he said it was fine. Perfectly normal for a boy of my age. So I'm reassured by this. Dad says it's okay, it must be okay. And. So. He tells me about this tribe in Africa. He says that in some cultures, sometimes boys have sex with men and not because they're gay. It was practice for the boys, for when they got older. He said this tribe in Africa believed they needed to do this in order to even be able to have sex with women at all later. And my mind is completely blown by this, but again, I feel special. He's telling me secrets—grown-up secrets."

I put my snow on the side table and pull out another tissue. Lauren waits in silence as I rip this one into strips. I don't make snow. I crumple the strips into a ball and set it back on the table. Propping my elbow on the arm of the chair, I hold my head in my hand, shielding my eyes. My forehead is sweaty, and I've got that feeling in my chest like the air's been knocked out of me.

"And I asked him how that worked. How can a boy have sex with a man?"

A minute passes, and Lauren says nothing.

"You get it? *I* asked *him*."

"So you think that at ten years old, you had the power to seduce your father?"

I sit back upright then slouch into my chair. "I guess not, but I still played into it, don't you think?"

She looks at me, her face hanging in a limp frown. I'm light-headed. Breathing too fast. I can't believe I just told her all of that.

"Yeah, I know, I get it," I say. "I was a kid. It wasn't my fault, and whatever else."

"Is that how you feel or how you think you should feel?"

"What?"

"That it wasn't your fault."

I grab another tissue and proceed to rip it. I wish it was louder, like paper when it tears.

"Jake," she pauses like she's trying to get my attention. I don't look at her. I keep ripping the tissue. "It wasn't you fault."

And those stupid words hurt. My eyes burn, and I look up toward the ceiling, suck in a deep breath. "You don't know all I did. Ten years of it."

"It wasn't your fault."

"You don't know all I did."

"You were a child. It was your father's job to set limits and teach you what was appropriate. It was not your fault."

I close my eyes and shake my head. I can't help it, I'm crying.

"It wasn't your fault."

# CHAPTER THIRTY-FIVE

There's a knock on the door, and Ben answers it. I'd been loading dinner dishes into the dishwasher, but I pause to peek. On the other side is some kid. Ben's age, I would guess, but he's taller than him by a good few inches.

Ben folds his arms, leans against the doorframe, and says, "What are you doing here?"

The kid shoves his hands in his pockets, looks up, and says, "You know I warned you about what would happen if you followed us again. I told you Tim would kick the shit out of you. So why'd you do it?"

This must be Dylan, Ben's former more-than-friend, author of the Ben-Gay tumblr, and betrayer of secrets. The idiot kid who's been converted into some bully's minion.

Ben turns back and sees me standing behind him. "Go away, Jake. This doesn't concern you."

"Benny, you need to close the door. There's no need to give this little shit the time of day."

"Go away, Jake. This doesn't concern you!" He says again, and it's clear he's only going to flip the fuck out if I push any further.

I step back into the kitchen, far enough away that Ben can't see me, but I can still hear what's going on.

Ben says, "Why are you here?" again.

Dylan says, "Just checking if you're still alive after that beating he gave you."

"Why do you care? I seem to remember you standing there like a dumbass watching the whole thing."

"I did warn you."

Why Ben is even entertaining this conversation is beyond me.

"I've left you alone," Ben says. "I don't want to have anything to do with you anymore. Why are you here?"

"See, the thing is, you went and filed a police report about us. Do you even know who Tim's dad is?"

"Do you think I care who Tim's dad is?"

"Well, his dad and my dad go back a long ways, and his dad is a cop."

"So what?"

"I'm just saying. If I were you, I wouldn't bother pursuing that any further."

"So, you've come here to threaten me again?"

"I'm not threatening, I'm warning. Tim doesn't even know I'm here. If he did, he'd probably do to me like he did you, okay? I'm doing you a favor."

I'm remembering back to that time I went to Ben's school with Mom. The cop who charged me with negligence said he had a kid Ben's age right before he punched me in the jaw. Maybe his kid's name is Tim.

Ben says, "All I was ever trying to do was just talk to you, but you never answer my texts and you never step more than two feet away from them. What is that? Why is that?"

"They're my friends," Dylan says. "We hang out."

"You were supposed to be my friend," Ben says.

"Quit acting like a girl," Dylan says. "You ever stop and think maybe that's why no one can stand you? You're a whiny bitch. You probably even lied about that stuff with your dad because you wanted the attention. That's just sick, you know it? It's sick."

I don't know about Ben, but I've heard enough.

"I never lied," Ben says. "I don't lie."

I storm over to the doorway, yank Ben back inside quickly enough that he can't get any complaints out, get right in Dylan's face, and say, "You or any of your little punk friends set foot anywhere near him again, if you so much as lay your eyes on him, I won't care one bit whether the law wants to do anything about it, because I promise you I will do something about it. You can tell your shit friends and your dad and their dads that I said they can all go fuck themselves. Got it?"

I don't leave space for an answer. I just slam the door.

The slam of the front door is followed almost immediately by the slamming of Ben's bedroom door upstairs. I make my way up to his room and knock.

Nothing.

I try to open the door, but he's got it locked. I knock again.

Then from the other side comes screaming. "Why can't you stay out of things and mind your own business? You were so good at it before! Why do you have to get in the way of things now? Dylan is still my friend, and now you've just messed that up! You don't care about me! You only care about yourself!"

"Nothing you are saying right now makes any sense," I tell him. "Look, can I come in?"

"No!"

"Well, will you come out then?"

Nothing.

"Benny?"

Nothing.

"I'm not going anywhere until you talk to me."

"Suit yourself."

I sit and lean back against his door. "That little shit who came to the door is not your friend."

"You're not helping."

"I'm telling you the truth. Friends don't treat people like that."

"Why don't you shut up about things you don't know anything about? He wasn't just my friend, but why would you even care?"

"Look, I get that, Benny. Okay? I'm sorry."

He doesn't respond.

"Say something." I reach behind me and knock on his door again.

"Leave me alone," his voice cracks. "Please, just leave me alone."

\* \* \*

The following morning Ben is speaking softly and carrying a big stick. Only he doesn't know I'm listening. The kid is talking to himself, pacing around the living room with that stick of his horizontal across the back of his shoulders, one hand hanging on either end. I don't know what he's saying. He's too quiet for me to make it out, but it's a lot whatever it is.

On another turn around the room he stops. He sees me watching him from the bottom of the stairs and says, "What?"

I shake my head. "You want to go for a drive?"

He slides the stick off his shoulder, holds it like a staff, and says, "Sure." That easy. Like he's forgiven me already. Seems odd, but I'll take it.

I hand him the keys and say, "We really need to get around to getting you that permit."

We go south today. We go a good six hours south, into California to see the redwoods. Trees so fat they dwarf the car widthwise.

It's warm out, but not hot. It rained here, probably last night. Everything is just a little damp. The pine smell is strong, and the air is humid with evaporation. We haven't had a good rain in a while back home. I hadn't thought about it in so long I didn't realize how much I missed it.

We follow a trail through the woods. Ben brought the stick with him. He stabs at the ground with it as we walk, but looks up the whole time, trying to see the tops of the trees.

"Do you remember the last time you were here?" I say.

"I was here before?"

"Yeah, first road trip I ever took you on. You weren't even in school yet."

Ben looks all around like he's trying to check the place for familiarity. "I don't remember."

"I think we hit every rest stop on the way down. Your bladder only held about an ounce back then, and I didn't want you pissing in my car."

He stops staring at the trees for a minute and smiles at me.

"*Holy moly*, you kept saying, *holy moly*. You'd never seen trees that big."

He was so happy, back then. Nothing hurt him yet. No one hurt him yet.

About halfway through our hike that day, he'd asked, "What if one of the trees falls?" His eyes got big. "Jake, what if one falls? Will we die?" And he stopped walking. So I stopped walking.

He grabbed at the bottom of my jacket with his tiny hand, and I said, "You'd hear it, you'd see it coming, and there would be plenty of time to get out of the way."

"But they're so big," he said, "I can't run that fast."

"I can," I said. "And I'd carry you with me."

He wouldn't let go of my jacket after that. His short-legged pace kept tugging me at an odd rhythm. I'd nearly step on his feet, nearly trip over him. So I put him up on my shoulders.

Back then I still told myself I wasn't going to let Dad get him. I would watch for warning signs. I would see it coming, and before Dad tried something I would jump in last minute. I would save him. When the time came that I needed to, that's when I would act.

But I didn't. I ran and left him there, let that big evergreen crash down on him.

Ben disappears for a minute, circling the base of a tree three times as wide as he is tall. He reappears around the other side, stands with his back next to the tree, and holds his stick at the end, pointing it all the way up above him.

I tell him, "You were scared last time you were here." He turns and looks at me. "You thought one of the trees would fall and get you."

Ben lowers his stick, taps it at the ground. He laughs. "I could totally outrun a falling tree."

* * *

There're string beans, peas, cucumbers, tomatoes, beets, and yellow peppers all close to ripe in Mom's garden. Weeds are in check, and I'm watering everything.

Mom faces the side of the house, her hand tracing down the siding, saying something to Ben that I can't hear. Ben just stands there with his arms crossed, nodding. And that's when I notice. I don't know why I never saw it before, but he's taller than Mom by a good few inches. The kid's been growing.

I turn the water off. Mom turns back around my way. She says, "I was thinking about painting the house. I don't suppose you and your brother would be willing to help me out with that soon? I want to get it done before fall, and that's coming up pretty fast."

I nod. "We can do that. Don't think you have enough paint for it, though. Only saw one bucket in the shed last time I was in there."

"I know. I'm going to go pick some up this week. Thought I'd go for a new color."

She watches me wind the hose, then tells us to come in for some lemonade.

A tall, icy glass perspires on the table, and I let it. I don't touch it, don't mess up the beads of condensation with my fingers.

Mom asks, "What's wrong?"

What's wrong is I can't stop thinking about Savannah. "Nothing, things are okay."

Ben stares at the side of my face. He opens his mouth a couple seconds before his voice breaks out from it. "You should go try to talk to her. Just one more time. Give it one more chance."

"Benny, she wouldn't even speak to me. Tore up my letters. Slammed the door in my face. You don't go back after something like that."

"One more time," he says. "Just try one more time."

I shake my head.

"It wouldn't hurt to give it one more chance," Mom says. "If you guys had a fight, maybe she just hadn't cooled off yet."

Mom doesn't know a damn thing about it, and I don't know why Ben would care. He doesn't even like her.

Ben says, "Just try talking to her one more time, that's all, just once, and if it doesn't work, I won't bring it up again, I promise."

I don't know why he's so adamant, what he thinks he understands that I don't. But I let the possibility sit in my head. I say, "Maybe."

# CHAPTER THIRTY-SIX

It's getting late, and I'm about to turn in for the night. I've been reading for the last hour or so. Or re-reading really—I need new books. The phone rings. Caller ID says it's Mom.

I pick up, "Yeah?"

"Jake?" she says. "I can't find my medicine. I've looked everywhere. I don't know—I can't find it." She's breathing heavy, and her words are coming out all strung together.

I tell her I'll be there in a couple minutes.

Ben's up in his room, and I knock on his door.

"What?" he says.

"Can I come in?"

There's shuffling, and he opens the door, "What?"

"I've got to run to Mom's. She's lost her pills and is starting to freak."

He looks sideways, so I look sideways. Nothing there.

"You want to come?" I say.

He shakes his head.

"All right, well, I don't really know how long I'll be. Answer your phone if I call you, okay?"

\* \* \*

Mom is pale. There's no color in her face at all, and she's shaking and wet with sweat. I tell her to sit down and take it easy. "Where do you remember leaving them last?"

"In the bathroom. I always leave them in the bathroom cupboard. They were there this morning. I know they were there this morning." Her voice gets louder with each word.

"I'll look. I'll look."

I start in the bathroom, in the mirrored cupboard with the cracked porcelain handle. I haven't opened it in years. On the frosted glass shelves there's toothpaste, Tylenol, some old prescriptions of other stuff, Dad's razor and shaving cream, dental floss, Vaseline. No Valium. I slam the thing shut a bit too hard.

Mom calls from the other room, "You find it?"

"Still looking."

The bathroom is small. There aren't many hiding places. It isn't on the counter. It didn't fall in the pile of towels on the floor. I dig through the garbage bin. Nothing but old Q-tips, cotton balls, and wads of tissue. I wash my hands. Mom appears at the bathroom door.

"Is there anywhere else you might have left them?"

She shakes her head. "I don't feel well." Her face is whiter than it was before, and she's breathing shallow like people do when they're trying to hold back vomit. She stumbles past me, falls on her knees next to the toilet, and proceeds to hurl. That sound of her gagging and choking, the vomit splashing into the toilet, is too much. Not sure what to do here. I grab a washcloth out of the towel closet in the hall and run some cold water on it. I hand it to her as she slumps back to sitting, leaning against the tub, her mouth and nose dripping.

"I'm going to check the rest of the house," I say. "Maybe you accidentally left it in another room."

She holds the washcloth in a fist up to her face. She looks scared, and I remember seeing her like this before. All of a sudden I'm remembering getting up to use the bathroom in the middle of the night, and she was there on the floor right where she is now. Her eyes were red, and her hair was messed, and her robe wasn't closed quite all the way. I've got that feeling again like the itch of a memory trying to come back. I stare at her a good few seconds waiting to see if déjà vu fills me in.

Nothing.

I continue my search, starting from one end of the house

and combing through in an attempt to be systematic. I upturn the cushions on the peach floral sofa as the sound of Mom dry heaving nearly sends bile up my own throat.

It feels like Dad's here somehow, like he's going to turn the corner from the hallway any minute and ask what's going on.

I check the kitchen—the countertop, the cupboards, the pantry, the garbage there, too.

Nothing.

My hands shake. I peek in the bathroom to check on Mom, and she's leaned up against the tub, eyes closed, mouth hanging, panting like a dog. It's way too late to try to call a pharmacy for a refill.

One last place to look, and that's her bedroom. Her and Dad's bedroom. I pause in the doorway, my hand on the doorknob, and the memory itch is back. I walk through the door and can smell the old man. It's been months since he lived here, but the room still reeks of him.

Mom cries out my name, long and slow and desperate. She says, "Please."

I kick around a pile of dirty laundry to see if the pills maybe ended up there. I check the drawers in the nightstand. I shake the blankets on the bed. Lift the pillows. She hasn't washed Dad's pillowcase since he left. The old man's sweat and drool still coat it, and I'm dizzy, and I've touched it with my hands.

I stare at my sweaty palms, opening and closing them, blinking hard. I don't need this right now. Mom calls my name again. I stare at the bed, and it feels like I'm fourteen. Dad is standing behind me. I can hear his words in my head. You're helping your mother. But he doesn't mean in the way I am now. I close my eyes, and it doesn't just smell like Dad in the room. There's more. There's Mom.

I need to snap out of this. My mind is slipping. Flashback. This is another flashback starting. But this one's the landmine. I can't do this right now.

I run back to the bathroom. Mom looks so weak and sick. I say, "We-we're going to the hospital."

I help her to standing. One hand at her back and the other at her elbow, I feel like I'm guiding a ninety-year-old woman, not someone in her early fifties. I walk her out to the living room and set her on the couch. I find her shoes and help her get them on. She clings to my arm as I walk her to the car. I face away from the sour vomit smell of her breath. Her heart beats so fast and hard I feel it through her skin, and my heart's racing, too, like it's a competition. Her hands are wet and clammy.

I get her in the car, and off we go to the hospital.

We don't wait long. Mom looks like she might keel over in the waiting room and disappears with a nurse, behind double doors as I'm left answering questions with the receptionist. I draw nothing but blanks—and on the obvious stuff, too, like date of her birth, but they manage to find her in their system. My hands are wet, with my sweat and hers and Dad's pillowcase. I wipe them on my jeans.

Every time I look around the waiting room, I see people staring at me.

"I have a William Smith listed as the emergency contact. Is that still correct?" the receptionist asks.

I say, "No," and give her my information instead.

As soon as I'm done with her, I'm told to have a seat and wait. Instead I go straight to the bathroom, locking the door behind me. I body slam myself into the tile wall, smack it a few times with the palms of my hands, kick it for good measure, and slide down to sitting on the floor.

I look at my hands again, opening and closing them. They're dirty. They feel dirty. I stand up and go to the sink, pump out a giant palmful of foaming anti-bacterial soap and start washing, letting the water get near scalding. My face shines with sweat and panic in the mirror. I turn the water cold, fill my hands up with it, and splash it on my face, let it drip off my chin, off my nose down into the sink. It looks like tears because my face is so red. I pull a bunch of paper towels out of the dispenser and dry off. I grab the sides of the sink, stare up at the ceiling, focus on my breathing, and try to calm the fuck down.

I should call Ben and tell him where I am and what's going on. That will give me something to do.

I leave the bathroom, find a phone, and call. Something about getting ready to speak to Ben clears my head a little. But voicemail picks up. The clock on the wall reads almost eleven. Maybe he fell asleep.

Returning to my seat, I grab the nearest magazine—a National Geographic. The cover article is something about earthquakes, but I'm not reading any of the words. Just staring at each page for a minute or two before flipping so I don't get caught in eye contact with anyone. Then I hear my name. A nurse in bubblegum pink scrubs and a long black braid stands in the doorway that Mom was taken through. I've seen this nurse before, some months back during the leg-crater incident. I get up and follow her back to a room with Mom in it. Mom looks calmer. She's lying in a bed hooked up to an IV, not sweating and panicked anymore. The nurse tells me they're keeping her overnight. She can probably go home tomorrow, but the doctor is probably going to recommend that she wean off the Valium.

Mom looks tired. I say, "I should let you get some rest. It's late."

She nods. "Thank you, Jake, for helping again."

* * *

I get home to a dark and quiet apartment. I get a glass from the cupboard and pour some water. I'm tired, but I doubt I'll be able to sleep. I head upstairs to my room anyway, to lie down if nothing else.

But at the top of the stairs I find an envelope taped to Ben's door with my name on it. My first thought is that he's maybe run away. I pull the envelope off, and am about to open it up when there's three very loud knocks on the door downstairs. I run down and peek through the peephole, and it's Larry fucking Daly. He knocks hard again and says, "I know you're in there, Jacob. Open up."

And for whatever reason, I do.

But I've still got the letter in my hand, and I don't know what it says, and I'm worried about Ben.

My fingers undo the envelope and slip the letter out as Larry says, "I had a little conversation with your pal Ronald, and I think I've started piecing some things together."

My hands shake as I unfold the letter.

"You set him up, didn't you? Only the fucker's too stupid to know it."

My eyes go down for a second and I read:

*Jake-*

*First off, don't open this door. I don't want you to see me like this. There won't be anything you can do anyway. Just call someone to take my body away...*

I look up at Larry and say, "Oh fuck."

"That's right, oh fuck."

"No. It's a suicide note." I hold it out for him to see. He grabs it, and then I'm running up the stairs.

It's not even a second before I'm through Ben's door, turning the light on in his room, yelling, "Ben!" at his limp body lying flat on his back on his bed. I grab his shoulders and shake him, "Ben! No, no, no, no, no." He's breathing. He's still fucking breathing. I saw his chest lift up. I put my ear near his mouth and feel his breath—faint, but there. I shake him again, "Benny, wake up, wake the fuck up!" I slap his cheeks, pull his eyelids open but his eyes are rolled back up in his head.

That's when I see it, there on the floor next to his bed, an emptied package of Valium. Mom's Valium. And three cans of beer. Three empty cans of beer. He's going to die. He's going to fucking die.

Larry's voice says, "Quit shaking the kid. That won't help him."

I turn around and see Larry coming through the doorway.

He says, "Get your phone. You need to dial 911. Right. Now."

But I just grab my hair, and I have no words, no breath.

Larry gets right in my face and yells, "Get your goddamn

phone and call!"

I run downstairs, grab the phone, and start dialing 911 as I run back up. The ringing on the other end of the line seems so slow. I get back to Ben's room, and Larry is standing over him with his ear to Ben's mouth, listening for breath.

"Oh god, did he stop breathing?" I say.

"Calm the fuck down. He's okay for now. Panicking isn't going to help him any. You dial yet?"

"They're not answering."

"They will." He steps aside, and I sit next to Ben, smooth his hair out of his face with my fingers, watch closely to make sure he's still breathing, and the operator picks up.

I spit out in speed talk, "Need an ambulance right away. My brother—he's fifteen—just swallowed a whole package of Valium, and he's unconscious." I rattle off my address, and I'm being told to remain calm. They're asking for dosage, and Larry hands me the package. I say, "I don't know how many were in there, but it's the ten milligram ones. Could have swallowed as many as fifty. The package says fifty." They ask about alcohol, and I say, "Three beers. Maybe."

I place my hand on his chest. He's breathing so slow and light. I put fingers on his neck to feel his pulse. So slow and light. I can't let him die. I can't let him die.

I'm being reassured over the phone. Paramedics are on their way.

My brother. My baby brother. My fingers are on his neck again. The time between every warm heartbeat feels like death.

And just like that, one long breath comes out slow and doesn't go back in. I pat his chest.

Nothing.

I check for pulse on his neck, and Larry is back over doing the same, puts his hand on Ben's chest and his ear to Ben's mouth.

I shout into the phone, "He's not breathing! He's not breathing!"

The lady on the other end asks if I know CPR.

Larry says, "We need to move him to the floor."

I tell the operator, "No, no I don't."

I stand up, and Larry puts his arms under the kid, lifts him gently to the floor, kneels beside him, and starts breathing into his mouth. I tell the operator, "Someone else here does."

The operator says the ambulance is almost there and someone will need to let them in. I hear the sirens approaching.

Larry checks Ben's pulse. He says, "Shit," and pounds on Ben's chest.

He's dying. He's really dying.

I run downstairs and open the front door just as the paramedics pull up. I tell the operator they're here, and the phone call ends.

"He's not breathing, and I think his heart's stopped!" I shout at them as they run toward me with medical gear in hand.

They follow me up the stairs where Larry is straddled over Ben doing chest compressions.

They tell Larry and me to step aside, and they check for a pulse. One of them resumes chest compressions while the other quickly attaches a pulse monitor and unpacks a defibrillator. There's a flatline beep that must be Ben's dead heart, and they cut open his shirt and attach electrodes, say, "Clear," and shock him, say, "Clear," and shock him again, and his heart starts up in a slow rhythm. One of them sticks a tube down Ben's throat and attaches a bag to it. He squeezes air into Ben's lungs.

I am numb. All the way through.

They ask me the same questions I already told the operator. Dosage—how much, any alcohol. And I repeat, "Ten milligram ones, a box of fifty, but I don't know how many were in there before he took them. Three cans of beer." And Ben looks so small.

The paramedic squeezing air into Ben's lungs says, "We need to move him now and get this stuff out of his system before he crashes again." The other paramedic runs back downstairs, and returns with a backboard. They move him onto the board and haul him off, just like that. I follow them down the stairs, and as they load him into the back of the ambulance, one of them shouts, "He's crashing again!"

The doors close, and they speed away as the sirens blare off toward the hospital.

I stand in the doorway in stupid disbelief until Larry says, "Get your ass over to that hospital!"

I nod and grab my keys and wallet and leave Larry alone in my apartment. He could burn the place down, and I wouldn't care.

At the hospital I walk up to the reception desk and say it's me again. Found my Mom's Valium. My kid brother just OD'd on it. And I don't even know if he's still alive.

The receptionist says they're working on him, and she has me sit down so I can give her all of his information. I tell her he's probably in their system. He was born here. She asks for a current address, and I give her mine.

She asks me if I'm the father.

"What?" I say, "No, brother."

I'm told the doctor will talk to me when there is news.

So I wait.

And wait.

And the waiting is god awful. I want to have hope. I want to believe he made it, but I saw his heart stop. Twice.

So I wait for someone to come out and say it and make it all the way real. And then what? Just go home? I have to tell Mom somehow. We're going to have to plan a funeral, and I don't know how to do those things. I can't bury my baby brother. I can't.

The same nurse in pink scrubs comes through the double doors and calls out my name, this time a spark of recognition in her eye, but she doesn't say anything. I follow her back to some little private meeting area inside. I'm told to wait again. My own heart is about to stop. There's no good reason to have me back in a private room like this.

A doctor walks through the door. He looks so serious. So deadpan. I'm shaking.

He asks me if I'm Jacob Smith. I say yes. He asks what my relationship is to Benjamin. I say that I'm his brother—he lives with me.

The doctor nods, "We have him stabilized."

"St-stabilized?" I rub my hands over my face. My whole body hurts with warm relief. "Oh, thank you. Thank you."

The doctor says, "But he's far from being out of the woods. His heart stopped three times, and we don't know how long his brain has been deprived of oxygen. He's in a coma, and we have an MRI scheduled in the morning to assess the damage. Right now we don't know the outcome. He might recover completely, but there's also a very real possibility that he may never wake up."

"I need to see him. Can I see him?"

The doctor nods, and I follow him down the hall, through a door, and there's Ben lying flat on his back, eyes closed, limp, a big tube coming out of his mouth, an IV, a beeping heart monitor, and an inhaling and exhaling machine.

To the side of his bed there's a chair with a soft seat and back and wooden arms that wrap around in a square and become the legs. I pull it out and face it towards his bed. I lean forward with my elbows on my knees.

Ben looks dead. Pale and unconscious. But the periodic beep of the heart monitor tells otherwise. The hiss and crush of the breathing machine keeps him alive. But he might be brain dead. He looks so small under the blankets, wires, and tubes. I stare at his eyes. The closed lids. I stare waiting for them to open, but they don't.

My insides burn, and soon I can't get enough air. Next thing I know, I'm bent forward almost falling out of my seat, hanging on for dear life to the side rail of Ben's bed. My blinking eyes see the tile floor, see the wheels of the bed. It all gets more patchy and gray with every blink.

A voice says, "Are you okay?"

I don't have enough air for words.

A hand is on my shoulder, and that's enough shock to my system that I manage to sit upright again. It's the pink nurse. "Are you okay?" she asks again.

This time a breathless "Yeah," makes it out as I nod furiously, unconvincingly.

She says, "How's your leg, by the way?"

"My leg?"

"When was that, sometime in January? You came in—infected leg wound. Pretty sure it was you. I'm good with faces."

"Oh. Leg's fine. It's fine."

She says, "It's late. It might do you some good to go home and get some rest. You've been here enough for one night. First your mom, and now this."

I nod again but don't move because my limbs feel like distant noodles, and I'm not sure my legs would support me if I tried. I start shaking my head no.

The nurse says, "His condition is not likely to change anytime soon. He's perfectly stable for now, and we won't know any more until the MRI in the morning." She says I'd do best to get some rest so I'm put together for then.

Maybe she has a point. But if I go home, I know I'm not going to sleep. I don't know what to do. I just sit. The nurse pokes around at the machines and enters stuff into a computer. She leaves, and it's back to the only sound being the beeping and the hiss-crush.

The monotony and the late hour slowly drive me insane. When it's coming on four in the morning, I finally peel myself from the chair and make it out the door.

Walking down the hall to the exit feels empty. Hollow. I'm going home to an empty apartment for the first time in a while.

I find Ben's suicide note on the floor at the top of the stairs when I get there. I didn't read past the first few lines earlier. I pick it up and step into the doorway of his room. The light's still on. The empty Valium blister packs are still on the floor, as are the three beer cans. I sit at the foot of his bed, unfold the letter, and read it in its entirety.

*Jake-*

*First off, don't open this door. I don't want you to see me like this. There won't be anything you can do anyway. Just call someone to take my body away.*

*You are probably wondering why. Maybe you can guess why. Living hurts too much. I know you've been trying to help me, and I appreciate everything you've done, it's just that school is coming up again soon, and I just can't do it anymore.*

*I'm sorry.*

*I don't want you to blame yourself. This is what I want. I've given it a lot of thought, and I really think it's for the best. So try not to take this too hard. I want you to be happy, and I think you can be, and it will probably be easier without me anyway.*

*I still think you should try to talk to Savannah again. You don't need to be alone.*

*I also think you should stop doing whatever it was you were doing to that Larry guy. I don't want you to end up getting in trouble or end up in jail with Dad.*

*I forgive you. For everything. But I don't forgive Dad, and I don't forgive Mom, and you can tell them that.*

*Thanks for everything, Jake. You've been the best brother.*

*-Ben*

The letter makes my skin sting. I lie down on my side and read it again, then toss it to the floor and stare at the empty beer cans.

# CHAPTER THIRTY-SEVEN

There's ringing. The phone downstairs. I blink my eyes open and am confused—first at where I am, then I figure out it's Ben's room. Then I wonder when exactly it was I fell asleep and what time it is. The phone's still ringing, and it could be the hospital, and in a matter of seconds I'm downstairs saying hello into the receiver, gripping the edge of the counter because the head rush of waking so suddenly has me tipping dizzy to one side.

I don't recognize the voice on the other end, but it asks me if I'm Jacob Smith. I say yeah. It is the hospital, but it's not about Ben. It's Mom. I almost forgot about her. She's ready to be discharged and needs a ride. The clock on the stove reads 11:00 a.m.

\* \* \*

I get to the hospital, but Mom can wait because Ben's MRI was supposed to be this morning. The receptionist gives me a visitor's badge and a room number, and then I'm in his doorway.

But he's not alone. It seems Mom found him.

She stands by his bedside, hands clasped in front of her, staring through him. Her clothes aren't on straight—the buttons on her shirt are all off by one. Her hair is unbrushed. She slowly turns my way. Her face is pale and looks to have aged a decade since last night. She shakes her head and says, "How did this happen?"

"What did they tell you?"

"No one's told me anything. I asked where my son was—I was asking for you. You were supposed to pick me up. I asked where my son was, and they brought me here. How did this happen?" She reaches a hand out and brushes the backs of her fingers against Ben's cheek. She places her hand on top of his.

I pull up a chair and ask her to sit. She shakes her head.

Ben looks the same as last night. He hasn't moved at all.

Mom stares right at me, waiting for me to say something.

"Your Valium," I say. "He took it. The whole package."

She still looks like she's waiting. Then it's as if every muscle holding up her face dissolves beneath her skin. What's left is a ghost, a vapor-essence of what she was. She's going to disperse and fade away.

She pulls her hand away from Ben's. Then she says to me, "What took you so long, anyway? I've been waiting for a ride home all morning."

"They were supposed to have done an MRI. That should tell us how he's doing. Did they say anything about that to you yet?"

"I can't do this," she says. "I can't be here. Take me home."

"We can ask the nurse—maybe talk to his doctor and find out the results. Don't you want to know—"

"Please take me home. It's been a long night."

Mom is liable to make a scene if I don't comply. There isn't anything I can do for Ben either way, so I nod.

We get in my car, and Mom smiles like normal moms do—that look like I've done something endearing.

She says, "You don't look like you got much sleep. You should be taking better care of yourself."

I drive her home, stopping on the way to fill a prescription. Valium. Reduced dose. They want to wean her off it slowly. That will surely work well.

Once she's a settled zombie of disbelief, I go straight back to the hospital. I ask to speak to someone. I need to know the MRI results.

I meet with the doctor in the little private room again, and he says, "The MRI looks okay, but sometimes damage doesn't show up right away. Your brother is still stable. At this point it's just a waiting game. Odds are he'll wake up—could be a few hours, could be a few days, could be longer."

I'm flooded with the same warm relief I felt when I found out he was still alive, and I have to take deep breaths so I don't break down.

The doctor continues, "When he does wake, we can run some neurological tests and get a better picture."

"What kind of damage?"

"One thing your brother has going for him is his age—younger people and kids tend to recover more fully from these types of brain injuries. But he might have some short term memory loss or some difficulty processing language and thoughts. There might also be muscle weakness and coordination problems. If these aren't too severe, many times patients recover fully with therapy. But again, we won't really know where he stands until he wakes up, so it's best to be prepared for anything."

I nod. The doctor tells me to feel to free to ask questions whenever. I nod again, and he leaves.

I go to Ben's room and sit in the chair next to his bed. "Benny?" I whisper. He doesn't so much as flinch. I grab his hand. His fingers are cold, and I'm mad that the hospital staff let him get cold. I tuck his other hand under the blanket and pull the blanket up higher to his chin.

Once I'm settled, warming his hand in mine, listening to the beeping of the heart monitor and the hiss-crush of the breathing machine, it all hits me again. How he could be dead right now. How I can hardly call this alive.

I squeeze his hand and whisper, "Benny?" again.

He looks peaceful. Like the cliché—like a baby. But it is what he looked like when he was a baby when he slept—like nothing's getting at him. Maybe it's good that he gets that for a little bit. Peace.

Every time I look away from him, I keep thinking I hear him wake up, I hear him stir, see him move out of the corner of my eye, but it always turns out to be the sounds or the motions of the machines, or my imagination and wishful thinking. I stare at him hard each time after, but he never budges, never flinches.

He said he forgives me in his letter. But I don't forgive me.

When Ben was a baby I used to sneak into his room at night and watch him sleep, just like this, but without all the machinery. I'd stare at his face and try to figure out who he looked like more. I didn't want him to look like me, but he did. I'd whisper to him. I told him I'd protect him—from Dad, from the world. But it's so much easier to say that to a sleeping baby than it is to an older kid, and besides, words are empty when you don't back them with action.

"Benny?" I say again. Still no response. I squeeze his hand again. It's warm now. I've warmed it. I tuck it under his blanket and lean back in my chair and stare at his pale, peaceful face.

"I'm sorry," I whisper. The hiss-crush of the breathing machine is the only answer I get. I remember being fifteen and feeling so protective of him. I feel that way again now, with that same intensity, for the first time since. He's more than my brother. That's how this feels. More to it than just having the same parents.

I need to make some big changes, I just don't know what they are yet.

"You need me to fix things, I'll fix things," I tell him. "You don't need to die for me to do that. You don't need to fucking die."

# CHAPTER THIRTY-EIGHT

I perch in the scotch pine across the street from Larry Daly's house, thinking about Ben and his letter.

This is me not running away, not fleeing the mess I made. This is me saying I'm not going to spend my life hoping Larry Daly never finds me, worrying about who has what evidence, settling on the hope that he'll forget about it after a while. This is me fixing it. This is me dropping out of the tree and knocking on Larry Daly's door on a Monday evening after I watch his car pull into his garage. Three loud, solid, I'm-not-scared knocks.

And I wait.

I don't even hear anyone moving inside the house behind the door when it suddenly opens and Larry bursts out of it like an enraged bull dog. He steps forward, all the way clear of the doorway. I step back, and he closes the door behind him.

His fat, wide head is red, taut, with big angry eyes. "And what brings you here?" he says without moving his jaw.

At least he doesn't have the shotgun with him.

I am wordless at first. What was it I was going to say? "I-uh, was just going to explain everything?"

"The neighbors don't need to see this." Larry looks around, up and down the street. "Into my garage." He walks past me over to his garage door, pulls it open, and stands under it, the bottom edge nearly resting on his head. He waits for me to step in, then slams the door behind us, leaving us in the dark.

Larry's going to kill me. That's what the neighbors don't need to see. He's going to fucking kill me.

A shop light overhead hums, flickers on, and now I can see everything in Larry's perfectly organized garage. Hanging on a rack by the door to his kitchen is the shotgun. And Larry stands between me and his shotgun.

"Don't wet yourself," he says. "I've got a cable lock on it, and the key's in the house." He leans back against the wall, right next to the gun, looking me up and down. "Besides, I could snap you like a twig with my bare hands if it came to that." He nods at me. "Is the kid okay?"

I nod, "He hasn't woken up yet. But they think he will soon." I have to watch my breathing so I don't disintegrate while talking about it. "He'd probably not have made it if you weren't there. Go figure."

"Is that the only reason you're here?"

I shake my head. "No. We've got some air to clear."

He cracks his knuckles.

He folds his arms.

He stares me down. Silent. Waiting for me to make a move.

"So, a few months back I kind of followed you home one night."

"You kind of followed me home? You either did or you didn't. Which was it?"

"Did."

"And?"

"That tree across the street? I sat up in that tree across the street."

"In the fucking tree?"

"Yeah, in the tree."

"And?"

"I'm the one who messed up your garage. And sent the letters."

"So it *was* you." He works his jaw around, limbering it up in preparation for biting my jugular. Any minute he's going to lunge forward and go all rabid, snap me in two just like he said, and I won't be able to get away in time. It would take too long to pull up the garage door. He says, "And?"

"And it was stupid? It was wrong. And I want to apologize. I'm sorry. I meant no harm by it. It was just a prank. And I'm done with pranks. And I'm sorry. I'm sorry."

"Why? Why did you do it? Why did you feel the need to fuck with me like that?"

"I was a moron. You'd come into work complaining about me, and at the time I had a lot of family crap going on, and I just, I don't know, it's what occurred to me to do at the time."

"What family crap? I want to know—what fucked you up so bad you turned into an asinine delinquent? What fucked the kid up so bad he tried to off himself?"

"It's kind of personal."

"Sneaking into my garage at night is kind of personal."

I suck in a deep breath. "I had to testify against my dad. That week when you were getting all pissed that I hadn't been at work—that's what I was doing."

"And what was your dad on trial for?"

I can't look at his eyes. The interrogation is too much. "I had to testify for my brother."

"You didn't answer my question."

"What?" I look back up.

"What was your dad on trial for?"

I fold my arms. Squeeze my biceps hard under my fingers. I'm going to leave bruises but it's all I can do. I look around at the shelved golf clubs, the tools all hanging neatly in categories. Wrenches, hung in descending size, hammers, screw drivers. "Um. I'd rather not talk about the specifics of that."

I look back at Larry. His eyes grow big again. The veins on the sides of his head throb more blood into his red face. He shifts position like I've just disrespected him, and he's about to make me pay for it. I don't care.

"Did he beat the kid?"

"What?"

"Your dad—did he beat the kid?"

I shake my head and look sideways.

"So he's a molester."

"You know, really, it's none of your business." This is another one of those moments where I try to sound assertive, and it comes out all weak. Like an awkward freshman reading a book report in front of the class. It's amazing Larry can even hear my words at all.

"There's more, then, isn't there? He went further than that."

And I freeze. I'm staring at the concrete floor. I can't move.

Then he says, "If anyone ever did that to my kid, I'd ass-rape them with the barrel of my shotgun, and that'd only be the beginning."

"He's not my kid. He's my brother."

I look up. Larry can see right through me. He knows about me. It's written all over my face.

"You trying to backtalk me?" he says.

"What are you going to do?" I say. "Snap me in half? You going to beat the shit out of me?" And here I manage to insert enough confidence that my voice is now in the normal range for speaking.

"Don't tempt me, asshole."

Maybe he's right. Probably not a good idea to tempt him.

"Why did you come here?" he says.

"I needed to apologize. I needed to fix this."

"Why? What changed? Why now?"

I shrug.

"Come on. You can do better than that."

"My brother. It's for my brother. I've got to—got to get my shit together."

He looks me up and down. "Takes some real balls to come here. You know what happened to the last guy that came here?"

"Yeah, about that." I close my eyes, take a deep breath. "See, I set him up. I guess I just wanted to see what would happen. I had no idea you'd actually shoot him."

"Jacob, tell me why I shouldn't call the cops on your ass right now."

Fuck. I don't need to go to jail over this. That's one specific thing Ben mentioned in his suicide note that he did not want.

"I'm not going to," he says. "I'm tired of dealing with the fucking law, and the fact of the matter is, that Ronald puke was unarmed. Just the same, I still want to know. Why do you think I shouldn't call the cops right now?"

"Look, I'll pay for what I did in whatever way you want—law or no law. You can even kick the crap out of me, and I won't tell—just don't kill me."

"If you want to fix things, you take care of that kid. When he wakes up he's going to need you more than he ever did. Don't let him turn into a drain on society. Don't let him end up like that Ronald puke. You make sure that kid finishes school and does something with his life, even if it's a struggle."

I nod. "I will, I will, I will."

Then Larry tenses up. Full enraged bulldog. Jabs a finger in the air at me. "I'm letting this go because of your brother. But you won't get another chance. Fuck with me again, and you can be sure I'll have your ass!"

* * *

The pain in my gut is so sharp I almost black out. The acid fire of vomit fills my mouth, but I manage to swallow it. I'm on the floor in Ron's apartment, curled in a ball, staring at the furry underside of his fridge, trying to get my breath back.

I didn't see it coming. I figured things went so well at Larry Daly's, maybe I should make amends with Ron as well.

Ron was happy to see me. Just smiled and nodded while I told him everything. Then he drove his fist into my gut.

He is not weak.

"Dude." He's standing over me. "That was so not okay."

His cane cracks me hard in the back of the head, and I forget all about my stomach. I make the sort of whimper sound you might expect from a struck animal.

A wet drop of his spit hits my cheek. "My leg is fucked for life because of you!"

The cane smacks me on the kneecap, and I'm out of my body. Ron sits down at his table. I lay curled, drowning in a pool of hurt.

"Sorry about that," he says. "But we're even now. Besides, the babes are all over me for this leg these days. You would not believe how many blowjobs I've gotten this week alone. No hard feelings?"

I plant my hands on the floor and push myself up, roll over sideways to get my ass under me, and sit leaning back against the fridge. My head throbs so bad I can't keep my eyes open at first.

When I can intake sensory data from the environment again, I lift my hand up off the floor. My palm is coating in something dark and sticky. I look over at Ron sitting at the table, staring back at me.

"Dude, you're white as a fucking sheet. Don't blow chunks on my floor."

I slip the leg with the unwhacked knee under me and manage my way up to standing. Another head rush swallows my brain, and I brace myself on the sink until I get my bearings.

"We cool now?" he says.

"Sure."

\* \* \*

Tonight will make two days since Ben's been dead to the world. I sit with him for three hours straight, and he still doesn't so much as flinch. I stay until it gets near evening, until the nurse convinces me there probably won't be any change any time soon.

But I don't go home. Ben had another request in his suicide note.

# CHAPTER THIRTY-NINE

As if I wasn't nervous enough just coming to Savannah's house, I've got to wait parked on the curb down the street. A silver BMW in her driveway blocks my way, and I'm waiting for it to leave. But it's more than just a car. I only know one person who drives a car like that.

I crack my window open to keep my car from turning onto an incubator. But I'm still sweating torrents. The street is so quiet. It's getting dark out.

I haven't exactly worked out what I'm going to say to her. Maybe she'll listen long enough for me to get through what I can remember of the letters. If my mouth will even form words when I need it to.

The smiling bulldog of Larry Daly steps out her door. The optimist in me says maybe he was here for something work related. I duck low in my seat in case he looks my way as he gets in his car and drives toward the freeway. I don't know what the bulldog would do if he caught me looking like I was stalking Savannah. I've got to wonder about how easy he let me off the hook. Something's creepy about that.

Now that Larry's gone, Savannah's white door is happy and inviting, saying, *Come knock on me, Jake. You know you want to.* What a tease, that door. It wants me over there, but a bitter Savannah will pop out behind it and remind me I suck as a human. But just the same, I get out of my car and knock on the door. It opens.

I'm not even a bit prepared to see her again—her blue eyes, one angry eyebrow, one crumpled burnt one on top. My mouth moves with no sound.

She looks at me confused like she was expecting someone else. Then she says, "Jake," like she's surprised, peeks her head up and down the street. She steps back inside, and says, "Come in."

I make it in the door. That's at least farther than last time.

I'm directed to sit on her couch.

Savannah reaches behind a black and white picture on a shelf up over the TV. The picture looks like maybe her as a kid—maybe five years old—with her brother at the beach wearing sunglasses. She pulls out a stack of papers, drops them on the coffee table in front of me, and says, "We need to talk." Then she walks toward the kitchen and asks, "Do you want some wine?"

"No, I'm good."

My writing is all over the papers. They're the letters I wrote for her. The letters she tore. The ones Ben took. All taped back together.

Ben did this.

I turn around and watch Savannah pour red wine into two bell shaped glasses on the counter. She's not wearing the wig today. Her hair is growing back. It looks normal, just really short. A red dress hangs loose over her body down to just above her knees, and I don't think she's wearing a bra. Larry must have noticed her nipples, too.

She returns to the living room, a glass in each hand, hips making little circles in the air. She sets a glass in front of me, sits in the chair at the end of the coffee table, one leg folded under her, sips at her wine, points a red fingernail at mine, and says, "Don't get any ideas."

And this is funny to me, even as nervous as I am. I smile.

She presses her lips flat, takes another sip of wine, waves her hand holding the glass around in a circle at the pile of letters. "You put him up to it?" she asks.

I look at the pile, then to her.

"Your brother. Did you send him here with the letters?"

I shake my head.

"Just checking." She takes another sip of wine.

I've been so oblivious to the workings of Ben-land. I've been so stupidly blind to everything. I feel like I'm about to vomit. I lick my lips in hopes of getting them moving. My hands shake in my lap.

"So why are you here, then?" She looks up at me, and her eyes get big. "Jesus, Jake, you look like you're about to pass out."

I can't help but think about Ben. How it's been two days, and he's still not awake.

She sets her glass on the coffee table, moves to sit next to me, and grabs a shaking hand. "What happened? Something happened."

I lick my lips again and manage a whisper. "It's Ben."

"What's Ben? What happened?"

I look into her eyes, her distorted burnt face, and my voice cracks. "He tried to kill himself. He's in a coma. He's lying in the hospital hooked up to machines, and he looks dead."

"Whoa… When did this happen?"

My eyes close. I can't open them. Her hand rests on my shoulder. I say, "Can we not talk about this right now? It's not why I'm here."

"How can we not talk about this right now? Why are you here? You should be at the hospital."

I open my eyes again. "I've been at the hospital. I've been there staring at him looking dead for the last two days. I'm here because of what he wrote in a note right before swallowing a whole pack of Valium."

She pushes my wine glass closer to me, and pats me on the shoulder.

I take a deep breath. "He was insistent that I try again to talk to you." I wave my hand at the letters. "I'm guessing this is why."

She gives me her asymmetrical eyebrow raise, sighs, and takes a sip of wine. "I read them," she says. "Your brother is a pretty amazing kid—that he did that for you."

I nod. My face burns. "I don't need you to forgive me. I just needed to tell you everything." The sting of anxiety is all over my skin now. Words hold too much power. One little slip, and that's it.

"Jake, there's a part of me that wants to help you, really. There's part of me that feels awful about everything you've had to deal with. And Ben... Jesus. But the tripping, Jake? My face? I get that you didn't intend for it to happen like it did, but what am I supposed to think?"

"I am so, so sorry."

"I know. I believe you said that a couple hundred times in the letters. Damn it, Jake. You always look so confused and innocent. You're like a toddler who sticks a fork in the electrical socket because he doesn't know any better."

My eyes stay trained on the letters splayed across the table.

She sighs again. She sets her wine glass down and edges closer to me. "Quit looking so sad," she says.

"Sorry." I can't look at her.

"You're making me feel guilty now."

I shake my head. "No, you didn't do anything."

"You have such faith in me."

"And why shouldn't I?"

"I'm not a very nice person," she says.

"That's not true."

"Jake, I was a complete ass to you even before we were dating. And I'm not just talking in general. It was my idea to have Rick give you the screw."

"It was just a joke. I get that."

"It was a cruel joke. Besides, you know how everyone thinks I'm a slut?"

"That's not true."

"Jake, you don't love me. You love some idealized version of me you carry around in your head."

"That's not true."

"We're so wrong for each other. It would be a mess. I'm not good with serious relationships. You're not good with life. Let's be realistic."

I grab for the wine glass and swallow most of it in one go.

"Yeah," she says. "You need to learn some healthy coping

techniques."

I set the glass back down and look at her.

She says, "How many new scars do you have since I left?"

"None."

"I don't believe you."

I stand up, pull off my shirt, put my arms out, and turn a circle for her. "None," I say.

She tilts her head briefly, then grabs her wine glass.

I reach my hand down for hers. She cautiously places her hand in mine, stands up, and I kiss her fingers.

She pulls away and returns to the chair.

"Sorry," I say.

She shakes her head. "It's not you."

It's not me.

She throws a hand up in the air. "There are things about me I'm not so proud of."

Larry. "Right before I came over, I saw Larry leaving. Does that have anything to do with it?"

"Larry is unhappy in his marriage," she says.

"Just now you fucked Larry? I was sitting out in my car, waiting to knock on your door, and you were fucking Larry?"

"I told you I'm nothing like the ideal you seem to be worshipping in your head. I've never claimed to be. You decided that, Jake. And besides, my personal life really isn't any of your business anymore."

"I'm sorry. I didn't mean it like that." I sit back down, close my eyes, and rub my hands over my face.

I hear her get up, walk toward the kitchen, walk back. I open my eyes to see her standing in front of me, filling my glass back up and then hers, and she sits next to me again.

"It's fine," she says. "Like I said, we're too different for it to ever work anyway."

I open my mouth but there are no words. I close it again.

"Say something," she says.

She slowly sips her wine, rests her feet, ankle on ankle, on the coffee table. I put my shirt back on, and we sit in awkward silence for a good few minutes before she gets up, stacks the letters neatly, and sets them back behind the picture.

"You should go," she says. "You should be with your brother."

"It was good to see you," I say, standing up.

She nods. "I'm glad you stopped by, really."

She moves toward the door and opens it for me. "If there's anything you need, anything I can do, you can still call me."

I nod.

"Call me anyway and let me know what happens with your brother," she says.

I nod again. "Yeah."

# CHAPTER FORTY

It starts with me thinking I'm imagining things again like I have been the last few days. But then I see it straight on—Ben's face scrunches a moment and relaxes. "Benny?" I say, but he doesn't respond.

I grab his hand and squeeze.

Nothing.

But a few minutes later his thumb twitches. Then he pulls his arm up, pulls his hand out of mine, smacks himself in the head with the back of his hand.

I don't think I've ever been so happy.

The nurse comes in, and I tell her "He moved. I think he's waking up."

She says, "It's about time."

I say, "No kidding."

She checks the machines and tells me his heart rate is up. She says, "It might take a bit before he's fully conscious. Give him time to come around."

His face scrunches up again and relaxes. "Did you see that?" I say.

She nods. "I'll let the doctor know we might have a live one soon."

She leaves, and I say, "Benny?" again. "Benny can you hear me?" A knee bends up, then straightens. He smacks his face again. I grab his hand, pull it off his face, hold it, and there's almost a bit of a grip back. It doesn't quite feel like I'm holding a dead hand anymore.

This goes on for the next hour or so. Then finally, finally, his eyes open. He looks right at me, then his eyes close again. He pulls his hand out of mine, reaches more purposefully towards his face, and touches the tube coming out of his mouth. A leg starts kicking back and forth. His eyes flit open again and look around, then at me. He pats frantically at the tube in his mouth, fighting it like it's choking him, looking to me to save him. "Relax, relax," I say. "It's okay, it's okay." I pull his hand away and pin it down. "I'll call someone, okay? I'm going to call the nurse, okay?" He blinks hard and reaches up at the tube with his other hand and kicks a foot weakly back and forth. I hear the heart monitor accelerate. I push the call button for the nurse and tell them he's up and can someone come in quick, please. I hold Ben's hands down. He keeps blinking and squirming, but he's got no strength. "Don't fight it. You're okay. Someone's coming."

The nurse comes in, and I tell her I think he wants the tube out. She repeats to him my command to relax and says she'll get the doctor. Ben's eyes are watering by the time the doctor comes in with the nurse. He isn't squirming as much, but I can tell he's uncomfortable.

The doctor disconnects the tube from the machine. The nurse positions the back of the bed so Ben is propped up to near sitting. Then the doctor tells Ben to exhale hard while he pulls the tube out.

Once the tube is out, the nurse is quick with an oxygen mask as Ben grabs at his throat and coughs.

Ben keeps looking to me, to the doctor, to me, to the doctor. The doctor checks his blood pressure, heart rate, and such. He looks at Ben and says, "Do you know where you are?"

But Ben just stares at him.

The doctor says, "Can you tell me your name?"

And still Ben just stares. Then his eyes go to me, then back to the doctor.

"Why isn't he talking?" I ask.

The doctor looks at Ben and points to me and says, "Do you recognize this person?"

Ben looks at me again and nods, and I feel a small rush of relief.

The doctor says, "Can you speak to us? Can you say his name?" He pulls the mask off Ben's face a little and waits.

Ben looks at me like I should answer and doesn't say anything.

"All right," the doctor says. "We'll give him a little more time to come out of it. I'll send the neurologist over in a bit to do a full assessment, and we'll go from there." He turns to me, "Just keep trying to talk to him. He's probably got a bit of a sore throat." He turns to Ben, "Is your throat a little sore?"

Ben just stares.

"I'll send the nurse in with some ice water."

They leave, and it's just me and Ben and no more breathing machine. I say, "Hey, Benny, you're okay, right? You're okay."

He pulls at his mask, and I help him move it aside. He speaks in the faintest, hoarse whisper, "Jake?"

"Yeah?"

"I need to pee."

"I'm pretty sure they have you set up so you can go where you are."

Ben stares at me confused a moment, then lifts up the blankets and peeks under the covers. Then he peeks over the side of the bed at the half-filled urine bag. He shakes his head.

When the nurse comes back in with ice water I ask if she can undo the catheter. Ben's eyes get all big. The nurse says she'll have to consult the doctor and disappears.

Ben says he needs to pee again.

"Well, you can go where you are or you can wait."

He shakes his head and lies back. He looks away from me, staring at the wall. I let a few minutes go by then ask him if he's okay again.

He turns back my way slowly then says, "What happened?"

"You don't remember?"

He shakes his head.

"Well, what's the last thing you do remember?"

His eyes focus on the empty air in front of him like he's thinking.

Then he says, "What day is it?"

"Wednesday."

He says, "Is it summer?"

"Yes, it's summer. It's August."

"What happened?"

"Well, you've been unconscious since Sunday, and you just now woke up."

"What day is it?" he asks again.

"Wednesday."

The doctor comes in.

I tell him Ben has started talking.

He proceeds to tell us how the nurse can remove the catheter, but they might just have to reinsert it. Ben isn't acting completely coherent, and they haven't assessed what his motor function is. "So we could remove it now, at the risk of having to redo it, or wait until we know more."

Ben says, "Now."

The doctor looks at me. I say, "It's what he wants."

The nurse returns and removes the thing. She asks if he'd like to use a bedpan or try to test out his legs and walk to the bathroom.

He whispers, "Walk," pulls the oxygen mask all the way off, and hands it to the nurse. She sets it aside.

"Okay," she says. "We're going to take this slow and easy, all right?"

The nurse lowers the rail on the side of the bed, and Ben sits up and scoots over to the edge, sliding off until his feet touch the floor. He pulls his arms out in front of him and examines the IV coming out of his left wrist. He gives it a little tug like he wants it gone.

The nurse says, "No, we can't take that out yet. We can carry the bag with us."

The nurse hooks his IV bag onto a pole on wheels. Ben still stares at the tube coming out of his arm, and he presses all around it with his fingers. The nurse asks him how he's feeling, and he nods without looking at her. She points out where the bathroom is on the other side of the room, and I grab Ben's right arm as he leans away from the bed with his full weight on his legs. He's wobbly like a drunk and grabs the pole with his other arm.

We move forward a few steps, then without warning he untangles his arm from mine and reaches over for the IV needle. He rips the thing right out of his arm, and a red stream of blood follows.

He loses his balance, and I grab him from behind under his armpits. He screams, "Let me go!" and tries to wrestle himself free, but he doesn't have the strength or the coordination. My foot slips on something wet on the floor, and I almost go down and drop him. There's a puddle under the kid, and at first I think maybe it's somehow IV fluid, but the whole front of his gown is wet and smells like piss. The nurse helps me get him back onto the bed as he keeps yelling, "Let me go! Let me go!" but his voice is so hoarse. We get him back on the bed, and he grunts in angry frustration, making sounds like a whimpering animal.

The nurse calls for assistance, and a male nurse shows up. Ben puts up a weak fight as they change him and his sheets.

The nurse says, "We need to put in a new IV and redo the catheter."

Ben says, "I'll rip them both out."

She says, "If you can't calm down, we will have to use restraints."

He says, "Die, bitch!" and snarls like a wild dog.

I say, "Something's wrong. He isn't normally like this."

The male nurse says, "Could you please wait in the hall, sir?"

As I head out, Ben yells as loud as his hoarse voice will let him, "Don't leave me here! Don't fucking leave me here!"

I sit in a chair in the hall for half an hour listening to Ben struggle and cry as they tend to him. When I go back in, he's lying on his back with his wrists and ankles tied to the bed in restraints. The IV is back. The catheter is back. Ben's will is broken, and his eyes are all red.

"You okay?" I say.

He says, "What happened? Why am I tied down like this?"

"I wouldn't let them do it if I didn't think they were trying to help. Trust me, Benny, you weren't acting like yourself."

His nose runs, and I grab a tissue and blot it. I sit back in my seat at his bedside.

He says, "What happened? Why am I here?"

"You really don't remember any of it?"

He shakes his head.

"You swallowed a bunch of pills. You almost died. Hell, you did die, but they brought you back."

He closes his eyes and just lies there crying.

# CHAPTER FORTY-ONE

The neurologist was optimistic and said that most of Ben's symptoms should resolve, including the want to call the nurse a bitch and tell her to die. The restraints are removed, and Ben falls asleep after all the testing is done.

I sit up watching him. Past two in the morning, I start drifting in and out of sleep myself. But all of a sudden he moves and lets out a scream. I stand up, and his eyes are rolled in the back of his head, and he's jerking back and forth.

"Ben!" I say, but he keeps jerking and grunting and showing only the whites of his eyes.

I call in a nurse, and she turns the lights on, and says he's having a seizure. She calls for the doctor.

The jerking goes on for what seems like forever before it slowly dies down. Then Ben lies there limp. His eyes start focusing again. They prop him upright, and the doctor checks him out. He asks Ben if he knows where he is, but the kid's gone mute again.

Ben looks around like he's aware of the world, but he won't answer anything. Then he starts whispering, "I'm really tired," over and over.

The doctor says it's best to let him rest. He speaks with me out in the hall and says they'll run an EEG in the morning to check his brain activity and see if they can figure out what type of seizure it was. He says it's even possible Ben's weirdness earlier was the result of seizure activity.

* * *

Early morning Ben has electrodes all over his head. A few hours later he's got a prescription for anti-convulsants.

I'm alone in the room with him again, and again he asks me what happened.

I give him the full story this time. How I found him passed out after getting back from taking Mom to the hospital. How the paramedics had to restart his heart more than once. How he was in a coma for three days.

He just stares up at the ceiling the whole time.

"Are you mad?" he says.

"No, absolutely not."

"What day is it?"

"Thursday."

He nods. "What does Mom think about this?"

"Don't worry about what Mom thinks. It doesn't matter."

"But she knows, right?"

"She knows."

"Then how come she's not here?"

"I don't know, Benny. She's not feeling well."

He swallows and takes a deep breath. "When do you think they'll let me go home? I want to go home."

"I don't know. I think they were going to move you to the psych ward later today."

Ben blows a long breath and crosses his arms.

"You did just try to kill yourself."

He won't look at me.

"When they do move you, visiting hours are different," I say. "I won't be able to just be here whenever."

"How long will I have to be there?"

"I don't know. Hopefully not long."

# CHAPTER FORTY-TWO

Mom pours a glass of milk. She sets the milk in front of me and takes seat on the other side of her dining room table.

"How's work?" she asks.

I tell her, "Work's fine," which is vacuously true.

A pained smile contorts her face, and she opens her mouth as if to ask something, but closes it again.

"Ben's awake now," I say.

She breathes deep as if catching her breath. "Oh, good."

"He's still in the hospital," I say.

She shakes her head. "I still don't—I don't understand what happened."

"Overdose, Mom. It was an overdose."

She leans forward, elbow on the table and forehead in hand. "After everything else, I can't believe he's abusing drugs now, too."

"He's not. It was kind of a onetime thing." I keep telling myself, *She's crazy. You know this. Don't let it get to you.*

She sits back up, oddly composed and matter-of-fact. "You do realize he's just doing this for attention, right?"

The anger writhing inside of me grows and grows. It takes all I have not to scream at her. "He left me a suicide note, Mom. He wanted to die."

She sighs as if I'm being difficult for no reason. I keep trying to figure out how the hell she got like this. I was at my parents' house a mere week before Ben spilled the beans on Dad, and I remember Mom being worried when he came home late. Now she's just mildly irritated that he almost died.

"His heart stopped three times," I say. "And he was in a coma for three days, and he's been having seizures. I watched him stop breathing. I watched them shock his heart back into rhythm before taking him away in an ambulance."

I hardly even raised my voice, but she won't look at me now, and her bottom lip is shaking. She bites it. I'm being stupid. I need her not to shut down. Ben needs to know he still has a mom. She still loves him on some level. That's the whole reason she's a mess. She can't reconcile that love with her need for a perfect family.

"You should come see him," I say.

She shakes her head.

She would sooner disown the both of us than acknowledge what happened in this house and what Dad did. Being a mother betrayed by her sons is easier than being a mother who let her own children be raped under her roof for years by the man she chose to marry. Just like it was easier for me to pretend I didn't know about what was happening to Ben. I needed everyone to believe my family was normal—I was normal. My dad was normal. He loved me. I had a place in the world of humans. If anyone found out all the things he and I did in my bedroom at night, it would have ripped away what measly identity I had built for myself. I'd turn into something abominable, a piece of shit, an idiot victim, a dirty fucking moron. I'd fall apart and disappear. I knew it down in my gut. Giving up the secret would completely destroy me.

"It would help him," I say. "It would mean a lot."

"He doesn't want me there. You know that."

"He does. He was asking about you today."

Mom sits up straighter, but doesn't look me in the eye. She nods and puts on a pleasant smile like this is a casual conversation about nothing of any real consequence, and says, "Bring him by for a visit when he's better."

* * *

Ben is asleep when I walk in, curled up on his side, his hands in fists up near his face. He looks like how I'd find him on the floor of the old apartment in the morning after the 4:00 a.m. sad puppy episodes. I take my seat next to him. I want to wake him to talk, but I'm sure he needs the rest. So I just sit and try to get comfortable, lean back in the chair and fold my arms. Nearly an hour goes by before his eyes open, and he looks at me.

"How are you feeling?" I say.

He says, "I had another seizure," and lifts up his forearm and shows me a long bruise he got from apparently smacking the bedrail in the process.

The sight of it puts a lump in my throat. "What did they say about that?"

He shrugs and sits up, his hair messed and his eyes tired.

"How'd your day go otherwise?" I say.

He rubs his face and yawns. "I told them I want to go home as soon as possible. They said they might put me on anti-depressants, and I'm going to have to keep seeing a therapist—like you do—except every day for a while after I leave."

I nod, and he plays with his bed sheets in his hands. Then I say, "Maybe this isn't the time to bring this up, but I read your note—the suicide note you left. Do you remember writing it?"

He nods but doesn't look at me.

"Just so it's clear, things would not be better if you weren't around."

He just keeps playing with the bed sheets.

"And...I'm sorry I didn't realize how bad you were hurting. And I'm sorry I haven't always been there for you when I needed to be, but I'm not letting that happen ever again, okay? It won't happen ever again."

He lies back down on his side and pulls the blankets all the way up over his head. I lean over and peel the covers off him. He doesn't fight it. I put my hand on his shoulder.

Then he says, "Jake, don't take this the wrong way, but I don't feel like being touched right now."

# CHAPTER FORTY-THREE

I fall asleep fast because I've not gotten more than an hour or two the last several nights.

But this is not restful sleep.

This is another nightmare.

And I know it is, but I can't wake up from it. Dad's here, and so is Ben, and not a one of us has anything on.

Dad stands with his hand on the kid's shoulder, and I hear Ben's words from earlier. *I don't feel like being touched right now.*

My limbs are lead, and I can't move.

Dad's other hand, the one not on Ben's shoulder, reaches over and tugs Ben's dick. Ben's eyes close, and his head tics to the side like mine always does.

And I can't move.

Dad nudges the kid down onto all fours. His fingers scoop Vaseline out of a jar. The same jar in Mom's bathroom cupboard.

They say Vaseline is odorless. Vaseline is not odorless. The smell is so strong I feel like I'm going to vomit.

I don't want to see this, but in my dream my eyes don't close, they won't blink. My head won't turn. Ben's face is buried in a pillow, and Dad goes at him.

I can't move, but I'm shaking where I stand. If my limbs weren't locked immobile, they'd crumble under me. My heart feels like a bass drum loud in my chest, and every beat hurts like a heart attack. I feel dizzy, like I should be falling, but I don't.

I hear my own voice, but I'm not speaking. I hear my voice

saying, *Alpha, beta, gamma, delta.* A new letter with each thrust of Dad, and the scene before me turns into a painting. The motion is brush strokes swirling into an impressionistic picture.

Then it all comes into clear view again. I've gotten closer to the both of them somehow, and Dad has just finished.

Dad looks at me and points to Ben. He says, "It's your turn."

Everything about me hurts right now. That drum pound of my heart is up in my head, and I feel like I'm dying. I keep trying to move to get away, but I can't.

Lauren's voice says, *You're a grown-up now. You can make it stop.*

Finally, finally I think I'm waking up, but I'm in my old room at Mom and Dad's house, stuck now in another layer of dream. I am not a grown-up. I can't make it stop. The door opens, and the old man whispers, "Shhh..."

I know how this goes. I've had this dream before.

He's got a pair of beers in hand, and when he closes the door behind himself, it's so dark in the room I can only make out his location by scent and sound. The caps twist off the beer, and I know to sit up and put my hand out for one. It's icy cold in my warm palm, and I take a sip despite hating the malt aftertaste. Despite feeling every moment is the moment—the time to finally say stop. To break the pattern. But I can't seem to. I can't get that word out.

The old man gulps, and there's that hollow plunking sound when his lips leave the bottle. A small sigh after he swallows, then a cold hand traces below my belly button, slips inside my underwear.

The old man says, "Shhh... You're fine." And I try to relax and move the tension elsewhere, and I take another sip of beer.

He swallows the rest of his brew and sets the bottle on the floor. I'm back on the bed on my elbows, and he pulls away from me. He stands up and says, "Come with me. I need your help with something."

"What is it?" I say.

"You know how your mother wants another baby? I can't seem

to make that happen."

I get out of the bed in the dark, and his hand on my shoulder guides me down the hall to the open door to his and Mom's room. I stand at the doorway, and see Mom lying on her back in the bed.

Dad says, "You're helping your mother." He put special powder in a pill capsule, and she swallowed it down. Now her eyes just stare, unfocused. "She won't remember," he says.

All I hear is my own heart beating like I could die from it. I close my eyes, and I'm falling. I'm fainting into an oblivion, and when I open my eyes again I'm on my back in my bed in my old room in the dark. Dad sits next to me. He smoothes my hair back with his cold hand, and he says, "You did good. You'll see. Like I said, she won't remember." He tells me he's proud of me, but I feel dead inside. I feel like nothing.

I blink, and I see my room now, and I'm in disbelief that I actually made it to awake. I want to get out of bed, to run, to get away from the awful feeling of that dream, but I'm paralyzed. I can't move. I can't get enough air.

Finally, finally, I can lift my arm, slow, like it was pinned to where it was with rubber bands. Then everything follows from that, and I'm out of bed and out of my clothes and into the bathroom, into the tub running water to warm it for a shower so fast that the head rush makes me black out for a second, and I blink my eyes back open from the bottom of the tub. The pounding of my heart up in my head isn't the only pain there now. I must have cracked my head against the tub on the way down. And there's blood. My arm's bleeding, I'd guess from hitting the faucet.

The water I'd started running is ice cold, and I'm fully awake now. I stand up, shivering like I'm convulsing until the water heats up, and I can let the shower spray burn me. Then I double forward, vomiting. The hot water mixes with the blood, mixes with the vomit at the bottom of the tub, and I'm on my knees in it, and my eyes are watering, and I can't see, and I can't stop heaving. It's all coming back to me. The landmine. What Dad meant by helping Mom.

# CHAPTER FORTY-FOUR

Friday morning I'm in Lauren's office telling her it's been a rough week. I give her the rundown, and her eyes get big like she's actually impressed with my tales this time. She asks how I've been sleeping, and I laugh but it's not really a laugh. I almost burst into tears right there in front of her. I tell her, "I won't be doing that again for a while."

"What?" she says.

"Sleeping—I won't be sleeping again. Not after last night."

"What happened last night?"

I tell her I need some air. "Can I open the window?"

She nods, and I get up, walk over to the window, open it, and stare out of it with my hands on the windowsill, my back to her.

"Did you have another nightmare?"

I don't know what to say. It's all fragmented, and it's too new. When I finally speak, all I've got is a whisper. "I don't think I can do this right now. Please, can we talk about something else?"

I hear her scratch away at her notepad for a minute. She says, "Can you tell me what happened to your elbow?"

I lift my arm and examine the scabbed gash. "I know what you're thinking. I'm not going to say it didn't cross my mind like a freight train, but that's not what this is. I fell. In the tub—I think I hit it on the faucet."

"How about we talk about Ben a little more? Is he coming home to stay with you again when he leaves the hospital?"

"That's the plan."

"Are you ready for that?"

"I'm more than ready for that." The knot tied around my throat starts to ease. I tell her I'm looking into seeing if he can go to a different school this fall since he's staying with me. I live in a different school zone than Mom does. It might not work, though. Since I'm not his legal guardian I have to go through all the hassle of the transfer paperwork, and get Mom to sign it, and then it still might not go through.

"It sounds like this is really important to you."

"You have no idea."

"Can you come sit back down? Are you feeling a little better?"

I walk back over and let the chair envelope me.

She says, "Have you given any thought to legal guardianship?"

"What do you mean?"

"Well, your brother lives with you. You take care of him. You seem to end up dealing with his problems as a parent would. You were the one by his bedside at the hospital. From what you've told me, your mother doesn't have much interest in raising him beyond cordial Sunday dinners. If she agrees to it, going to the court for legal guardianship is a fairly straightforward process. Then you wouldn't have to worry about the school zones, and you wouldn't have to worry about any other legal stumbling blocks down the road."

"I didn't even—I guess it never really occurred to me that was a thing I could do."

"Is it something you'd want? Do you think you'd be ready for that?"

"It makes sense. It makes more sense than anything."

"I don't know all the details, but if you stop by the courthouse, they can probably get you set up with the appropriate paperwork."

I nod.

The courthouse. My favorite place.

I head there right after I leave Lauren's office and obtain the paperwork. And since I can't see Ben again for a few more hours, I figure now is as good a time as any to bring up the idea with Mom.

I drive to her place, but sit in my car a few minutes before going in, trying to decide how exactly to present it in a way that she'll agree to.

Inside the house, I sit on the recliner while she sits on the sofa. I have to turn her TV off to get her attention, but I can't look her in the eye. I keep thinking about the dream I had, and I'm scared she'll see what happened written all over my face. So I mostly look at the arm of the couch as I talk to her. I take the approach of making it like I'm doing this as a favor to her and not to Ben. I tell her that it would take the burden off of her and make her life easier.

"I'll be able to deal with any trouble Ben finds himself in," I say. "Nothing will change, really. We'll still come visit like we have been."

She has this distant look like she's considering it for the longest time. Finally she says, "I don't want to deal with the courts. This sounds like it will be a mess."

"The only thing you have to do is sign the paperwork in front of a notary. We can do that Monday. I'll drive you there."

She looks deep in thought again, and then nods. "I suppose I can do that," she says.

* * *

Ben looks much more alert this evening. His skin is pink, and his eyes don't seem so tired.

I stare at him, maybe a little too hard, but after that dream last night I'm looking for signs that what I'm remembering is real. He tells me his doctor said they were probably going to let him go tomorrow.

"That's awesome," I say. "Have they been helping at all?"

He shrugs. "I feel like they take me seriously. Which is nice. To tell you the truth, I kind of like the idea of having someone to tell everything to."

I nod. "You know you can always talk to me, too, right? Sometimes it might be hard for me to hear what you have to say, but I'll always listen."

"Yeah…" he says and stares down in his lap.

"So, I went to the courthouse today. I want to be your legal guardian since you're staying with me now."

He lifts his head. His face brightens, and he says, "You would do that?"

"You'll be able to switch schools, too, since we live in a different school district than Mom does."

His eyes go back and forth like he's thinking, then his shoulders slump.

"We don't have to," I say. "I'll leave the decision up to you."

"What does Mom say about it?"

"She's willing to sign the paperwork," I say.

He nods.

"What is it?" I say.

"She still doesn't care," he whispers.

I put my hand on his shoulder. "Whether she does or not, I do. Don't let her get to you."

\* \* \*

After visiting hours, I go home. My whole body feels tired. I consider the beer in the fridge. I consider drinking enough to pass out, and maybe then I wouldn't dream.

No.

The thought of shopping for razor blades crosses my mind, but I can't do that anymore.

I go to my room and retrieve Prometheus from his tank. I put him on my shoulder as I pace around the apartment. His tongue flicks at my neck.

Ben might be coming home tomorrow. It occurs to me his room is still just as it was when he was taken away in the ambulance. In fact, the whole place is more than a bit disheveled. Prometheus bites me on the earlobe as if to say *Put me back in my tank and clean this dump.* So I put him back on his half-log, toss him a few crickets, and spend the night cleaning the apartment from top to bottom.

Late morning I get a call from the hospital telling me they're ready to discharge Ben. I bring a change of clothes for him to wear home and get over there as quick as I can.

When we get home, he stops at the top of the stairs, nervous about going into his room. I open the door and show him it's all cleaned up. No empty beer cans, no empty Valium box. I washed all his dirty clothes and bedding, dried them with fabric softener, and put them away. He smiles with relief.

Ben is still tired from the whole ordeal of the past week and spends a good portion of the weekend sleeping. I check on him hourly like a newborn baby to make sure he's breathing.

Monday morning we get dressed and ready to pick Mom up to go get papers signed. On the drive over I tell Ben, "Don't let her insanity fuck with your head. If she says something asinine, just ignore it, and we can vent about it later."

"I can't make any promises," he says.

He waits in the back of the car while fetch her. When she gets into the front passenger seat, she turns around, smiles at Ben, and says, "Hello, Benjamin. I'm glad to see you're all better."

Ben opens his mouth like he wants to say something caustic— perhaps, *I'm not all better*, or, *No thanks to you*, or, *You lying bitch, what do you care?* But I clear my throat to get his attention, and he just says, "Hi, Mom."

She's wearing the same dark clothes of mourning she wore to the grand jury hearing. We drive to the courthouse in silence.

Signing papers in front of the notary and handing them to the court clerk is surprisingly uneventful.

Mom says, "This wasn't easy for me," as we get back into the car, like maybe she actually put some thought into what it all means. Ben looks right at me with a sort of hopeful sadness on his face at the sliver of possibility that his mother still loves him.

I tell her, "I know."

Once we're all in the car and on the road again, she puts a hand on my forearm and says, "Ben is lucky to have you."

I lock eyes with Ben in the rearview mirror and try to offer him a small smile, but he looks like he might go sad puppy on me at any moment. We drop Mom back off and head home.

After dinner, Ben and I sit across from each other at the table, and we had been talking about painting Mom's house, but we paused, and now he doesn't seem able to speak.

I say, "Benny? You okay?"

He looks me right in the eye but says nothing. Then he looks through me with the stare of a blind person. He hums one long, endless note.

"Ben?"

All I get is the note. The kid's having some sort of seizure again. I move his dish away from him and move to stand beside him, ready to pull him down to the floor should he start flopping like a fish. But he doesn't. The humming stops.

"Ben?"

He turns his head slowly and looks at me, confused.

"You okay?"

He looks down and pulls his hands up out of his lap, opening and closing them, and they're damp. His pants are all wet.

"We'll get you cleaned up, and we'll call the doctor, okay? No big deal, right?"

He doesn't say a word, just sits there.

"Come on," I put my hand on his shoulder. "Come get a shower?"

Finally he nods. He gets up, and I follow him upstairs. He starts undressing in the bathroom with the door open, and I find him some clothes and a towel and set them in there for him, close the door, and wait right outside in case he needs anything.

# CHAPTER FORTY-FIVE

Sleep still scares me. I spend the vast majority of the nighttime hours talking to Prometheus like some crazy person. We don't even talk about anything interesting—vague plans for possibly finding a new job. We recall what bills have yet to be paid this month. We consider if the car is due for an oil change.

In the morning I'm on the couch in the living room, intending to close my eyes for only a few seconds, but I make the mistake of going all the way under, falling into a dream.

Soon a feeling infiltrates every bone, every muscle in my body. My flesh, my bones no longer feel like my own. They're crawling with *him*. We do share DNA after all. He has me more ways than one. And I don't like the foreign feeling in my bones, how they're filled with helium and about to float out of my body.

Then comes the sensation down in my gut. In my lower intestine. Really, my ass. I feel like clenching the sucker so tight I never shit again. And I want to cross my legs like a girl. I want to cover my nuts and dick. Because I'm naked in this dream, and I can't get away because I'm naked. Where would I go? If anyone sees me they'll see how dirty I am.

There's a long hallway with walls and windows and blind corners, and I need to run. But I have to duck at the windows and crawl on my hands and knees until I get past, then stand back up and sprint. I'm breathing hard, but there's an echo to my breath. It's him. He's breathing. But not breathing like he's been running hard. He's breathing like when he'd go at me, breathing like he was when he went at Ben in my dream from the other night. I can't see him. But I know he's close. Now I'm wondering where Ben is. I keep running, ducking under the windows, my knees hitting hard on the floor.

I turn a corner and find Mom, but double back before she can see me. I stand with my back against the cold wall, panting.

His breathing gets louder. I smell his sweat and the beer on his breath. My tongue rolls around the inside of my cheek.

Then I hear Ben's voice, calling my name. "Jake," he says. "Jake?" And my body shakes back and forth. It's not me making my body shake. I flail my arms around trying to stop it, trying to steady myself, and Ben's voice says my name again. But it sounds different this time. My eyes blink open.

Ben stands over me, staring, his hand on my shoulder, and it scares me, and I swat his hand away without thinking. He looks confused, and I realize I'm awake, on the couch in our apartment. I say, "Sorry," and sit up rubbing my face. He just saved me.

My stomach is sick. I go to the kitchen and pour myself a large glass of water and drink it down. As if by instinct, I know what I need to do, and I need to do it right now.

I grab my boots, sit back on the couch and lace them up.

"Where are you going?" Ben asks.

I finish tying my boots. "I'm driving out to visit Dad."

"What? Why?"

"Because I have some things I need to say to him."

"You going to tell him off?"

"You want to come?"

He shakes his head.

I go to the kitchen again for more water. Ben flops on the couch.

The sleep deprivation is really fucking with my head. I'm not thinking straight. "Get dressed," I say.

"I'm not coming."

"I'm not about to leave you here alone just yet. That didn't turn out so well last time. You don't have to see him. You can wait in the car."

"I don't want to go." He crosses his arms.

I set my glass down hard on the table, and sit in a chair. "Do we have to do this today?"

"Why do you need to talk to him anyway?"

"I don't know. He's in my fucking head every time I try to fucking sleep, and I need to tell him to get out of my fucking head."

"What was your dream about just now?"

"Rainbows and butterflies."

He says, "Whatever," gets up and stomps up the stairs.

I follow and get my foot in the door just as he tries to slam it shut. He sits on his bed. I sit on the floor facing him.

"You lied," he says. "When I was in the hospital you said that we could talk about things, but you still won't. Rainbows and butterflies, my ass. I had to wake you up, remember?"

I sigh. "Some things I don't even know how to find the words for. Sorry."

"It's called rape, Jake. It's called being fucked in the ass by your own dad. It's called, why do I have hemorrhoids when I'm only fifteen? What's so hard about saying that?"

His words knock the air right out of me. I stare at him, but can't bring myself to speak.

"It really is that hard for you to say. Why is that?"

I throw my hands up in the air. "I don't know. It's embarrassing. It's humiliating. It's disgusting. It's degrading."

"Do you think I'm disgusting? Do you think I should be embarrassed and humiliated?"

I shake my head. "No. That's not it at all. Just come with me so I don't have to worry about you. Let me do this. Then tonight we'll talk. You can ask me anything. I promise."

He stares at me for a moment, then says, "Fine."

I leave his room to let him get dressed, and then I look through my bookshelves for a book. I figure I'll bring him some reading material for when he's waiting in the car. I pick *Ancient Greece*.

# CHAPTER FORTY-SIX

Dad sits across the table from me. I expected a Plexiglas window of separation, but no. He's there in a familiar but slightly changed way. Dressed in blue denim. He's let his beard grow. And he's thinner, too. I already feel my stomach cramping, and I'm dizzy with it.

I feel like he and I, we have this little secret. It's no big deal. It wasn't anything wrong. Just a secret. I stare at him. The familiarity in his face. Every feature. The brown eyes, the thin mouth. I see my dad, I see myself, I see Ben in that face. I see the normalcy that was living at home. The normalcy that was having him in my bed at night. The normalcy of eating breakfast at the table with him in the morning. The normalcy of going camping. The normalcy of his mouth around my dick. The normalcy of handing him my report card. The normalcy of his dick in my mouth. The normalcy of drinking a beer with my dad. The stories he'd tell and how I'd hang onto every word.

He is the first to break the silence. "It's good to see you," he says. "Haven't had any visitors ever since your mother decided she was done with me."

I know his voice too well, and cringe for a second at the sound of him. I nod.

"How is your mother?"

"She's fine. She's like she always is."

"Is Ben staying with you or with her?"

"Me."

"Tell me you at least visit her—check on her."

"We do. She's fine."

"I've filed an appeal."

I shake my head.

"You got something to say?"

My instinct is to shut down, but I fight it. My heart beats behind my eyes. *You're a grown-up, Jake.* "No. I wanted to tell you no. Because I never did. And I should have."

His eyes narrow, and all the wrinkles on his aging face bunch up and deepen.

"And, I don't forgive you. Ben doesn't either."

He leans back. The corners of his mouth turn up just a bit. "Does Ben forgive you? Do you forgive you, Jakey?"

"I remember, now, you know. I'd forgotten, but now I remember everything." I look him right in the eye this time. "And I do mean everything."

"I was never bad to you, son. I took damn good care of you. You know that. I was always honest with you. You were always honest with me. We only did what felt right. Are you going to deny that now? We only kept it secret because other people don't understand."

"Stop it," I say.

"Stop what? If you love your brother. You remember where he came from. Would you really change that? The real bitch of it is, no one's done anything wrong here except make a big deal out of something that's a family matter. If either of you boys ever had a problem with anything, you could have talked to me about it first. But the fact is, neither of you ever did."

"You know you almost killed him? He tried to off himself last week and came within a hair of succeeding. You did that, Dad. You did that."

"I've been locked up for the last several months. Don't try pinning a damn thing on me. If anything I should be having your ass if you were the one taking care of him. So you tell me, Jacob—why did you let that happen?"

I feel it in my hands, in my knees, in my face. I'm absolutely livid. Leaning forward, in a voice just above a whisper I say, "If there weren't guards watching us right now, I'd fuck you with the toe of my boot until your ass bled in buckets. I'd stomp on your fucking dick. I'd crush your nuts with pliers. When you get out, if you so much as come near any of us, that's what I'm doing." Then I get up and head for the exit.

As I walk away, he says in a voice far too calm, too everyday, "Good to see you too, son."

I get back to the car with my insides on fire. Ben is sitting in the passenger seat with the book open in his lap, watching me. He has a pen in his hand and has been defacing the pictures in the book, enhancing the gore of the battle scenes. He says, "How'd it go?"

I close my door and put the key in the ignition and turn it.

"Not so well?" he says.

I put on my seatbelt, release the e-brake.

He says, "That's okay, because we can talk about it tonight when you promised I could ask anything."

I look over at him.

"Okay, then," he says.

"Buckle," I say, and he does.

My hands are so sweaty it's hard to grip the steering wheel. I don't know that I've ever been so angry. I can't go home. So I go to the river, park the car, leave Ben behind, and run into the woods. Kick the trees. Rip branches off, snap them over my knee, fling them off into the air as hard as I can. I grab the biggest boulders I can lift on shore and chuck them as far into the water as they will go, letting them splash up giant fountains.

I go until my arms are sore from throwing and hitting, my legs are sore from kicking, my toes are stubbed and burning inside my boots. I go until my knuckles are worn so raw they sting and bleed.

Then I sit exhausted on the sand and rocks with my legs splayed out in front of me. Then I lie flat on my back as the tears come. My body heaves as sobs force their way out. I let it take over. I let everything leave me that wants to leave me.

When I finally get over myself, I find Ben sitting up the hill near the car on a fallen log, book in lap. He isn't reading. He's watching me. I don't know how long he's been watching me. He follows me back to the car, and we both get in.

He says, "Better?"

I wipe my face with the bottom of my t-shirt and nod.

"Want me to drive?" he says.

I try to inhale the loose snot back up into my sinuses. "You can't, Benny. The seizures. The doctor said you can't drive until it goes away."

He sighs and slumps back in his seat.

Back home, Ben disappears up into his room, saying he needs a nap.

I decide to call Savannah.

She says, "You actually called like you said you would."

"I miss you."

She says, "Are you okay? You sound weird for some reason. Is Ben okay? Did he wake up?"

"Yeah, yeah, he's up and home with me again. He's okay."

"And what else is going on? There's something else."

"No, I-uh... I went to see my dad today."

"Really? How'd that go?"

I laugh, but it's a nervous laugh. "I told the old man off."

"Are you okay?" she says.

"I'm angry. I'm so angry."

She's quiet a moment, then says, "Do you want me to come over?"

"No, no. I-I just wanted to hear your voice."

She says, "Do you have any plans for the weekend?"

"Ben and I are painting our mom's house."

"I see," she says.

"You could come. If you want. It won't be very exciting, but you could come."

* * *

321

Ben makes a spaghetti dinner, complete with garlic toast. But my stomach is too weak to eat much. When he finishes eating, I clear the table and sit back down across from him.

"Okay," I say. "Ask anything."

He puts his arms on the table and leans forward. "What was your dream about last night?"

"Rainbows and butterflies."

He leans back, "Fuck you."

"I didn't tell you what the rainbow did to the butterflies."

He crosses his arms, and stares at me skeptically.

"Well, the rainbow gives the butterflies this fermented nectar, so they get a little loopy. Fly in spirals and such."

Ben waits for more.

"Then he's chasing them down this hall. The rainbow chases the butterflies, and they're separated. He's chasing the older one who's trying to find the younger one. Now, the rainbow is invisible sometimes, even though he gets close. The butterfly can feel he's close because the rainbow has this hot breath that smells like the fermented nectar. And sweat. He smells like sweat and sex. And the butterfly, he knows exactly what that smells like because he's had all of that right up in his face."

Ben just keeps staring at me, waiting for more.

"I can't do this," I say. "Do you really want to hear this?"

"Yes."

I wait a second to see if maybe he'll change his mind before I continue, but he doesn't. "In this dream," I say, "I can taste him. And I'm running, butt-naked, trying to get away. But there're windows, so I have to duck under the windows so no one sees me. Then I turn a corner and there's Mom, so I have to double back. And I'm trying to find you. I hear you calling my name. And I smell him. His breath is huffing away on the back of my neck. My body starts shaking. And I wake up. You woke me up. That was it."

Ben sits there motionless, his eyes watering.

"What else? What else do you want to know?"

"What did you say to Dad today?"

"To be honest, I was so pissed, I don't even really remember. Something about crushing his nuts with pliers and stomping on his dick."

"And I missed that?"

"You didn't miss much. Just me flailing out of control, and him not budging. I thought I'd maybe find some kind of resolution, maybe a sign that he felt bad about all of it, but he doesn't."

"What did he say?"

"Stupid shit, mostly. He doesn't seem to think he did anything wrong. And you know the really fucked up thing of it? The way he's so confident about it, I almost believe him."

"Well," Ben's voice cracks. "He can go to hell."

"There's something else," I say.

"What?"

"While you were in the hospital, I had a dream—a nightmare. But it was more than that. It was a memory. Something I'd forgotten, or at least locked up somewhere in my brain where I couldn't see it anymore. But it involves you, so maybe you should know." He looks fragile, too young for too many things, and I'm thinking maybe I should have kept my mouth shut just now.

"I'm not a baby," he says. "I can handle it, whatever it is."

"Wasn't that long ago you were still a baby."

"What is it? Just tell me."

I don't know that I can let this out. I'm trying to think of something else to tell him, but it's all I've got on my mind.

"You promised," he says. "You said you'd tell me anything."

"Fair enough. But when I tell you, you can't hate me for it. You can't go all crazy because of it, okay? Promise me."

He nods.

"I don't believe you. Promise me."

"I promise."

"Just so you know, no one knows about this except for me and Dad. Mom doesn't even know, all right?"

"Mom doesn't seem to know a lot of things."

"Trust me on this one. When you hear what I have to say, it'll blow your mind that she doesn't know, and that's what makes this all the more fucked up."

"Okay. So what is it?"

I watch him a moment, looking for a sign that maybe he'll change his mind. But he doesn't so much as flinch. I say, "Before you were born, Mom had wanted another baby for years, and for whatever reason Dad couldn't do it. He couldn't get her pregnant. And she really, really wanted another baby."

He says, "So then where did I come from?"

I shake my head, and I'm losing it again. My eyes start to water, and I hide my face in my hands.

"What was it? Where did I come from?"

I wipe my face with my shirt, sit back upright and suck in a long breath. I look right at him. I say, "One night Dad comes into my room, and I'm expecting, you know, the usual, except he tells me to get up." I sniff, I look up at the ceiling, hoping gravity will keep any more tears in. My voice shakes so bad I don't know if Ben can even make out my words. "So I do, and I follow him into Mom and Dad's room, and Mom's lying there, naked, staring at the ceiling like she doesn't know where she is, and he tells me he slipped her some special drug concoction so she won't remember anything." I suck in another breath.

Ben says, "You saw Mom naked?"

"Are you listening to what I'm saying? I did a lot more than see her. But to be honest, I don't remember much of anything about that night either, which is weird because I remember plenty of other crap. What I do know, is you were born nine months later. So there, that's it. That's the secret."

"What are you saying?" he says. "Are you really saying what I think you're saying?"

"Dad just kept saying, 'You're helping her—you're helping your mother.'" I get up and walk into the kitchen, start running cold water in the sink. He follows. "I'm sorry," I say.

"It wasn't your fault," he says. "It was Dad."

I grab handfuls of cold water and splash my face. I grab a paper towel and dry off. "Look, you can't ever tell Mom about this, understand? She can't know. Promise me."

He nods. "I promise." And then he shakes his head. "So what, you—you're my real dad? But also my brother? So I'm, like, inbred?"

I look him right in the eye. "Don't let it fuck with your head. It's already fucked with my head enough for the both of us. There's nothing wrong with you. Don't even think that for a second. It doesn't matter where you came from."

He stares at the floor, not even blinking.

"I'm sorry," I say. "You okay?"

He nods and smacks a rolling tear off his cheek.

"Really okay?"

He nods again, and says, "I guess there are worse things. I'd rather have you as a dad than him anyway." He looks up at me and smiles, but his smile quivers away, and he's back to staring at the floor. He says, "I'm not going to start calling you Dad."

"Please don't."

He pulls a paper towel off the roll to wipe his face.

I pull him in for a hug, hold him tight, and say, "We're going to be okay." He hugs back like he used to all the time when he was little, and I say, "You're the best thing in my world right now, Benny. The best thing."

# CHAPTER FORTY-SEVEN

I don't know what's going to happen when Ben goes back to school on Tuesday. It's a new school so maybe he won't come home beat up again, but all bets are off if he seizes and pisses himself during class. I have temporary guardianship until the court finalizes the permanent paperwork in another month or so.

At Mom's house, Dad's toothbrush and shaver still sit on the bathroom counter. His jacket still hangs by the door. But Mom's frantically thrilled to have us over painting today. We're over-hydrated with lemonade, and it's still early. Don't know when or if I'll be able to look her in the eye again, but she hasn't seemed to notice.

Yellow.

Mom chose yellow paint for the house.

Savannah came over in jean shorts and an old t-shirt. She already has yellow paint in her hair, and she smiles with the sun behind her head.

Over by the garden, Mom has half a dozen brown paper bags out. She's harvesting—filling the bags with produce. I'm pretty sure she expects us to take most of it home even if it'll rot before we can get to it all.

Ben has taken a painting break over by the garden and sits on an upturned five gallon bucket whittling the end of the long stick he found behind our apartment complex to a sharp point.

I pour some more paint in the tray and dip my roller in. Savannah nods toward the garden, "What's your brother doing?"

Ben holds the stick up over his shoulder, parallel with the ground. Like a doru. He is a Spartan hoplite. We all flinch as he lets out a battle cry, runs at the garden, and stabs the spear into the soil. He leaves it standing there, pulls at the tangled wad of string bean plants, and winds some of the vines around it. He's given the stick up to the garden.

Savannah dips her roller in the paint tray.

Mom moves to pick the tomatoes.

Ben looks up and salutes me.

Visit jakeandben.com for more about these characters, links to short stories and other works, and updates about future releases in this series.